THE VEIL

Ivy Brannon

Content Warning

For the fighters

SAMHAIN
November 1
YULE
December 19-22
AUTUMN EQUINOX
September 19-22
IMBOLC
February 1
LUGHNASADH
August 1
SPRING EQUINOX
March 19-22
LITHA
June 19-22
BELTANE
May 1

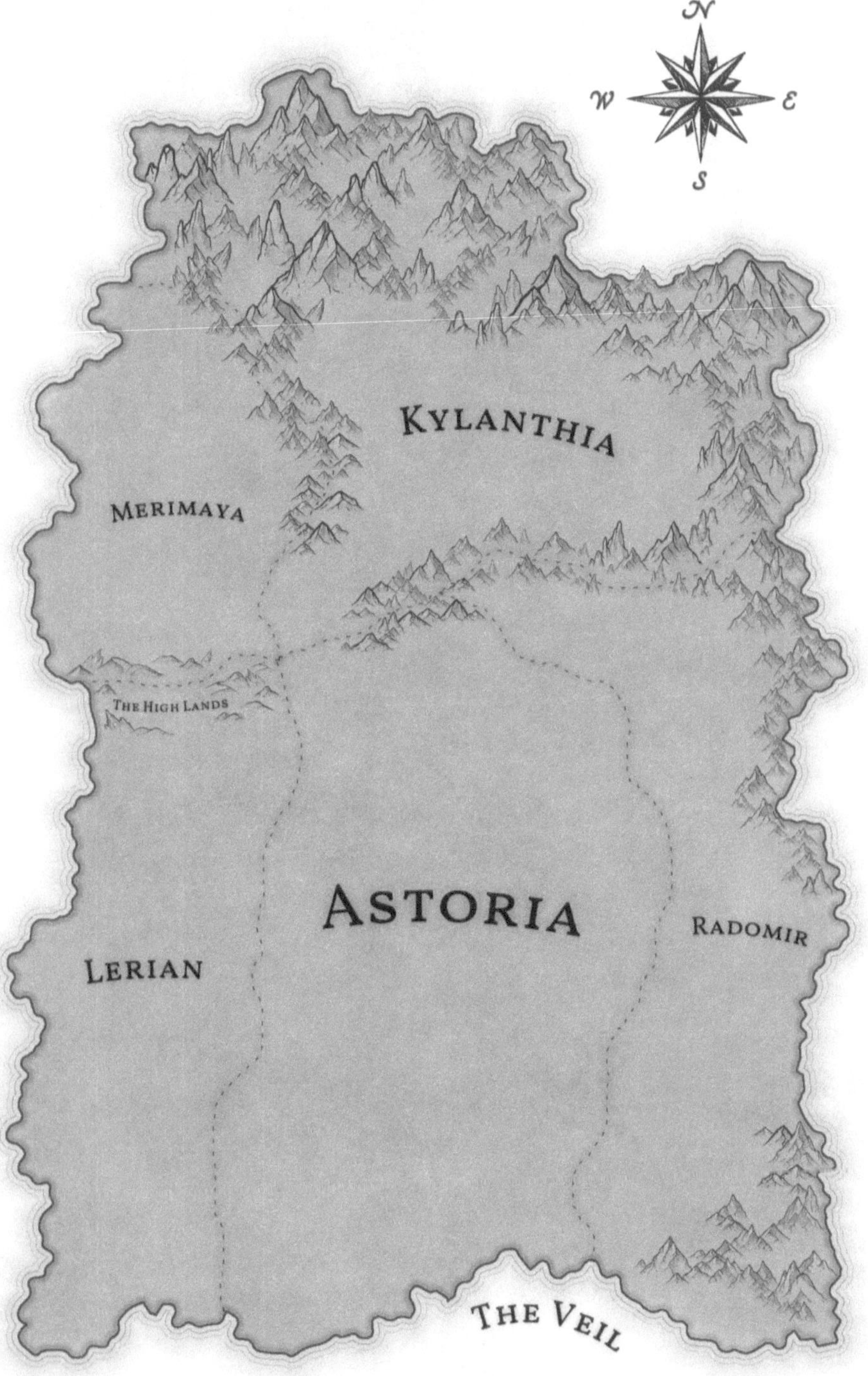

N
W
E
S
KYLANTHIA
MERIMAYA
THE HIGH LANDS
ASTORIA
LERIAN
RADOMIR
THE VEIL

THE VEIL

Chapter 1

Samhain marked the end of harvest and the first day of winter.

The days leading up to it had been relatively warm still, but the leaves on the trees had begun to change colors weeks ago, and usually by the time darkness fell, the chilled air would cut right to the bone. Tonight was no exception.

Camped in a small glade for the night, I hunched beside a small crackling fire with my three brothers, blowing into my hands and rubbing them together in an attempt to bring some warmth back into my fingers. They were starting to turn an unnatural shade of blue, even though I'd bundled up in my father's old winter coat and draped one of the threadbare blankets we'd brought from home over my skirt. My youngest brother, Wynnric, clung to my side, shivering miserably in the nook between my arm and shoulder. He'd just celebrated his sixth birthday last week, but somehow he seemed even younger tonight as he huddled close and whimpered in fear when a wolf howled in the distance. I brought my hand to his back and rubbed it in circles to comfort him.

"It's alright, Wynn, he won't hurt us."

"But what if he's hungry?" Wynn asked, looking up at me with those big turquoise eyes of his, now round and watery with worry.

"Well, we're hungry too," my younger brother Dominic chimed in, glancing up from the hunting knife he was sharpening, "and it's four against one, so I'd say our odds are pretty good."

He grinned and winked at our brother, which helped Wynn relax slightly. I looked over at Dominic and mouthed the words *thank you*. He nodded knowingly.

At nineteen, there was no denying Dominic was a man now. He looked the part, with his lean physique and a dusting of stubble on his chin and upper lip, and although he hadn't lost the playfulness of his youth yet, he'd grown strong and handsome seemingly overnight. It was strange suddenly seeing all the young women in our village fawning over him. It felt like just yesterday he had been the snotty, whiny child pulling my braids and blaming it on our older brother, Jaras.

Our eldest brother was, as usual, not paying much attention to us.

If Jaras was cold, he didn't show it. He sat slightly removed from the fire, his cloak draped haphazardly over his bony shoulders while he stared blankly into the flames. He occasionally sipped from a flask at his hip, the flickering shadows accentuating the deep, dark circles under his hazel eyes. He'd been attractive once, but when our parents passed away he turned to drink and cards, and it was starting to show. Tonight he looked pale, gaunt, and utterly miserable.

I frowned. I probably didn't look much better. I'd been working myself ragged all summer and harvest, tending the fields at Lord Olin's estate during the day and assisting the scullery maids in his kitchen at night. With our parents gone and Jaras doing little else besides frequenting the local tavern, Dominic and I were responsible for our family's survival. He would be gone hunting for days on end, while I would wake up before dawn to make breakfast for Wynn prior to work, and arrive home just in time to squeeze in one reading and writing lesson with my little brother before he went to bed.

"Are you really going to be hunting for wolves?" Wynn asked, a tinge of worry still coloring his voice.

Dominic slid his knife back into its sheath and tucked it in the outer pocket of the canvas pack resting beside his bow and arrows. "No, not on this trip."

Wynn let out a heavy sigh of relief. "Good."

"What's the matter?" Dominic laughed, nudging him. "You don't think you could handle a wolf?"

"I could!" Wynn protested. He lifted his chin proudly, but scooted a little closer to me. "I just wouldn't want Lina to be scared, that's all."

I exchanged a glance with Dominic as we stifled our laughter.

"That's very gallant, Wynn." I had to consciously fight against my lips as they attempted to curve into a smile. "You're quite the gentleman. Thank you."

"You're welcome." Wynn beamed and snuggled further into my side. I smiled and kissed his mop of blond hair, smoothing one of the rogue ringlets that twirled off the cowlick at the back of his head. Wynn's wild curls had always seemed to have a mind of their own, and no matter how much our mother had fussed over them when she was alive, they refused to be tamed. It was clear not much had changed in two years.

"Well, you won't need to worry about Lina pretty soon," Dominic said, readjusting the blanket over his lap and nestling against his pack. "I'm going to use this trip to teach her how to hunt."

"Women don't hunt."

We all turned to look at Jaras, who scowled into the flames and took a large swig from the flask.

"They do too," I bit back.

"Name one woman who hunts," Jaras argued.

His condescending tone sent a twinge of irritation through me. I shoved the feeling down and pursed my lips.

"There are plenty of huntresses in history. You'd know that if you actually picked up a book every now and then."

Jaras scoffed, but kept his gaze fixed on the fire.

"Besides," I continued, my tone sharpening, "*someone* needs to go out with Dom. There are four mouths to feed in this family, so unless *you'd* like to go, it looks like that person has to be me."

"I could hunt with Dom!" Wynn chirped.

Dominic leaned in and captured Wynn in a playful headlock. "When you're older, you and I will go out all the time. We'll be the finest hunters this land has ever seen!"

Wynn grunted and pushed and shoved until he managed to wriggle out of Dominic's grasp.

"But I don't want to wait until I'm older!" he whined. "I want to do it now!"

"You're too little, you know that."

Wynn stuck out his bottom lip in a pout, prompting Dominic to laugh, throw his arm around our little brother's shoulders, and haul him in to a loving squeeze.

"But how about instead you help me gut whatever Lina and I catch, huh?" He ruffled Wynn's hair. "I'll teach you how to skin it and pull the meat off the bones. Does that sound like a deal?"

"Women don't hunt," Jaras repeated.

My irritation returned, and this time I had to grip a corner of the blanket and viciously twist it in my fist to keep from saying anything. Luckily, Dominic spoke for me.

"Lina's smart and strong and quick on her feet. She has all the qualities of a good hunter. She'll do great out there."

I offered my younger brother a grateful smile. He responded by giving me a small nod back. Dom had always been the peacemaker of the family. Or he tried to be, at least. Unfortunately, peace was not a concept Jaras and I seemed to understand.

"She wouldn't need to be out there in the first place if she'd accepted Lord Olin's proposal," my older brother snapped.

Panic sank an icy claw into my chest at that name. I quickly swallowed the lump forming in my throat.

"You know why I couldn't do that," I whispered, my words hoarse.

Jaras rolled his eyes. "I don't know why it's such a big deal. Everyone knows you gave away your maidenhead years ago."

My face flushed with sudden rage and humiliation. Someone always had to bring that up. People made it seem like I was some promising race horse who'd broken its leg and had nothing else to offer.

"You'd have better suitors if you hadn't," Jaras continued, taking another hefty swig from the flask and smacking his lips at the aftertaste, "but here we are. Olin is as good an offer as you're going to get."

For Wynn's sake, I tried to stay calm.

"Lord Olin," I said, furiously gritting my teeth against the name, "is a vile old man who doesn't understand that when a woman says no, she means it."

"You should feel lucky anyone still finds you desirable," Jaras grumbled. "Tainted *and* well past a marriageable age."

I took a shuddering breath, attempting to block out the image of Olin's cracked and rotting teeth as he grinned and grabbed me roughly, his sour breath making me gag. That had been right before I'd bashed him in the head with a fireplace poker, run as fast as I could back home, and burst into the house to demand my brothers take me hunting *immediately*.

Dominic shifted uncomfortably and ground the heel of his boot into the dirt.

"I don't know if twenty-three would be considered *well* past marriageable age..." he mumbled.

"Everyone her age has at least two children by now," Jaras countered.

I sighed and grabbed a long stick to poke at the dying coals in the fire. "Gods forbid your sister doesn't utilize her womb and becomes an old hag." I glared up at Jaras. "How does that affect you? What do you care if I marry or not?"

"Lord Olin has means," Jaras replied gruffly, his bloodshot eyes narrowing in my direction, "enough to pull us out of the shit situation our parents left us in."

I couldn't take it anymore.

My rage flared, and I threw the stick aside as I leaned forward and snarled, "Your constant boozing and gambling isn't helping the family's financial situation either!"

Jaras sat upright, his eyes glinting with fury. He opened his mouth, prepared to pummel me with a scathing response, but Dominic cleared his throat to interrupt us. Jaras and I peeked over at him. Dom subtly angled his chin to Wynn and arched his eyebrows. When I looked down at our youngest brother, concern etched his cherubic face as his bright eyes bounced between the two of us.

"Maybe Wynn should go get some more firewood," Dominic stated, staring at me pointedly.

Guilt stabbed my chest. Jaras and I hated each other, but there had always been one thing we agreed on: we kept Wynn out of it. We never let our little brother see or hear our frequent disagreements and screaming matches. Wynn was sweet and innocent, and even though he'd lost our parents at such a young age, he wasn't beaten down by the world yet. It would happen one day, but gods forbid we be the ones responsible for it. So I blamed the bitter cold and the hunger in my belly for my temporary lapse in judgment and plastered a cheery smile on my face.

"Good idea, Dom. Wynn, do you know what to look for?"

Wynn bounded to his feet. "Yep! Dry wood with no sap because it pops."

"Very good." I smoothed his hair once more. "Don't wander too far, alright?"

"Yeah." Dominic leaned forward, resting his elbows on his knees. "You wouldn't want to get snatched up."

Wynn froze with one foot in the air, then lowered it and slowly faced our brother. "... Snatched up?"

"That's right." Dominic's hazel eyes glittered mischievously. "Haven't you heard the stories? There are monsters in these woods. Every Samhain, they come down from the mountains in search of little boys and girls to steal away and take home for dinner."

"*Every* Samhain?" Wynn asked, his voice wavering.

Dominic nodded gravely, the corners of his mouth twitching as he fought against a grin. "That's right. Legend says one night a year, on Samhain, the veil between our world and theirs lifts. Anything can come into our world as it pleases, free to run wild... free to *feed*." He slurped loudly to further his point.

Wynn gulped and warily scanned the forest surrounding us. A thick fog had started rolling in from the mountains and was now spreading through the trees. Its eeriness was only amplified when the wolf howled in the distance once more.

"But... but tonight's Samhain," Wynn squeaked.

"Is it?" Dominic sat back and crossed his arms. "Uh-oh. Better be careful, then."

I rolled my eyes and lightly punched my brother in the shoulder. "Dom, stop! You're scaring him."

Dominic burst out laughing. "Oh, come on! He's not scared! He's a Calder! Calder men don't get scared. They're big and strong and brave. Isn't that right, Wynn?"

"Uh-huh..." But the way Wynn continued to watch the woods told a different story.

"Do you want me to come with you?" I asked gently.

"Don't coddle him," Jaras snapped. "You do that enough. He has to learn how to be independent. Go on, Wynn, before the fire dies."

Wynn hesitated, but after an icy glare from Jaras he dutifully shuffled towards the tree line.

"Shout if you need help finding your way back!" I called after him.

My little brother nodded and disappeared into the night.

I turned back to the fire and rearranged my blanket over my knees. "Gods, Dom, are you *trying* to traumatize him?"

Dominic laughed again and stretched his hands closer to the fire. "It's a rite of passage. Father did the same to me when he took me on my first hunt."

"Of course he did," I sighed. "That explains why you're so messed up."

"You think you're so much better than us," Jaras sneered, "but the same blood runs through your veins."

Silence fell over the campsite.

Dominic lowered his gaze and picked at a loose string on his trousers.

"She was just joking, Jaras," he muttered. "We're playing around."

"No, I see it!" Jaras flung an accusatory finger in my direction. "I see the way she looks at us. The way she looks at everyone. She acts like she's too good for everything. Not even a lord is good enough for her to marry."

My blood boiled at his words. "That lord *attacked* me!"

"You weren't hurt."

"That doesn't matter!" I shrieked. Tears stung my eyes, whether from the rage or pain and panic from the memory, I wasn't sure. My hands balled into fists, digging my nails into the skin. "Lord Olin is a fucking monster!"

Jaras rolled his eyes. "Now you're just being dramatic."

The tears finally slipped out and spilled down my cheeks. How could I make my brother understand I insisted on this trip because I was terrified for my safety at home? Would he even care if I explained that while I was running from Lord Olin's estate, the lord had screamed after me, swearing that he'd find me and finish what he'd started? Doubtful. My brother's eyes were devoid of any compassion as he took one look at my tears and laughed before bringing the flask to his lips.

My rage surged.

I darted forward, grabbed the flask out of Jaras's hands, and tossed it into the fire.

"You bitch!" he shouted, roughly shoving me off and lunging for the flames. I lost my footing and stumbled backwards. When I hit the ground, the back of my head cracked against a rock, and searing pain shot through my skull. I cried out and coiled into a heap as stars exploded across my vision.

"Lina!"

Dominic rushed to my side and carefully scooped my head into his lap. Jaras didn't even seem to notice my blood pooling in Dom's hands. He was too busy using the stick I'd been poking the fire with to flick the flask out of the embers and onto safe ground.

"What the hell is wrong with you?!" Dominic shouted. He

grabbed my blanket and lifted it to my head, blotting at the wound.

Jaras sat in a huff. "It's just a scratch. She'll be fine."

Dominic sighed as he eased me into a seated position. "You have a problem, Jaras."

Jaras just rolled his eyes and took another drink.

Gingerly, I felt at my blood-soaked hair and winced as my fingers found the ridges of a bloody gash. I glared at my elder brother through the flames separating us. "Our parents would be ashamed of you."

Jaras sniffed and shrugged. "Then it's a good thing they're not here, isn't it?"

Suddenly, a bloodcurdling scream cut through the forest.

The three of us shot to our feet, Dominic's eyes growing wide.

"Wynn..." he breathed.

Dread washed over me.

Without waiting for the others, I bolted into the forest.

"Wynnric!" I screamed as I tore through the brush. My head pounded, and branches snagged at my hair and clothing, one protruding bough even nicking my cheek enough to draw blood, but I barely felt it.

"Wynnric!" Dominic shouted. He raced through the woods not far from me, maybe fifty paces to my left. "Wynn, where are you?!"

The fog thickened, making it impossible to see where we were going. My brothers and I charged on in the direction of the scream, stumbling more and more as our surroundings disappeared into the mist. To my right, Jaras tripped over a raised root and grunted as he went down, but I didn't stop to help him up.

"Wynn!" Dominic called out again, his voice cracking, "Wynn, please, say something!"

My shins collided with a mossy stump protruding from the forest floor, but I grit my teeth against the pain and sprinted onward.

Not Wynn. Gods, please not Wynn!

He was the good one. Out of all of us, he was the good one.

Jaras had his issues.

I was stubborn and impulsive and had fought with my parents and older brother about everything my entire life.

Dominic could never take anything seriously, so much so that it made having an emotional conversation with him utterly impossible.

But Wynn? Sweet, angelic Wynn? He was as pure as the driven snow. We couldn't let anything happen to him.

I *would not* let anything happen to him.

I fumbled through the forest, continuing to trip over rocks and roots and brambles until the trees began to thin. All at once they dispersed, and I staggered into a clearing. I bent over and braced my hands on my knees, attempting to catch my breath. As I squinted through the dense fog ahead, shadowy outlines slowly came into view.

"Wynn?" I called out.

"Lina!" My brother cried, terror choking his voice.

A gust of wind whipped through the forest, lifting the fog just enough to reveal something that made my blood run cold.

A band of ten marauders surrounded my brother, each more rough and menacing than the last. A boorish brute of a man missing an eye seemed to be their leader, and cowering beneath his hand, a crude knife at his throat, was my little brother.

The man grinned when he caught sight of me, showing off a mouthful stained teeth. They reminded me of Lord Olin's, and the thought immediately had bile churning in my stomach.

"Well, well, well," the man chuckled. "What do we have here? Two for one?"

I raised my hands to show I wasn't armed.

"Please," I panted. "Please, don't hurt him."

My other brothers careened out of the forest behind me, stopping dead in their tracks at the scene in front of them.

"Oh, we wouldn't hurt him," the leader crooned, tightening his grip on the back of Wynn's neck until my brother whimpered in pain. My stomach lurched at the sound.

"This one'll fetch a pretty penny at auction," the man continued. "There's good money to be had in little boys like this one."

"We can pay you!" Dominic blurted. "We don't have much, but we have blankets and a few family heirlooms back at our camp. Our father's hunting knife, and a finely crafted bow and arrows. It's yours, all of it!"

The man pressed his blade further into the skin of Wynn's throat, causing my little brother to cry harder. "That's not nearly enough. This one's worth five times that."

"Take our sister, then."

My knees nearly buckled.

Dominic and I whipped our heads to stare at Jaras in disbelief, but he refused to look at us. His mouth was set in a firm line, his expression disturbingly cold.

"What?" The man laughed, as if he too was just as shocked by the words as Dom and I were.

But Jaras didn't even flinch.

He simply jerked his chin in my direction and repeated, "My sister. Take her instead of the boy."

Air whooshed out of me like someone had just punched it from my lungs. My stomach clenched, my throat tightened, and if I had eaten dinner, I would have vomited right there in front of everyone. Instead, I gaped at my brother and furiously fought the tears stinging my eyes.

The raider glanced over at me and looked me up and down. His lewd, lingering gaze made my skin crawl.

"She's desirable," Jaras continued, "don't you think? Men will pay good money for her too."

The man sucked his teeth, still ogling me. "Virgin?"

"Yes," my brother lied.

A ringing started in my ears.

"Jaras—" Dominic began, but our elder brother held up his hand, silencing him.

This wasn't happening. This couldn't be happening.

"*Please,*" Jaras pressed, stepping closer. "Take my sister, and the blankets and bow we have back at camp. Just not the boy." His eyes softened as he glanced at Wynn, and for the first time since I could remember, Jaras showed a sliver of emotion. "Please, take anything but him."

Tense silence settled over the glade.

Finally, the man holding Wynn chuckled again, shaking his head grimly before fixing his beady eye on me.

"Miss..." he sighed. "I don't envy you. You've gotten a poor lot in life if *this* is who you're required to call family." He gestured to Jaras.

My bottom lip quivered, but I tried to stay strong.

The raider kept his firm hold on Wynn, but removed the knife from my little brother's neck.

"I'll tell you what," he said, his gaze flicking to Jaras before settling on me once more. "How about we do you a favor?"

He let out a single sharp whistle, and as stealthily as a wraith, one of the members of his band materialized out of the fog, grabbed my older brother from behind, and rammed a blade into the center of his back. Jaras gasped and went rigid for a few breathless seconds, his stunned gaze locking on mine before he let out a strangled cough and sputtered a mouthful of blood.

"There!" The leader of the band cackled. "Family no more! Problem solved."

Wynn's horrified scream echoed into the surrounding mountains.

I froze, unable to look away as my older brother's eyes rolled back in his head and he toppled to the ground, twitching and spasming as his life drained away.

Beside me, Dominic let out a guttural wail before charging towards our brother's attacker.

Everything went in slow motion after that.

Wynn continued to scream as he watched blood pool around Jaras's body, his cries growing distorted in my ears.

Dominic clashed with our fallen brother's killer, his fists and fury his only weapons, but he was no match for the man twice his size, or the knife swiftly rammed into his stomach. Dominic crumpled to his knees and gasped for air, his hands flying to his abdomen as blood gushed from the wound.

Wynn's screams turned to heaving sobs. His voice was a distant echo when it wailed my name.

The rough grip of one of the marauders finally snapped me out of my daze. His hand latched around my arm and dragged me towards him. I knew that movement. I'd felt it before, in Lord Olin's kitchen. My body recognized the man's intent and responded before my mind could catch up. Instinctively, I kicked and thrashed, but the man still managed to bring me to the ground.

"No! *No!*" I screamed, pushing at him as he pinned me on my back and clawed at my clothing.

But he was too strong, and there was no fireplace poker to defend myself with this time.

"This'll all be over soon," my attacker whispered in my ear.

I choked on a sob as the man fumbled for the button of his pants. Miserably, I shut my eyes tight and braced for the worst.

But another scream rang out through the night.

... Only this one didn't belong to Wynn.

It was a high-pitched, otherworldly shriek that made everyone, including the man on top of me, freeze.

My attacker scanned the fog-laden forest around us, his brow furrowing in confusion.

"What the hell was—"

His words were cut short as a shadowy figure darted by. The man choked, then looked down at me, his eyes round with surprise. I watched in horror as he brought a hand up to touch his neck. A deep gash had been carved across it, a sliver of red blooming at its center. The man gurgled as the blood overflowed, dribbling faster and faster before bubbling out of his mouth and pouring from the wound. The stream of hot liquid rained onto my chest and face, filling my nostrils with its metallic sting. I rolled out from under the man a split second before he collapsed to ground and convulsed in his death throes.

I hauled myself to my hands and knees, catching sight of Wynn not far away. He met my gaze.

"Wynn, run!" I screamed.

Then the world turned into chaos.

Dark shadows flashed all around us, too fast for me to identify. Whenever they collided with one of the raiders, the man ended up gasping and gurgling as his blood spewed violently from a fatal slit to the neck. We were under attack by an unseen foe, and the once hardened men reverted to frightened children as they cried for their mothers and begged mercy from their gods.

Frantically, I crawled towards the edge of the clearing, keeping my stomach flat to the ground while I dodged the writhing, blood-soaked bodies of men as they dropped around me. I'd nearly reached the tree line when something clamped on to my ankle and dragged me back into the clearing. I screamed, fumbling for anything to defend myself with. My hand collided with a fist-sized rock, and I latched on to it. Wrapping my fingers tight around its jagged surface, I flipped over onto my back, coming face-to-face with what was responsible for the annihilation around me.

A spindly creature with slimy pale green skin and bulging black eyes grinned down at me. It was unlike anything I'd ever seen, and I froze again, unable to speak or think or feel anything besides terror. All I could do was stare up at the creature and wince as its mouth drooled globs of thick, sticky black sludge onto my face.

"Pretty human," it slithered. A long forked black tongue dropped out of its mouth and trailed along the length of my jaw. Its breath reeked of rotting flesh, the stench forcing my head to the side as I gagged.

The creature let out an amused snicker.

"I will enjoy this," it hissed.

I managed to face forward again, but shrank back as the monster opened its mouth wider, then wider still, until its jaw unhinged like a viper's. Row after row of needlelike teeth stared back at me, black drool dripping from their points to mix with the blood and tears on my cheeks.

A nauseating wave of realization swept over me:

There would be no escaping this time.

I couldn't run from this the way I had from Lord Olin, and my brothers weren't here to help me. I was going to die, and it would be brutal and agonizing.

The fear paralyzing my body told me to shut my eyes and pray the gods took me quickly, but deep inside another voice called out too. It was much quieter, almost entirely drowned out by the fear, but it spoke urgently.

Fight, it whispered. *Fight like hell.*

Those words sparked a fire in my soul, igniting a flame of determination that tore through my limbs and replaced terror with adrenaline.

I wasn't done living. Not yet.

I grit my teeth, tightened my grip around the rock in my hand, and smashed it into the side of the creature's head. It let out that horrible, high-pitched screech from earlier and rose on its knees, allowing me enough time to clamber out from under it and scramble towards one of the marauder's mutilated bodies. The man's dagger was still at his side, and I snatched hold of the hilt and ripped it from its sheath.

When the creature recovered, it grabbed my ankle and pulled me back again, but this time I was ready. As it unhinged its jaw and prepared to strike, I rolled over and jammed the dagger into its open mouth as hard as I could. The blade found its mark, the tip piercing up and through the creature's skull.

The monster gaped and twitched, its body going rigid as the light of life dimmed in its eyes. I dislodged the dagger and yanked it backwards, accidentally slicing my wrist on one of the creature's dripping fangs in the process. I sucked sharply through my teeth, wincing as my skin split and heat shot up my arm. Pushing past the pain, I shoved the monster's lifeless body off me with a grunt and scrambled to my feet.

Panting heavily, I took in my surroundings. The darting green figures had gone, leaving me alone in the now quiet clearing. I lasted all of ten seconds taking in the slaughter before the stench of steaming blood wafting off the corpses forced me to bend over and viciously dry-heave. When I composed myself, I returned to my surveying, holding my breath as I searched for any sign of a small mop of blond hair.

But Wynn wasn't here.

He must have escaped during the madness and run into the forest. Hope surged through me, and I stumbled away from the massacre and started for the trees.

"Wynn!" I called into the night.

My foot caught on something along the ground, and I tripped, falling face-first into the dirt with a groan. Pain sliced across my cheek, and judging by the way dust and gravel clung to my skin, fresh blood now coated my face. I pushed myself upright and maneuvered to see what I'd stumbled on. A tortured sob wrenched itself from my throat when I saw what it was.

Jaras looked back at me, his eyes wide open but devoid of life, nothing but an empty shell without a soul. My memory replayed all the times he and I had fought and screamed at each other, the two of us saying the most hurtful things we could come up with just to get a reaction. My stomach roiled with guilt, and in that moment I regretted every second.

But there was nothing I could do for my brother.

Not this one, at least.

I mustered my strength, hauled myself upright, and refocused on the woods ahead.

"Wynnric!" I called again, shuffling forward until I'd forced myself into a jog.

When the trees thickened around me, everything became unnervingly quiet. Even the crackle of leaves and twigs beneath my boots seemed to be swallowed up by the night.

"Wynnric!" I yelled. The dense blanket of fog muted my words.

I tripped again, this time over a jagged rock that sliced into my shin. I fell to the ground and groaned, but weakly dragged myself back to standing. I pushed on, but my vision was blurry and my head felt ten times heavier than it had before. I tried to shake off the sensation, but the farther I went, the stronger it grew. Soon I had to cling to mossy tree boughs and boulders to steady myself.

"Wynnric, where are you?!" I shouted. My voice was muffled in my ears.

Still I trudged on, but with every step my breathing grew labored. The world spun around me, leaving me dizzy and disoriented. I fumbled for a branch to hold on to, but it snapped beneath my weight, sending me hurtling towards the earth. It took me a few seconds to process that I was tumbling down a muddy slope before I landed with a splash and a grunt in the shallows of a swift-flowing river. The icy water soaked through my winter coat and stung my skin. I tried to lift my head, but it now felt too heavy to hold upright. I attempted to drag myself out of the river, but I was too weak and collapsed. The current tugged at me, threatening to pull me deeper into its clutches. My body eventually went numb, and it became harder and harder to keep my eyelids open.

I was so tired. More tired than I'd ever been in my entire life. I just needed a little rest to regain my strength, and then I'd crawl out of the river.

My heart echoed in my ears, its rhythmic thumps growing weak and drawn out.

Unable to fight the exhaustion any longer, I let my eyes flutter shut. I'd just begun to drift away to a quiet, peaceful place, when the weight of realization washed over me.

This is it. This is where I die.

But then I heard voices.

Chapter 2

Maybe I was hallucinating, or hearing the voices of my ancestors in the Underworld calling me home.

But I wasn't imagining it.

Someone was coming closer.

More than one someone.

Still groggy and fighting unconsciousness, I stayed as still as possible in case the voices belonged to more of the strange creatures from before. But as they neared, my fears faded. They didn't sound like slithering, green-skinned monsters. They sounded like two men.

"Are you sure?"

"Yes. Stop asking that."

"But—"

"Look! Right there!"

Twigs snapped and leaves crunched as footsteps padded closer. Water splashed as someone waded towards me. My eyes fluttered open, but in my blurred vision, all I could see was two shadowy silhouettes hunched over me.

"Oh, gods. She doesn't look good..."

A hand grasped my arm where it had been sliced open by the monster's teeth.

"The venom's spreading fast. She needs a healer."

"We should just leave her."

"Xavier, look at her! She'll never survive!"

"But if dawn comes—"

"I'm aware, Xavier! Make yourself useful and ride ahead to Valdir. Tell him to gather any healers he can."

There was a moment of silence as the other voice hesitated.

"*Now*, Xavier!"

"Yes, sir."

One set of footsteps quickly retreated. Then a pair of thick, muscular arms wrapped around me and hauled my body from the river's icy grip.

"It's alright," a deep voice murmured in my ear, "I've got you."

Then my vision went black.

I WAS in and out of consciousness.

Flashes of images passed before my eyes, but I was unsure if I was dreaming them or if they were actually there.

I saw a pair of deep blue eyes staring down at me, filled with worry and concern.

I saw my fingers tangled in a horse's mane while a set of large hands rested on top of my own to keep them in place.

I saw a dark castle looming on the horizon at the base of a mountain, with waterfalls trickling underneath its bridges and balconies.

And finally, I saw a gilded staircase lit by black candelabras that bobbed past me as someone carried me up its steps. Maybe it was my imagination, but I could have sworn the faintest strains of music played in the distance. When my eyes shut this time, my head lolled to the side and came to rest comfortably against something firm, clad in satin and velvet. It smelled of musk and wood and spice, and even though I'd never smelled anything quite like it, it instantly made me think of home. I lost myself in that feeling and once again drifted into the beckoning darkness.

"Soren!"

The sudden booming voice made me gasp, and my eyes snapped open.

I blinked rapidly, experiencing a brief moment of clarity. I was on my feet now, groggily teetering side to side. Someone stood behind me and held onto my shoulders to keep me upright. They pressed their chest to my back to steady me further, providing a warm wall for me to lean against. When my vision began to clear, my filthy, waterlogged boots came into view, their soles oozing mud all over a glossy marble floor. Still in a daze, I lifted my eyes, taking several seconds to process my surroundings.

We were in a mirrored ballroom embellished with gold trimmings and black candles, similar to the ones I fuzzily remembered from the staircase. They illuminated the entire room in a golden glow, revealing a sea of black, burgundy, and orange swirling around me, chaotic and overwhelming. I rubbed at my eyes, then rubbed them again. I was staring at... fabric?

Yes. Fabric. Expensive, luxurious material forming extravagant skirts and tailored jackets.

Fascinated, I watched the decadent velvet, silk and tulle spin around me, and something in my mind finally clicked.

Dancing. I was surrounded by people dancing.

"Soren!" the voice called again.

I pulled my gaze from the ball gowns and suits sashaying

around the room and looked up. A man pushed through the crowd towards me. He wore a rust-red overcoat trimmed in black fur, and had rich brown skin with gray eyes that narrowed as they scanned my face.

"Xavier explained what happened," he said urgently, stopping in front of me. "This is her?"

"Yes. She's in rough shape," replied a deep voice behind me. It was the same voice from before, the one that belonged to whoever had pulled me from the river. "Can you help her?"

"I'm not sure." The gray-eyed man frowned and rubbed the stubble on his chin. "I've never dealt with her kind before, and neither have my healers. But I'll see what they can do." He bent and looked me in the eyes, offering a kind smile as he did. "Miss? Miss, can you understand me?"

A sluggish nod was all I could manage.

"Good." The man smiled again, his friendly expression brightening the room even more than the warm candlelight. "Can you tell me your name?"

I swallowed and scraped my tongue over my cracked lips. When I opened my mouth, my voice was still muffled, like someone had stuffed rags in my ears.

"Lina..." I mumbled. "Lina Calder."

Suddenly, an eerie wave of dread washed over me.

My skin prickled, the hair on the back of my neck stood on end, and a voice at the back of my mind shouted that something about this moment, this place, was wrong.

My eyes drifted around the room again, locking on the sea of orange and black.

That. That didn't feel right. But why?

I squinted, focusing intently on the guests in the ballroom. Their clothing was rich and elegant, finer than anything I'd ever come in contact with. Even the clothing of the lords and ladies going to and from Lord Olin's estate couldn't compare. I expected the ensembles to be accompanied by impressive jewelry, but when my gaze moved upwards, my heart nearly stopped.

This was the first time I had really looked at the faces of those in the room, and to my horror, there was not one among them who looked human.

Monsters straight out of the folktales the grannies in my village told us as children now swirled around me.

Instead of smiles, fangs flashed in the candlelight.

Instead of hair, horns spiraled skyward.

Instead of eyes and cheeks and noses, skulls and snouts and scales peppered each face.

I wanted to scream, but the wind squeezed from my lungs, and just as I had with the marauders earlier that night, I froze in terror. Someone said my name but they sounded worlds away. The hands on my shoulders shook me, but I couldn't move. My name was called again, echoing louder this time, but it was drowned out by a ringing in my ears. Everything moved in slow motion once more, and when the horrifying figures stopped their dancing and turned to look at me, their monstrous faces blurred and churned together to form one single hellish hallucination.

It was enough to finally push my mind and body over the edge.

My eyes rolled back in my head, my knees buckled, and I collapsed onto the cold marble floor where I faded into oblivion.

When I regained consciousness, the two voices from the forest were back, still bickering like an old married couple.

"Gods! Could you *please* stop pacing? What has gotten into you?"

"*That. That* has gotten into me! How are you so calm when *that* is just lying there?"

Cautiously, I opened my eyes just a sliver, enough to subtly peer through my lashes and analyze my surroundings in secret before anyone realized I was awake.

I was in a large study, lying on a green velvet sofa across from a solid mahogany desk. The room had wall-to-wall bookshelves, satin drapes in rich jewel tones, and gold-plated accents on every surface. I'd never seen such a lavish space. Not even Lord Olin's estate had this kind of wealth, or anything remotely close to it.

Two figures stood at the other end of the room. One faced me, but the other had his back to the couch. The one who faced me was dressed in a burgundy suit with black accents. He looked around the same age as I was or a little younger, with shaggy dark brown curls, large forest green eyes, and a smattering of freckles across his face. He was in the process of gnawing on his thumbnail and anxiously striding back and forth in front of the desk.

"Never thought I'd see the day when a woman had you stumbling all over yourself," the figure with his back to me said, amusement in his voice.

Even though I couldn't see his face, judging from the way he spoke and held himself, he was older than the man in burgundy. While that man paced nervously, this one stood tall and proud with his broad shoulders squared and his head confidently lifted. He wore a black shirt and silver brocade vest, while ash-brown hair cascaded onto his back in messy waves.

"It's not just a woman," the man in burgundy growled, "it's a *human* woman."

"And?"

"And it's nearly dawn!"

"I'm well aware."

"Then wake her up! She's running out of time!"

"There's no need. She's already awake."

A flutter of panic shot through my heart.

I'd been caught.

I opened my eyes fully as the men turned. The one in burgundy gulped nervously, while the other simply fixed a pair of dark blue eyes on me, the light sprinkling of facial hair around his mouth curving upwards with his lips as they formed a charming smile. He appeared to be in his early thirties, and except for a raised white scar along his left cheek and one through the tail of his right eyebrow, there wasn't a single flaw on his exquisite face. He was easily the most attractive man I'd ever seen, and I wasn't sure if my stomach flipped because of that or because my head spun as I gingerly pushed myself into a seated position.

The handsome man in black hurried over and knelt beside me as I sat up, placing a hand on my back to support me.

"Easy, miss. You've been through a great deal."

"Where am I?" I croaked. I licked at my chapped lips, prompting the jittery burgundy man to grab a goblet of water and bring it over. His hands shook as he extended it. My brows knit together in confusion, but instead of calling attention to it, I accepted the water and lifted it to my mouth.

"You're under the protection of King Valdir of Radomir," the man beside me said as he watched me drink. "He's a dear friend. His healers saved your life."

Radomir? I'd never even heard of it. How far had my brothers and I accidentally trekked into the woods if the names and locations no longer sounded familiar?

... My brothers.

The memory of Jaras's blood pooling on the ground while

his eyes dimmed of life flashed into my mind. A wave of nausea hit me, and the claw of panic in my chest tightened into a fist. Instantly, I battled frantic, gulping breaths.

"Easy," the blue-eyed man repeated, his deep voice calm and soothing. "You're alright. You're safe now."

He rubbed small circles on my back, just like I would do to comfort Wynnric when he was scared.

Oh *gods*, Wynn!

My eyes grew wide, and I shot to my feet, my vision exploding with bright stars at the sudden movement. The world spun, and my already uneasy stomach twisted. I groaned as my knees gave out, but the handsome man caught me in his arms and gently eased me back to recline on the couch.

"Fascinating," the man in burgundy muttered, squinting at me. "She's so weak. If it were any one of us, we'd have been fully healed hours ago."

"You're not helping, Xavier," the other man snapped.

Burgundy suit leaned against the desk and crossed his arms, sulking like a sullen teenager.

"My brother," I rasped. "Where is he?"

The handsome man's brow furrowed. He peeked over at Xavier, who shrugged and shook his head. The man turned back to me.

"You were the only one we saw."

"I need to find him." I went to sit up, but the man firmly held me down.

"You need to rest."

"She needs to *leave*," Xavier said, stomping his foot. "If we don't get her across the river in a few hours—"

"*Enough!*"

Both Xavier and I jumped at the man's outburst. He composed himself by taking a deep breath and letting it out slowly.

"We will get her across in time, Xavier," he stated. "I'm sure she doesn't want to stay here either."

Xavier nodded sheepishly, not meeting the man's eye.

"Please..." I wriggled out of my savior's grasp and finally managed to bring myself to seated. "I have to find my little brother."

"Miss," the man sighed wearily, raising his eyes to the ceiling. "I'm sure your brother is fine. He's probably safe and sound back at your camp, having himself a nice hot meal—"

"We were attacked," I blurted, my voice breaking. Tears welled in my eyes and spilled out onto my cheeks. "We were attacked," I repeated feebly. "My other brothers, they..."

I choked as my throat tightened, and my heart ached so badly I thought I might die from the pain.

"They were killed. And then there were these strange things..." I motioned to the bandage on my arm and shook my head. "I don't know what they were, but they... they slaughtered everyone. But Wynn ran, he got away. Please, he's only six. He's only six..."

I broke down then, melting into a hysterical, blubbering heap on the sofa. The weight of everything I'd experienced that evening finally hit me, and I sobbed miserably, losing myself in the hopelessness and despair that came flooding in. It took a few seconds before I noticed the hand that had gently landed on my shoulder. I looked up to find myself staring into the handsome man's deep blue gaze. He was frowning, but compassion warmed his eyes.

"Please," I whimpered pitifully, "you have to help me."

The man's jaw clenched as he studied my face. Then he slowly reached out and delicately brushed his knuckles across my cheeks to wipe away my tears. For a brief moment, the tenderness of his touch eased the aching in my chest ever so slightly.

When he lowered his hand, the man let out a heavy sigh and glanced at Xavier.

"Find Valdir and see if he'll pull some of his men from the ball. You'll go back to where we found her and start your search there."

Xavier nodded dutifully, then faced me. "Does your brother look like you?"

I shook my head. "Not really. He has blond hair, not brown. And he has blue eyes. His name is Wynn. Wynnric Calder."

Xavier nodded again and exited the room.

I turned back to the man beside me, my bottom lip quivering as I tried to rein in my emotions. He offered me a small reassuring smile.

"We'll do everything we can to find him. You have my word."

"Thank you, sir," I said earnestly. "Thank you so much. I'm in your debt."

The man waved away the comment. "There is no debt. And please, call me Soren."

He extended his hand. When I took it, the rough calluses on his palms brushed against my own. He might look like a nobleman, but those calluses, the scars on his face, and his commanding presence made me think this man was also a warrior. I became keenly aware of how small and frail my hand looked in his.

"I'm Lina."

Soren smiled. "It's nice to meet you, Lina."

He bent his head and lightly pressed a pair of warm, pillowy lips to the back of my hand. When he looked up through hooded eyes, he added sincerely, "I wish it were under better circumstances."

I swallowed, thinking of Wynn alone in the woods somewhere, shivering and crying out for me and our brothers. "Me too."

Soren's smile disappeared, and he released my hand. He then glanced down at his own, toying with a silver signet ring around his index finger.

"Lina," he began hesitantly, "do... do you know where you are?"

I looked around us at the extravagant study. "You said it was called Radomir, didn't you?"

"Yes," Soren replied. He paused for a moment, his brow furrowing as he searched for the right words. "Have you ever heard of it?"

"No. My brothers and I must have wandered farther into the mountains than we thought."

"Yes," Soren mused, a distant look coming over him. "Much farther."

He took a deep breath before scooting a little closer to me. "Lina, are you also aware of what day it is?"

I nodded. "Samhain."

"So you're familiar with the holiday?"

"Yes."

"And..." Soren frowned. "Are you familiar with the lore behind it?"

I nodded again. "Once a year, the veil between the human world and the Otherworld is lifted, allowing passage between both." I shrugged. "An old wives' tale used to scare children into behaving."

Soren's lips pressed into a tight line.

"You..." I squinted, studying his expression. "You don't actually believe in all that?"

"I do," he said softly.

I scoffed.

Wonderful. I've been saved by a madman.

Soren leaned back into the sofa and raised an eyebrow.

"Is that so hard to believe?" He motioned to my arm. "You were attacked by something you'd never seen before, weren't you? Something... otherworldly?"

I peeked down at the bandage around my right wrist. Images of the black-tongued, bug-eyed creature flashed across my mind. I quickly shut my eyes and shook my head to chase them away.

"How do you explain that?" Soren asked.

When I opened my eyes again, he was staring at me intently.

"I... I don't..."

"Think about it, Lina," Soren pressed.

Reluctantly, I relived the massacre.

The chilling screech that made everything in the forest stand still.

The shadows moving at inhuman speed.

The creature's slimy skin pressing on top of me as it swiped a putrid black tongue across my face.

There was no logical explanation for any of it.

My eyes widened, and I looked back up at Soren. Slowly, he leaned forward and gently took my hand.

"They're not just stories, Lina," he said earnestly. "It's real. All of it."

The door to the study flung open, and Xavier burst back into the room, his chest heaving.

"One of Valdir's men saw a group of Nethers heading west shortly before he arrived," he panted. "There's a good chance they crossed paths with the boy. I think we should go after them first, before they get too far."

Xavier ran a hand through his hair, slicking one of the thick curls off his forehead and tucking it behind his left ear. Something glittered there, catching my attention.

Two small silver hoop earrings hung from the top of Xavier's ear.

An ear that curved into a point at the top.

I opened my mouth and let out a horrified scream.

Xavier stuffed his hands into his pockets and sighed. "Well, looks like she just figured it out."

"Lina!" Soren said, squeezing my hand tighter in an attempt to ground me. "Lina, it's alright!"

But then my gaze caught on a pointed ear tip poking through his own brunette waves.

I ripped my hand from Soren's grasp and roughly pushed him away before scrambling backwards off the couch.

"What the *fuck?!*"

Soren stood and raised his hands in defense. Behind him, Xavier groaned and started pacing again.

"*What the fuck?!*" I repeated.

I snatched a heavy gold bookend off a nearby shelf and held it above my head, ready to strike, and warily backed away.

"Lina," Soren said cooly, "you need to calm down—"

"Don't tell me to fucking calm down!" I screeched, my back colliding with the bookcase behind me. "What the fuck are you?!"

"I didn't expect human women to swear so much," Xavier mused.

Soren shot him a dirty look, then returned his attention to me.

"Lina, I will explain everything, but first I need you to calm down. Just let go of the bookend."

I hurled the gold slab at Soren's head.

He dodged it, then frowned impatiently.

"Well, you didn't say *how* she had to let go of it," Xavier muttered, trying to hide the smirk tugging at one corner of his mouth.

I whirled and ripped books off their shelves, lobbing them wildly at the men across the room.

"Lina!" Soren ducked out of the way of a large flying tome in the nick of time. "Lina, that's enough!"

"Stay away from me!" I shrieked.

I needed to get out. I needed to find Wynn.

Desperate for an escape, I frantically searched the study. The pointy-eared men stood between me and the only door, but there was a large window to my left. I had no idea how high up we were, but maybe if I crawled out onto the window's ledge, I could find a way to climb down.

I threw one last book in their direction, this one glancing off Xavier's kneecap and pulling out a yelp of pain, before I saw my chance and bolted for the window. I fumbled for the latch, and once my hand found it, I yanked the window open. A gust of wind instantly tore through, nearly knocking me off my feet.

"Lina, wait!" Soren barked.

I squinted against the draft and cautiously stepped onto the ledge. When I looked down, I saw I was much, *much* higher up than I expected. I could barely even make out the ground below. Bone-chilling wind whipped at me, sending my hair swirling around my face and making me lose my balance. I grasped the side of the window frame to steady myself.

Gods save me, I prayed.

"Lina, please!"

I glanced over my shoulder at Soren. His eyes were round with worry, his arm extended towards me.

"Please," he repeated, "if you ever want to see your brother again, you're going to need our help."

I peeked back down at the ground, the height making my head spin.

"We're not going to hurt you," Soren said softly. "I promise."

A lump formed in my throat. One wrong move or misplaced

step on this ledge and I would plummet to my death. On the other hand, this man, or whatever the hell he was, seemed genuine, and he had already saved my life once. I didn't like it, but the choice was clear.

I took a deep breath and let it out slowly. Then I stepped back from the window and shoved it closed before brushing past Soren and his outstretched hand. I returned to my spot on the sofa and plopped down, but not before grabbing one last book for protection and clutching it tight to my chest.

"Alright," I huffed. "What the *hell* is going on?"

Chapter 3

After Xavier had left to go in search of Wynn, and I had taken Soren's advice and calmed down slightly, Soren politely offered me a change of clothes and a warm meal. The clothing I accepted, eager to peel off the dirty, bloodstained material clinging to my body. When I slipped on a simple, long-sleeved blue dress instead, a weight lifted from my shoulders. I still desperately needed a bath to wash the evening off me, but this would do for the time being.

The meal was a nice gesture, but I was far too anxious to keep anything down. I did, however, agree to a steaming cup of peppermint tea, which eased my roiling stomach and warmed my chilled bones from the inside out.

"Better?" Soren asked, taking a seat on the opposite end of the couch. He'd lit a fire in the hearth and tied back the top half of his hair, revealing more of his sculpted cheekbones and square jawline.

"A little," I said, sipping gingerly at the contents of the mug, "but I'd be even better if you told me what's happening. Have I gone insane? Is that what this is?"

"No," Soren chuckled. "But I understand how it would feel that way. As Xavier's behavior earlier demonstrated, we're not accustomed to seeing your kind either, but at least we know you exist. I can't imagine what you must be feeling."

I let my gaze drift over his near flawless face, the strange pointed ears, his expensive clothes...

"What the hell are you?" It took me a moment to realize I spoke the words out loud.

Soren laughed again.

Embarrassed, I hurriedly shook my head. "I'm sorry, I... I didn't mean—"

"It's fine, I understand." Soren gave me a reassuring smile. The light from the fire flickered and danced in his eyes, somehow making him more attractive.

"There are many different words in many different dialects," he continued, "but the most common and preferred term is Fae."

I nodded slowly, a dull ache forming in the center of my forehead as I worked to process the information.

"And the thing that..." My voice trailed off, and I glanced down at the bandage on my arm.

I couldn't do it. I couldn't say the words, couldn't talk about or dwell on the horrors from tonight anymore. So instead, I gestured to the wound.

"*That*. What was that? Was that a Fae too?"

"No. We call them Nethers."

I stared at Soren blankly.

"It's a broad term," he explained, readjusting in his seat and draping his arms over the back of the couch. "Ultimately, you'll find two separate groups in this realm. There are creatures like me and Xavier and Valdir, and then there are others. Our legends say they originated in a place called the Netherworld and escaped here through a crack in the ground, hence why we refer to them as Nethers."

"And they all look like that one I saw in the forest?"

"No. There are different types, just as there are different types of Fae."

"Then how can you tell the difference?"

Soren's face grew serious. "Nethers are vile, evil creatures. There's no mistaking one if you come across it."

I shivered. There was definitely no mistaking the creature that had attacked me in the woods tonight.

"What about the ones in the gowns?" I asked, suddenly remembering the eerie ballroom with monsters swirling around me.

"Those were Fae nobles. Samhain is a dark holiday, so each year, Valdir holds a dark ball to celebrate it. Xavier and I were on our way there when we found you. What you saw were just masks and costumes. I apologize if they scared you."

While we'd been talking, I hadn't noticed the faint sound of music in the distance, but now that I was paying attention, my ears locked onto a haunting melody of violins and flutes floating up from below.

"Well, I'm sorry for making you miss your ball," I mumbled.

Soren waved the comment away. "I've been going to these for two hundred years, they're all the same. I'm not missing anything. I'm just glad you're alright."

I nodded and stared into my tea.

Wait, did he just say...

My head jerked up. "*Two hundred years?*"

Soren gave me a sheepish smile.

I sniffed and shook my head, returning my attention to the tea and lifting it to my lips. "So the stories really are true. You're immortal."

"I wouldn't say immortal," Soren muttered.

When I looked at him over the top of my mug and raised an eyebrow, he shrugged.

"We can die, it just takes a little more effort."

I let out a wry chuckle, which caused a dazzling grin to spread over Soren's face.

"Look at that! She *can* smile!"

"Well, there hasn't really been much to smile about today," I countered.

"No, I suppose not." Soren's face fell. After a few moments of silence, he leaned forward earnestly. "You've been very brave, Lina. I hope you know that."

A familiar sting started behind my eyes. Brave? No. Frantically, desperately scrambling for a chance at survival? Yes. But if I was being honest, I'd been doing that for a long time. My brothers and I had been fighting to survive ever since our parents passed away.

"I don't feel very brave," I whispered.

"No one ever feels brave."

I peeked up at Soren. The confidence in his voice and the knowing look in his eyes made me wonder how many battles he had seen. How many times he too had felt that frenzied burning in his soul, that inner fire forcing him to push onward, to fight like hell and *live*, no matter what.

"Don't worry." Soren sat back in the sofa again and offered me another reassuring smile. "Soon all this will be nothing but a bad dream. Xavier is a skilled tracker. I have no doubt he'll find your brother and have you two back before dawn."

I tilted my head to the side and narrowed my eyes. "Why do you keep saying that?"

"Saying what?"

"Dawn. Xavier kept mentioning it too. He seemed nervous about it for some reason. What's the significance of the dawn?"

When Soren finally broke his silence, he chose his words carefully.

"Samhain is the one night a year when the veil between our worlds is lifted. But when Samhain is over, that veil goes down again. And if you and your brother have not passed over the boundary in time..." He took a deep breath. "Then I'm afraid you won't be able to return to your own realm until the veil lifts again."

My stomach dropped. "Which would be—"

"The next Samhain."

"So you're saying," I said slowly, "if I don't find Wynn before morning... we'll have to stay here for an entire year?"

Soren nodded solemnly.

Attempting to fight the panic rising in my chest, I licked my lips and swallowed. "How long do I have?"

He didn't answer my question. Instead, he slipped my hand into his and tenderly skated his thumb across my knuckles.

"Don't worry, Lina. We'll find him."

I ripped my hand from his grasp and sat taller. "I said how long do I have before I'm trapped in this *godsforsaken place*?"

Soren frowned and averted his gaze. "Three hours, give or take."

"*Three hours?!*" I shot to my feet. "Then what are we doing just sitting here? We should be out there looking for him!"

"There's nothing you can do." Soren rose to his feet as well. His voice grew alarmingly forceful, showing a glimpse of the hardened warrior once more. A general, maybe, judging by his tone.

"You'll just get in the way if you go out with Valdir's men. Besides, scores of Nethers still prowl the forest near the boundary. Samhain is the only time they have guaranteed access to human flesh, so they'll be on the hunt for it tonight. Your scent will just lure them in and put you in danger. You'll stay here so you can regain your strength—"

"I can't just sit here and do nothing," I pleaded.

"You have to," Soren replied firmly.

I wanted to be strong. I desperately wanted to be the girl who wasn't rattled by anything, who kept her cool even when a war raged within. But I had always felt everything too much, and was completely at the mercy of my emotions. And now, countless emotions churned inside me.

I was worried about Wynn.

I grieved my lost brothers.

I feared this strange place I had stumbled into.

I had no idea how to handle it all at once. So, yet again, I broke down.

A strangled sob wrenched from my throat as I crumpled to the floor. Frantic gasps accompanied the tears that burst from my eyes and streamed down my face, saturating the bodice of my new dress. Soren hesitated for a moment, then cautiously knelt beside me and reached out a comforting hand. The second his palm slid to the curve of my back, my mind flooded with recent memories of the violent men who'd felt entitled to me and my body. Even though Soren had done nothing wrong, I acted on instinct.

"*Don't*," I blurted, recoiling and shoving him away. "Don't touch me!"

Soren's brow furrowed. "I'm sorry, I—"

"Just don't," I repeated as firmly as I could. "*Please*."

Soren obediently dipped his head and sat back on his heels. There, he watched me brace my hands on the floor as I sputtered and wailed, releasing every shard of bitter heartache embedded in my soul. I don't know how long I cried, or if my miserable, screaming sobs were heard by others outside the study, but after a time, something warm and soft came to rest on my shoulders. When I looked up, I caught Soren stepping away from the throw blanket he'd lifted off the sofa and draped over me. Quickly and respectfully, he backed up to give me space, then resettled on the floor a good distance away. For some reason that simple gesture and kind, nonthreatening movement sent me into another spiral of emotion.

"Thank you," I whimpered, pulling the blanket tighter.

Soren nodded and offered up a small, tender smile.

To my surprise, I found myself returning it.

Suddenly, the door banged open.

We both jumped, but I relaxed when Xavier passed through the doorway. His curls were mussed and his eyes wide. Soren instantly rose to his feet.

"What's wrong?" he asked.

"It's the boy," Xavier panted, struggling to catch his breath.

"You found him?"

Xavier shook his head. "No, but we found out who has him."

I huffed a sigh of relief. "Oh, thank the gods."

"Soren..." Xavier trailed off. He gulped, his gaze nervously bouncing between the two of us.

"What is it?"

Xavier frowned and fidgeted with a button on his cloak, clearly not wanting to say the words in front of me.

"Xavier!" Soren demanded.

"He's been claimed as a Changeling."

CHAPTER 4

"WHAT'S A CHANGELING?"

I jogged after Soren and Xavier. The two talked urgently among themselves a few strides ahead of me as we made our way towards the stables by way of a torch-lined tunnel beneath Valdir's castle.

"I thought you knew all the old wives' tales?" Soren called over his shoulder before turning back to Xavier and lowering his voice. "Have they sent the Auf into the human realm yet?"

"I'm not sure. All I told them was you demanded an audience and wanted to discuss the boy. They argued, but I quoted our laws. They know they're required to obey, even if it is Samhain."

"Good man. Where are we meeting them?"

"Same place we found her. Soren, if they've already sent the Auf over—"

"We'll cross that bridge if we come to it."

"What's a Changeling?" I repeated, shouldering my way between the two of them.

"It's when a human child is stolen and an identical Nether

child called an Auf is left in its place," Soren replied. He didn't look at me as he spoke; instead, he stared straight ahead, his jaw set and a determined glint in his eyes.

"Why would they do that?"

"A multitude of reasons. Sometimes the Auf is sick, and they think it will heal in the human realm—"

"Sometimes they're just bored and want to wreak havoc," Xavier added.

"And other times it's simply because they desire the human child."

I stopped in my tracks. "Desire it?"

Soren and Xavier stopped walking too.

"They're fascinated by it," Soren clarified. "They want to raise it, mold it... play with it, in a way."

"Or eat it."

Soren shot Xavier an icy glare. "That's *very* rare."

The anxiety gnawing away at me intensified. The men continued down the tunnel again, and I trailed after them, desperately trying to focus on anything other than the image of Wynn being eaten alive.

The tunnel opened into a cavern where horse stalls and troughs had been carved into the dark gray stone of the mountain. Soren entered one of the stalls and coaxed out a large steed, then threw a quilted saddle pad onto its back. Xavier retrieved the horse's saddle and slid it into place.

"Should I come with you?" he asked, firmly cinching the beast's girth strap.

"No," Soren replied, "I ride faster alone."

"But if something goes wrong—"

"I'll be fine," Soren said, clapping a hand on Xavier's shoulder. "You've done enough."

Xavier frowned, clearly not pleased with the answer. In response, Soren playfully mussed his hair. It was a move I'd seen Dominic do to Wynn countless times, and a pang of sadness shot through my heart at the realization Dom would no longer be there to do it when Wynn was grown.

"Go on," Soren told Xavier. "It's a holiday. Enjoy what's left of the ball."

"Are you sure?"

"For the final time, *yes*." The playful brother disappeared, and the hardened general returned. He grabbed a bridle and slid it over his steed's head. "But don't have too much fun. We ride back tomorrow."

Xavier finally brightened, a mischievous smile spreading over his handsome features. "No promises." He turned to me. "Goodbye, human. A little advice before you go?"

Xavier pulled off his thick maroon cloak and threw it over my shoulders, fastening the top snugly at my neck. "Someday do yourself a favor: pick up a weapon, and learn how to wield it. You can't rely on books as your only defense. Your aim was shit."

His words were followed by a charming wink and a cheeky grin.

"Not the time, Xavier," Soren warned.

"Right." Xavier nodded dutifully and backed away. "Good luck, then."

"Thank you," I said, managing a grateful smile.

He dipped his head in acknowledgement, then bounded up the tunnel to the castle with the giddy excitement of a child being called to dinner.

"Come on," Soren urged, patting the horse and extending his hand to me. I slipped my fingers into his palm and he led me over, steadying me as I put a foot in the stirrup and hauled myself up. Soren settled in behind me, wedging me tightly between his thighs. When he took up the reins, he lowered his mouth to my ear.

"Hold on tight," he commanded.

He then slapped the leather straps, sending us speeding through the stable and out a door that deposited us at the base of Radomir's mountain fortress.

I had to shut my eyes as we raced through the woods, darting and weaving through a twisted maze of tree, briar, and rock. I had no idea how Soren and his horse saw where they were going; the night was at its darkest point and thick with fog, but somehow they expertly maneuvered the forest, making impressive time as we headed back towards the river I'd collapsed in just hours before. I glanced up at the night sky.

Still no signs of morning light.

A flicker of hope cut through the worry in my chest. Maybe, just maybe, I could get Wynn back in time to cross the boundary before the veil went down again. We could find our brothers and bury their bodies, say a prayer to the gods that they would find peace in the Underworld, then return home to pretend this had all been a horrible nightmare.

I frowned at the thought of home. What would we do now that Dominic and Jaras were gone? Jaras hadn't contributed much since our parents' passing, but Dominic had been crucial to our survival. He was the reason we hadn't gone hungry the past two years. Without him, how was I going to feed Wynn? I could make enough money working in the fields to buy a few loaves of bread every week and maybe the occasional block of cheese, but I doubted that would be enough to live on.

A queasy pit opened in my stomach as I considered the prospect of accepting Lord Olin's proposal. I couldn't deny it would take care of our problems. At least, it would take care of Wynn's problems. Under a lord's care he could get an education. He'd be fed, he'd be clothed, he'd have a roof over his head, he'd have a shot at a decent life. And I... well, I'd be fed and clothed and have a roof over my head too. Sure, I'd have to lie beneath that awful man every night, used for nothing but a tool to produce his heirs...

I fought back tears, unable to even finish the thought. Could I do it? Could I put myself through hell if it meant my brother never had to want for anything ever again?

"We're coming up on the river," Soren declared, his voice in my ear knocking me from the dark place my mind had drifted to.

The cold night air had chilled my hands and face, and his warm breath on my neck was such a shock that I shuddered.

"What are we looking for?" I asked. Warily, I searched the surrounding darkness, praying to the gods it wasn't more of the creatures I'd run into before. The wound bandaged on my wrist twinged at the thought.

"We aren't looking for anything." Soren yanked on the reins, causing his horse to dig its hooves into the ground and skid to a halt. He leapt off the beast, then offered his hand so I could do the same. "They'll come to us."

I gulped and dismounted, gripping Soren's fingers like they were a lifeline as he led the way through the woods. It was still dark, but the forest had lightened just enough for me to see basic shapes and objects.

Suddenly, Soren stopped walking and brought a finger to his lips. I froze and listened closely, trying to make out what he'd fixated on, but all I could hear was the chirping of birds eager for dawn and my own frantic pulse pounding in my ears.

Soren leaned closer.

"No matter what happens," he whispered, "let me do the talking. Understand?"

I nodded obediently.

Soren squared his shoulders and looked out at the woods with a hardened gaze.

"Show yourself!" he roared, his voice booming through the

trees. His firm command sent a flock of black birds shooting up from a nearby thicket and scattering into the sky. Afterwards, an eerie quiet settled over the forest. Everything stilled. There were no birds, no insects, no rustling of leaves from a breeze. The silence was as heavy as the fog.

Then she appeared.

A woman stepped out from behind a tree. At first glance, I wouldn't have assumed she was a Nether. She looked like any other woman, except she appeared to be on the edge of starvation. Her disturbingly thin frame was draped in an old gray wool shawl and tattered dress. There was no way to tell how old she was. At first glance, she could be mistaken for someone in her early twenties like me, but the hollow cheekbones and sunken eyes were of someone much, much older.

She simultaneously looked like youth and death.

The woman grinned, exposing a mouth full of grimy teeth, and pulled something from behind the tree.

Gripped in her gnarled fingers was the wrist of a small, blond boy.

"Wynn!" I cried, rushing forward.

But Soren's hand landed on my shoulder and quickly yanked me back.

"What are you doing?" I protested, shrugging him off. "That's my brother!"

"I told you," he snapped. "Let me do the talking."

I wilted and faced Wynn again. He was unharmed, thank the gods. No wounds marred his skin, and aside from a few smudges of dirt on his face...

I frowned and peered closer at my brother's expression. He stood beside the woman, slack-jawed and milky-eyed, staring off into the distance at nothing in particular.

Something wasn't right.

My brother's eyes should be clear and round and filled with

fear. He should be calling out to me the same way he had when the men captured him earlier.

"What—" I began, but Soren cut me off.

"He's spellbound."

I didn't know what that meant, but I could tell it wasn't good.

"Blessed Samhain," Soren called to the woman. He bowed his head politely, but his voice was curt.

The woman opened her mouth and spoke, and when she did, a shiver skittered down my spine. Her voice was somehow that of a little girl and an old woman, simultaneously a whisper and a scream.

"Indeed it has been," the woman said. She brought a dirty, pointed nail to Wynn's face and traced it lovingly down the side. "Very blessed."

I instinctively lunged at the woman, but again Soren caught me by the shoulder. This time, he kept his hand there.

The woman looked me up and down curiously, but spoke only to Soren.

"Bold of you to summon us outside your own territory, Soren of Astoria. Planning to rise up and expand your dominion into Radomir?"

"You will speak to me with respect!" Soren snarled.

Both the woman and I jumped at his tone. Afraid to meet his gaze head-on, I peeked at the man out of the corner of my eye. The steely gleam in his gaze would have even the most menacing soldier cowering in fear. And cower the woman did. Her body shook like a leaf as she bent her head and averted her attention to the ground.

"Our apologies, Your Majesty."

My eyes widened.

Majesty?

The man whose head I'd hurled a book at was *royalty*?

Everything clicked. The regal stance, the no-nonsense tone, the sinewy figure and those impossibly perfect features... I could easily imagine a crown on this man's head while he ruled lands and commanded armies.

"This is a special case," the king went on. "Valdir granted me leniency."

The woman's hand clamped firmly around Wynn's wrist. The urge to sever that damn limb right off her body swelled inside me. Somehow sensing my thoughts, Soren tightened his grip on my shoulder.

"Enough talk," he said. "What will it take for you to return the boy?"

The woman threw back her head and cackled. "Not even the king of Astoria can command us to return a Changeling on Samhain. It was agreed upon during the first summit—"

"I know the rules," Soren barked, his razor-sharp tone once again making the woman flinch. "I'm not commanding you, I'm asking. Has the Auf already crossed the boundary into the human realm?"

"Yes, Your Majesty."

Soren frowned. It was clearly not the response he'd wanted to hear, but he quickly composed himself. "What will you take in exchange for him?"

"Are you trying to barter with me?" The woman asked, a delighted smile spreading across her hollow face.

"Yes." Soren spoke through gritted teeth. It sounded like he was losing his patience.

"Hmm..." The woman clicked her tongue and trailed another dirty finger over my brother's face, but Wynn didn't move. He continued to stare straight ahead, eyes dull and his face blank.

"Nothing," the woman crooned, fondly twirling one of

Wynn's locks. "There is nothing we would want in exchange. We like him. We want to keep him."

I had to bite the inside of my cheek to keep from screaming at her to take her hands off my brother.

"There must be something—"

"There is nothing!" the woman shrieked.

I recoiled at her outburst, but Soren just bristled.

"You said yourself you know the rules, Your Majesty," the woman barked, bringing herself up to her full height. "You know returning the Auf is the only way. A life for a life."

Before I could stop myself or process the words tumbling out of my mouth, I blurted, "Take me!"

Soren whipped his head around to face me. His eyes were round with surprise and fury, but I ignored him and stepped forward.

"Take me instead of my brother."

Soren muttered a curse under his breath.

The woman looked me up and down again, sniffing the air in my direction. She then pulled back, hissing like a snake, and gripped Wynn tighter.

"You are too old. We require an equal life exchange. A child in exchange for a child."

"Please," I begged, my throat tightening. I desperately willed myself not to cry. "I would be of more use to you than him. I can cook and clean and sew, and I'm strong too. I tended the fields back home—"

The woman hissed again, startling me and causing me to jump backwards. Soren threw a hand to my lower back to steady me.

"We do not desire the child for labor!" the woman stated, as if insulted I would even suggest such a thing. "However..."

She slowly reached out and unfurled a hand.

"If the sister of the Changeling boy wishes to watch over

him and ensure he is taken care of, she is welcome to join us. Come." Her finger curled, beckoning me nearer. "We will not harm the boy. You have our word."

I hesitated for a moment, prompting the woman's thin lips to crook into a soothing smile.

"Do we have a bargain?" she cooed.

I swallowed hard.

Wynn was all I had left. And I was all *he* had left. Even if we were in a strange land, full of creatures that made my skin crawl and my stomach churn, it was my responsibility to look after him. It was my fault he was even here at all. If I hadn't let Jaras rile me up, Wynn wouldn't have needed to wander off so he wouldn't hear us arguing. And if I hadn't attacked Lord Olin and asked my brothers to take me hunting to avoid his wrath, then Wynn wouldn't have been in the woods in the first place.

No. I will not abandon him.

Without a second thought, I stepped forward and reached for the woman's hand. Just before my fingers brushed hers, however, Soren grabbed my wrist and tore me away.

"Do *not* accept that bargain," he growled.

The woman let out an indignant hiss at his words.

Soren shot daggers at her with his eyes as he dragged me backwards. "She's trying to trick you. A child's mind they can shape and mold, but someone like you is good for nothing but slavery, or worse. You'd just be a toy in their sick, twisted games."

The woman's lips curved into a sickly sweet grin. "And what a fun toy she'd be."

At that, a hot, bubbling rage tore through my veins.

I was sick and tired of being seen as an object, good for nothing but the pleasure of others.

Lord Olin thought it.

The marauder had thought it.

Now it seemed the Nethers thought it too.

And I'd finally had enough.

I wrenched free from Soren's grasp and lunged forward to grab Wynn's hand, attempting to rip him away from the woman. She screeched and latched on to him like a leech.

"Give... me... my... brother!" I grunted, tugging at one of Wynn's arms while the woman clung to the other. We probably looked like two dogs fighting over a bone.

"Lina, stop!" Soren snapped. "Let the boy go! Let him go!"

He wrapped his arms around my waist and dragged me off Wynn with alarming strength. I kicked and squirmed, but Soren hauled me a few paces away like I weighed nothing.

Her eyes wide and wild, the woman used her free hand to rip a crude knife from the waistband of her gown and defensively thrust it in our direction.

Soren's eyes narrowed.

He set me down, raised his own arm, and flicked his wrist in a sweeping motion. The knife flew from the woman's hand and landed somewhere deep in the forest.

I blinked furiously, trying to process what I'd just witnessed.

"You did *not* just threaten a Fae king..." Soren's voice shook with restrained rage.

Undeterred by the warning in his words, the woman stood tall and released her grip on Wynn so she could point forebodingly in Soren's direction.

"Mark my words, Soren of Astoria: your time is coming. Too long have we hidden in the shadows. You and your kind will pay a steep price for all you have done to us."

She continued to speak, but I didn't hear her.

With her focused on Soren, I saw my chance. I mustered my courage, bolted forward, and punched the woman square in the face.

Then I grabbed Wynn, turned tail, and ran.

Behind me, the woman shrieked like I'd just stabbed her in the back. Soren yelled too, demanding I stop running and come back, but I ignored him. I dragged my brother through the woods, forcing my legs as fast as they could move. My dress snagged and caught on the underbrush, but I tore through it, focusing on the sound of the river in the distance. The sky was lighter now, which meant we didn't have much time. I wasn't even sure where this mystical boundary was, but I vaguely remembered something Xavier had said about crossing the river, so that became the goal.

Something solid collided with my back, and I went down hard, landing on my stomach with a grunt as the wind was knocked out of me. I groaned and rolled over, only to find the spindly woman crawling on top of me, her sunken eyes bulging and her teeth bared. I had no idea how such a frail woman had caught up to me so fast.

"You will not take the Changeling from us!" the woman screeched.

To my horror, she wasn't frail at all. Her hands wrapped around my throat and tightened, squeezing my airway shut with inhuman strength. I choked and gasped, scratching at her hands and kicking frantically, but I struggled in vain. Stars scattered across my vision, and my lungs screamed for air.

Suddenly, the woman was knocked aside by an unseen force and hurtled off me, sliding along the forest floor before colliding with the trunk of a large oak tree. My throat finally free, I gasped in a lungful of air and pushed myself upright as Soren charged towards the woman. She hissed and lunged at him, but with a deft flick of his wrist he sent her flying into another tree.

"A life for a life," the woman rasped, hauling herself up from the ground and glaring up at the king. "The boy is ours."

Still recovering from the woman's stranglehold, I crawled,

coughing and sputtering, onto all fours. While she spoke to Soren, I peeked over at my brother. Wynn was worlds away, his eyes still glossy and lost in a daze. Those eyes lit a vicious fire deep in my soul.

My sweet, innocent brother would not be taken and corrupted by those *things*. Not over my dead body.

I looked over at the woman once more...

And saw red.

There was no rational thought in my mind anymore.

No mercy.

No compassion.

Nothing existed except vengeance.

While the woman's back was to me, I stood upright and staggered towards her, my eyes fixing on a large mossy rock resting behind her. Soren clocked my movement, his brow furrowing. He followed my determined gaze down to the rock, but by the time he realized what I was doing, it was too late.

"Lina, don't!" he shouted.

He threw out a hand to stop me, but I had already grabbed the stone, hauled it over my head, and smashed it into the base of the woman's skull with all my strength. A sickening crack rang through the forest, and the woman crumpled to the ground. I went to hit her again, but Soren darted between us.

"Stop! *Stop!*" He ordered, pushing me backwards.

I dropped the rock, my chest heaving. Soren and I stared at the body on the forest floor. The woman lay still. Limp.

Lifeless.

"Oh gods, what have you done?" Soren breathed.

I only had a few moments to process the blood on my hands before a shrill screech cut through the forest. We searched our surroundings, but there was nothing except the trees and the sky, which was growing lighter by the second.

"Shit." Soren turned to me, the urgency in his gaze sending a chill down my spine. "*Run!*"

I went to grab Wynn, but Soren scooped my brother into his arms and slung him over his shoulder before sprinting in the direction of the river. I hiked up my skirts and tore after them.

The screech sounded again, closer this time.

"Hurry!" Soren yelled over to me, leaves puffing up behind him as he deftly leapt over rocks and fallen branches. My brother bounced along his shoulder like a knapsack.

"There's an ancient burial ground on the other side of the river," the king continued. "It marks the edge of the boundary. You'll need to reach it to be in the human realm when the veil comes down."

Soren nervously glanced up at a dangerously bright sky.

"Hurry!" he repeated.

The screech rang out again. It felt like it was directly on top of us. I looked around the woods in a panic, but saw nothing.

A ribbon of blue shimmered between the trees.

The river.

We're going to make it. We're actually going to make it!

Just a few more paces, and we would reach the bank and wade across to the other side.

We were almost safe.

We were almost home.

We skidded to an abrupt halt when a woman stepped out from behind a tree in front of us.

... The same woman I had just killed.

And then another identical woman stepped out from a different tree.

And then another.

Then another.

Horrified, I turned in a circle as scores of women with sunken faces stepped out from behind every tree in the forest.

Paralyzing fear seeped through my body, making me quake like a frightened child.

The woman in front of Soren stared him down. When she opened her mouth to speak, her voice came from all around us.

"We want what is owed."

Soren tightened his grip on Wynn.

"A life for a life," the woman continued, chillingly calm. "You know the laws."

A muscle in Soren's jaw twitched.

He took a deep breath in through his nose and released it through his mouth to calm his ragged breath. Then his shoulder blades tensed, and he lowered his head. He looked ready to pounce, like an animal preparing for the kill. I readied myself for the power he was about to unleash with nothing but a flick of his wrist. Or maybe, judging from that furious glint in his eye, he might just tear them all apart with his bare hands.

Good, I thought bitterly.

But then Soren's grip loosened, and he gently slid Wynn off his shoulder and onto solid ground.

My stomach dropped. "What are you doing?!"

I stepped forward, but Soren put up a hand up, halting me. Stone-faced, he passed my brother off to the woman in front of him. She smiled down at Wynn, tenderly caressing his cheek before looking back at Soren and bowing her head.

"Thank you, Your Majesty."

The hair on the back of my neck stood on end as the woman turned her icy gaze on me.

"Now for the sister."

My heart nearly stopped.

"She was just protecting her brother," Soren said quickly.

"A life for a life," the woman repeated. "Two lives are owed this Samhain. One for the Auf in the human realm..." She pointed at Wynn. "And one for our slain sister." Her knotty finger shifted to me.

I froze. Too terrified to run, too terrified to cry, too terrified to do anything but stare at the woman with a claw in my little brother's shoulder. To my relief, Soren moved between us, blocking me from the woman's view.

"I'm not going to let you touch her."

"Settle the debt, or pay the price."

"I *said...*" Soren hissed through clenched teeth. "I am *not* letting you touch her."

The woman blinked at him, then looked to her sisters surrounding us. All of them seemed to have a silent conversation. Finally, the woman glanced back to Soren and smiled sweetly.

"So be it."

She then snapped her fingers and vanished with the others, Wynn disappearing along with them.

It was just me and Soren alone in the forest once more, the last remnants of fog evaporating as the first rays of dawn peeked over the horizon, sealing my fate.

CHAPTER 5

ON THE RIDE BACK TO VALDIR'S CASTLE, I'D BEEN TOO preoccupied with sobbing my eyes out to feel much besides grief. But by the time we returned, all my tears had dried, my eyes were swollen and puffy, and I was furious.

I stormed after Soren as he stomped up the grand staircase flanked by the black candelabras, their wicks now burned down to nothing.

"How could you?!" I shouted at his back. "How could you hand over a defenseless boy to those *things*?"

Soren didn't look at me. He continued down a gilded hallway, his face fixed in a cold expression.

"You heard them. The boy won't be harmed."

"And you believe them?!" I shrieked.

Soren slammed to a halt and whirled to face me. "*Yes*, I do."

I recoiled slightly but stubbornly kept my chin lifted.

"I'd like to think I know a thing or two more about the creatures in my own realm than you do. They honor their word, which means they will be keeping their word about spilling your blood in payment of the debt owed."

I tried not to show how uneasy that comment made me, but my nervous gulp gave me away.

Soren let out a furious grunt and raked his fingers through his hair. "Why the fuck didn't you listen to me? I told you to let the boy go! Things were already tense enough with the Nethers."

Despite my desire to hold my ground, I shrank as he shoved his face in mine and bared his teeth like an animal.

"Congratulations on your stupidity, Lina Calder," the king spat. "You may have just started a war."

Tears stung my eyes, but I refused to let them fall. For once, I would not cry. I wouldn't give this man the satisfaction of seeing he'd broken me.

Soren turned away and pounded his fist against a nearby door.

"We'll go to Astoria," he huffed. "Maybe I can negotiate a truce or work out some other form of payment."

I stubbornly folded my arms over my chest. "I'm not going anywhere with you. I'm going after my brother—"

"Fine!" Soren snapped, spinning to face me once more. "That's just *fine*. If you would rather take your chances out in the woods on your own, be my guest. You're going to be *very* popular with the Nethers."

I pursed my lips defiantly. "Then I'll stay here with Valdir."

Soren barked out a laugh so condescending it had me fighting the urge to cower in shame. "Oh, yes. Do that. I'm sure he'd be more than happy to host some strange human girl who ruined his ball and trashed his study."

He banged on the door again, harder this time.

"You're... you're..." I searched for a word that would cut just right but came up blank. I miserably settled on, "You're *mean!*"

Another snide chuckle puffed from Soren's lips. "I'm in politics, sweetheart. That's part of the job description."

The door creaked open.

A half-naked Xavier, looking a little worse for wear, stood in the doorway, grasping a sheet around his hips and blinking at the daylight pouring in. Behind him, three Fae in a similar state of undress, two males and one female, stirred on the bed.

"Hey," Xavier muttered groggily, "how did it go?"

"Get dressed. We're going home."

Soren and I didn't speak for the rest of the day. He'd insisted I ride with Xavier on the way to their home territory of Astoria, so I spent all day glaring at the back of his head as we galloped through the forest. If I hadn't been so consumed by my anger, I would have noticed how much more vibrant the colors were in this realm than the human world. The heavy moss on the rocks and trees of Radomir diminished, revealing branches practically glowing with the vivid reds and yellows of autumn, and the glittering streams and ponds we passed became even more dazzling shades of blue and green. No one would have suspected such terrible creatures lurked in the shadows of these woods, preying on unsuspecting men and innocent little boys who got lost in the night.

It was dusk by the time we arrived at the castle. Though the world around us had darkened, I could still see the pale stone fortress rising up between towering trees, the windows in its majestic spired turrets aglow with cozy candlelight. It was a stunningly beautiful sight, straight out of a painting, but I felt nothing as we passed through the ivy-adorned archway in the exterior wall and halted in a cobblestone courtyard.

Soren immediately slid off his horse, handed the reins to a servant who'd dutifully hurried over, and sauntered towards the castle.

"Show the girl to a room," he ordered over his shoulder as he made his way up the front steps. "Then both of you wash up and come to dinner."

"Yes, sir."

Xavier obediently dismounted and offered a hand to me, but I ignored it and slipped off on my own. I shot one last imaginary dagger into the back of Soren's head as he disappeared inside the entryway before trailing behind Xavier.

The interior of the castle was just as elegant as the outside, with vaulted ceilings, intricate silver chandeliers, large hearths with crackling fires, and a wide mahogany staircase that split off in opposite directions at the top. It looked how I imagined a luxurious hunting lodge might, only twenty times larger and complete with gilded accents and sensual fabrics and furs.

"Come on," Xavier said, gesturing for me to follow him up the stairs.

We started up the steps, taking a left when they split, and made our way down a candlelit hallway with dark wood paneling and intricate paintings hung along the walls. We stopped in front of a door halfway down the hall, its surface carved with intertwining vines and leaves. Xavier turned the handle and pushed the door open, arcing his arm in an elaborate sweep to usher me inside.

"Here we are," he sang.

The room had the same dark wood paneling as the hallway, as well as a four-poster bed with a maroon canopy, two overstuffed chairs, an armoire, and a vanity. There were luxurious rugs and tapestries on the walls, furs and silk thrown over the bedding and chairs, and a roaring fire in the hearth at the far end of the room. Not even the nobles in the human realm lived in this kind of luxury, but as I looked around at the grandeur I was meant to live in, I felt no flutter of excitement or gratitude.

There was nothing except the miserable, heavy ache of despair in my chest.

"I hope you'll find it satisfactory," Xavier said. He nonchalantly leaned against the doorframe and gestured over his shoulder. "If you need anything, I'm down the other hall. If you want company, you're welcome to stop by any time, day or night. I happen to do my best work at night—"

I slammed the door in his face and locked it.

Then I walked over to the bed, crawled on top, and shut my eyes tight.

I DIDN'T LEAVE the room that night or the next two days.

Off and on I would hear a knock at the door, but I ignored it. I cried occasionally, but mostly I just slept. My whole body hurt, whether from the Nethers' attack or the ride from Radomir to Astoria, I wasn't sure. My heart hurt too, and no matter how much I slept or cried or screamed into my pillow, the weight in my chest refused to let up.

The nightmares didn't help.

I always woke from my slumber sweaty and gasping for air, haunted by the horrors in the woods and the image of my brothers' cold, dead eyes that played over and over in my dreams.

I was dreaming of Lord Olin morphing into a green-skinned, black-tongued Nether when I woke on the morning of the fourth day.

My eyes snapped open as someone pounded furiously on the bedroom door. I grabbed a pillow and slammed it over my head to stifle the sound, figuring whoever was at the door would eventually grow tired and give up like all the others had before them, but I was wrong. After a minute straight of knocking with no signs of letting up, I growled and removed the pillow.

"*Alright!* I'm coming!" I shouted, kicking back the covers and swinging my legs over the side of the bed. I stomped across the room, begrudgingly unlocked the door, and tore it open. Almost immediately I was nearly bowled over by a tall, slender Fae who barreled inside.

"Oh, *gods*, it's stuffy in here!" he said, looking around the room dismally. "The windows *do* work, you know."

The man flitted over to one of the lattice-paned windows, unhooked the latch, and pushed it open. A cool breeze instantly wafted in, rustling his straight, waist-length white hair. He shut his eyes and took a deep breath in.

"Ah! Much better."

When he turned around, I examined him more closely. He had snow-white skin, elongated pointed ears, smoky gray eyes, and an angular face with cheekbones so sharp they could cut glass. He struck a dashing figure as he strutted around the room dressed in breeches and a floor-length silver overcoat that billowed behind him. He was simultaneously masculine and feminine, and by far one of the most ethereal and uniquely stunning creatures I'd ever seen. Perhaps the most beautiful part about him was the smile he wore. It was warm and sincere, and it brightened the room just as much as the rays of morning sun shining through the window.

"Now that we've got that out of the way," the Fae said, clasping his hands in front of him, "we can move on to introductions. Hello, Lina Calder. My name is Meer. It's a pleasure to meet you."

Suddenly, I became very unsure of what to do with myself. I had no idea what the customs were in this place. Was this a noble? Should I bow my head? If I accidentally disrespected him, would he get mad and eat me? After what I'd seen on Samhain, nothing seemed too far-fetched.

"I'm head of household staff," Meer explained, noticing my uncertainty. His tone softened. "If there is anything you need during your stay with us, anything at all, come to me and I'll sort it out for you, alright?"

His head tilted to the side as he studied me, eyes filling with compassion. "I've been told you had quite a harrowing holiday."

I nodded stiffly.

Meer clicked his tongue and wrapped a willowy arm around my shoulders before steering me towards a door at the far end of the room.

"You poor thing. Well, I can think of no better salve for the soul than some freshening up. What do you say? How does a nice hot bath sound?"

As Meer led me across the room, we passed the vanity. For the first time in days, I caught a reflection of myself. My eyes were bloodshot and red-rimmed from crying, I had dirt smeared across my face, and parts of me were still coated in dried blood.

Whose blood it was, exactly, I couldn't be sure.

I sucked in sharply at the thought, prompting Meer to squeeze me tighter.

"There, there," he said tenderly, "you're alright. It's all over now."

I nodded, which earned me another encouraging smile from the Fae.

Meer pushed open the door at the end of the room, revealing an adjoining washroom. At the center of the room was a large copper tub already filled to the brim with steaming water and sweet-smelling bath salts. Three beautiful handmaidens also stood in the room, poised and ready, armed with sponges, scrubbing brushes, picks and combs.

"These lovely ladies here are Wood Sprites. This is Laurel," Meer said, beckoning to the tallest of the maids, who was dressed in a modest dark green dress that popped against her deep tan. Her golden brown hair had been swept into a tight bun, but a few rogue ringlets had sprung free and dangled near her temples and the nape of her neck.

"And this is Cassia," Meer continued.

The shortest of the maids politely bent her head. She had dark skin and wavy, black hair that contrasted perfectly with the happy yellow dress she was clad in, and her kind eyes were the same shade of turquoise blue as Wynn's.

"And finally, we have Acacia."

The last maid grinned and bobbed a curtsy. Her dress was the same color as her pin-straight, plum-purple hair, and when she smiled, her cheeks turned a bright shade of rosy red.

The Sprites looked like any other women, except for the fact their skin glowed a little brighter than a human's, the color of their hair and eyes was more vivid, and just like the others I'd encountered in the realm, a pair of pointed ears poked out on either side of their heads. Theirs, however, were more long and slender than those of any Fae I'd met so far. It was something I hadn't grown accustomed to yet, so an awkward wave was all I could manage.

"These dear girls will be making you right as rain while I head out to find you something more suitable to wear." Meer pinched the sleeve of my simple blue dress between his fingers and tutted. "I'm assuming the king chose this for you. There's your first mistake. If you must let one of those big brutes pick an outfit for you, make sure it's Xavier. He has much better taste in fashion."

Meer grinned at his joke, but I could only blink in response. He sighed and gave me another warm squeeze.

"We'll have you laughing again soon, dear. Mark my words, we'll have a sparkle back in those eyes before you know it. Now, I'm going to leave you in the capable hands of the the Sprites here." He gently passed me off to the handmaidens. "I'll see you shortly, alright?"

After giving me one last encouraging smile, Meer was gone, and the Sprites got to work.

At first, I was wary of having three strangers in the room while I bathed. I'd never had handmaidens before. Only nobles and royalty had need of them, not peasants whose baths consisted of sitting in a small basin and splashing handfuls of cold water on themselves. But the women effortlessly put me at ease.

Acacia was the friendliest out of all of them. Her bubbly personality blazed the trail of conversation as she scrubbed at my feet and fingernails with a coarse bristle brush. Cassia would laugh at Acacia's jokes and occasionally throw in quips of her own while she rubbed at my skin with a plush washrag, and Laurel was quiet and stoic as she massaged soap into my hair and scalp, but I frequently heard her attempting to stifle laughter of her own. Eventually I trusted them enough to relax into their touch, and slowly all the tense and aching muscles in my body loosened.

I'm ashamed to admit how long it took for me to get clean. Back home, *when* we were lucky enough to bathe, my brothers and I all had to share the same bathwater, so on top of the blood and filth from the events on Samhain, the Sprites were scrubbing away twenty-three years of leftover grime. The bathwater was disgustingly dark by the time they finished, but when I stepped out of the tub, smelling of citrus and sandalwood, and Acacia wrapped me in a fresh, fluffy towel, I was clean, *actually* clean, for the first time in my life.

Once I was out of the bath, the Sprites removed the bandages around my arm, and I could finally see the damage inflicted by the Nether on Samhain. The wound had miraculously healed, most likely thanks to the work of Valdir's healers, but in its place remained a long raised black scar running vertically down my wrist. Bile roiled in my stomach as I realized that every time I saw it, it would serve as a reminder of all the horrors I witnessed that night. I made a mental note to wear as many long-sleeved clothes as I could so I'd never have to look at it.

The Sprites had moved me from the washroom to the vanity in the bedroom and were in the process of rubbing me in scented oils and spritzing me with perfume when Meer swept back in.

"I didn't know what you liked," he said as he spread an assortment of dresses, overcoats, trousers, tunics, and shoeboxes across the bed, "so I just brought it all. Anything capture your fancy?"

My eyes drifted over the rich fabrics. Not even my best dress at home had been remotely as nice as these. I did like the look of a green velvet gown with sheer flowing sleeves and almost pointed to it, but an image of Wynn flashed into my mind, sparking a pang of guilt. Here I was worrying about which pretty thing I should wear, while my little brother was off with a legion of monsters doing gods know what to him.

Meer watched my face fall and, as if reading my thoughts, he waved away the Sprites, who obediently dipped their heads and left the room. Meer moved behind me and took up a silver hair brush resting on the vanity.

"May I?" he asked softly.

I hesitated for a moment, but after studying his earnest

expression, I nodded. Meer smiled wide in response and began delicately combing through my hair. I'd cut it short early in the spring so it wouldn't cling to the sweat on my back while I worked in the fields, but it had since grown out and now grazed the tops of my shoulders. It was usually a dull shade of brown, just like Jaras and Dominic's, but the harsh sun this summer had brought out natural streaks of auburn.

Meer toyed with the damp strands, his long fingers working the top half of my hair into an intricate plait.

"You've been through so much, Lina," Meer murmured, his kind eyes finding mine in the mirror. "Enjoying life doesn't mean you've stopped worrying about young Wynnric, or that you don't grieve for your other brothers. In fact, I think you'd be doing them a disservice not living your life to the fullest when they're no longer able to."

The familiar pinch behind my eyes forced me to break Meer's gaze and focus intently on the fists clenched in my lap. His hands finished in my hair and gave my shoulders a gentle squeeze.

"You are good, Lina," he whispered, "and you deserve good things. You don't need to suffer more than you already are. It's not a crime against those you've loved and lost to let yourself be happy sometimes."

An unintentional whimper crept up from the depths of my soul, and I quickly clapped a hand over my mouth to keep my emotion at bay. Meer rubbed my arm in encouragement, and when I finally dared to meet his gaze in the mirror again, he gave me one last smile.

"Personally, I think you'd be devastating in the green dress." He winked, then headed for the door. "Breakfast will be ready soon. I hope you'll join us."

When the door shut behind him, I sat with his words for a long time. Then I stood, made my way over to the bed, and picked up the velvet gown.

By the time I'd dressed, another knock sounded at the door. Assuming Meer or one of the Sprites had forgotten something, I walked over and opened it without hesitation.

It wasn't Meer on the other side, but Soren.

When our eyes met, I immediately went to shut the door, but he slammed his hand against the solid wood to hold it open. I grunted and used all my strength to try and push the door closed, but it refused to budge. The man was infuriatingly strong. Eventually, I gave up and glared at the king instead.

"What?" I spat.

Soren bristled slightly, but attempted to keep his expression composed. "Breakfast is served."

"I'm not hungry."

"Yes, you are. Your stomach's been growling since Samhain." At my confused look, Soren gestured to his ear. "Fae. Heightened senses. I can hear it."

Gods, I can already tell that's going to get annoying.

"Fine. Let me rephrase that. I don't *want* to eat."

Soren's eyes narrowed, and he exhaled sharply through his nose. "I don't know whether you're starving yourself to be self-destructive or to try and punish me, but either way it's foolish and doesn't help you or your brother."

I frowned and crossed my arms. "You're not used to being told no, are you?"

"No, I'm not." He shoved the door open wider and gestured to the hallway. "After you."

Realizing that arguing with him was pointless, I begrudgingly accepted defeat and stomped out of the room, making sure to trample the toe of Soren's boot with my heel as I did.

When we arrived in the dining room, Xavier was already wolfing down his breakfast with the ferocity of an animal that hadn't eaten in weeks. When Soren and I entered, however, he jumped to his feet and respectfully bowed his head. Although his mouth was stuffed full, he still managed to mumble, "Good morning."

I ignored him and slid into one of the tufted chairs at one end of the long mahogany table. Xavier glanced at Soren, who rolled his eyes and shook his head before taking his seat. Xavier sat too, his gaze bouncing warily between the two of us as an uncomfortable silence settled over the room.

I moved to pick up a fork, but hesitated at the assortment of elegant silver cutlery framing the plate. Never before had I seen so many utensils placed in a setting, and for some reason the idea of choosing the wrong one instantly had me sweating. It made me keenly aware of how out of place I was here, not just as a human in a land of Fae and Sprites and creatures made of nightmares, but also as a commoner surrounded by wealth and luxury, a world I blatantly didn't belong to. A wave of insecurity crashed over me, and it only worsened when, out of the corner of my eye, I caught Soren watching my struggle.

"The second fork from the left," he finally informed me, jerking his chin towards the setting.

My cheeks heated with humiliation, but a rebellious flame inside me flared in response, forcing me to meet Soren's gaze and snatch up a spoon from the opposite side of the plate. He shook his head again.

"Charming," he muttered, refocusing on the eggs, sausage, and potatoes in front of him. I attempted to do the same, but the screech of Soren's fork and knife scraping against porcelain grated on my ears. I let out an annoyed huff and pushed my breakfast around in circles, partially because I still didn't feel like eating, but mainly because it was nearly impossible to do with the spoon in my hand.

Rebellion, it seemed, was good for making a point, but not so great for the appetite.

The room fell silent again, filled only with the scrape of silverware and the palpable tension rippling between Soren and me. Xavier, chewing tentatively, continued to watch both of us until the quiet became too much for him.

"So." He cleared his throat and swiveled in his chair to face me, smiling brightly. "What's it like being a human?"

Without looking up at him, I replied, "Currently it's shit."

The silence returned, heavier this time.

Clearly not someone used to spending long periods without talking, Xavier fidgeted in his seat. He picked up a bowl of salt and its serving spoon, but decided against it and put it back in its place. Then he grabbed a pastry off a nearby platter. Then took a second. Then he changed his mind and exchanged them for two sticky buns. When he slurped at his tea, both Soren and I couldn't help but glare at him. It was enough to make the younger man snap, and Xavier set the cup down, propped his fist under his chin, and again attempted conversation.

"Have you been around long?"

Across the table, Soren let out an exasperated sigh and pinched the bridge of his nose.

I raised an eyebrow. "Are you asking how old I am?"

"Yes." He squinted at me. "I'm guessing eighty-five."

"What?" My forehead wrinkled in confusion. "No, I'm twenty-three."

Xavier nearly choked. "Did you say twenty-three?!" He laughed heartily and sat back in his seat. "Oh, wait, that's right! I forgot you humans age differently in your world. Gods, look at you! You're just a little baby!"

"Manners, Xavier," Soren mumbled.

I awkwardly shifted in my chair. "Why? How old are you?"

"Seventy-six," Xavier replied. He took a ferocious bite of sausage and shot me a wink. "Just hitting my sexual prime."

Silverware clattered, prompting Xavier and I to look over at

Soren. He folded his hands and rested them on the table, staring at Xavier pointedly.

Xavier wilted and quickly wiped his mouth with his napkin. "I, uh... think Meer's calling me. Excuse me."

He stood and gave me a stiff bow before darting out of the room, leaving me alone with the king. Once again we were plunged into agonizing silence, and just when I thought *I* would be the one to snap, the king cleared his throat.

"I apologize for Xavier's inability to read a room," he said tightly.

I prodded at a large chunk of scrambled eggs on the plate in front of me. "He's quite the character."

"Yes, he is."

"Your brother?"

Soren considered, then replied, "No."

"Lover?"

I could have sworn Soren almost laughed.

"*Gods* no."

"Then what is he to you?"

Soren went quiet.

I rolled my eyes and started smashing a piece of potato with the curve of my spoon. "Well, you're just a delight in the mornings, aren't you?"

"Miss Calder," Soren said abruptly, the firmness of his voice making me jump. When he spoke again his tone was low and calculated, like he was holding back from saying the words he really wanted to. "I understand you're going through a difficult time. I've lost people close to me as well. So has Xavier. But please keep in mind we did not *have* to help you on Samhain. I did not *have* to defend you against the Nethers in the woods, and I did not *have* to put my neck on the line by offering you sanctuary in my home. You don't have to like me, Miss Calder, but you *will* respect me."

I bristled and tossed my spoon to the table. "Clearly someone can't take a joke."

"Someone can, and they would have laughed had they not sensed the contempt behind it."

I scoffed. "More of those heightened Fae senses, huh?"

"It doesn't take heightened senses to see you're angry with me. I know you don't understand them, but I had my reasons for what I did. What happened to Wynn was the best option for him. Your brother is safer than you are at this point."

My frosty exterior evaporated as I paled at the sense of doom his words carried.

"Now I swear to you, I will do everything in my power to try and find a way your brother can be returned to you, and I will search for a solution that absolves you of your debt. However, I can make no promises about the outcomes of either. If you hate me for that, then so be it. You're free to wallow in your anger and self-pity on your own time, when it doesn't affect me or those living under my roof."

And with that, Soren pushed his chair away from the table and stormed out of the room.

I sunk in my seat and stared at my battered breakfast, feeling shockingly similar to a child who'd just been given a good scolding.

Chapter 6

After the conversation with Soren at breakfast, I knew if I returned to my room I would just sit there stewing and end up making myself more miserable, so I took the opportunity to cool off by exploring the castle grounds. This time around, seeing it in broad daylight, I was in awe. It seemed the castle was made to perfectly blend in with the forest outside its walls. Hanging vines clung to many of the pillars and exterior walls, and countless verandas and courtyards opened onto gorgeous gardens filled with old-growth trees, manicured hedges, and lush ponds. I was standing beside a long reflecting pool just off the great hall, admiring the flurry of bright red leaves that were drifting down from a nearby maple tree to land on its shimmering surface, when I stumbled across Meer.

The Fae was passing through the courtyard, his alabaster fingers curled around the handle of a large wicker basket full of fresh fruit, when he stopped in front of me.

"Hello, Lina Calder. Good to see you up and about. Don't you look lovely." He eyed my green dress and winked knowingly before gesturing to the castle around us. "What do you think of the grounds?"

"They're beautiful," I replied.

I meant it, too. Although my blood still boiled at the thought of Soren handing my brother over to the Nethers, there was no denying the king of Astoria kept a stunningly beautiful home.

Meer beamed. "I thought you might like it. The moment I heard your story, everything made sense."

"What made sense?"

"Why you're here."

I'm here because your king gave an innocent boy to a horde of monsters and I had nowhere else to go.

But I kept the thought to myself and instead blinked expectantly at Meer. He clicked his tongue, slipped an arm through mine, and began walking with me as he explained.

"You see, His Majesty has a little habit of picking up lost souls. He gives them a safe haven here. A place to heal. Take me, for example. I was attacked and left to die by a particularly nasty group of Nethers, and when His Majesty found me on one of his hunts, he brought me here to mend before offering me a position on his staff."

I glanced over at Meer. It was hard to imagine anyone wanting to harm such a kind, gentle soul.

"And then there's Xavier, of course," Meer continued.

"What about him?"

"They didn't tell you?"

I shook my head.

Meer wrinkled his nose and scoffed. "Gods, Fae men can't communicate to save their life." He patted my hand. "Well, a number of years ago, His Majesty lost his younger brother, Prince Silvain, in a battle against an especially nasty Nether uprising. No one is exactly sure what happened, but Silvain's entire battalion was wiped out."

We passed beneath another old maple as a chilly autumn breeze rustled its boughs and released a sprinkling of leaves into the air.

"It was a brutal massacre. No one in Silvain's battalion lived to see the victory. But one low-caste soldier survived longer than the rest, and he stood by the prince, bravely defending him until the bitter end. That soldier was Xavier's father."

One of the descending leaves caught in my hair, prompting Meer to let out a small chuckle and lift a hand to gently pluck it away.

"After the battle," he went on, "His Majesty heard about the soldier's loyalty and sacrifice, so he went to pay his respects to the family. But when he arrived at the home, he discovered the only person the man left behind was a seven-year-old son. His Majesty adopted the child and raised him himself. He taught him all the airs and graces of a nobleman, even though there wasn't a drop of noble blood in him."

Against my will, the ice around my heart thawed slightly. Wynn hadn't been much younger than Xavier when our parents died. The day it happened, my brother had been confused at first, the information not processing fully in his young mind, but when it finally did, he was devastated. I imagined Xavier must have had a similar response. That was something no child should ever have to go through.

"Well, he seems to blend right in," I mused.

Meer chuckled again. "He learned from the best. His Majesty was a shining star at court when he was younger, too."

I remembered the night we met, the way Soren had kissed my hand and looked up at me with those hooded eyes. It would be easy to picture him doing the same to woo a lady at court. I quickly shoved the image from my mind. It made

Soren much more charming and magnetic than I wanted to view him.

"Xavier is young and excitable," Meer continued, "but he has a good heart. And make no mistake, he's a skilled warrior as well. His Majesty made sure to teach him everything he knew in that regard too."

"The king has seen many battles?"

"Unfortunately, yes." Meer frowned. "Relations between Fae and Nether have always been complicated, to say the least. And just as Xavier shines at court, His Majesty shines on the battlefield."

That explained the glimpses of the hardened warrior I'd seen in Soren on Samhain. The one who barked orders and whose eyes had been stubborn and callous as he sealed my brother's fate.

"So you see?" Meer gestured to the courtyard around us. "Even though you're a stranger in a strange land, I think you might fit in here more than you realize, Lina Calder."

Meer's kind words and the warmth in his smile managed to crack the ice around my heart even more, but something broken and angry still pinched there, refusing to let go of the bitter cold.

"My brother was lost too," I muttered. "Why isn't he here then? Why did your king abandon him?"

The joy in Meer's eyes dimmed.

"Oh, Lina," he breathed, halting his stride and lowering his basket so he could take my hands in his. I didn't meet his gaze, choosing instead to keep my eyes fixed on my shoes.

"Believe me, the king wanted to help your brother." Meer's head angled to the side as he looked at me, compassion cushioning his voice. "But there are laws in place, ones set in stone at the dawn of time. Breaking them would have terrible consequences. It was a difficult decision, but a necessary one."

Meer rubbed my arms comfortingly, giving me the strength to finally peek up at him. An encouraging smile waited for me.

"Come with me," Meer said brightly, beckoning me to follow him with a nod of his head. "There's something I want to show you."

I obediently trailed behind as Meer took up his basket again and drifted into the castle, leading the way towards the grand staircase near the entry. When we'd made our way upstairs and turned down the hallway to the right, Meer stopped in front of the first door we came to and pushed it open.

"After you," he declared.

I entered and looked around the room. I was in a study, significantly smaller than the one in Radomir, but with its dark wood furnishings, massive hearth with a marble surround, and a leather sofa and chairs draped in fluffy white furs, it felt just as luxurious.

"This is His Majesty's private study, but I figured when he's not using it, you might like to take a look through some of the reading material." Meer pulled a dusty book from a shelf and flipped through its worn pages. "I thought we could search for any information on how to help your brother. There has to be something of use somewhere in here." He replaced the tome and shrugged. "I thought doing something productive might make you feel better."

I offered Meer a tiny grateful smile and reached out to squeeze his hand.

"Thank you," I said earnestly.

Meer gave me a tight squeeze back. "Of course. Now…" He lifted his basket high and shook it cheerfully. "I'm going to deliver these to the cook and see if she'll make us something to nibble on. We can't search with an empty stomach, can we?"

Two hours later, I was buried in a stack of books while Meer was carving up a spiced pear tart for the both of us. For the first time in days I actually felt like eating, and the scent of clove and cinnamon wafting up from the dish was making my mouth water. I eagerly accepted a serving from Meer, shoveling a spoonful into my mouth with one hand while tracing the other over a page of intricate symbols in one of the books.

"What is this language?" I asked. "It looks beautiful."

Meer peeked over my shoulder. "That's the ancient Fae tongue. Just give those ones to me, I'll go through them."

I slid the text over to Meer's side of the table, grateful to have one less thing to go through. I was literate, but I was a fairly slow reader, and the texts that had piled up were starting to feel overwhelming. Thank the gods I had Meer, who was significantly more educated than I was.

It took me by surprise. In my world, servants wouldn't traditionally have the ability to read and write. The fact that my brothers and I had the skill was rare, and it had only come about because I'd found a novel lying trampled in the mud of the main village road when I was ten. It must have fallen off the cart of a nobleman or merchant on his way to market. I'd brushed off what debris I could, brought it home and laid it out to dry, then spent the next year carrying it everywhere I went. When I came across someone of a higher class than myself, I'd hold the book open, point to a passage, and politely ask them if they could tell me what it said. I lost track of how many laughed in my face or brushed me aside, but some had taken pity on me and slowly read aloud so I could follow along with them. I'd memorize what they said, then run home and copy down the letters.

Eventually, I could put together basic sentences of my own,

and taught Dominic and Jaras what I'd learned. When my mother found out, she'd threatened to throw away the book, insisting no man would want to marry a literate wife, but my father had intervened. He'd told her it was a harmless hobby, it was benefiting my brothers, and I could simply keep it a secret from my future husband if I needed to.

Meer, on the other hand, hadn't needed to be so stealthy with his education. When I asked him if it was normal for servants in the Fae realm to read and write, he'd shrugged and said, "Unfortunately many of us can't afford it, but His Majesty supplies tutors for anyone on his staff who wishes to learn, and nearly everyone in his employ has taken him up on the offer."

It was yet another story about Soren that made the ice around my heart threaten to melt completely, but the image of him handing my brother over to the Nethers kept the remnants of my hatred fixed firmly in place.

Refocusing on the present, I flipped open the weathered cover of my book and examined the table of contents. "Thank you again for helping me. You really didn't have to."

Meer waved away the comment and poured us both a cup of the ginger tea he'd brought up earlier. "That's what friends are for."

I gave him a small smile, then flipped through the pages in search of any mention of Changelings.

We read in silence for a few moments before Meer spoke again.

"So," he said, turning a page and taking a dainty sip of his tea, "do you have a lover waiting for you back in the human realm?"

I jerked my head up from my book, mouth agape at the boldness of his question.

"What?" Meer asked innocently.

I shook my head and sank deeper into my chair. "I'm just not used to speaking so lightly about such... intimate things."

"Oh, that's right!" Meer propped a fist under his chin and squinted at me. "I heard humans have a rather close-minded view on intercourse. Is it true you're only allowed relations with one partner?"

"Um..." I prayed my cheeks weren't as red as they felt. "Well, there are some who don't believe in that, but for the most part... yes, a young woman is expected to save herself for her husband only."

"I see." Meer nodded thoughtfully. "And do you have a husband?"

"No."

"So you're a virgin?"

My cheeks were *definitely* red now.

"Not... exactly," I mumbled, averting my gaze.

"Not exactly?" He squinted in confusion. "What does that mean? You either are or you aren't. So? Which are you?"

Gods, please just let me melt into the floor, I prayed.

"I... am not."

Meer gasped and leaned forward eagerly. "Lina, you little rebel!"

I peeked up at him, expecting to be met with the same judgment I typically was in the human realm when people found out about my past, but Meer simply smiled at me, his gray eyes twinkling with delight.

"You needn't feel ashamed, Lina." He patted my hand. "I doubt you've done anything that could surprise a Fae. Life gets boring when you live as long as we do. We do *much* to keep it interesting."

A wave of relief washed over me, and I even found it in myself to chuckle a little.

"But now I'm curious…" Meer raised a mischievous brow. "Have you had one lover? Or multiple?"

I leaned back in my seat and crossed my arms, trying my hardest to resist Meer's contagious grin.

"… Multiple."

Meer squealed in delight, causing a laugh to finally bubble up out of me.

"Lina Calder," Meer said, nudging me playfully, "maybe a little part of you is Fae after all."

Someone knocked at the door, and we both looked up. Xavier stood in the doorway, casually leaning against the doorframe.

"What's this? A party in Soren's study? Why wasn't I invited?"

He sauntered into the room, rolled the sleeves of his shirt up to his elbows, and helped himself to a slice of tart.

Meer sighed and examined his fingernails. "Oh look, Xavier's sniffing around a beautiful young woman. What a surprise."

Xavier bent and planted a kiss on Meer's cheek. "Who says I'm not sniffing around you?"

Meer smiled coyly up at him. "Oh, sweetheart, you couldn't handle me and you know it."

"Keep telling yourself that."

Xavier took his dessert and plopped on the sofa, nestling into the cushions and propping his boots up on the armrest. "It's good to see you actually reading the books instead of throwing them, Lina."

He spooned a chunk of pear into his mouth and smirked at me.

I kept my eyes glued to the text on the table and flipped to the next page. "It's good to see you doing something besides following the king around like a puppy, Xavier."

Meer threw his head back and cackled gleefully. "Oh, I like her. I *really* like her."

Xavier pouted and waggled his spoon at the both of us. "I'm not sure I like this new alliance. It's got trouble written all over it."

"Xavier, darling, when have *you* shied away from a little trouble?" Meer asked, batting his long white lashes sweetly.

"Since it washed up in Radomir on Samhain and started wreaking havoc." Xavier popped another piece of tart into his mouth. "Soren's been impossible to reason with since she showed up."

"What's the matter?" I casually flipped to the next page. "Are you two having a lovers' quarrel?"

Meer nearly spat out his tea as he laughed again. Xavier scowled and thrust his spoon in Meer's direction like a tiny sword.

"I blame you for this new attitude of hers."

I smiled to myself. I hadn't realized it before, but Xavier reminded me so much of Dominic. They were the same height and body type, had the same playful energy, and Xavier even shared the signature Calder freckles dotting our cheeks and noses. Bantering with him felt like second nature. It made me miss Dominic terribly, while simultaneously making me feel like he was still here with me in spirit.

"I'm in full support of Lina taking her power back in whatever way she can," Meer stated.

"I support that too, but I'd prefer if she took her power back in a way that was much less painful for me." Xavier finished off his dessert and tossed the empty plate to the side.

"What would you suggest, then?"

"I told her before. She should pick up a weapon."

"Will you teach me?"

Both Meer and Xavier turned to look at me. I stared at

Xavier, my mouth set and my shoulders squared, more sure of this than I had been of anything in a long time.

I didn't want to survive by the skin of my teeth anymore.

I didn't want to freeze when those I loved needed me the most.

I didn't want to be at the mercy of my fear or rage, or at the mercy of anyone else.

I wanted to confidently hold my head high and know I was competent and strong and a force to be reckoned with.

"Meer said you're a skilled warrior," I pressed.

"I am," Xavier replied, his eyes narrowing.

"So teaching me the basics should be easy." I shrugged. "Unless you're scared you couldn't do it."

Xavier's lips slowly curled upwards into a devilish grin. "Tomorrow morning. Wear something you don't mind getting blood on."

I HADN'T SLEPT much thanks to the constant nightmares of bony Nether women with sunken faces chasing me through the forest, but when morning came I still bounded out of bed. I ate a quick meal of eggs, bacon, and porridge, then met Xavier outside in the courtyard off the great hall. Thankfully, Soren hadn't been at breakfast, so I was able to remain in a good mood.

Per Xavier's request, I wore something I could get dirty: my knee-high brown boots, a pair of dark green trousers, and a white lace-up top. He was dressed similarly, but once I positioned myself across from him like he asked, he immediately whipped off his shirt.

"Really?" I asked flatly.

"What?" Xavier shrugged. "It's for optimum movement."

I rolled my eyes. "Sure it is. But it's a little chilly for that, don't you think?"

"Movement warms up the body. Besides, this is how I always train."

I sighed impatiently and tapped my foot, trying not to make eye contact with Xavier's six-pack. He raised an eyebrow and gave me one of his cocky, lopsided grins.

"You're welcome to take your top off too."

I glared at him. "Let's just start."

Xavier snickered. "Alright." He pulled two daggers from the sheaths at his hips and spun them in his hands before passing one to me. "We'll begin small and work our way up."

I carefully took the knife, tightly wrapping my fingers around the hilt. I liked the way it felt in my hand. The slight weight of it, the cool kiss of the metal against my skin.

It felt like power.

"I also want to learn to hunt," I declared. "My brother was going to teach me, but he... well, he didn't get around to it." I pushed the image of Dominic crumpling to the ground beside Jaras out of my mind. "Can you teach me how to do that too?"

"Unfortunately, I'm shit with a bow. I'm much better with my hands." Xavier shot me a suggestive wink, prompting me to roll my eyes again.

"You'd be better off having Soren teach you," he continued, tossing his dagger deftly from one hand to the other. "He's a great shot. Best hunter I've ever seen."

I frowned.

Well, it seems I won't be learning to hunt, then.

Xavier clocked my bitter expression and scoffed. "You'd think you would show a little more gratitude towards someone who saved your life. *Twice*, I'd like to point out."

"I didn't ask for a moral lesson, I asked you to teach me to fight," I snapped. "Are you going to do that, or not?"

Xavier chuckled. "Fiery. I like it. Alright, human." He took a fighting stance. "Keep your chin down to protect your neck, left fist up to block your face. Let's get to work."

~

Xavier and I trained for hours. He taught me basic footwork and blocks, both of which could be used in hand-to-hand combat as well as with a weapon, and then we switched to offensive maneuvers. He was right about the movement warming us up; by the end of the first hour, sweat was dripping off my forehead and down my back. By the second, my shirt was soaked through.

"No, you've got to step forward first, block with your left, and *then* come in for the kill with the right."

I attempted the action again, but still stumbled and lost my balance. I sighed in frustration.

"That's alright, you'll get it," Xavier encouraged. "Go through it slow. Forward... block... slice. Good. Now faster. Forward—"

"Xavier!"

We both turned. Soren stalked towards us, his expression grave. Gone was his usual finery. In its place were furs and fighting leathers, bracers, and a large broadsword strapped to one hip, while a dagger hung at the other.

"What's wrong?" Xavier asked, taking one look at his king and immediately standing at attention.

"Get dressed," Soren ordered. "A patrol saw a group of Nethers near the border. I want to see if they're the same ones we encountered in Radomir."

Xavier nodded and snatched his knife from my hand. "Practice everything we went over on your own, Lina. Next time we'll pick up where we left off."

He sprinted towards the castle and disappeared inside, leaving me and Soren alone in the courtyard.

The Fae king looked me up and down, taking in my flushed face and the sweat-drenched shirt that clung to my chest and stomach.

"It's nice to see you channeling your rage into something useful."

Irritation shot through me at his words, and I lifted my chin defiantly. "Don't worry, there's still plenty left to channel other places."

Soren sniffed wryly. He stared at me for a few weighted seconds before unsheathing the dagger at his hip. He extended it to me, the silver filigree vines circling its hilt glittering as they caught the sunlight.

"Show me," Soren ordered.

I blinked in surprise. "What?"

"Show me what Xavier's taught you so far. Try that last move you were working on."

"No," I said, taking a step back.

"Why?"

"You're just going to magically bat it away like you did with that knife the woman in the woods had."

Also I hate you and don't want you near me, I wanted to add, but bit my tongue.

"I won't use my magic. I promise."

I chewed the inside of my cheek as I considered. Soren blinked at me expectantly, then gave the dagger a taunting shake.

"Fine," I huffed, stepping forward and reaching for the knife.

"Go full speed," Soren commanded. "Actually try to cut me."

"What? No!" I yanked my hand away. "I'll hurt you!"

Soren chuckled. "No you won't."

At that, my blood heated.

"I *might*," I said indignantly.

"No, you *really* won't."

My blood warmed to a full blown boil.

Alright, Your Majesty, you want to play this game? Let's play.

I clenched my jaw, ripped the dagger from Soren's hand, and held it at the ready like Xavier had instructed me. My body hummed at the prospect of wiping the arrogant expression off Soren's face.

"Full speed," Soren repeated.

I tightened my fingers around the hilt, mentally repeating the sequence I'd just learned. Then I moved.

Step, block, slice—

On the last maneuver, just before I thrust the blade into Soren's neck, he kicked my standing leg, causing my knee to buckle. I yelped in alarm as I toppled to the ground.

"Keep your weight evenly distributed," Soren cooly instructed. "If you lean on your front foot like that, you'll lose your balance."

I growled and pushed myself off the cold stones of the courtyard before spinning and lunging at Soren again. This time, he easily sidestepped me and rammed an elbow to my back, sending me hurtling to the ground. I landed on my stomach, grunting as the wind whooshed from my lungs. I coughed, gasped in a breath, then rolled onto my back to glare up at him.

"What the hell was that?!" I sputtered.

"You're too emotional. Emotions can blind you and cause you to make mistakes," Soren stated. "You have to learn how to control them. Better to take a moment to reset and analyze the situation, then adjust accordingly."

My cheeks burning, I scrambled upright and attacked once more.

Step, block, slice—

Again, Soren roughly knocked my leg out from under me, sending me to my knees in front of him. Judging by the stinging pain that followed, the skin there was now thoroughly scraped. I scowled up at the man looming over me.

"You had all your weight on that front foot again," he said with a shrug.

I sighed and hauled myself up a final time. I got into position: chin tucked, left hand ready to block, right hand gripping the dagger firmly, weight distributed equally on both legs. Then I took a deep breath, focused, and exhaled calmly...

Step, block, slice—

My blade collided with the bracer around Soren's wrist as he brought it up in the nick of time, stopping my knife mere inches from his throat. I stared at him intently, chest heaving as I attempted to catch my breath. He stared right back, a slow smile spreading over his lips.

"Good," he murmured. "Very good."

I stepped away, still panting, and offered him the dagger hilt-first. Soren glanced at the blade, then shook his head.

"It's yours."

I opened my mouth to protest, but he turned and started back for the castle, calling over his shoulder as he went.

"Keep it on you at all times. You might need it."

Chapter 7

That night, I put the dagger Soren had given me under my pillow before I climbed into bed. I felt significantly better having a weapon on me that I knew how to use, and I hoped that knowledge would also put my subconscious at ease while I slept.

It was just wishful thinking. I still had nightmares.

I dreamed that I found Wynn. A dense fog pulled away, revealing him standing alone in the middle of the forest. His back was to me. I called out his name, but he didn't answer. I walked closer, and just as I reached out to touch him, he turned. His eyes were black, and when he opened his mouth, his teeth dripped black sludge and a long forked tongue snaked from his mouth to lash at me like a viper's. I fell backwards, landing in a crack in the ground beside two dead bodies: Jaras and Dominic. I screamed, but no sound came out. When I tried to move, my brothers' bodies came to life and grabbed me by the throat, choking me until I couldn't breathe, then pulled me down, down, down into the ground until the crack swallowed me whole.

I woke in the middle of the night, my face smothered in a pillow, screaming and sobbing. Shaking violently, I bolted upright and wiped my eyes, attempting to calm my gasping breaths. I inhaled through my nose and exhaled through my mouth, then did it three more times. Tears continued to stream from my eyes, and my breathing stayed rapid and shallow.

Shoving back the covers, I stepped out of the bed, slid my feet into a pair of fur-trimmed slippers, and threw a velvet dressing gown over the chemise I'd worn to sleep. I then went to the door, opened it as carefully as possible to avoid it creaking, and padded into the hall.

I tiptoed down the stairs and made my way towards the kitchen. My tears had stopped by the time I got there, but my heart still raced, and my body shook so intensely it looked like I'd been caught in the snow without a coat. I'd forgotten to bring a candle down with me, so I fumbled through the dark, stubbing my toes on table legs and whacking my knees on counter corners as I searched for something to take the edge off. When I stumbled into a shelf with a collection of bottles containing what appeared to be some form of liquor, I breathed a sigh of relief.

"Thank the gods," I whispered.

I snatched up the first bottle on the shelf and headed back towards my bedroom. From past experience, I knew the only way I would be able to relax was if I numbed my frayed nerves with alcohol. Maybe that was the reason Jaras had drunk so much. Maybe there had been too much pain inside, more than he knew what to do with, and he'd wanted to dull it the way I was now. Maybe all those years I had just misunderstood my brother, and treated him horribly because of it.

I shook the guilt-ridden thought from my mind and started up the stairs. When I got to the top and turned left towards my bedroom, a deep voice spoke from the darkness behind me.

"What are you doing up?"

I screamed, dropped the bottle, and spun to find myself face-to-face with Soren. He'd silently materialized out of his study and now leaned against the wall, arms crossed in front of his chest.

I smacked a hand to my racing heart. "You scared the shit out of me!"

Soren glanced at the ground and stooped to pick up the bottle, which had rolled to a stop at his feet. He blinked at it, then returned his gaze to mine.

"This is cough syrup."

I squared my shoulders. "I don't care what it tastes like, I just—"

"No," Soren said, a hint of amusement in his words, "I mean this elixir is literally used to treat coughing fits."

"Oh." I frowned.

We stood in silence for a few moments before Soren sighed. "Come with me."

Cautiously I obeyed, trailing a few steps behind him as he led the way to his study. The room was faintly lit by embers smoldering in the hearth, but when we entered, Soren waved his hand and the fire roared to life, showering the room in warm gold light.

"Neat party trick," I mumbled.

Soren ignored my snide comment and instead reached into a bottom drawer in his desk to pull out two glasses and an elegant crystal decanter containing a brown liquid.

"This is the best you can get," he said, shaking the bottle.

He set the glasses on the table, then poured a healthy amount of the liquid into each before holding one out to me.

"Although, I should warn you. I'm not entirely sure what kind of effect it might have on a human. It could act like a powerful sedative, for all I know."

I hesitated, but eventually accepted. "A sedative is exactly what I need."

He swirled his drink in his hand, eyes fixed on the contents inside. "Can't sleep?"

I shook my head. "Nightmares."

Soren nodded pensively, then lifted the glass to his lips and took a sip. I did the same. The liquid burned all the way down my throat, but the aftertaste of vanilla and maple and the way it warmed my stomach from the inside out made the pain worth it.

Soren finished off his drink, poured himself a second, then retreated to the sofa in front of the fireplace. I perched on the back of one of the leather armchairs and studied him while we both continued to sip.

This was by far the most disheveled I'd ever seen the king. He was barefoot and dressed only in black pants and a partially unlaced crimson shirt, exposing a sliver of his wide chest. His long, wavy hair was pulled back in a messy knot at the nape of his neck, but several pieces had fallen forward and hung around his face. Highlighted in gold by the dancing flames, watching the fire with a somber, far-off look in his eyes, there was no denying the man was breathtaking. So breathtaking in fact, that I'd forgotten my distaste for him and was so mesmerized by his statuesque appearance that I almost didn't hear him when he spoke again.

"I owe you an apology."

I snapped out of my trance. "Huh?"

Soren didn't look at me. Instead, he frowned and absent-mindedly tapped a finger against the side of his glass. "I'm sorry for how I acted at breakfast yesterday. What I said was too harsh. Everyone grieves differently, and I'd forgotten that."

Oh, right. One of the many reasons to be angry with him.

I opened my mouth to say something snippy and biting, but paused at the sincerity glimmering in his eyes.

"Apology accepted," was what I said instead.

Soren dipped his head in thanks but kept his attention fixed on the fire. We sat in silence a few moments longer before I decided to break it.

"Is everything alright with the Nethers? You and Xavier ran off so fast today."

Soren frowned, then waved the question away. "You don't want to know about all that. You've got enough on your mind as it is. It's just..." He sighed and chuckled wryly, then lifted his glass to his lips. "My father made this all look so fucking easy."

"He didn't prepare you for the crown?"

Soren finally met my gaze. The flames danced in his irises the way it had on Samhain, and while that night I had been too distressed to take much notice, I now found myself captivated by the flickering shades of navy and gold.

"No, he didn't," Soren said softly. "Nothing could ever fully prepare you for this."

He seemed tired as he said it. And maybe... was that a hint of fear in his eyes? Part of me wanted to inch closer to get a better look, to find out what else hid behind this seemingly perfect exterior, but I peeled my gaze away and took a swig from my glass as we again fell into silence. When I eventually found the courage to speak, my words were barely above a whisper.

"I... I never said thank you. For saving me."

"You don't have to—"

"No, really." I forced myself to meet Soren's stare. "Without you, I'd be dead. I'm sorry I didn't say anything before, it's just... it's been a really hard couple of days."

A gruesome picture of my brothers flashed across my mind, and the ache in my heart deepened.

"I understand." Soren offered me a sad, knowing smile. "And you're welcome."

"I'm still mad at you, though," I added quickly.

The chuckle that rumbled up from Soren's chest had no right sounding so seductive. "I can live with that."

I nodded, then downed my drink and stood, clearing my throat. "Well, I should probably be going." I shook the empty glass. "You were right, this does act like a sedative."

That was a lie. It didn't act any differently than alcohol in my world, and I wasn't tired at all. I was wide awake, and for some reason, maybe the drink or the way the firelight made Soren's eyes look, the warmth in my stomach had spread slightly lower.

"Good night," I blurted, starting for the door.

"Good night, Miss Calder."

I froze in the doorway, then slowly turned. I thought for a few seconds, fiddling with the small ribbon at the neckline of my chemise before deciding what I wanted to say.

"It's alright if you call me Lina, you know," I mumbled. "I'd prefer it, actually. Miss Calder just sounds so formal. And you don't have to be formal with me. I'm nothing special."

I peeked up to meet Soren's gaze, but when I did, he quickly returned his attention back to his drink.

"With all due respect," he murmured into his glass, "I don't think that could be farther from the truth."

His response sent an unexpected flush into the apples of my cheeks, so I ducked my head and faced the door to make sure he wouldn't see it.

"Lina?"

I glanced over my shoulder. Soren was looking at me again, his brows low over his eyes.

"You're safe. I had the castle's exterior walls spelled. No one comes in without my say. Nothing can get to you here. Not anymore. You have my word."

His words instantly soothed my aching soul. My tightly wound body relaxed slightly, and as I took a deep breath and released it, the claw of fear that had been a constant in my chest since Samhain didn't feel quite as heavy as it had before. I hadn't realized how badly I'd needed to hear that, or how badly I'd need to believe it.

That I was safe.

I gave Soren a smile, a *real* smile, and exited the room.

I did finally manage to go back to sleep that night, and I had the same nightmare as before. But this time, when the crack in the ground swallowed me whole, a hand burst through and pulled me out.

THE NEXT FEW weeks consisted of little else aside from fight training and poring over books. I would see Soren in passing and at breakfast and dinner, where we would have civil, verging on enjoyable, conversation. Many times he even said something that pulled a laugh out of me, but I disguised it by faking a cough. I couldn't have the man thinking all had been forgiven and forgotten. One night of shared drink in his study didn't change anything, despite how often I fought the urge to meet him there again whenever I'd wake up crying from more nightmares.

Most of my spare time was spent with Meer and Xavier. Meer's education, I learned, spanned more than just reading and writing. He was a sponge that had soaked up every crumb of information he'd ever been given, and he shared with me anything he thought might be useful. I was familiarized with the ins and outs of a court, the airs and graces involved, as well as general Fae history and politics.

There were five Fae territories, Meer explained to me: Astoria, Radomir, Lerian, Merimaya, and Kylanthia, and they were ruled by Soren, King Valdir, Prince Kaspar and Princess Syrena, King Ilris and Queen Ivari, and Queen Erith, respectively. Meer also revealed that, aside from King Ilris and Queen Ivari, all the rulers of the realm were relatively young and had come to power fairly recently, which made it an exciting albeit uncertain time in history.

I spent countless hours with Meer in Soren's study. Apart from the texts in the ancient Fae tongue, which I left for him to read, I had gone through nearly every book on the shelves and still found nothing that would help Wynn. I did stumble upon a few mentions of Changelings, but the solutions offered were to either locate the Auf and bring it back, or kidnap a different human child to offer in exchange for the original. I had become desperate enough that I wasn't opposed to the latter, but it still didn't change the fact I had to wait an entire year until the veil lifted before crossing over to the human realm again, which was unacceptable. Who knew what might happen to Wynn over the course of a year? I couldn't let myself think about what those things were doing to him wherever they were. Their location remained a mystery, and every time I pestered Soren about whether his patrols had come across them or if he'd received notice from the other territories that they'd been spotted, I got the same answer: it was as if they'd vanished into thin air.

So in order to keep from spiraling into the dark well of depression that constantly called to me, I channeled all my energy and focus into training.

Xavier worked with me as often as he could. He had me getting stronger, quicker, and more skilled by the day, and by the time three weeks had passed, I could have a decent sparring session with him and hold my own so long as he felt like taking it easy on me.

The days were growing cooler, but it wasn't nearly as cold as in the human realm this time of year. Or maybe it was, and the layers of velvet, cashmere, and fur I dressed in now made it less noticeable. It's amazing how much more enjoyable the cold can be when you're properly dressed for it. On one particularly chilly day, the clouds overhead were heavy and dark, threatening to release the first snow of the season, but Xavier and I still trained in the courtyard. The sweaters and jackets we'd bundled up in provided us with plenty of warmth, as well as some extra padding so we could hit each other a little harder than normal. Xavier now had me working on knee drives and shin kicks on top of everything else, which I loved and utilized often.

I blocked a slice from Xavier's knife with my own and drove a knee towards his gut, and when he blocked that, I quickly switched to a kick and landed a blow to his shins.

"Ow! *Shit!*" Xavier threw his hands up and limped away from me. "Truce! Truce! Give me a second."

I grinned and sheathed my dagger, wiping my damp forehead with my sleeve. "I'm getting good, aren't I?"

Xavier rubbed his shin ruefully. "You're alright. Don't get cocky. I wasn't going full speed."

"Excuses, excuses," I teased.

Meer wandered outside holding two goblets of water for the both of us.

"I swear..." He tutted. "You two are going to turn each other black and blue."

"Well, luckily for Xavier he looks good in blue."

His pain forgotten, Xavier stood upright and winked. "You think I look good, huh?"

"Only when I beat the shit out of you, which is why I do it so much!"

I lunged at Xavier again, but this time he dodged my blow and slammed a knee to the side of my thigh, instantly giving me a dead leg that had me crumpling to the ground.

"I told you not to get cocky," Xavier chided, taking a hefty swig from the goblet Meer offered him.

"That's enough!" Meer grumbled as he helped me stagger to my feet. "Xavier, you may heal in twenty minutes, but please remember Lina is delicate. If you ruin her appearance before the harvest celebration, I will personally tear you limb from limb."

"Take it easy, Meer." Xavier nudged him playfully. "I like it rough, but not that rough."

Meer let out an exasperated sigh and raised his eyes to the heavens. "Gods, give me patience because this child is testing me today."

"What's the harvest celebration?" I asked.

Xavier's eyes lit up. "It's this grand event Astoria holds every year to celebrate a successful harvest and usher in the Yule season. There's dancing and drinking and a huge feast, and Fae from every territory come to celebrate."

"The Fae can and will find any excuse to hold a ball," Meer added.

"It's not as important of an occasion as the Yule Ball," Xavier continued with a shrug. "That's our biggest event all year. But the harvest celebration is still fun. You'll like it."

"Well, it's important this year."

Xavier shot Meer a wide-eyed look. Meer responded by glaring back. They stared at each other tensely, communicating with nothing but their eyes, until Xavier shook his head and Meer pouted and stomped his foot. My gaze bounced between the two of them before I squinted in confusion.

"What am I missing?"

"Nothing," Xavier snapped.

Meer grunted in disagreement.

"Meer..." Xavier's voice was a low warning.

The head of staff simply pursed his lips and lifted his chin. "I'm telling her."

"Telling me what?"

Xavier clapped his hands over his ears. "Nope. I'm not listening to this. Soren can't be angry with me about something I didn't hear."

He spun on his heel and retreated into the castle.

I turned to Meer. "What's going on?"

The Fae slipped his arm through mine, and together we began leisurely strolling the courtyard.

"Lina, the king hasn't spoken to you about what's been happening with the Nethers, has he?"

"No." The memory of Soren's somber expression in the study all those weeks ago and that distant look in his eyes appeared in my mind. "Is it bad?"

"It's never good with those creatures," Meer said with a shake of his head, "but I'm afraid the events on Samhain put a target on His Majesty's back. More so than usual."

"Why?"

Meer stopped and placed both hands on my shoulders. "You remember what I told you when you first came here? That there were laws put in place at the beginning of time?"

I nodded, the conversation vaguely coming back to me.

"Those laws state that one night a year, there's a truce. The Nethers are permitted free rein of the five territories. They can move without fear of persecution, they're free to hunt, they can do whatever they'd like. The only condition is the Fae must not interfere with their activities or harm them."

"Samhain," I murmured, realization washing over me. "The one night the Fae can't touch them is Samhain."

Meer dipped his head in acknowledgement. "And *this* Samhain, a human woman killed one of their kind, but a Fae king defended her. They demanded her blood, and the king gave her sanctuary. He broke the rules that night. For you."

My heart sank to my stomach. I'd been so focused on everything happening to me and my brother that I hadn't thought about how others might be affected by the events of that night. Soren's words the morning after Samhain suddenly rang in my ears:

You may have just started a war.

I swallowed hard. "What does that mean for the five territories? For Soren?"

Meer sighed and hung his head, a lock of silky white hair hair falling in front of his face with the motion. "We're not entirely sure yet, but tensions are high. Nether attacks are growing more frequent. There are rumors some have even begun creating alliances with each other. Hostility between Fae and Nether has been building for years, it just needed a spark. And it seems—"

"I'm the spark."

Guilt hollowed a hole in my chest.

Meer nodded, then gave me a sad smile. "His Majesty instructed us not to tell you. He said it would just cause you more distress, and that you'd been through enough already."

I remembered Soren in his study again, how he'd waved away the question when I asked about the Nethers.

You don't want to know about all that. You've got enough on your mind as it is.

While I *would* have liked to know what was going on, I could see now that Soren's intentions had been good.

... Maybe the king wasn't as horrible as I'd originally thought.

Maybe.

"I didn't know," I mumbled. "I'm sorry, I didn't mean to start anything."

Meer wrapped a comforting arm around my shoulders. "You couldn't have known. Don't worry, everything's going to be fine. His Majesty will work it out, he always does. You can't blame yourself."

Easier said than done, I thought grimly.

Meer began walking again, taking me with him. "Regardless, this ball is crucial for the king. His allies will be there, as well as many of the nobles who will send their people to fight for him if the worst should happen. He needs to save face, show them that he stands confidently by his choice. He must prove to them he made the right decision."

I frowned. "The right decision saving me."

"Yes." Meer sighed and rolled his eyes. "Politics are just the worst."

My mouth went dry as the familiar clutch of panic grabbed at my chest. "So everyone is going to be watching me, and judging me for plunging their lands into turmoil?"

"All I'm going to say is," Meer said carefully, "it's very important for His Majesty that you prove you are someone worth saving."

I took a deep breath and let out a shaky exhale. "No pressure."

"I have an idea!" Meer chirped, spinning to face me and clapping his hands in excitement. "How about we take a trip into the local village and get you fitted for your dress for the celebration?"

"But I have plenty of dresses already."

"None like this." Meer's eyes glittered with excitement. "We need you to make a splash."

THE NEXT DAY, after the Sprites had helped me wash the morning's training session off me, Meer and I prepared to head into town. Xavier eagerly asked if he could accompany us, which I thought was odd until we arrived at the dressmaker's shop and a pretty, perky middle-caste Fae greeted us at the front desk. Xavier immediately sauntered over and flashed her one of his signature smiles, and by the time the dressmaker had measured and pinned me into a basic pattern, the two of them had mysteriously disappeared. When the appointment was finished, Xavier and the assistant reappeared, only now they looked extra smiley, a little sweaty, and very flushed.

"You're unbelievable," Meer snapped the moment we left the shop and shut the door behind us. He climbed atop his horse and shot an icy glare in Xavier's direction.

Xavier hauled himself into his mare's saddle too, attempting to hide his mischievous grin but failing miserably. "I have no idea what you're talking about."

"Mm-hmm," Meer grumbled, shooting him one last disapproving glance before trotting off.

Xavier winked at me and clicked his tongue, nudging his horse forward.

I chuckled to myself and shook my head as I followed them.

We rode down the village's main cobblestone street, then passed a handful of thatched roof cottages on the outskirts before turning down the rural path we'd taken earlier, which acted as a shortcut through the woods to the castle.

"I just want you to remember," Meer called over his shoulder, "that even though the king isn't here, you still represent him. Everything you do is a reflection of His Majesty."

"Exactly," Xavier chuckled. "Who do you think I learned it from?"

I peeked over at him and raised an eyebrow. "What exactly are you saying?"

"I'm *saying* Soren is the stuff of legends, in more ways than one, and he wanted me to follow in his footsteps. So..." Xavier gestured to himself proudly. "Here we are."

I laughed again. "Xavier, are you saying your king is a slut?"

"*Was*," Meer cut in abruptly. "But His Majesty has matured since then. Besides, that's a terrible word. Instead let's just say... His Majesty was once an exceedingly voracious lover. He, however, did it with class, unlike *this* one." He pointed a stern finger at Xavier and narrowed his eyes into slits. "*This* one is completely and utterly shameless."

Xavier grinned and trotted forward to torment Meer while I fell silent and replayed the statement *His Majesty was once an exceedingly voracious lover* over and over in my mind. The images it brought up made the cool day feel significantly warmer.

I was lost in thought for several minutes before I noticed Meer and Xavier had stopped talking at some point during my daydream, and now rode ahead with stiff backs as they surveyed the forest around us.

"Everything alright?" I called ahead.

"Everything's fine!" Meer cheerily yelled back.

But Xavier slowed so my horse caught up to his, and when I came up beside him, he lowered his voice.

"Act natural," he whispered, keeping his eyes forward. "Pretend like nothing's wrong."

"*Is* something wrong?" I mumbled out the side of my

mouth. Warily, I peeked at the woods. Nothing seemed out of place.

"Listen. What do you hear?"

I cocked my head and listened for a few seconds. "I don't hear anything."

"Exactly." Xavier's eyes scanned the tree line ahead. "Not a bird. Not the rustle of a leaf. Not the whistle of wind through the trees."

I turned my attention to the forest again. He was right. It was unnaturally calm. The only time I'd ever experienced such a thick blanket of silence was underwater, or in the fog, or on Samhain when I came in contact with...

"Nethers," Xavier said grimly.

My heart began to pound in my chest. I tried my best to appear composed and stared straight ahead the way Xavier was, but my horse's reins trembled in my hands.

"Where?" I asked tightly.

"Behind us." Xavier's eyes flicked to the trees on our left and right. "To the sides as well."

I gulped. "Meer—"

"Knows. He's going to make a run for the castle. You're going with him."

"What about you?"

"I'm going to keep them from following. You're what they really want."

My breath caught in my throat.

"Stay calm," Xavier ordered. "They'll smell your fear. Control it."

I gulped and forced myself to take a deep breath.

Xavier squared his shoulders, determination flaring in his eyes. "Now I'm going to count to three, and on three you're going to dig your heels into that horse and—"

"Wait, are you armed?"

"Yep." He peeked over and winked in my direction. "Fists and feet."

"Here, take this." I reached for Soren's dagger at my hip.

"Stop!" Xavier hissed. "You'll give us away! Besides, you might need it. I'll be fine."

"Will you, though?" I whispered back. "How many are there?"

He didn't answer, but his grim expression told me what I needed to know.

"On three," Xavier repeated firmly.

"No, you need—"

"One..."

"We can't leave you!"

"Two..."

"*Xavier!*"

"Three!"

Xavier flung out his hand and slapped my horse's flank as hard as he could, sending it hurtling up the path.

CHAPTER 8

THE ONLY SOUND IN MY EARS WAS THE HORSE'S HOOVES POUNDING against the earth and my own panicked breaths.

The world blurred as it flew past. Meer was just a sliver of silver on the path in front of me as he led the way towards the castle, darting around bushes, trees, and bends in the trail at a breakneck pace. I focused on that flash of silver and white, letting it guide me like a beacon as we fled our unseen foe.

A deep, inhuman bellow thundered behind us, so loud and violent that the ground vibrated, shaking the trees and rattling my bones. Icy terror shot through my body, making it impossible to think straight or feel anything besides fear. Meer's voice brought me back.

"Faster, Lina!" he shouted over his shoulder.

I'd been so afraid that I'd stopped breathing. I forced myself to take a deep inhale, then slapped my horse's reins against its neck and dug my heels into its sides. The beast needed no further urging. It ran as fast as its legs would permit, chomping at the bit like it too feared whatever was behind us.

I'd almost caught up to Meer when Xavier's scream echoed

through the forest. My stomach dropped at the sound. When he screamed again, my eyes pinched. When he screamed a third time, agony strangling his voice, tears streamed down my face.

"Keep going, Lina!" Meer commanded from ahead.

I held back a whimper and slapped my horse's reins once more.

The next time I heard Xavier, my heart nearly stopped.

Because this time, he spoke. And he sounded close.

"Lina!" he cried, "Lina, come back! Please! I need your help!"

I gasped. Xavier was clearly hurt, but he must have given his attackers the slip.

"Lina, please! Help me!" Xavier begged. His voice was closer this time. He had to be right behind us.

I set my mouth in a determined line. I couldn't let someone else I cared for fall into the hands of the Nethers. I wouldn't leave him like I'd left Wynn.

I started to turn my head and call out to Xavier when Meer's voice rang out in front of me.

"Lina, don't! Don't slow down!"

"He needs our help!" I shrieked. "We can't just—"

"*It's not him!*"

I froze.

... And then I heard my brother.

"Lina!" Wynn cried, his voice directly behind me. It was so close I felt like I could reach out and touch him.

"Lina, please!" he sobbed. "I'm scared!"

"*It's not them, Lina!*" Meer yelled. "I promise you! Do not slow down!"

When Wynn screamed, I nearly fell off my horse. The air whooshed from my lungs, and I crumpled forward as tears poured from my eyes and blurred my vision. I could barely see

Meer on the horse in front of me.

"Lina, they're going to hurt us!" Wynn wailed.

Xavier screamed in pain.

"Keep going, Lina!" Meer commanded.

Wynn let out a tortured sob.

"Lina, it hurts so bad! Please help me!"

I began to weep hysterically.

"Come on, Lina! We're almost there!"

"Lina, save me!"

"Save your brother, Lina!"

"Lina, please! Don't leave me! Not again!"

"Don't leave us, Lina!"

"*Lina!*"

Meer and I burst through the castle gate, and the voices abruptly stopped.

Our horses skidded to a halt in front of the main entry as Soren raced down the front steps to meet us. I threw myself out of the saddle and ran to the king, my knees buckling underneath me when I reached him. Soren caught me before I fell, firmly gripping both of my arms and forcing me to look him in the eyes with a gruff shake.

"What's wrong?" he demanded. "What happened?"

All I could do was point a trembling finger towards the forest and gasp out a single word:

"Xavier."

I didn't need to say anything else.

Soren's gaze hardened. He released me, ripped the dagger from the sheath on my hip, then hauled himself onto my horse and kicked it, sending it tearing out of the castle and back into the woods.

I slumped to the ground as Soren disappeared into the trees, my body shaking uncontrollably as I broke down in frantic, gasping sobs. Meer ran over and knelt beside me, wrapping me in his arms and rocking me back and forth as he gently stroked my hair.

"It's alright," he shushed. "You're alright, you made it. It's over now. It's over..."

I have no idea how long we sat there, curled on the cobblestones in front of the castle, Meer rocking me like a babe, but I had finally stopped crying by the time Soren reappeared.

My horse nowhere to be seen, Soren stumbled through the gate, Xavier's limp form draped over his shoulder. Both of them were covered head-to-toe in blood.

Meer leapt to his feet.

"Is he..." His voice cracked, and he clapped a hand to his mouth, unable to bring himself to say the words.

"Alive," Soren panted, his legs trembling beneath Xavier's weight. "But just barely."

Meer nodded, his face growing serious. "Right. Get him up to his room. Lina, fetch a pitcher of water."

Obediently, I scrambled off the ground and bolted into the castle. I flew into the kitchen, bumping into maids and cooks as I frantically searched for a pitcher, then gathered an armful of towels, rags, and bowls. Supplies in tow, I sprinted up the stairs two at a time and found Soren and Meer in Xavier's bedroom.

Soren carefully laid Xavier on the mattress, finally revealing the extent of the damage inflicted by the Nethers. On top of vicious bite marks all over his body, Xavier's abdomen had been sliced diagonally from hip to chest, his skin peeled back to reveal a glimpse of his internal organs. The sight had nausea rising in my stomach, and I had to duck my head into my shoulder to stifle a gag.

Soren stared at Xavier intently for a few seconds before heading for the door.

"Where are you going?" I asked.

"One got away," he mumbled.

"It was just one, Your Majesty," Meer said. "Please, Xavier would want you here. Stay with him in case the worst—"

Soren whirled to face us.

"*One got away!*" he roared.

The fury twisting his expression and vengeance gleaming in his eyes turned him into an entirely different person. He wasn't a king or a warrior. Hell, he wasn't even a man. He was nothing but a mass of bloodlust and violence, and even Meer flinched under his gaze.

Without another word, Soren charged out of the room.

When he'd gone, I braved another look at Xavier's mutilated body.

"Is… is there a healer coming?" My voice came out as a pathetic squeak.

Meer knelt beside the bed and rolled up the sleeves of his overcoat. "I am the healer."

He gingerly pulled back the bloody shreds of Xavier's shirt, revealing more of the deep wound on his stomach. It wasn't so much the sight of the twisting mass of intestines that bothered me, but the smell. The tang of blood and bile was so potent that it stung my eyes, and I couldn't fight the queasiness any longer. I immediately bent and vomited on the floor. Meer didn't seem to notice.

"Bring the water," he ordered, snapping his fingers in my direction.

I wiped my mouth and shuffled over with the pitcher.

"Pour me a glass."

I did so, my quaking hands making me miss the cup, spilling some of the water onto the floor. When I finally managed to get the glass full, I moved to lift it to Xavier's lips, but Meer stopped me.

"It's not for him." He held out his hand. "It's for me."

Confused, I handed him the cup. He downed the contents in three gulps.

"I need to be hydrated for this," Meer said, returning the empty glass. He then hovered his hands over Xavier's body, spread his fingers wide, and shut his eyes.

A white light started radiating from Meer's palms. As it pulsed, its rhythm similar to that of a heartbeat, Meer mumbled in a strange, lilting tongue. The louder his words grew, the stronger the light became. Soon, Meer spoke with a clear, confident voice, and the light spread over the entirety of Xavier's abdomen. Meer's hands shook, and his eyes squeezed tighter as a vein bulged on his forehead and beads of sweat slowly trickled down his temples. His typically snow-white skin flushed as he strained, and his cheeks turned an unnatural shade of purple. I wanted to help but had no idea how, so I said a silent prayer to the gods and watched with bated breath.

Meer eventually collapsed, gasping for air, and his pulsing white light disappeared. I dared a peek at Xavier's wound.

It didn't look any different.

"It takes time," Meer panted, reading the disappointment on my face. "They're the smallest of changes."

"So what now?"

Meer extended his hand towards the pitcher of water, beckoning for more. "Now we do it again. And fast."

MEER WORKED on Xavier for an hour, and each time he brought forth his healing light, it was a struggle. By the time he finished, the light was flickering and there were dark bags under Meer's eyes. He finally stood up, drank an entire pitcher of water, and shakily left the room, insisting that he needed to sleep before he could do anything more.

Wanting to feel useful even after Meer left, I stayed and dressed Xavier's injuries. Meer had healed them significantly, but they were still bad enough that looking at them for too long made my stomach turn. I bandaged the wounds as best I could and pulled a blanket over Xavier in the hopes it might make him more comfortable. Then I sat on the bed beside him and gently stroked his hair as I hummed a lullaby my mother used to sing to Wynn. I lost track of how long I sat there, but it must have been hours, because when Soren returned, the sun had set and the room was dark.

I was sitting next to Xavier, rubbing my collarbone while lost in thought, when the king's low voice startled me.

"How is he?"

I jumped and looked over at the darkened doorway. Soren stood silhouetted by the glow of candlelight behind him. When he stepped inside, my breath caught.

The king was drenched in fresh blood, still clutching the hilt of the dagger in an iron grip.

"He's still breathing," I said, mustering an encouraging smile.

Soren's tense shoulders instantly relaxed as he let out a shaky exhale. He walked over and looked down at the pale body in the bed. Soren stared at Xavier for several long, tense beats before he spoke again.

"I thought I lost him."

His voice was raspy and hoarse, like he'd been screaming.

I turned to Meer's pitcher of water and poured Soren a glass. He accepted it with a trembling hand. I watched him while he drank, taking in his stained shirt, the dagger, the blood coating his arms and matting his hair.

I should be terrified of a man who looked like this, who had just done gods know what in those woods. And maybe I would have been if it weren't for the way he was watching Xavier. His eyes glinted with emotion while his face wrinkled with compassion and worry. I could have sworn he even sniffled a little.

Soren felt my gaze on him and glanced over.

"How much of that blood is yours?" I asked softly.

Soren was silent for a long time. His eyes were distant, brows pinched low over them. Finally, he shook his head and croaked, "I don't know. I... don't remember much."

I swallowed and nodded, hesitating for a moment before lifting my hand to his. Slowly, gently, I pried his fingers away from the dagger, then carefully laid it on the bedside table before gesturing to his shirt.

"Take that off. Let's see if you need a healer too."

"I'm fine."

"*Soren.*"

The king blinked at the ground. After a few seconds, he reached down to the hem of the blood-soaked linen and stiffly peeled it over his head, grunting at the pain the movement caused him.

My eyes roved over him, lingering on his wide chest and the defined lines of his stomach. There were a few nasty gashes, but nothing life-threatening. I tried to avert my gaze, but it stayed fixed on the breadth of bare skin. Here, painted in flickering candlelight and the gore of battle, Soren was a terrifying work of art, the perfect depiction of a god of war returned victorious. Only his eyes betrayed his true identity. They were not those of a cruel or ruthless god. Instead they shone with fear, pain, and hurt, but somehow that made him even more beautiful.

Shaking the thought from my mind, I dragged my attention away from his body and took the soiled shirt from Soren's hands. I balled it up, stuffed it under my arm, and cleared my throat, praying the darkness prevented him from seeing the flush that had crept up my neck and into my cheeks.

"Looks like you'll live too."

Soren nodded listlessly, then lowered himself to the ground so he was curled on the floor beside Xavier's bed.

I froze, unsure of what to do next, but as Soren stared up at his friend, looking less like the vengeful god and more like a terrified child, I slid off the edge of the bed to join him.

"I thought I lost him," Soren said again. His voice was barely audible, and for a split second he seemed so much more fragile than he was.

His vulnerability had me instinctively scooting closer. "You didn't, though."

"But I could have."

"But you didn't," I repeated, firmly this time.

Soren nodded. After a few seconds, he slowly reached out and took my hand. My breath caught as he gave it an earnest squeeze.

"Thank you for staying with him," he muttered, his voice gravelly.

Soren's touch caused a tingle to spread up my arm, the intensity of his gaze only strengthening it.

I swallowed and quickly looked away. "Of course. He saved me, it was the least I could do."

Soren released my hand, but a faint tingle remained.

I cleared my throat again and forced my attention elsewhere. I looked back up at Xavier to examine his features. That nose and his mop of brunette hair were identical to Dominic's, and all those freckles splattered on his face looked exactly like mine.

"He reminds me of one of my brothers," I murmured.

I hadn't meant to say the words, but in the peace of the moment, I'd let my guard down and they'd sneaked out.

I peeked over at Soren. A small, sad smile had formed on his face, and his eyes glazed slightly as he drifted to a far-off memory.

"He reminds me of my brother too."

We fell silent, both of us staring up at Xavier and losing ourselves to our separate thoughts. Maybe it was that stillness, that moment of serenity after all the chaos, or maybe it was something else, but the walls around my heart ached to come down. It didn't make sense, but suddenly a violent warrior clothed in another's blood now felt like the most peaceful person in the world.

"It's my fault they're dead," I whispered.

I felt Soren's gaze land on me, but I didn't look over at him. I couldn't. My tears were already threatening to overflow, and I knew without a doubt if I peered into those soulful eyes of his, they would break me.

"My brothers. I'm the reason they're dead."

I fought to control my quivering chin and buried my hands in my lap, praying Soren wouldn't notice the way they shook.

"I worked for a man who... well, he asked me to marry him, and when I said no, he became violent. He said I should be grateful that he even noticed me, because I was nothing. A nobody. Worthless and tainted. Then he... he tried to force himself on me. I fought him off, but he said he'd find me and finish what he started. So I ran home and asked my brothers to take me on a hunting trip over the holiday. I'd always wanted to learn, but when that happened... I felt like I *had* to, because I knew when I got back I was going to have to defend myself."

There was no fighting the tears anymore. One slipped out, followed by another, then another, and then they wouldn't stop.

"We were in the woods that night because of me," I whimpered. "If I hadn't taken them out there, my brothers would still be alive. Wynn wouldn't be with those monsters. Your world wouldn't be talking about a war. And Xavier wouldn't..." I choked on the words, gesturing to the unconscious figure in the bed. "He wouldn't look like that. Everything is my fault."

I took a shuddering breath, afraid to meet Soren's gaze. When I finally did, he stared at me a few seconds longer before gently reaching out and brushing away my tears, the same way he had the night we met. When he pulled his fingers from my cheek, he quickly looked away.

"Several years ago, my father asked me to represent him on a diplomatic mission to Lerian. I refused, claiming it was because of a feud I have with the prince there, but in truth I was just being selfish and didn't feel like going. So my father went instead. He was killed on that trip."

Soren swallowed and peeked up at Xavier. "Before that, there was a battle. My little brother Silvain led a battalion under my command. I miscalculated the Nethers' move, and accidentally left my brother and his men exposed. They were slaughtered, every last one of them. Because of my mistake."

Soren exhaled slowly. "Both of those things ate away at me for a long time. Some nights, they still do."

He then looked to me, leaned forward, and replaced his hand on my cheek, wiping away one last tear with his thumb. His touch was warm and soft despite the thick calluses on his hands, and before I could second guess myself, I shut my eyes and nuzzled his palm, savoring the feeling of his skin against mine.

"It's not your fault, Lina," Soren said gently. "And I know from experience that hearing someone say that doesn't magically take the pain away or make you believe it. But it's true."

I sniffled, prompting Soren to tenderly stroke my cheek.

"It is *not* your fault," he repeated.

"Starting a war with the Nethers is," I argued.

Soren fervently shook his head, then shifted his hand from

my cheek to my chin, which he gripped firmly and lifted so I looked him in the eye. "War was inevitable, it was just a question of when. You didn't do anything wrong. You were defending someone you love, and there is nothing wrong with that. You hear me? *Nothing.*"

Just like that night in his study, I hadn't realized how badly I needed someone to say those words to me. The weight that had been a constant in my chest over the past three weeks lifted a little more, and without thinking I slipped my arms around Soren's waist and sank into him. Caught off guard, he froze for a moment, but soon his arms tightened around me, enveloping me in a sturdy embrace. I melted under the warmth and weight of his arms, relaxing to the soothing beat of his heart in my ears. Buried beneath the bite of sweat and blood, a woody scent wafted up from his chest. It was as if the whole of Astoria, all its rivers and old-growth forests, had somehow been bottled and dabbed across his skin. I nestled further into it, the smell only adding to the sense of safety and comfort in Soren's embrace.

Then, I made a choice.

The ice inside finally melted fully, and I decided this man was good.

Yes, he handed Wynn over to the Nether woman.

Your brother is safer than you are at this point, he'd said. Today had proved that. Soren must have known the Nethers would eventually come for me, and by handing Wynn over, he'd kept him out of harm's way.

This man was generous, even when he didn't have to be.

He was selfless, and had a heart for the broken and lost.

He fought for his loved ones with a ferocity as admirable as it was terrifying.

And he understood why I felt like I had blood on my hands, because he felt the same.

"Soren?" I murmured into his chest.

"Hmm?" His breath was hot on my neck, sending the tingle from before through the rest of my body.

"Xavier said you're a good hunter."

"I am."

I was quiet for a few moments, suddenly afraid to ask. But Soren already knew what I wanted to say.

"Would you like me to teach you sometime?"

I nodded, and his arms tightened.

"It would be an honor."

My heart swelled, and I sat upright, smiling earnestly up at him. "Thank you."

Our eyes locked, but I forced myself to look away. "I should probably get some rest."

I pushed myself off the ground and started for the door.

"Lina?"

I glanced back over my shoulder.

"He's going to be fine." Soren gestured to Xavier, a grin finally lighting up his face. "The harvest celebration is coming up, and he never misses a party."

I chuckled a little. "Good night, Soren."

"Good night, Lina."

I gave him one last smile and exited the room.

That night, I had a nightmare. But by the end of it, I'd slain all the monsters and found Soren in his study. Together we sat in front of the fire, wrapped safely in each other's arms, until the sky brightened with the dawn.

Chapter 9

I didn't see Meer over the next few days. My Sprite handmaidens, Laurel, Cassia, and Acacia, informed me that every spare moment Meer had was spent either working on Xavier or preparing for the upcoming festivities. I hadn't seen Xavier either, as everyone in the castle was under strict orders from the king not to disturb him while he was on the mend. I was alone for the first time in weeks, and I spent my days wandering the grounds and its gardens, practicing my fight training by myself, and attempting to avoid falling into a downward spiral of anxiety and depression. I still hadn't uncovered any information on how to get Wynn back, and the idea of monsters lurking in the woods just outside the castle walls, thirsting for my blood, haunted my dreams at night.

When I woke from my nightmares, I often found myself wandering to the closed door of Soren's study and watching the warm light of the fire flicker through the gap beneath the door. I wanted to knock. I liked to imagine that if I did, Soren would come to the door, and when I told him I'd had another bad dream, he'd offer me a drink like he had before and we'd sit next to each other, sipping in silence as we both stared into the flames. My mind would occasionally drift to more than that, to him pulling me into his chest and holding me in that safe, peaceful place in his arms, with his face buried in my hair and his warm breath on my neck. But I always ended up losing my nerve, shaking the thought from my mind, and retreating to my room before I could ever bring my knuckles to wood.

The day of the harvest celebration, the castle was a flurry of activity. Servants were up at the crack of dawn adjusting decorations, making food, preparing refreshments, straightening guest bedrooms, and obsessively cleaning the entire property. I was overwhelmed by the hustle and bustle, and no matter how hard I clung to walls and corners, somehow I always managed to get in the way. By lunch I had decided to hide in my bedroom for the rest of the day. By midafternoon I had talked myself into avoiding the ball entirely, but in the late afternoon, Laurel, Cassia, and Acacia barged in carrying a giant dress box and insisted I was going whether I liked it or not.

The Sprites were masters of their craft. In no time they had transformed me physically and mentally; Laurel was in charge of getting me into my dress, Cassia did my hair, and Acacia painted my face, while the three of them took turns plying me with snacks, wine, and positive affirmations. By the time they spun me to see my reflection in the vanity mirror, I had to blink a few times to make sure the woman staring back was actually me.

Cassia had twisted my hair into an intricate weave at the nape of my neck and stuck it full of crystal pins. Acacia had colored my lips a bright berry pink and placed a shimmering gold powder on my cheekbones and eyelids, making my eyes pop. The real star, though, was the dress. Meer and the dressmaker in the village had designed a masterpiece. I was laced into the corseted bodice of a blush gown, the flowing tulle skirt sparkling as the light caught tiny crystals sewn into its layers. Dainty lavender floral appliqués dotted the bodice and its off-the-shoulder sleeves.

"I..." My brain turned to mush as I attempted to formulate words. "I look like... like..."

"Springtime," Acacia chirped.

"A Fae," Cassia said.

"She looks like a queen," Laurel declared firmly.

The other girls nodded and mumbled in agreement.

I took a deep breath and let out a long, slow exhale before picking up an armful of the massive skirt. "How the hell am I supposed to walk in this?"

"Ideally you have a handsome man to hold on to," Acacia tittered.

"Would she settle for me?"

I whirled.

Meer stood in the doorway. He looked exhausted, but his smile still brightened the room.

"Lina," Meer breathed, placing a hand to his heart as he walked over, "you are the most exquisite creature I have ever laid eyes on."

"Oh, stop it." I batted him away, attempting to hide the fact his comment warmed my entire soul.

"I'm serious!" Meer passionately fluffed my full skirt. "Gods, I'm good."

I threw my head back and laughed.

Meer beamed. "Would you look at that! As promised, there's that sparkle in Lina Calder's eyes! I told you we'd get it back, didn't I, ladies?"

The Sprites nodded proudly.

I squeezed Meer's hand, trying to ignore the pinching behind my eyes. Meer saw right through me, and his eyes began to water too.

"Now, don't you start!" Meer huffed. "You'll get all of us going. And believe me, you do not want to see Laurel cry. It is *not* a pretty sight."

Laurel scowled at him and flipped him her middle finger. I laughed again.

"Shall we?" Meer asked, holding out his arm to me.

I took it, blushing at the way my hands had started to tremble. Meer squeezed my wrist comfortingly.

"Don't worry, Lina," Acacia called after us. "They're going to love you like we do!"

I looked back at the Sprites one more time. They smiled and blew me kisses and wished me all the luck in the world, then Meer ushered me into the hall.

As we neared the staircase, Meer showered me with last-minute information.

"King Valdir of Radomir and Queen Erith of Kylanthia are here. They're His Majesty's allies. Valdir you've met before, but Erith is a fresh face, so play extra nice with them. Make sure to smile constantly. Drink white wine or clear liquor so it won't stain your dress if you spill, and whatever you do, do not strip naked and jump in the reflecting pool. You'd be surprised how often it happens."

I chuckled. "Well, you don't need to worry about that one. I don't think I could take this dress off without any help."

"Oh! That's another thing! Whatever you do, do *not* have sex with anyone."

"Meer!" I laughed, smacking his arm playfully. "Really? You think so little of me?"

"No, darling, I think so little of everyone else." Meer raised an eyebrow. "All eyes are on you tonight, and if you do well, *everyone* will try to bed you. Partially because I made you look fabulous, but mainly because no one's had human before.

Curiosity will get the better of them, and everyone will want a taste."

As Meer talked, we passed a pair of Fae nobles in the hall. Both the male and female looked me up and down lasciviously.

"See?" Meer clicked his tongue in disdain. "Shameless."

When we arrived at the top of the staircase, my heart nearly pounded out of my chest as we surveyed the ocean of Fae mingling below. Everyone wore shades of maroon, olive green, mustard yellow, burnt orange, and navy, their extravagant gowns and dapper suits accessorized with colorful leaves in their lapels and acorns entwined in their hair. I stuck out like a sore thumb.

In a sea of autumn, I was the spring.

"Meer, what did you do?" I growled out of the corner of my mouth.

Meer winked back. "I told you that you'd make a splash."

He then gestured to the stairs, and I had no choice but to grip his hand and follow as he descended. I tried not to think about everyone's eyes turning towards me, and instead focused on putting one foot in front of the other. I could think of no worse fate than tripping in front of all these people. I'd rather be handed over to the Nethers in the woods than slip and fall on my ass on these godsdamned stairs.

We neared the bottom of the steps, and a figure emerged from the crowd. They were dressed in a green velvet doublet with embroidered leaves down the center. When I recognized them, my heart leapt.

"Xavier!" I squealed.

All the etiquette Meer had been teaching me over the past few weeks went out the window, and I threw myself into Xavier's arms, squeezing him tight. He didn't seem to mind, though, and laughed heartily as he spun me in a circle.

"You didn't think you could get rid of me that easy, did you?"

"Wishful thinking," I teased.

Xavier grinned, and it sounded like he genuinely meant it when he said, "You look lovely, Lina. Meer and the Sprites have outdone themselves."

I turned to smile proudly at Meer, but he'd already retreated up the stairs. He caught my eye at the top and waggled his fingers in a cheeky wave before disappearing into the depths of the castle. I returned my attention to Xavier.

"Would you like to dance?" he asked, extending his hand.

"Uh…" I hurriedly shook my head. "No thanks."

Xavier shrugged. "It's either that or socialize. And something tells me making small talk with strangers would be Lina Calder's own personal hell."

I hated when Xavier was right. He could always tell when he was, and that cocky, lopsided grin would spread over his face as he raised an eyebrow in a silent taunt. Usually I would wipe the expression off him by smacking him across the back of the head, but unfortunately tonight there were witnesses. So instead, I uncomfortably shifted from one foot to the other, fumbled with one of the appliqué flowers on my dress, and lowered my voice.

"I don't know how to dance," I mumbled.

Xavier leaned in. "Sorry, what was that?"

I sighed and raised my voice. "I said I don't know how to dance. I never learned. Back in my world, only the nobles learned, and my family was the farthest thing from that."

Undeterred, Xavier gestured to the ground. "It's easy, I'll show you. Watch my feet. If I step forward with my left, you step back with your right. Then we go to the side, then you go forward as I go back, then to the side again, and that's where you'd start to turn. See? Easy."

He looked up and smiled, extending his hand again. "Want to give it a try?"

"You're not going to let up, are you?"

"Nope."

I chuckled. "Alright, fine."

I reached out to accept, but someone else slipped their hand into mine first.

My breath caught as I met a pair of deep blue eyes.

Tonight, Soren looked every inch a king, dressed in a dark crimson jacket with silver embroidery and gray fur accents. His hair was in its usual style, half pulled back in a messy knot, but on top of his head he wore a thin crown of silver engraved with vines and leaves.

"May I?" Soren asked.

Had his voice always been so low and silky?

My lips parted, but I couldn't seem to form words. Instead, I glanced over at Xavier. He let out a dry chuckle, raised his hands in defeat, then sauntered through the crowd towards a group of male and female Fae twice his age. He performed an extravagant bow, then said something that made all of them blush and giggle like little schoolgirls.

"Shameless," I mumbled, smiling to myself.

When I faced Soren again, his fingers tightened around mine, and he whisked me in the direction of the ballroom. The crowd parted as we walked through, servant and noble alike all turning to watch us curiously. If Soren hadn't been beside me, I would have felt like a fawn walking through a den of wolves. But once again his confident, commanding presence had a strangely calming effect.

"Did you really have to go and shatter Xavier's dreams like that?" I muttered, keeping my voice quiet so only the king could hear me.

Soren smirked. "He'll be fine. He's been itching to show off his new scars to everyone anyway. Besides, I couldn't let that boy's ego get any bigger than it already is. If he was the first Fae to dance with a human, he'd never let anyone hear the end of it."

"So you're actually doing everyone a favor by stealing the title for yourself?"

"Something like that."

"How selfless of you."

Soren let out a small chuckle and took his place on the dance floor. I could still feel everyone's eyes on us, and a wave of insecurity washed over me.

"Like I told Xavier, I'm not going to be any good," I blurted. My cheeks and neck heated with a self-conscious blush. "I've never done this before."

"Don't worry. I'll go easy on you."

For some reason, those words made my blush deepen.

Soren raised his hand and signaled the musicians in the corner. They took up a slow, sweeping waltz.

I mentally repeated the footwork Xavier had just taught me, but as soon as Soren's hand grasped my waist and pulled me close, my mind went blank. All I could think about was the way his chest pressed against mine, how warm his hand was on my lower back, and how that intoxicating woody scent I'd smelled in his study was drifting down from his neck. My heart raced, but I assured myself it was only because I was nervous I would mess up.

As soon as we began to dance, however, I realized worrying had been pointless. Soren moved with fluidity and grace, and even when I confused the steps, he adjusted without missing a beat. I could have tripped over my own feet and he would make it look like it was part of the dance. I remembered what Meer had said about Soren being a shining star at court. In this moment, as we swept elegantly around the room and everyone stopped and stared, it was obvious.

"You're a natural," Soren declared.

I scoffed. "And you're very funny."

"I mean it. The training you've been doing with Xavier is helping you here. You've grown accustomed to complicated footwork." Soren smiled down at me, causing a warm flutter in my stomach. "He says you're getting pretty good."

I stuck out my bottom lip. "He's never told me that."

"He doesn't want you to get a big head."

I snorted. "*He* doesn't want *me* to get a big head?"

Soren threw his head back and laughed. It was a contagious sound, and I caught myself giggling along with him.

"It is a bit hypocritical, I'll admit." Soren returned his gaze to mine. His eyes sparkled, the reflected light from the chandeliers glittering in the rich blue of his irises.

"I'm glad you've been working with him, though." Soren's tone softened. His voice was earnest, as was his expression. "It seems to have helped you quite a bit over these past weeks. You're a long way off from that girl I found in the woods."

I nodded thoughtfully. "I guess I was just tired of feeling defenseless. It feels good to do something about it."

Soren threw me into an abrupt spin, then tugged me back to him, our bodies fusing together once more. The movement left me breathless.

"I respect that about you," Soren murmured.

The warmth returned to my stomach, and this time it spread lower.

I wonder if those heightened Fae senses can pick up on arousal.

A sudden bolt of panic cut through me at the thought. I was probably fine now, but if he did that move again, spinning me and bringing me back into his chest... gods, I might be in trouble.

If Soren did sense anything, he didn't show it. His face remained relaxed, his posture proud and regal, and he casually changed the subject as we continued floating across the dance floor.

"Have you kept that dagger on you like I asked?"

"I have."

"At all times?"

"Yes."

"So you have it on you now?"

I glared up at him and cocked an eyebrow. "Where would you suggest I conceal a knife in this dress? Unfortunately, there's not a whole lot of room left in this bodice."

Soren's gaze flicked to my chest before returning to my eyes. The move made my stomach flip.

"Between your thighs, then," he purred.

The warmth in my stomach took the word "thighs" as an invitation to settle there instead. I blinked up at Soren, unsure if he realized the effect of his words. His cool expression gave away nothing.

I quickly composed myself. "Why is having a dagger on me necessary right now, anyway? Are you suggesting I might be attacked at your own party?"

Soren shrugged. "You never know when an enemy might attack."

I blinked.

The exterior walls are spelled, he'd said so himself. No one can touch us here.

Then it dawned on me.

You're playing games, I thought smugly. *Alright, Your Majesty. I can shine in your court too.*

"Well, with all these skirts, I'm not sure I could reach a dagger between my thighs by myself." I sighed, staring up at him with innocent, doe-like eyes. "I'd need some help retrieving it."

A smile tugged at one corner of Soren's mouth. "We'll have to find you someone willing to assist, then."

"Oh?" I coyly tilted my head and arched my eyebrows. "Have anyone in mind?"

Soren's palm pressed harder into my lower back, moving me closer. My heart skipped a beat, but I forced my face steady, keeping up the pretty fawn facade.

"We all know Xavier would happily step up to the task."

"Yes, but there is the small matter of him reminding me of my brother, so that's out of the question."

"That would be a bit uncomfortable, wouldn't it?"

"It would. So we'll have to find someone else, it seems."

"Well, have a look around." Soren nodded to the crowd. "Take your pick. The whole room caught their breath when you walked in. I think everyone in here would gladly volunteer to slip between your thighs. And I do mean everyone."

The song ended and the crowd applauded, but Soren and I didn't move. Our bodies were still pressed together, and our eyes remained locked.

Apparently, I didn't need him to spin me again to be in trouble.

And suddenly, it wasn't a game anymore.

"Your Majesty..." I looked up at him through my lashes. "If you're trying to tell me you think I'm beautiful, you can just come out and say it."

Soren hesitated for a moment, his throat bobbing as he swallowed. Then, he opened his mouth.

"Soren!"

A booming voice across the ballroom forced us to break away. The brown-skinned, gray-eyed man I foggily remembered from Samhain strode towards us, waving eagerly and grinning from ear to ear. His long braids had been woven in and out of the intricate, swirling gold crown atop his head, and his robes were made of the finest silk and fur.

A woman trailed behind Valdir. She was tall and slender, with waist-length white-blonde hair and angular ice-blue eyes. Her head was adorned in a silver circlet set with a teardrop-shaped rough diamond that dangled onto her forehead. Wearing a silver satin gown that tied around her neck, she was so striking that my jaw went slack at the sight of her.

"Valdir!" Soren beamed as the duo approached us, then embraced the man by giving him a warm clap on the back. "So glad you could make it."

He then turned to the woman and took her hand. Her long nails were painted the same dark burgundy as her mouth.

"Erith, as always, you look ravishing."

A sliver of jealousy shot through me as Soren's plush lips grazed the woman's knuckles. Erith didn't seem to care about Soren's lips the way I did, though. She watched him with a blank expression, then turned her cold gaze on me.

"This is the human?"

Her flat, disapproving tone made me want to bristle, but I remembered what Meer had said about playing nice with Soren's allies. So I smiled sweetly and bowed my head out of respect.

"Lina Calder, Your Majesty."

"Valdir, you've met Lina before," Soren said.

"Of course, on Samhain. Good to see you're feeling better, Miss Calder."

"Much better. Thank you, Your Majesty."

I desperately tried to remember the lessons on small talk Meer had given me, but my mind was drawing a blank. So I pathetically tacked on, "Sorry about ruining your study."

Valdir let out a hearty laugh. "That's perfectly alright, my dear." He grabbed Soren's shoulders and shook him playfully. "If I had woken up to this big old brute, I would have thrown a tantrum too."

Soren grinned and shoved Valdir off him. For a moment they looked like boys roughhousing instead of two powerful kings. I giggled at their antics and glanced over at Erith. She was still staring at me with the same icy expression. I fought the urge to cower in the corner and offered her another smile. She didn't even blink.

"Miss Calder," Valdir continued, draping his arm around Soren's shoulder, "I'm afraid you'll have to excuse us. We have business to discuss."

My heart sank at the idea of milling around the room alone. I would have much preferred to keep dancing with Soren, where I was safe in his arms and it smelled liked the autumn woods and there was more innuendo about things slipping between my thighs. But instead, I took Meer's advice and plastered a smile on my face, painting the perfect picture of a damsel worth saving.

"I understand. I'll see you later."

Soren grimaced apologetically and allowed Valdir to drag him away. Erith shot me one last glare before prowling after them. The vicious clack of her heels accompanied them all the way out.

I took a deep breath and scanned the ballroom, accidentally making eye contact with a pair of beautiful Fae women in the corner. One winked at me suggestively while her companion licked her lips.

I pretended I hadn't seen and hurried off in search of *anything* to drink.

Chapter 10

Soren didn't want to leave.

He was enjoying Lina's company too much. Tonight it felt like she had finally stopped hating him. Over the past few weeks, Soren had spent every waking moment trying to think of a way he could explain his actions on Samhain to her. He wanted her to know it had killed him to hand over Wynn to that Nether woman. It felt like part of his soul died when he slipped that boy off his shoulder and gave him away, but a Changeling wouldn't be touched. They were toys to the Nethers. Wynn would be nothing but a little doll, dressed up and paraded around while they doted on him. Hell, he'd be treated like a fucking prince. Meanwhile his sister was here, being hunted like an animal.

A fiery rage swelled in Soren's chest. He hadn't told Lina, but he'd sworn an oath to track down every last one of the Nethers who'd taken Wynn and slaughter them like cattle, same as he'd slaughtered the ones who'd brutalized Xavier. He'd completely obliterated them when he found his friend in the woods. They'd just sliced Xavier open and were about to feast on his insides when Soren charged in.

He'd lost himself in that fight. He barely had any memory of it. When he'd finally come to his senses, the bodies of the Nethers were nothing but bloody chunks coating the leaves around him. He'd told Lina emotions could blind her and cause her to make mistakes, but sometimes, at least for him, it was the opposite. Sometimes emotions could turn you into something else, something capable of destroying the monsters because you became a monster yourself.

He'd turned into a monster again when he'd carried Xavier to safety and returned to hunt down that final Nether. He'd found it, but he made sure to focus and remember everything he did that time. He'd done to it exactly what they'd done to Xavier. He'd taken his time with that one, and he'd done it with a smile.

Soren peeked back at Lina one last time before he followed Valdir out of the ballroom. She'd managed to find Xavier and was laughing at something he said as he handed her a glass of wine. There, in that soft light by the window, she had such a radiant, youthful glow about her.

Soren frowned and trailed after Erith and Valdir as they headed upstairs towards his study.

Fuck. Twenty-three years old.

To a human, twenty-three might feel like a significant number. But to the Fae, twenty-three years was nothing but a blink in their long lives. Deep down, Soren knew this meant he should see Lina as ignorant and inexperienced. Nothing but the innocent fawn she'd teasingly played the role of while they danced. But from the moment she awoke in Valdir's study, Lina had shown she was so much more. Was she a lost soul? Yes. And maybe that was what had first drawn him to her in the woods. But that night she'd also shown him she was a fighter. A survivor. She was passionate and tough as nails. She was by far the most fascinating woman he'd ever met, and he'd met *a lot* of them. Meer had offered Soren an explanation the other day when he'd asked about it. He said he'd read something about how the scent of a human is intoxicating to a Fae due to an ancient instinctual prey drive, but Soren had tuned him out at that point. He wasn't fascinated with Lina just because she was human. He was fascinated with her because she was... well, *her*.

They entered the study, and Valdir immediately went for Soren's hidden stash of liquor, the same one he'd shared with Lina. She'd looked beautiful that night, too. Even with her hair mussed and her eyes swollen from crying, she took his breath away. He'd had to keep his eyes glued to the fire the whole time she was in the room so he wouldn't get caught staring at her.

Tonight, though...

Gods, it almost hurt his eyes to look at her. Soren's heart had begun to race the moment he saw her with Meer at the top of the stairs. Lina's heart had sped up when she saw him, too. He could hear it pounding, could practically see it beating out of her chest, which he had to physically stop himself from gawking at. That corset lifted and shaped her in all the right ways, and it was ruining him. He could barely focus on anything else. Keeping eye contact would have been impossible if she didn't have such beautiful eyes. He hadn't realized they were hazel before. He'd thought they were green, like Xavier's, but when you looked close, they were made up of green and blue and amber and gold all melded together. They were complex, just like she was.

Gods, he could stare into those eyes all night.

"Soren!"

Erith's voice knocked Soren from his thoughts. He looked up at her and blinked.

"You're distracted."

"No, I'm not."

A lie.

"You are," Valdir agreed. He handed Soren and Erith the drinks he'd poured and sprawled in one of the overstuffed armchairs by the fire, propping his feet on a footstool. "You have been ever since that human came into your life."

"You're imagining things."

Another lie.

Erith downed her drink in one swig and barred her arms over her chest. "If you're not going to be honest, this meeting is pointless."

"You asked me to meet with you during a party, Erith," Soren snapped. "Of course I'm distracted. I should be downstairs being a good host."

"That's not what you really want to be doing downstairs, is it?" Erith sneered. "I think you'd rather be doing something else. Some*one* else."

Soren tossed back his drink too. The liquid burned the back of his throat and warmed his stomach, only adding fire to the one building inside.

"Just come out and say what you're trying to say," Soren barked. "It's embarrassing watching you try to be coy."

"Fine. Your dick is going to get people slaughtered."

"Not that it's any of your business, but I haven't touched Lina."

And he hadn't. Although he couldn't deny he'd been tempted. That night in his study he'd been tempted. She'd been wearing nothing but a painfully thin chemise and velvet robe, and the second he'd seen her in the firelight he'd imagined laying her down in front of the hearth and ripping both items off with his teeth. He was tempted again when they sat on the floor beside Xavier's bed. With her arms wrapped around him, her face nuzzling his bare chest, he'd considered taking her back to his bedroom, dragging her into the bath with him, and fucking her senseless after the blood had been washed clean from his skin.

But he couldn't do that.

He provided her sanctuary. He protected her. He took care of her. If he did anything beyond that, it would be inappropriate. Not to mention it would complicate things too much. That wouldn't be fair to her. She was grieving her brothers, she was being hunted by Nethers... the poor girl had enough to think about. No, he couldn't touch her. He *wouldn't* touch her, no matter how badly he wanted to.

Erith scoffed and shook her head. "So you start a war for her, and she's not even warming your bed?"

Soren's anger swelled, and he clenched the glass in his hand to ground himself. "If war comes, it's not because of her. This has been brewing for thousands of years. You know that."

"It was avoidable!" Erith hissed. "The Nethers just want to be treated normal, that's all! They want to stop being discriminated against and treated like they're monsters—"

"They *are* monsters!" Soren growled. "They've slaughtered our people for millennia! You know better than anyone! How many citizens has Kylanthia lost in their attacks? How many loved ones have you had to clean up the remnants of after the Nethers had their way with them?"

Erith stood tall, her eyes as cold and cruel as the mountains in her territory. "You know, I actually thought you would be different than your father—"

Unable to control himself any longer, Soren snarled and hurled his glass at the bookcase beside Erith's head. She barely flinched as it smashed and scattered onto the bearskin rug at her feet.

"Don't you *ever* compare me to my father again," Soren said through gritted teeth, his body shaking with rage. "I am *not* him."

Erith pursed her lips and stormed out of the study without another word.

Valdir watched her go, then took a sip of his drink and smacked his lips. "That went well."

Soren sighed and collapsed on the sofa to bury his face in his hands. Valdir nudged him with his foot.

"You two should just fuck already."

"I'd rather stab myself in the eye."

Not a lie.

Silence fell over the room. After a few moments, Valdir swirled the liquid in his glass and spoke again. "She made some good points, though."

Soren lifted his head and glared at Valdir. "She's delusional."

Valdir smiled, but it was strained. "I just think we should try and see all sides. Is making peace with the Nethers really a worse option than full-blown war?"

"Making peace with the Nethers is *impossible*. You've faced them in just as many battles as I have. You know firsthand the horrors they're capable of."

A haunted look came over the king of Radomir's face. There were countless conflicts he could have been thinking of. "Yes. Yes, I do."

"You should have seen how they acted with Lina's brother too. Lower Nethers, practically harmless, but even *they* refused to see reason. There was no bartering with them. They were devoid of any form of compassion."

Valdir shrugged. "It was Samhain, and they claimed him as a Changeling. They were completely entitled to—"

"Did you know they're banding together now?" Soren sat upright and faced his friend. "It's not just the one group coming after Lina. The other day, Xavier was attacked by an entirely different kind. That means they're communicating. They're working together. They've never done that before. What happens if all of them decide to form a singular army? What then? They need to be stopped, once and for all."

Valdir nodded thoughtfully. "A singular army would be terrifying."

"It would."

"So there's no changing your mind, then?"

"No."

Valdir sighed again and shook his head. "Well, you better pray you can change Erith's. You'll need Kylanthia's armies by your side if you're going to have a fighting chance. Unless you plan on suddenly allying with Lerian so you have *their* armies to back you."

Soren scoffed. "Ally with Lerian? You're funny."

They chuckled grimly and fell silent once more. Soren eventually glanced over.

"And what about you?" he asked softly. "Would you be by my side if the worst came?"

Valdir was quiet for a long time. Finally, he cleared his throat and leaned forward. "Soren, you know you're the brother I never had. I admire you, I respect you, and I'll follow you anywhere..." His dark brows knit with concern. "But this is *war* you're talking about. And over what? A human?"

"This started long before her, and you know it."

Valdir nodded. "I do know. But..." He scooted closer and lowered his voice. "Just think of what a gesture it would be if you gave the Nethers what they wanted. Think of what it would mean to them! If we did something like that, we might *actually* have a shot at peace."

Soren's stomach twisted in revulsion. "You're saying you

want me to hand over an innocent woman to be butchered like some animal sacrifice?"

Valdir shrugged. "Well, she's not *innocent*—"

"She was defending her brother!" Soren barked.

Valdir stared at Soren for several tense seconds. Finally, he looked away. "You're right. I'm sorry. I don't know what I was thinking."

He downed the rest of his drink and smiled brightly. "I think I should stay for a few weeks. Get to know Lina better. I think I've misjudged her. She sounds like an incredible young woman, and if she means that much to you, then I'd like to give her a chance."

"She *is* incredible." Soren's rage receded, and he clapped his friend on the back. "You know you're welcome here for as long as you'd like."

"Thank you. Now, if you don't mind..." Valdir stood and rubbed his hands eagerly. "I've got a party to get to."

XAVIER AND I HAD A GAME.

It was called *Are They Making Eyes at You or Me* and it was a drinking game. If we caught someone looking at us, then Xavier was sent to investigate, which was code for flirt shamelessly. If he had success, then I had to take a drink of my wine. If the Fae was uninterested and continued to look over at me, then Xavier had to take a drink of his wine. We ran into a problem, however, because more often than not when Xavier investigated, he discovered the subject in question was, in fact, interested in having both of us at the same time, in which case Xavier and I both had to drink. Before long, we were both pleasantly buzzed and giggling in the corner like children.

One thing I'd forgotten was that alcohol of any kind made

me unbearably horny. In fact, half my experiences with men back home had started because I drank a half a bottle of wine, which wasn't enough to get me drunk, but it *did* get me bold enough to swallow my nerves and make the first move. Tonight's wine was having a similar effect, and although I told myself I wasn't going to do anything with anyone, the heat between my legs had different plans and would frequently leap in protest of my inaction. The feeling only amplified whenever I was close to Soren, and the man wasn't helping the situation. He asked me to dance throughout the night, and each time I could have sworn he held me tighter and his hand drifted a little lower on my back. Maybe alcohol had the same effect on him as it did me.

By the time we reached the final dance of the evening, his palm rested just above my tailbone, and our bodies were pressed together so tight I could feel his hips through my petticoats. As the song finished and the crowd applauded for the musicians as they took a bow, I could focus on nothing but Soren's intoxicating scent and the eager pulsing between my thighs. Everyone began saying their goodbyes and sifting out of the room, but Soren and I remained where we were, still lost in each other's eyes.

I should let him be a good host. I should let him stand at the door and say "farewell" and "thank you for coming" to each guest as they leave the castle. I should be prim and proper and quietly return to my bedroom. I should behave.

With that goal in mind, I prepared to tell Soren that I had a lovely evening and he should go say goodbye to his guests. So naturally I clasped my hands behind my back, opened my mouth, and said,

"Walk me to my room?"

Damn wine.

HER HEART WAS POUNDING.

He could hear it.

And *gods*, could he see it.

Soren swallowed and tried to stare at anything besides the pulsing of Lina's breasts as he accompanied her upstairs. He silently reviewed his plan: walk her to her room, drop her off at her door, retreat before he did something he regretted. As they neared the top of the stairs, he repeated that plan over and over in his head.

Once they got to the landing, however, Lina peered up at him through a row of dark lashes, and Soren immediately forgot what the plan was.

They turned down the hallway towards Lina's room, and Soren felt sudden pressure to fill the silence. He made sure to adopt his most professional tone.

"You did very well tonight."

Lina sneaked a glance at him, insecurity flickering over her face. "I did?"

"Yes. Everyone was extremely impressed with you."

She breathed a heavy sigh of relief, and Soren's heart swelled. He hadn't realized it had been eating away at her so much.

"Good. I wasn't sure because I didn't always follow Meer's rules."

Soren laughed. "Meer gave you rules to follow?"

"He did."

"Dare I ask what these rules were?"

"Well, he said to play extra nice with your allies."

She'd excelled at that. Valdir had been smitten with her by the end of the night. So smitten, in fact, that Soren made a mental note to tell his friend not to try anything with her.

"You definitely succeeded there."

"And he said I should never stop smiling."

She never did, and Soren couldn't stop watching her because of it. He had never seen her so happy.

"You were a ray of sunshine all night."

"And he told me not to let anyone seduce me."

Soren froze.

WE'D STOPPED in front of my door.

Soren stared down at me, his back rigid and his mouth pressed in a tight line. I stared back, my brows raised innocently, but we both knew what I was doing. My stomach fluttered with anticipation.

"And..." Soren swallowed and licked his lips. "You followed that rule?"

"I'm not sure yet."

The king didn't say anything. He just continued to stare, and for a moment I wondered if I had imagined everything.

Maybe I was the only one feeling this overwhelming pull tonight.

Maybe I was the only one who thought our moments together in the study and Xavier's room had meant something more, that we had developed an emotional connection.

Maybe it was just the alcohol messing with my head, or my own delusions making me think this man, this powerful, regal creature, would ever be interested in someone like me.

But then Soren's chest rose and fell faster, and his gaze dropped to my mouth.

"Lina..." he began, taking a step closer but still not touching me.

My ache for him became maddening. I wanted him pressed

into me like we'd been on that dance floor. I wanted his hand in mine and on my lower back… hell, I wanted his hands all over me. I wanted him on top of me, in me. I wanted every part of him, and I wanted it *now*.

Unable to resist any longer, I brought my body into his, the warmth of his chest and the pressure of his hips against mine making me release a small breathy moan. If the Fae could sense arousal, there would be no hiding mine anymore. The move elicited a groan that rumbled up from somewhere deep in Soren's chest. He exhaled sharply through his nose and lifted a hand to my face, brushing a loose strand of hair behind my ear before cupping my jaw. I shut my eyes at the tingle his fingertips sent rippling across my skin. My mouth parted as his thumb traced delicately over my bottom lip, making it quiver with desire. He leaned forward…

… And pressed his lips to my forehead.

"Good night," he murmured against my skin.

Then he walked away, leaving me alone in the hall, feeling like an idiot, and swearing I'd never touch another drop of wine for as long as I lived.

SOREN HAD NEVER BEEN MORE grateful for Valdir.

His friend's presence at the castle over the next weeks was a wonderful distraction, and Soren desperately needed one. Things with Lina had been strained, to put it lightly. The woman had been completely avoiding him, sometimes going so far as to have Meer make up her plates at mealtimes so she wouldn't have to see him at breakfast or dinner.

Soren felt horrible for putting her in such an uncomfortable position. He hadn't slept the night of the harvest celebration; he'd been too busy mentally kicking himself for letting things go as far as they had. He shouldn't have agreed to walk her to her door, but he couldn't resist. He'd felt drawn to her like a moth to a flame, and it had taken every ounce of strength in his body not to shove her against that door and take her right there in the hall. Still, even that caress and the kiss on her forehead had been too much. It had gone too far, and Lina's current behavior was *exactly* what Soren had wanted to avoid.

Nevertheless, he found himself missing her. At every meal, he'd keep one eye on the doorway, praying she'd appear in it, and every day he'd walk by her bedroom, even though it was out of his way, in the hopes he might bump into her. He even went so far as to watch her and Xavier train from the window in the mornings, just so he could catch a glimpse of her. He was desperate for any form of contact, even if she was angry and snippety with him like she had been the first days after she'd arrived.

One morning after breakfast, Soren got his wish.

He was about to head out on a ride with Valdir to enjoy the first snowfall of the season when he rounded a corner and almost collided with Lina. She was either flushed from the snow or blushing, but either way she had the rosiest cheeks he'd ever seen, even rivaling those of her bubbly little handmaiden Acacia. Soren asked Lina if she was cold and offered her his cloak, which was just his pathetic excuse to find something to talk about. Lina casually refused and ducked past him, so Soren panicked and ended up blurting, "Do you still want to go hunting?"

When she turned and looked at him, he hurriedly explained that he, Xavier, and Valdir were going the next day and they wanted her there. He actually didn't know if *they* wanted her there, but *he* wanted her there, and if they had a problem with that, it was too bad because he was the king, damn it, and he was allowed to invite whoever he wanted.

So Soren waited with bated breath as Lina considered. After what felt like an eternity, she agreed, and the vicious pit gnawing away at his stomach subsided. For the first time in weeks, he felt like he could breathe.

Soren was acting completely fine, and I couldn't decide if I was thankful for that or extremely annoyed. When I accidentally ran into him one snowy morning, I felt like I might die of humiliation, but he was completely unaffected and calmly asked me to go hunting with him, Xavier, and Valdir.

Just like that. As if nothing had happened between us.

My cheeks still burned at the memory of us in the hall after the harvest celebration, and I desperately wanted to forget it the way Soren apparently had. So I agreed to the hunt and hoped that maybe, just maybe, if I pretended like everything was fine, then it eventually would feel that way.

Valdir, it turned out, was a good distraction. He was boisterous, intelligent, and genuinely intrigued when he asked for details about the human realm. Xavier was also his usual cheeky, bouncy self, so it was hard to be awkward or uncomfortable around the two of them together. Soon the tension between Soren and me lessened, and we were all laughing and swapping stories and taking turns poking fun at each other, although Xavier received the brunt of the teasing. I realized not a lot of hunting is actually accomplished on these kinds of trips, and they were mostly just an excuse for men to spend quality time with each other. It was something these particular men desperately needed after the stress of the past few weeks.

By afternoon, we hadn't caught anything and I still didn't know how to shoot a bow, but I *had* learned plenty of embarrassing stories to hold over Xavier's head. It was Valdir who suggested we should finally do something productive, claiming it would be a disgrace to return to the castle empty-handed, so he and Xavier set off to track a buck we'd glimpsed earlier in a glen while Soren and I stayed behind so he could finally teach me how to shoot.

"Elbow back," Soren called.

He stood a good distance away from me, leaning against a boulder with his arms crossed while he watched me struggle with the bow and aim it at a nearby tree trunk.

"It *is* back," I grumbled.

"No, it's to the side."

I grunted, shook my fur-trimmed cloak out of the way, and pulled the string again.

"Like this?"

"No, *back*. Bring it back."

I lowered the bow and glared at him. "You can keep saying *back* all you want, it's not going to make me understand it any better."

Soren chewed the inside of his cheek while he thought, then stood up straight.

"Should I just show you?"

I sighed in exasperation and extended the weapon. "Please."

Soren walked over and took it from my hand, nocking the arrow and drawing the bowstring back with perfect, precise form.

"Like this. See how my arm's positioned?"

I tried not to focus on how massive the muscles in his shoulders looked as they flexed in said position and instead shifted my attention to his elbow.

Soren handed the bow back to me. "Try again."

I nocked the arrow like he had and lifted the bow, pulling my arm back.

"No, you've got to bring your elbow—"

"If you say *back* one more time..." I snapped.

Soren chuckled a little before pushing my arm closer to my body so my elbow was pointed towards the ground. Then he circled behind me and put one hand on my shoulder blade to hold it in place, while the other hand drew my elbow backwards and up. His touch, even through the thick velvet of my dress, made my skin prickle.

"Elbow *back*," he whispered in my ear, a smile in his voice.

It immediately had a shiver running down my spine.

Soren stepped away from me and folded his arms. "Try that."

I cleared my throat and refocused, taking a deep breath before letting the arrow fly. It shot pitifully into the ground a few strides ahead. I sighed and stomped forward to retrieve it.

"Here," Soren said, coming up beside me again, "get in position."

Gods, the man sounded good barking orders.

I nocked the arrow and drew the bow, with my elbow actually back this time.

Soren slipped behind me, tracing his fingertips over mine on the string. "Don't hold it too tight here."

I loosened my grip slightly, hyperaware of his presence behind me and how warm his fingers were despite the cold.

"Good."

He gently ran those fingers from my hand to my arm and then down my back. My breath caught in my throat.

"Keep your hips straight."

Soren's other hand found my waist and gripped me tightly, angling me forward.

A dull ache formed between my legs.

"Don't lock this elbow."

He kept one hand on my waist while the other moved to the arm gripping the wood of the bow.

I swallowed and obeyed.

"Hold it steady." His voice was low in my ear, so close that it rustled my hair and sent another round of chills rippling through my body.

I desperately tried to focus on the target instead of the pounding of my heart and the pulsing between my thighs.

"Now aim."

Soren pressed forward slightly, his chest connecting with my back.

I inhaled through my nose and exhaled through my mouth, practically melting at the way his face was now nuzzled against my neck.

"Let go," he breathed.

I released the arrow, sending it whizzing straight and fast through the forest. It landed solidly in the tree trunk with a *thwack*.

But neither Soren nor I celebrated the victory.

We stood frozen, our bodies still fused together and Soren's hand still around my waist as each puff of his breath licked my ear. His breathing grew heavier, same as mine, and before I could stop myself, I lost control and ground my backside into his hips, causing a groan to rumble out of his chest while his fingers clutched me tighter.

"Lina," he panted against my neck, "I can't."

I shut my eyes and leaned my head back, moaning softly as his hands wrapped tighter around my waist and his velvety lips grazed my earlobe.

"I can't," he whispered again.

But his body was saying something else entirely. One of Soren's hands strayed towards the bottom of my breast while the other drifted down my torso. I was throbbing for him now, every carnal part of me desperately screaming for him, but I'd made a mess of things at the harvest celebration, and I didn't want to do it again.

This time, I *had* to behave.

So I mustered every ounce of self control I had and peeled myself away.

"Well then," I said, clearing my throat and smoothing my hair as I put a few paces between us, "what should we do instead?"

Soren exhaled sharply and rubbed his face, trying to compose himself.

"I have an idea!" I chirped. "How about a race back to the castle?"

That's right, Lina, run away from the problem, I thought bitterly, *just like you've been doing for the past two weeks.*

Soren saw right through me.

"Lina, don't. There's nothing to feel uncomfortable about, it's alright—"

"Loser has to muck out the stables," I interrupted before grabbing my horse's reins and hauling myself into the saddle.

"Lina," Soren said, his voice more firm this time, "really, it's fine. You don't have to—"

Without letting him finish, I slapped the side of my horse's neck with the reins, and we shot into the forest.

Maybe it was cowardly, but I'd never been good with words. I'd always get too caught up in my emotions and trip up, never saying exactly what I wanted to. Or I'd just end up crying. I needed time to compose myself. A pause to translate the storm inside.

I knew the quickest way back to the castle, but I chose the longer route so I could clear my head. I was toying with the idea of simply never speaking to Soren again and remaining locked in my room forever when my horse stopped in its tracks.

"Whoa! Easy..." I shushed, patting the beast's neck, but it

continued to shake its head and step backwards, whinnying nervously. Something had spooked it. Warily, I surveyed the darkening forest. My stomach dropped as I realized what it was my horse had sensed.

The woods were unnaturally quiet.

CHAPTER 11

SOREN SHOT ARROWS INTO THE TRUNK OF THE TREE UNTIL IT WAS nothing but splinters. Once again, he was furious with himself for letting things go too far. Everything had happened so naturally, so effortlessly, that by the time he realized how close he and Lina had gotten, it had felt impossible to stop. His biggest regret was not communicating to her why he couldn't let things go farther. He should have told her it wasn't personal. It was nothing against her, it was simply a matter of his honor.

He was really starting to resent that damn honor.

When he returned to the castle, Soren found Xavier and Valdir in his study, sharing his stash of liquor.

"Catch anything?" he asked.

"Nothing." Valdir pouted. "I blame the loudmouth over here, he scared everything off."

Xavier kicked the leg of his chair playfully. "Me? People can hear your laugh a league away!"

Soren sat beside them.

"What about you?" Valdir asked, pouring another glass and handing it to him. "How did it go?"

Horrible.

"Good." Soren nodded casually. "She shows promise."

"Where is the little archer, anyway?" Xavier asked, taking a swig.

Soren looked up in surprise. "You haven't seen her?"

Valdir and Soren exchanged glances.

"No..." Xavier's brows crinkled together. "We thought she was with you."

A pit formed in Soren's stomach.

"Meer?"

The head of staff had been passing the doorway with an armful of laundry and popped his head in. "Yes, Your Majesty?"

"Have you seen Lina?"

Meer frowned. "Not since you all left this morning. Why?"

Soren dropped the glass and bolted for the door.

THE ONLY THING I remembered was pain and darkness.

It surged towards me in a dense cloud and overwhelmed me, filling my eyes and nose and lungs and mouth, and suddenly I couldn't see or breathe or taste or think as everything went black.

I woke panting for air, my mouth parched with thirst and my brain scrambled. When my eyes snapped open, I frantically scanned my surroundings, attempting to piece together what had happened.

The first thing I saw was a large bonfire.

The second was my horse lying on the ground, its entrails ripped from its abdomen and scattered across the forest floor.

Something wet dropped onto my cheek, and I thought it must be snowing again, but when I looked up I gasped in horror. Some of the horse's intestines had been draped along the treetop, their contents now showering down on me while I sat tied to the trunk.

There is no pretending to be strong after witnessing something like that.

I let out a gut-wrenching scream.

"Look, it's awake!" a voiced hissed nearby.

"I want first taste!"

"No, me!"

"No, *me!*"

When I finally caught a glimpse of my captors, I truly believed I'd never felt real terror until this moment.

Something stepped in front of me. Leathery, charcoal-gray skin clung to its skeletal frame, while its glowing yellow eyes chilled me down to the darkest parts of my soul. It resembled some form of mummified corpse, and it smelled like the carcass of an animal that had been rotting for weeks. I couldn't call it a man, and I could barely call it a Nether. One thing I was certain of, though.

It was pure evil.

"Hello, human," the being greeted me. Its voice was a mix of a whisper and the hiss of a snake. "Your little brother's told us all about you."

The monster's stench filled my nose and throat, reaching into the depths of my stomach to rip out a gag.

"She's so easy to upset!" Another snakelike voice sniggered beside me.

I turned my head. Three more of the creatures prowled around me. I tried to fight the panic rising in my chest, but it was impossible. As soon as they skulked towards me, tears burst from my eyes and I began to hyperventilate.

One of the Nethers sniffed my face, then lapped up my tears like a dog. I choked on a scream, retching as that sour stench filled my nose once again.

"I like the sounds it makes," one crooned, raising a curved black claw to my cheek to stroke it lovingly.

"I want to know how it tastes," another claimed. The slits where its nose should be flared and constricted beside my neck.

"We're supposed to keep it alive!" the third hissed. "You know that! We're not allowed to kill it!"

"That doesn't mean we can't have some fun with it first!"

"I've always wanted to know what human tastes like." Before any of the others could object, the first Nether sank its teeth into my forearm and ripped out a chunk of my flesh. I let out an agonized scream as blood spurted from the wound.

The creature pulled back, crimson dripping from its shriveled lips.

"How is it?" one asked eagerly.

"Yes, how is it?

"Tell us!"

The monster wiped its mouth with its finger, sucked my blood from the tip, and shuddered at the taste.

"It's divine."

"I want to try!"

"No, me!"

"No, *me!*"

Two of the Nethers pushed and shoved each other, fighting over who would be the next one to taste, while the other quit wasting time and dove in. It buried its teeth deep in my thigh, forcing me to scream and crumple forward against my bonds. It tore a glob from my leg, a cruel smile spreading over its withered face as blood sprayed across it.

"Poor thing. Don't you know?" It brought its mouth close to mine, my skin still squishing between its molars. "We haven't even gotten to the fun part yet."

Slowly, it raised a hand to my shoulder and sank its claws into my skin, sending an excruciating pain searing through me like a lightning bolt. My body stiffened and convulsed, my eyes rolling back in my head as the pain ravaged my body. Suddenly it seemed like I was looking down from above, unable to feel the extent of my torture, unable to do anything but watch myself seize and jerk and froth at the mouth.

Fuzzily, I heard one of the creatures shrieking, "Not too much! We need it alive!"

Then I must have passed out, for how long I'm not sure, but everything went dark. When I opened my eyes again, one of the Nethers was shaking me.

"Wake up," it hissed. "Time to play some more."

In a daze, I came to. Within seconds I was shivering from fear and cold, and it took me a moment to realize my face was wet. Unintentionally, I'd started crying again.

When the creature saw my tears, it hovered its claw over my shoulder.

"It doesn't have to hurt so bad, human. Tell us the Fae king's secrets, and we will show it mercy."

"I don't know what you're talking about," I whimpered.

"Tell us of his army," the Nether hissed, inching its claw closer. I flinched in anticipation.

"Tell us, and it can see the Changeling one last time before it dies."

"What army?" My teeth were chattering so much they were shaking my vision. "I don't know anything about an army."

"It must! It's spent time in the Fae court, and the king cares for it. He must have confided in it!"

"You clearly don't know that much about men."

I have no idea how I still managed to have a sense of humor.

The creature wasn't amused, though. It narrowed its eyes and dug another claw into my shoulder, sending that agonizing bolt shooting through my veins once more. My body thrashed against the ropes restraining it, and again I faded towards unconsciousness.

I never reached it, though.

In my peripheral vision, something moved.

The Nether in front of me flew backwards, bringing an abrupt stop to the pain. Panicked screeching rang in my ears, and when I looked up, I thought I must be dreaming.

Soren and Xavier charged in with weapons drawn, mercilessly slashing and hacking the Nethers to pieces. Their violent dance was in perfect, deadly harmony, with Soren inflicting critical damage before sending a creature flying with a flick of his wrist. When it landed, Xavier dove in and finished it off.

Xavier was about to slit the throat of the final Nether when Soren stopped him.

"Wait!" he bellowed.

Xavier froze, panting heavily as he held his sword at the ready, its razor-sharp tip tickling the monster's throat.

Soren stooped and shoved his face a hairsbreadths from the Nether's.

"I'm going to keep you alive," he ground out, "but not out of mercy. You'll go back to whatever master you serve and tell them Soren of Astoria is coming for them, and he will not rest until he slaughters every last one of you."

The Nether spat in Soren's face.

"It only really needs its tongue to pass on the message," Xavier said, his glare narrowing.

"My thoughts exactly."

Soren lifted his sword and jammed it into one of the creature's eyes, twisting his blade until it screamed. Then he moved on to the other. When he was finished, he waved his hand, sending the Nether flying through the air. It collided with a boulder, then scrambled up and teetered blindly into the woods.

"Lina!" Soren ran over, sheathing his sword, and knelt in front of me. Gently, he cupped my face and lifted it to look at him. "Lina, it's alright, I'm here. You're safe now."

Xavier sliced the ropes binding me, allowing me to slump forward into Soren's chest. There I could do nothing but shake and whimper into the folds of his coat.

"She's bleeding too much." Xavier's voice was foggy, but he sounded worried.

Soren immediately stood, wrapped his jacket around my shoulders, and hauled me into his arms where I feebly clung to his neck.

"Ride back and have Meer prepare," he ordered.

"Yes, sir."

Xavier dashed away, and Soren tightened his grip around me as we began the trek back to the castle.

"Hold on, Lina. Stay with me."

Before I slipped into darkness, distant and echoing I heard my voice begging, "Don't let me go."

And I could have sworn Soren's voice whispered back, "Never."

IT TURNED out Meer's warm white light did more than just heal physical wounds. I expected to be mentally tortured by my experience in the woods, vividly seeing corpse-like creatures taking bites of my flesh in my nightmares, but I didn't. I remained in a deep, restful sleep. The darkness I'd drifted to made way for dreams of walking through meadows of wildflowers with Wynn, Dominic, and Jaras, who was laughing along with the rest of us.

When I eventually woke, my eyes fluttered open, and I groggily took in my surroundings. I was in my own bed in Astoria, bathed and dressed in a fresh chemise. I peeked down at my forearm. The long black scar from the events on Samhain still remained, but the bite wound from my ordeal in the woods had healed, leaving nothing left but a teeth-shaped indent. What surprised me more, though, was how calm my mind was. I felt rested, refreshed, and thoroughly at peace. There wasn't even a flicker of terror or anguish when I remembered my experience in the woods.

I angled my head to look beside me. Meer was kneeling beside my bed, dark circles under his eyes and his face flushed from straining, but he was smiling.

"Welcome back, Lina Calder," he said weakly.

Happy tears stung my eyes, and I reached out to give his hand a grateful squeeze. He bowed his head, acknowledging my silent thanks.

"How long was I out?"

"Nearly a week."

I sat up in the bed and rubbed my eyes. "Gods, that must mean it's nearly Yule."

Meer nodded. "Only a few days away now."

I accepted the glass of water he handed to me and took a sip. "How are things coming along for the ball?"

"There's not going to be a Yule Ball this year."

I lowered the cup from my lips. "But Xavier said it's the most important event of the year."

"It is."

"So why—"

"His Majesty has been worried sick about you, Lina." Meer's eyes softened. "When he wasn't where I am now, holding your hand, he's just been pacing his study like a madman. No one could talk to him about anything. He was inconsolable."

It took me a moment to process Meer's words. Imagining

the mighty warrior on his knees beside my bed, forgoing all his duties because the thought of losing me was too great…

A lump formed in my throat as my eyes stung again. I knew what Soren had come to mean to me over these past few weeks, but I had no idea I was anything to him. Especially not this.

Suddenly, life seemed too short to hold back.

I had to see him.

I needed him to know that I was no longer at war with myself, and the space between his arms felt like a safe harbor where I could find solace from any storm that passed my way.

I needed him to know I wanted him close, not just now, but at all times.

And I needed him to know that I was done pretending I didn't want him.

Meer seemed to read my flood of thoughts, and he gave me a knowing wink before patting my hand. "If you wanted to find him, I believe he's in his study."

I squeezed Meer's fingers one last time and slid out of bed. Then I raced to the door, threw it open, and sprinted barefoot down the hall, still dressed in nothing but my nightgown. I didn't care who saw me. At that moment, there was only one thing, one person, on my mind.

When I found Soren, his back was to me as he stared into the fire. The crystal liquor bottle lay empty beside him.

"Soren?"

He turned.

My mind suddenly went blank, and I was furious with myself for not rehearsing something to say on the way here.

But I didn't need words.

Soren stormed across the room, grabbed my face, and crushed his lips to mine.

He kissed me fiercely and unapologetically, making my stomach dip at the way his tongue swept into my mouth and his hands clutched me so tight I thought he might never let go. He only broke from my mouth for a moment, his lips parting to say something, but I didn't let him finish. I hauled him back into that ravenous kiss before he managed a single word, grappling at his muscled chest and the hem of his shirt to pull him closer. In response, he slammed my back into a nearby bookcase, knocking several tomes off their shelves in the process, and pressed his body firmly against mine before releasing his grip in feverish exploration of my body. I eagerly ground my hips into his, shuddering as I rubbed myself along the hardened object I found there.

Soren lowered his mouth to my neck, dragging his tongue along the sensitive skin before sucking firmly. My center tightened and I let out a breathy whimper. The sound was enough to make Soren finally lose whatever control he'd been clinging to. He growled hungrily and clawed at my chemise, shoving its skirt all the way up to my waist.

My body was throbbing, aching for him, furiously screaming at me for not having him inside me yet. I fumbled at the buttons on Soren's trousers, maddeningly impatient to remedy that.

"Soren, I—"

Valdir strode into the study, catching a glimpse of us against the bookcase.

"Oh, gods!" he yelped.

Soren and I gasped and peeled ourselves off each other. We hurriedly withdrew our hands and fixed our clothing while Valdir averted his eyes.

"I'm sorry! I am *so* sorry! I didn't... the door was open, I had no idea... sorry."

Soren cleared his throat and crossed his hands in front of him, attempting to hide the very large problem he now had. "We were just talking."

"That's definitely what it looked like." Valdir nodded, still refusing to look at us. "Definitely what I thought. Yes. Good. Happy to see you're feeling better, Lina."

"Thank you, Valdir," I mumbled, staring intently at the floor in the hopes he wouldn't see the humiliation flushing my cheeks, or the arousal flushing the rest of me.

"What's happening in the study?" A familiar voice shouted from the hall.

A head of dark brown curls popped into the room.

"Lina!" Xavier's eyes lit up, and he darted in to pull me into a hug. "Thank the gods you're awake!"

Soren huffed a sigh and tried to subtly readjust himself while I awkwardly patted Xavier's back.

Valdir clapped a hand on the nape of Xavier's neck, attempting to guide him away. "Xavier, I think we should let Soren and Lina talk."

"Talk?"

"*Talk.*"

Xavier's head tilted curiously. "What do they need to talk about?"

Soren sighed again.

"Maybe they're going to discuss the Yule Ball," Valdir offered. "Now that Lina's healed, there's nothing stopping us from having it. Right, Soren?"

"If it will get you lot out of this damn room then *yes*, I will give you your beloved Yule Ball, Valdir."

It was Meer's turn to poke his head into the study.

"Your Majesty, if the Yule Ball is happening, then I need to steal Lina away immediately so we can start working on her outfit. Do you know how hard it's going to be for me to beat that dress from the harvest celebration?"

Soren grunted and threw his hands up in exasperation. "So much for this being a private study."

Meer took my arm and raised an eyebrow at the king. "If you want privacy, Your Majesty, might I suggest learning how to shut a door?"

I barely had time to glance at Soren over my shoulder and wince apologetically before I was swept out of the room and thrust into preparations for the most important celebration of the year.

OF COURSE VALDIR pulled off a Yule Ball in four days.

Aside from Xavier, Soren could think of no one who loved a good party more. Because of that, he had delegated most of the planning to Valdir and Meer, and the two of them had thrown together a truly impressive fete.

When Soren arrived downstairs on the night of, he was welcomed by roaring fires in the hearths, with white furs, velvet throws, and crimson candles adorning every available surface. Boughs of evergreen and holly added pops of green and red to the mantels, tables, and rafters. All the nobles Soren invited had shown up as well, packing the castle with festive Fae bedecked in every shade of the Yule season.

When Valdir pushed through the crowd and found Soren, he proudly threw his arms wide.

"Aren't you glad you held a Yule Ball now?" he boomed.

Soren chuckled and slung his arm around Valdir's shoulders, clapping him on the chest. "You've outdone yourself, my friend. Thank you."

Valdir shrugged. "Well, you were a little distracted."

Movement at the top of the grand staircase caught Soren's attention. When he looked up, what he saw took his breath away.

"And clearly, you still are," Valdir mumbled.

But Soren didn't respond. He continued to stare at the top of the stairs where Lina and Meer stood together, just as they had at the harvest celebration. Only this time, Lina didn't look timid and nervous. Now she confidently held her head high, and when her eyes met Soren's, a blinding smile spread over her face. Soren's heart leapt at the sight, and he grinned back at her.

"Soren," Valdir whispered in his ear, "I hate to pull you away, but I need your help. I'm expecting a few friends who said they were coming last minute. Since no one can enter the castle walls without your permission, do you think you could—"

Soren waved him away, his eyes still fixed on Lina. "Do whatever you want, Valdir. Talk to Meer, he knows the spell that will allow guests in too."

"Thank you, my friend." Valdir put a hand on Soren's shoulder and squeezed, glancing up at Lina before giving him a knowing smile. "Have fun tonight. You deserve it."

Valdir disappeared into the crowd, and Xavier took his place. He followed Soren's gaze up the staircase as Lina and Meer began their descent.

Though everyone else was dressed in green and red, Lina wore white gloves and a gray satin gown with swirling silver embroidery studded with glittering crystals. The only pop of color came from the wreath of holly on her head and her painted cherry red lips.

Lips Soren couldn't help imagining doing some *very* dirty things with.

Xavier peeked over at his king and stifled a giggle.

"What?" Soren asked, his eyes still glued to the woman on the stairs.

"Oh, nothing," Xavier replied. "It's just... what was it you said to me on Samhain? Oh, yes! That's right... 'I never thought

I'd see the day when a woman had you stumbling all over yourself.'"

A cheeky grin spread over the young man's face.

"You're in trouble," he sang.

Soren playfully elbowed him in the ribs.

But as Lina stepped in front of him and his heart threatened to explode out of his chest, Soren knew Xavier was right.

MEER SQUEEZED my hand and smiled. "I'll see you after."

I nodded and watched him return upstairs before turning back to Soren. I had no idea Meer dressed me to match the king. Earlier, I'd wondered why Meer had insisted on this particular dress when I'd originally been eyeing a sleek gown made from red velvet. But with Soren in a slate blue satin jacket trimmed in white fur and adorned with a sprig of holly on the lapel, it all made sense.

He and I were perfectly coordinated.

Meer, you sneaky little...

Xavier shouldered his way in front of Soren, took my hand, and made a grand display of kissing it. "Lina, there'll be no drinking game tonight because you'll win every single time. All eyes are on you this evening."

I laughed and shook my head. "Xavier, you are—"

"I know, I know." He glanced back at Soren and winked. "Shameless."

Soren smiled, but when he spoke his voice was a warning. "Move."

Xavier snickered and obediently stepped out of the king's way.

Soren stepped forward to take my hand, brushed his lips

against my knuckles in a delicate kiss, and gazed up at me with a pair of obscenely seductive hooded eyes.

"You're beautiful, Lina," he said softly.

My cheeks were beginning to ache from smiling so much. "Thank you."

Soren straightened. "May I have the honor of your first dance?"

I nodded, my stomach fluttering as his fingers intertwined with mine before he whisked me towards the ballroom. The crowd parted for us, only this time around I walked confidently beside Soren, proudly peering out over the sea of red and green, no longer feeling like prey but, dare I say it... a queen.

When we arrived on the dance floor, Soren gave me a quick spin and pulled me close, effortlessly sweeping me into a graceful waltz.

"I haven't seen you since we were... interrupted." He licked his lips at the last word.

The memory of us pressed against the bookcase in his study caused a twinge between my legs.

"Meer kept me busy with the preparations."

Soren's eyebrows raised. "You had a hand in all this?"

"A little." I shrugged. "I wanted to help. To show my gratitude for everything."

Soren nodded, his expression darkening.

"Are you alright?" he asked earnestly. "After what happened in the woods?"

"I'm fine. In fact..." I pressed further into him. "I'd like to show you my gratitude for that too."

Soren's brows arched again. "Oh?"

I nodded and leaned in, brushing my lips against his earlobe as I whispered, "I've got that dagger on me tonight. Maybe later you could help me retrieve it."

Soren's fingers gripped me tighter as he exhaled sharply. I

smiled and leaned back, adopting a look of pure innocence. The wine the Sprites had given me while I was getting ready was up to its usual tricks. But this time, Soren didn't shy away. This time, he threw me into a deft spin and drew me firmly back into him, that low chuckle rumbling in his chest and sending vibrations through my entire body.

"Gods, the things I'm going to do to you, Lina Calder," he growled in my ear.

I bit my lip as my body hummed in anticipation. I had no idea how I was supposed to wait the whole night before I could have him. It would be agony.

Maybe I can pull him away. I could just drag him into a coat closet so he can bend me over and—

An earsplitting scream tore through the ballroom, followed by gasps of horror. We immediately stopped dancing and spun to see the cause, Soren instinctively reaching for his sword, only to find his hip empty.

The crowd parted to reveal the source of the commotion, and my knees nearly buckled as a wail ripped from my mouth.

A horde of Nethers, each one more hellish and hair-raising than the last, swarmed through the castle, while one creature towering over the rest of them paused at the center of the doorway. Shrouded in a flowing black cloak, it had an elongated, skeletal face and antlers, its hands made up of long, curved claws as sharp as scythes. The Nether looked out over the crowd and triumphantly raised something high for us all to see.

Twisted in an agonized expression, dripping blood across the ballroom floor, was Meer's brutally severed head.

Chapter 12

All hell broke loose.

Fae nobles screamed and scattered while the Nethers attacked, picking them off one by one. Across the dance floor, Xavier took one look at Meer and let out a devastated, gut-wrenching battle cry from the depths of his soul before grabbing two cake knives off the dessert table and launching into the fray. There, he morphed into a whirling, slashing flurry of violence, destroying anything unlucky enough to get in his path. Soren was armed with nothing but his own magic, but he too was a terrifying instrument of death, viciously hurling Nethers across the room and snapping their necks like twigs as they crashed against the walls and rafters.

Something grabbed my arm, and I spun, prepared to come face-to-face with a Nether, but instead I found myself staring into a pair of gray eyes.

A wave of relief washed over me at the sight of Valdir.

But instead of leaping into the melee beside his friend, Valdir tore me away from Soren and brought a long dagger to my throat.

"*Stop!*" Valdir's booming voice echoed throughout the room. The Nethers halted their onslaught.

Panting and wide-eyed, Soren looked wildly around the room. His eyes darted between the Nethers and Valdir's knife.

"Valdir, what—"

"I'm sorry, Soren," Valdir croaked, his expression pained. "I didn't want it to come to this."

Soren's eyelids flickered as realization washed over him, and he scoffed bitterly. "So these are your last-minute friends?"

"They just want the girl, that's all," Valdir replied. He tightened his hold on the dagger, causing the blade's edge to nick my throat. "If we make an example of her, they're prepared to consider peace."

"You backstabbing son of a bitch!" Xavier lunged at the king of Radomir, but Soren threw a hand to his shoulder to stop him.

"I'm sorry," Valdir said again, "but I can't let you plunge our world into war. I don't think we could survive it. Not against Erith's forces." He frowned and gestured to the Nethers surrounding us. "She's sided with them. She sent word to me last week. She's threatening to hit Radomir first if I don't comply. I didn't want to pick a side, but I had to."

I struggled against Valdir's hold, but he only gripped me tighter. I gasped as the blade cut deeper into my skin, drawing a thin line of blood. When I looked over at Soren, I recognized that glimmer of rage in his eyes, but they also held something else I knew far too well.

Fear.

"It's just one woman," Valdir pressed. "A single human life, or the lives of thousands of Fae if we go to war with Erith and the Nethers. Be logical about this. *Please.*"

Soren's eyes finally met mine. They were brimming with tears, and for a moment I thought he might be considering it.

But I hadn't been joking about the dagger between my thighs.

I flicked my gaze down to my skirt, then back up at Soren pointedly. He stared at me for a few seconds until the light of realization appeared in his eyes. He gave me a subtle nod of understanding.

"Fine." Soren lifted his head high as he returned his attention to Valdir, but his voice wavered. "You're right. We'll make an example of her."

"What?!" Xavier screeched indignantly.

Soren ignored him. "Just one thing... let me say goodbye properly. Please, just let me kiss her one last time."

Behind me, Valdir breathed a sigh of relief. "You're doing the right thing, my friend."

He removed the dagger from my throat and prodded it against my back instead, walking me forward. Soren made his way over too, meeting us at the center of the dance floor. Valdir released me and took a small step back.

"Make it quick."

Once again, all eyes were on me and the king.

Soren grabbed me by the waist and pulled me into a passionate kiss. While one hand cupped my face, the one at my waist trailed down my body, groping my backside, my thighs, and caressing my knee before moving back up to my waist, taking my skirt with it. By hauling my dress up, Soren had discreetly left me access to the dagger. Following his lead, I kissed him back, running my hands fervently down his chest, hips and pelvis. He drew me closer, pressing our bodies together so tight that no one was able to see my hands slip between my legs. When my fingers met the cool steel strapped to my thigh, Soren stopped kissing me and lowered his lips to my ear instead.

"You know what to do," he whispered.

I nodded.

I tightened my fingers around the dagger's hilt and remembered what Xavier had taught me. Then I took a deep breath, reined in my emotions, and spun.

Step, block, slice!

Valdir gurgled as my blade found its mark. Blood spurted from the fatal wound I'd slashed across his throat and bubbled out of his mouth. The surprise in his eyes looked exactly like Jaras's when the same thing happened to him, only this time around, I didn't freeze.

This time, when Valdir collapsed and the Nethers shrieked and resumed their onslaught, I leapt into the battle alongside Soren, weaving, slashing, and hacking without hesitation.

"Xavier!" Soren roared. "Knife!"

Xavier tossed one of the knives he'd been wielding to Soren, who deftly caught it and began inflicting carnage on anything that foolishly challenged him. Xavier fought his way over to us, and when we'd cleared a path, Soren grabbed my hand and rushed out of the ballroom towards the terrace, Xavier and a few remaining nobles following close behind.

We burst outside and raced across the grounds, headed for the stables. The nauseating chorus of screams from the Fae and screeches from the Nethers plagued us the entire way. Soren and Xavier saved as many as they could, but significant damage had already been done. I tried not to think about the countless bloodied bodies we leapt over on the way to the stables, but it became impossible when I saw three beautiful Sprites splayed on the cobblestones of the courtyard.

My handmaidens had met the same fate as my horse in the woods. Their bodies were limp, their eyes lifeless, and their insides streaked the freshly fallen snow with crimson.

I choked on a sob at the scene. My legs nearly gave out under me, but Soren wrapped an arm around my waist and dragged me onward. When we made it to the horses, he shoved me onto his steed's back, hauled himself up behind me, and kicked at the beast's sides. Xavier did the same, and together the three of us bolted out of the castle's walls and tore into the forest. The screams faded into the distance, leaving us with nothing but the sounds of the horses' thundering hooves and my own miserable weeping.

Time blurred together as we rode.

The night was bitterly cold, and even though I was wedged between Soren's thighs, the air still stung my skin and chilled me to the bone.

By the time we arrived at an encampment for one of Astoria's battalions, I was shivering violently. All three of us were. But that didn't stop Soren from jumping off his horse and immediately throwing himself into the role of commander, while Xavier dutifully fell in beside him. Soren barked orders, telling one messenger to raise the alarm and alert the other battalions scattered throughout Astoria, yelling at another to send reinforcements to the castle, and, finally, he demanded I be taken to his tent and given a clean set of clothes. I was whisked away from him then, too numb and cold and trauma-tized to protest.

A soldier shoved me into a large tent at the center of the camp with a pair of tattered mens trousers and a shirt that, I discovered when I pulled it on, was two sizes too large. They didn't have any boots that would fit my feet, so I had to wear the same blood-stained satin slippers I'd worn to the ball. Meer would have lost his mind at the garish ensemble.

Meer.

I collapsed on a pile of pillows and furs in the corner and

clutched my bloodied dress to my chest, as if doing so would magically bring my friend back to me. I shut my eyes against the image of the Nether gripping Meer's head in the doorway, but deep down I knew it wouldn't help. That was an image that would haunt me for years to come.

Exhaustion and depression finally took over, and, still holding the gown, I drifted into a weepy, restless slumber.

Over and over I dreamed of the events of that night.

I saw Valdir's eyes go wide as the dagger found its mark.

I felt his skin and tendons split beneath my blade.

I heard that awful wail rip from Xavier's mouth when he saw our fallen friend.

But mostly, I was tormented by the image of that antlered beast and Meer's lifeless eyes boring into me until I woke up screaming my throat raw.

Soren didn't join me in the tent that night. Whenever I jerked awake from a nightmare and scanned the tent, hoping to find him to curl up next to, I was alone. When morning came and he was still nowhere to be seen, I stepped outside the tent to look for him. I was immediately met by a soldier barring my way.

"For your safety," he explained stiffly. "By order of the king."

So I retreated into the tent with the plate of food I'd been handed and waited.

And waited.

And waited some more.

I sat in the tent for three days, repeating the cycle of crying and sleeping and trying to leave but being ushered back in by a stern-faced guard. I was permitted to bathe if someone accompanied me, but besides that I was forbidden to leave.

On the evening of the third day, I was dozing off again, still cradling the soiled dress, when the tent flap pulled back and Soren strode in. I immediately jumped up, ran to him, and threw myself into his outstretched arms. He held me tight, kissing my hair and rubbing my back as I cried into his shoulder.

I'd rehearsed what to say this time, but I couldn't get it out. All I could muster was, "I'm sorry," and I repeated it over and over until Soren broke away and caught my face in his hands, forcing me to look at him as he wiped away my tears with the pads of his thumbs.

"I told you before, this isn't your fault."

"It *is*."

"It's not."

"But Meer—"

"It's *not* your fault, Lina."

"Valdir—"

"Valdir made his choice. I would have done the same if I'd been holding the blade."

I sniffled and nodded miserably, and Soren brushed one last tear from my eye.

"Where have you been?" I mumbled.

I needed you here. I'm sad, and I'm scared, and I'm worried about you, and I care about you, and I want us to hold each other until we feel like everything's going to be alright.

But the words didn't come out. Instead, Soren's face grew somber as he moved to the other side of the tent and stripped off his jacket from the ball. Had he not slept since that night? The dark circles under his eyes suggested as much.

"I've been preparing my troops and making arrangements for you."

"Arrangements?" My head angled in confusion. "What arrangements?"

"You're going to Lerian."

"What?" I couldn't disguise the panic in my voice. "What are you talking about?"

Soren wouldn't look at me. There was no sign of the kind, compassionate man I knew. The callous warrior had taken over.

Soren crossed to a small copper basin and splashed water on his face, slicking it back through his hair.

"I'm going to *war*, Lina. A battlefield is no place for you. You'll just get underfoot. I've negotiated a deal with the prince and princess of Lerian, and they've agreed to take you in. You'll stay there until I can come for you and take you somewhere more permanent. There are a few noble families with rural estates in southern Astoria and Radomir who might be willing to have you, but it's going to take time to work out the details."

I shook my head. "I thought you didn't get along with Lerian?"

"Exactly why you'll be safe there. It's the last place the Nethers would think to look for you, and with Erith focusing on Astoria and Radomir, Lerian will go untouched for the time being.

"But..." I frantically looked around the tent. "But I don't want to leave Astoria."

"Lina," Soren sighed. There was a hint of impatience in his voice as he explained, "The attack on Yule was just the beginning. Astoria is the largest territory and has the strongest military presence. If you take Astoria, you can take everything. It'll be Erith's main target, which means there will be more attacks here, worse ones, until I can take care of this."

I furiously rubbed my eyes, trying to process the information Soren had just given me. "So... I'm just going to be passed around to different territories?"

"More or less, yes."

"For how long?"

"Until next Samhain when the veil lifts and you can return to your world."

My heart dropped, and a painful lump formed in my throat. Somehow, I managed to speak around it.

"But... I want to stay with you."

"I told you, it's not safe with me."

"Yes, it is!"

"I can't keep you safe, Lina!" Soren roared, whirling to face me.

I recoiled at his outburst.

Soren's chest heaved, but it wasn't anger coloring his expression. His gaze glistened with emotion, and when he continued, his voice cracked.

"I promised you the castle was safe, but they still got in. My people trusted me, counted on me, and I failed them. If anything happened to you too, I couldn't..." He took a shuddering breath. "I will never forgive myself."

The tears returned to my eyes. Cautiously, I made my way over, slid my arms around Soren's waist, and sank into his chest. His tense shoulders eased slightly as he melted into me too, his hands finding the arch of my back to draw me closer.

"I don't want to leave you," I whimpered miserably.

Soren kissed the top of my head. "I don't want you to either."

Slowly, I looked up. When our eyes met, I let myself drown in his soulful stare as I considered everything I wanted to say.

I wanted to say I refused to go, and I could make myself useful in the camp. I could wipe the blood from his skin after battle, and run my fingers through his hair until he'd relaxed enough to drift off to sleep, and if he had any nightmares, I'd save him by kissing him awake.

I wanted to say the concept of navigating this world in search of my brother without him by my side left me paralyzed with fear.

But mostly, I wanted to say I had no idea good men like him

even existed, and now that I'd found him, I never wanted to let him go.

Instead, I did something that encompassed everything I felt. I flung my arms around his neck and kissed him.

Soren's grip around me tightened, and I lost myself in him as I channeled all my emotion into that one moment. Our movements grew quicker, more heated, and soon Soren's hands started migrating to my hips. He stopped himself before he went too far, breaking away to look me in the eyes.

"We should stop," he panted. "My men will hear us."

I shook my head. "I don't care. I just want you."

That was all Soren needed to hear.

He hungrily dragged me back in and crashed his lips into mine, bringing one hand to the back of my head to hold me steady as his tongue swept into my mouth, while his other slipped between my legs. I let out a small whimper as his fingers found their mark, sending pleasure rippling through my center. Soren smashed his mouth against mine to silence me. I moaned against him, breathing sharply through my nose as he lightly stroked, gradually increasing his speed. My blood warmed, my body thrummed, and suddenly it seemed like if I didn't have him right here, right now, I would burst.

I pulled away and frantically tore at Soren's shirt, ripping it over his head and throwing it aside before fumbling with the laces of his pants. Soren stripped me of my own top before sweeping me off my feet and striding towards the pile of furs and pillows in the corner.

The way he delicately laid me in the plush cushions was a stark contrast to the frenzy of his kiss. His skin was warm and clammy as he firmly pressed his body on top of mine, grinding himself into the aching spot between my legs. I rolled my hips along with his, the pulse of pleasure deepening each time our bodies connected. I raked my fingernails down the muscles of

Soren's bare back, causing a groan to come grating up from the depths of his chest. He immediately pushed himself upright and ripped off my pants.

"I need to taste you."

Just the tone of his voice, gruff and commanding, was enough to make me weak, so when Soren threw my leg over his shoulder and slipped his tongue between my thighs, licking up my center before dragging it in precise circular motions, my body instantly started quivering. I gasped out, my fingers latching on to Soren's tousled waves as my back arched. Soren gripped my leg tighter with one hand, then used the other to grab the inside of my opposite thigh and shove it back down, pinning me in place as he edged me closer to a climax. The pleasure built, and when Soren's tongue finally brought me to my peak, my body shook uncontrollably as I threw my head back, prepared to cry out in ecstasy. Without lifting his head, Soren clapped a hand over my mouth. His palm muffled most of my cries, and only when the pleasure had waned did he remove it.

Soren rose from between my legs to kiss me deeply, drawing a moan from my lips at the taste of my satisfaction on his tongue. I was practically dripping with need. I furiously clawed at his pants to finally release what I'd been aching to have inside me for weeks. Soren slipped two fingers into my mouth to wet them, then lowered them to spread over the tip of his hardened cock. He positioned himself at my center, looked me deep in the eyes as his silken skin kissed mine, and thrust forward.

I gasped in pleasure, forcing Soren to smack another hand over my mouth. I nodded, and he cautiously released me before thrusting deeper. I bit my lip to stifle my moans while Soren buried his face in my neck to smother his own.

"*Fuck,*" he groaned against my skin, "you feel fucking perfect."

His words sent a jolt of sensitivity through me, making me break my silence to whimper his name. Soren responded by pulling out and flipping me onto my side before repositioning himself behind me. He slammed into me, gripping my hair with one hand while the other reached around to stroke me.

"*Shit!*" I cried into the pillow.

My body quaked again as every pump of his length built the pleasure inside until I erupted in ecstasy. I buried my face in the pillow as I came, shuddering as Soren pounded into me, his hand still working between my thighs until he coaxed out every last blissful ripple. My body was spent and thrumming with satisfaction, but I wanted more.

I slipped Soren out of me and shoved him onto his back, eager to give him the same release he'd just given me. I grabbed his cock and dragged my tongue along its length, forcing Soren to throw back his head and mutter a curse under his breath. Before I could take him all the way into my mouth, he impatiently dug his fingers into my waist, hauled me forward so I straddled his hips, and lowered me down. I gasped at how deep he slid, but once I'd adjusted, I slowly rocked my hips forward and back, whimpering softly at the knee-weakening sensation. To push my pleasure even further, Soren licked his thumb and brought it to the apex of my thighs, gently rubbing it in circles as I rode him.

Tightness coiled inside me once more. Soren's sweat-licked chest heaved, faster and faster, matching the pace of my rolling hips, proving he was getting close too.

Finally, he sat up and took my breast in his mouth, nipping and licking its peak, while I feverishly ground into him. Within seconds I was sent over the edge, the pleasure so intense that neither Soren nor I cared who heard us anymore. We both found our release at the same time, Soren's fingers digging deep into the skin of my back as we lost ourselves in passionate surrender.

We stayed there with our bodies entwined, clutching each other tight, until our hearts had stopped racing. Then Soren kissed me tenderly and rolled us over onto the pile of pillows where he nestled in beside me. I snuggled up to his chest, inhaling the sweet scent of wood and sex from his skin, and together, draped in nothing but each other's arms, we fell asleep.

That night I didn't have any nightmares.

CHAPTER 13

I woke to someone clearing their throat.

Groggily, I rolled over and blinked, expecting to see Soren, but I found the spot beside me empty. When I looked up, I gasped, grabbed a nearby bearskin, and dragged it over my naked body.

Xavier stood in front of me, covering his eyes with his hand.

"Good morning," he said stiffly. "I didn't see anything."

"What are you doing?!" I shrieked, snatching up a nearby pillow and chucking it at his head. "Get out!"

"I will. I just came to tell you to get dressed."

"Why? Where's Soren?"

"He sent me to get you. He's meeting with the prince and princess of Lerian."

I abruptly sat upright. "Wait, they're *here*?"

"Yes. They've come to take you back with them."

"*What*?" My heart sank. "I'm leaving *today*? I thought..." It became difficult to swallow as a sudden wave of heartache made my throat tighten. "I thought we had a little more time."

"There *is* no time, Lina. Erith's forces are already moving towards Radomir, and it's not a question of *if* the Nethers will ambush Astoria again, but *when*. It's now or never."

Xavier removed his hand from his eyes and met my gaze, his usual playful expression now grave. "I'm sorry, I know it's not ideal."

I nodded miserably, and Xavier exited the tent, leaving me to get dressed as a vicious pit formed in the base of my stomach.

When I was fully clothed, Xavier led me through a maze of tents and soldiers to a table and chairs set up beneath a canopy on the outskirts of the camp. Soren, dressed in his warrior's leather and heavy fur cloak, sat in one of the chairs, his face stern as he spoke with the Fae opposite him. I examined them closely, trying to remember everything Meer had taught me about the royal family of Lerian.

Prince Kaspar and Princess Syrena were fraternal twins, suddenly thrust into a position of power when their parents, the king and queen of Lerian, had disappeared without a trace several years prior. Together they shared equal reign of their ocean-bordered territory. The two appeared older than me but younger than Soren, and even by Fae standards they were absolutely gorgeous. They shared the same long curly black hair and tanned olive skin, but while Kaspar's eyes were downturned and a rich brown shade, his sister's angled upwards and were a stunning hue of sea green. The two siblings were dressed in flowing, draping fabrics in orange, red, and gold, and both were adorned in copious amounts of jewels. Perched regally in front of Soren, they looked exactly as I imagined royalty should.

It was the man standing behind them that I couldn't figure out.

Like the twins, he appeared to be in his late twenties, and aside from his ghostly pale skin, everything on him was black:

his leather coat and gloves, the countless knives strapped to each of his thighs, and his straight, chin-length hair, which was pulled back tight save for a few rogue strands that fell into his face. Even his angular eyes were such a dark shade of brown that they looked black. Those eyes constantly scanned his surroundings, analyzing, assessing, and missing nothing, and I felt them lock onto me long before I arrived under the canopy.

The man remained still, arms crossed and his face expressionless, as Xavier lead me over. What perplexed me most about him was an odd marking at the center of his neck. I wasn't sure if the symbol was a tattoo or a scar, but it was a design I'd never seen before. A spiked circle decorated the front of the man's throat, and inside were two crescent moons facing away from each other, while two lines jutted through their centers to connect them. The marking was strange and beautiful, much like the man himself, and I had to physically stop myself from staring at it.

When I arrived, Soren and the twins stood.

"You must be Lina," the woman said, flashing a radiant smile.

As she beamed at me, the thought drifted into my mind that, apart from Soren, she might in fact be the most beautiful creature I'd ever laid eyes on.

"The king has told us so much about you. I'm Syrena, and this is my brother, Kaspar."

The prince glanced up from examining one of the many rings on his fingers and offered a half-hearted attempt at a grin.

"And this..." Syrena gestured to the leather-clad man behind her. "This is our captain of the guard. Hale."

Hale didn't move. Instead, his piercing gaze continued to bore into me. I met his stare, but instantly regretted the decision. It was so intense I felt like the man might actually be capable of seeing into my mind. I quickly averted my gaze.

Beside me, Xavier scoffed. "It has a name?"

The princess of Lerian whipped her head around to glare at him. Her voice hardened, no longer a light, singsong warble as it had been before, but a tone as sharp and deadly as the blades at her guard's sides.

"Yes. *He* does have a name."

"Manners, Xavier," Soren warned.

Xavier huffily crossed his arms. "You're alright with this? You're fine with sending Lina off to live with them when *this* is going to be prowling around in the shadows?" He jerked his chin in Hale's direction.

The prince of Lerian finally spoke. "*This* has been a loyal servant of our court longer than you've been alive, low-born. Watch your tongue."

Both Soren and Xavier bristled.

"*Low-born?*" Xavier spat. "Name calling's rich when you call that *thing* a friend!"

Kaspar returned to casually studying his rings. "Call off your dog, Soren, or I'll have it put down."

Soren took a menacing step towards Kaspar. "I told you never to threaten—"

"Would all of you just shut up!" Syrena snapped.

Everyone turned to look at her.

"Please," she added.

The men continued to stew, but begrudgingly backed down.

"I apologize for my brother's behavior." Syrena spoke sweetly, but shot Kaspar an icy glare. "What I was trying to say before we got sidetracked is that we are more than happy to open our doors to you, Lina. *Aren't we*, Kas?"

Kaspar sighed and threw his arms wide, saying with forced cheerfulness, "My home is your home."

Syrena gave him a curt nod of approval, the line clearly one she'd coached him on.

"Thank you for taking her on such short notice," Soren said tightly. His gaze flicked warily to Hale, then shifted back to the princess. "I want your word she'll be safe."

Syrena didn't look at him directly, instead choosing to toy with the stack of gold-and-emerald bracelets decorating her wrist. "She'll be treated like one of the family. Hale will protect her the same as he does us."

Hale bowed his head in agreement, but Soren didn't seem convinced. He turned to me and took my hands in his.

"I won't be able to have much contact," he said softly, "but I'll try to send word as often as I can."

I nodded, furiously fighting the pinch behind my eyes. I did *not* want to cry in front of these people, especially not this arrogant prince or his guard, who didn't even seem to know what emotion was.

"When will I see you again?" I asked. My voice sounded like it belonged to a terrified child, mirroring how I felt inside.

Soren swallowed. "I can't know for sure. As soon as there's a break in the fighting and it's safe for me to leave my men."

I nodded again, blinking the tears away.

"I'll miss you," I said feebly.

Soren pulled me into his chest, and I wrapped my arms around him as tight as I possibly could one final time. He did the same, kissing the top of my head and nuzzling into my neck. Then, only loud enough for me to hear, he whispered, "Don't trust any one of them."

Dread swept through me at the ominous command, but I nodded all the same.

In my peripheral vision, Hale's head abruptly jerked upwards. He looked around, his dark eyes scanning the horizon.

"What is it?" Kaspar asked, his brow furrowing.

Hale's frown deepened. "We need to go. Now."

"What's wrong?" Soren asked urgently.

"Trouble to the east," Hale stated, ushering Syrena and Kaspar towards their horses. "If I were you, Your Majesty, I'd prepare your men for battle."

The king dipped his chin to Xavier, who immediately rushed back through the camp raising the alarm. Soren grabbed his sword and started jogging after him.

"There's a lesser known route back to Lerian just south of here," he called over his shoulder. "Take that instead of the main road."

Hale nodded and began to lead me away, but I shrugged him off.

"Soren!" I shouted.

Soren stopped in his tracks and looked back at me.

I couldn't fight the tears any longer. They streamed down my face as I sprinted towards him. When I reached Soren, I threw myself into his arms and kissed him like it was the last time I'd see him.

For all I knew, it might be.

We finally broke apart, and Soren took my face in his hands, pressed his forehead to mine, and whispered, "No matter how this ends, I wouldn't change our story. I would find you in those woods again and again, every life over. Because I love you, Lina Calder. With every fiber of my being."

Then he turned and disappeared into the frenzy of the war camp, leaving me too stunned to utter a response.

WE FLED the camp and only slowed when our horses needed to be watered. We'd found the path to the south Soren had mentioned, and once Hale deemed it safe and the horses were rested, we continued at a more casual pace.

Syrena was a talker. Most of the time, she rode alongside me, asking countless questions about the human realm and babbling on about Lerian, its wealth, its culture, and its rich fishing and trade industries. She also repeatedly brought up the idea of getting me some new clothes, and judging from the way I'd frequently catch her frowning at my oversized shirt and men's trousers, I was beginning to think she was truly disturbed by the ensemble. She would have been kindred spirits with Meer and the Sprites.

The other two in our party were not nearly as bubbly or social as the princess. Especially not the steely-eyed captain of the guard. Apart from his words to Soren back at the camp, Hale didn't speak again. Most of the time he rode ahead, as silent as a mouse but as watchful as a hawk. After I tried and failed to strike up a conversation with Kaspar, who made it blatantly obvious he wanted nothing to do with me, I chose to pass the time by attempting small talk with the captain instead.

I nudged my horse forward so we rode alongside each other, but Hale kept his eyes on the path.

"Hello," I said.

"Hello," he replied curtly. He still didn't look at me.

Silence fell over us once again.

This is going well, I thought miserably.

I looked around for something, *anything*, to talk about. My eyes landed on the design at Hale's throat.

"What does that mean?" I asked brightly.

Hale continued to face forward, but peeked at me out of the corner of his eye. "What does what mean?"

"Your..." I thought for a moment, unsure what exactly to call the marking, then gestured to his neck. "Tattoo. That symbol, what does it mean?"

Kaspar and Syrena, who had been speaking in hushed

tones behind us, immediately stopped talking. Hale stared ahead, his lips pressed in a taut line.

Confused, I glanced between him and the twins.

"I'm sorry, did I say something wrong?"

Syrena cleared her throat. "That's not really something we talk about—"

"It's not a tattoo," Hale said stiffly, "it's a brand."

Syrena shut her mouth and exchanged a wary look with her brother.

A muscle in Hale's jaw twitched, but his eyes remained fixed on the trail. "You don't have a name for it in the human tongue. It's a slur. Roughly translated, it means demon."

Without another word, he urged his horse into a trot, leaving me in its dust.

Kaspar and Syrena rode up beside me, watching Hale ride away with concerned expressions.

"I'm sorry," I muttered, "I didn't mean to—"

"You couldn't have known," Syrena said. She attempted an encouraging smile, but it didn't make me feel better.

I peeked at Hale again. "I take it he didn't have that done himself?"

Kaspar scoffed. "Do the people in your world make a habit of marking their bodies with demeaning phrases?"

Syrena glowered at her brother. "Shut it, Kas. She's trying to get to know us better. To be *polite*. A concept you should try sometime."

Kaspar scowled but didn't fight back, instead focusing intently on Hale's form in the distance.

Syrena sighed as she turned back to me.

"Fucking fairy princes," she mumbled under her breath. "Little pieces of shit, all of them."

I blinked at her sudden change in language. With her

poised, elegant exterior, it was the last thing I'd expected to come out of her mouth.

"Please excuse my brother," the princess continued. "He doesn't understand how to be anything besides an insufferable ass."

She sent another warning glare in Kaspar's direction before speaking again.

"We've known Hale since we were young. His mother was one of the palace handmaidens, and when she passed away, our mother made him her ward. He was fourteen at the time, just a year older than us, so we practically grew up together."

I nodded thoughtfully. "So the mark happened before then?"

Syrena's face fell. "Yes."

She fiddled with her horse's reins and smoothed her skirts as she tried to find the right words. Kaspar came to his sister's aid.

"Hale was fathered by a Night Sylph," he explained.

Syrena winced.

I glanced between the both of them. "I'm sorry, I don't know what that is."

"They're a type of Nether," Kaspar continued, his face growing serious. "They materialize into darkness and prey on sleeping women."

My stomach lurched. "Prey on them?"

"Have their way with them. When they're finished, they kill and eat their victims before dissipating back into the night."

"I can't even imagine," Syrena murmured, shivering. "The last thing you see in this life being that thing, floating above you, smiling as it..."

Her voice trailed off, and she shivered once more.

I thought of Lord Olin's cracked and rotting teeth hovering over me. My stomach roiled with nausea.

"But it left Hale's mother alive?" I asked. "Why?"

"A villager happened to find them when it was... *you know*... and they killed it before it could finish. A few months later, Hale was born."

"Why didn't his mother just lie about who the father was?"

The twins exchanged glances.

"Lina," Syrena began carefully, "since the moment Hale was born, it's been clear he's... different."

My brow furrowed. "Different how?"

"Well..." Syrena toyed with one of her bracelets. "When he was born, it was a shock to everyone. He didn't come out a Night Sylph, but he wasn't quite Fae either. He didn't turn into darkness like his father, but darkness came *from* him. No one had ever seen anything like it, and the response... well, it wasn't the best."

She glanced at the back of Hale's head, compassion flickering over her face. "We don't know the extent of what they did to him before he came to live with us. Understandably, he doesn't like to talk about it. But people can be more horrible than you could ever imagine."

I peeked at the figure riding ahead and tried to imagine the pain and horror of being branded against my will, and as a child no less. It was something out of my worst nightmares.

"Anyway..." Kaspar shook off the seriousness of the conversation with a casual shrug. "Our father said if Hale was going to live with us and we were to trust him, he had to be put to use. So he trained with Lerian's finest, and now look at him. Not bad for a low-born Nether bastard."

His crass words left a sour taste in my mouth, but I held my tongue.

"There's no need to be afraid of him, though," Syrena assured me. "You're completely safe with us, I promise."

"Also keep in mind," Kaspar added, narrowing his eyes,

"your secrets aren't safe, even if they're whispered in the dark. So do yourself a favor and behave."

I frowned, annoyed at the way his purposefully vague and ominous words hinted I was somehow the villain in this story. "Is that why you agreed to take me in? You want to learn my secrets so you can use them against Soren?"

The twins looked at each other and had a conversation with their eyes only the two of them could understand. Finally, Syrena returned her attention to me.

"Lina, what did he tell you about us?"

"Nothing."

Kaspar's lips curved into a smug grin. "Interesting."

I didn't know what exactly it was about this man that made me want to smack him, but the feeling was becoming overwhelming.

I shoved the urge down and decided instead to extract as much information as possible while the prince still felt like talking.

"All I know is Astoria and Lerian were once allies, but they aren't anymore. Why is that? Why are things so strained between your territories?"

Syrena fidgeted in her saddle, but Kaspar's expression grew even more amused.

"He really didn't tell you anything." The prince chuckled and shook his head. "The man certainly loves his secrets, doesn't he?"

Syrena shot her brother a pleading look. "Kas, *drop it.*"

I grit my teeth. "You didn't answer my question. What's your problem with Soren?"

Kaspar sighed like he suddenly didn't have the strength to put up with me anymore. "Miss Calder, with all due respect, you're a guest in our court. You'll be free to wander and do as you please, you'll be welcome at dinner and parties and be treated like you're royalty yourself. It's a privilege anyone in this realm would die for. But make no mistake, you are *just* a guest. Which means we are, in no way, shape, or form, under any obligation to talk to you about our court's politics or inner workings. Hell, we don't even have to talk to you at all. Do you understand what I'm saying?"

I frowned and raised an eyebrow. "Shut up and look pretty?"

"Oh good," Kaspar said with a charming smile. "So you're not as dense as you look."

That's how it's going to be, huh? I thought bitterly. *If this prick thinks he's going to get under my skin, he's in for a surprise. I grew up with Jaras. Nothing can get a rise out of me after what he put me through.*

So I bottled my irritation and matched Kaspar's sickly sweet expression. Syrena, however, was not content to brush off her brother's behavior. She let out a growl of exasperation and threw a solid, well-aimed punch into his arm.

"Enough! Go! Torment someone else!"

Kaspar glowered at his sister but reluctantly obeyed and rode forward to catch up with Hale.

"Fucking fairy princes," Syrena grumbled.

BY THE TIME DARKNESS FELL, Lerian was still a half day's journey, so we made camp for the night. The closer we rode to the border, the warmer the weather became. The evening felt more like a chilly spring day rather than the dead of winter, and there was hardly any snow in this section of the forest. Still, I was glad to warm my hands by the fire Hale had made, and I was even more thankful for the pheasant he'd caught and roasted over its flames. I'd barely touched food since the horrors on Yule, and as the rich scent of the bird wafted around me, my mouth watered and my empty stomach rumbled furiously. When dinner was ready, Hale cut off a few large chunks and placed them in bowls. He'd taken off his gloves to cook, and as he handed me a serving, something on the back of his left hand caught my attention.

The same marking from his neck had also been seared into the skin there.

"Thank you," I murmured, trying not to make eye contact with the scar.

He dipped his head in response and started towards Syrena's tent with another bowl.

"Hale?"

He turned.

"Um..." I shifted in my seat and racked my brain for the right words. "I'm... I'm sorry about earlier. For asking about the..." I gulped and gestured to his throat. "*That.* I didn't mean to make you uncomfortable. I had no idea, I just thought it was pretty."

Hale stared at me.

Not speaking.

Just watching.

He stared for so long that I had to fight the urge to fidget. When I was about to snap and break eye contact, Hale blinked.

"Pretty," he repeated. He said the word low and soft, like speaking it too loud might shatter the world around us.

I nodded slowly. "Yes."

Hale watched me a few moments longer, then quickly looked away. His voice returned to its usual timbre.

"Don't let anyone else hear you say that. You'll be labeled a demon lover. A witch."

I sniffed wryly and shrugged. "I've been called worse."

"I'm sorry to hear that." Hale's frown deepened. "People can be cruel."

My heart tugged at the haunted, far-off look in his eyes. "Yes. Yes, they can."

Hale rubbed his branded hand absentmindedly, then turned to go. "Enjoy your dinner, Miss Calder."

"Lina," I called after him.

Hale paused, then glanced back at me and respectfully dipped his head a second time. "Lina."

I smiled at him, but he continued on towards Syrena's tent before he could see it. When he presented her dinner, the two of them talked quietly for a few minutes, and gradually a hint of a smile appeared at one corner of the captain of the guard's mouth. It made me wonder what his full smile actually looked like, and if the princess was the only one he'd ever shown it to.

Chapter 14

Lerian had a temperate climate and was full of rolling hills, vineyards, and pastures, as well as a picturesque, rocky coastline. The territory was absolutely beautiful.

Its people, however, were not.

Sure, on the outside they were attractive. Many looked similar to Kaspar and Syrena with their dark hair and a range of olive complexions. But the way they treated Hale made them hideous to me. When he walked through their villages and town squares, they would spit at him, jeer, throw whatever they could get their hands on, or simply run into their homes and businesses, slam their doors, and shutter their windows. Syrena assured me the Lerian people rarely reacted to Hale this way. According to her, he usually followed behind the prince and princess and never had any issues. But due to the secretive nature of the trip, Syrena and Kaspar wore hooded cloaks to keep from being recognized, and I had to keep my ears covered to disguise the fact I was human. To any onlookers, it seemed like Hale traveled with three regular Fae.

My heart ached for him as we walked our horses through a

crowded coastal village. Hale led the way a few paces ahead, his chin high and his blank expression revealing nothing despite the actions of the villagers. I wondered how he did it. If it were me, I would have been sobbing hours ago.

Syrena glanced over at me, reading the look on my face. "Don't worry, it'll be over soon. We're almost home."

"Is it like this every time he goes out without you?" I asked.

The princess shrugged. "I wouldn't know. To be honest, he doesn't leave the palace that much."

"I can see why," I mumbled as Hale dodged a rotten apple that a sour-faced child had hurled at his head. "Isn't there anything you can do?"

"What would you suggest?" Kaspar sneered. "Should we make a law that people can't be mean to each other?"

I'd told myself at the start of the trip that Kaspar wouldn't get to me, thinking that twenty-three years with my older brother had given me thick enough skin to handle whatever the prince of Lerian threw my way.

But damn, the man had a gift.

He barely spoke to me, but when he did, his words were full of venom. When he wasn't saying something nasty or biting, he was shooting me dirty looks, scoffing when I replied to Syrena, or rolling his eyes if I tried to start up a new conversation. He constantly made me feel small, inferior, and stupid, and after his most recent comment, I'd had enough.

I planted my feet, dragging my horse to an abrupt stop. It snuffled in protest.

"What's your problem with me?" I demanded.

"We don't have a problem with you!" Syrena blurted. Her strained smile wasn't convincing.

"He does." I jerked my chin towards the prince. "So you might as well come out and say it."

Syrena laughed, but a glimmer of panic flashed in her eyes. "No, no, everything's fine. Kas is just—"

Kaspar spun and shoved his face in mine.

"You want to know what my problem with you is?" he hissed. "*You,* Lina Calder, are the reason thousands of people are about to die. All because your little friend in Astoria is an entitled prick with a savior complex who's starting a war because he wanted to try sticking his cock in a human hole for once."

The familiar fires of rage began coursing through my blood, and my hands instinctively curled into fists at my side. "If you hate me so much, why did you you even bother taking me in? Why don't you just hand me over to the Nethers, huh? Seems a hell of a lot easier."

Kaspar laughed in my face. "And be on the receiving end of Soren's wrath? Wonderful idea. I heard what he did to the last person who tried that."

I lifted my chin defiantly. "If you're talking about Valdir, Soren didn't kill him. *I* did."

Syrena gasped.

It was quiet for a few tense seconds. Finally, Kaspar sucked his teeth and gave me a scathing once-over.

"Well, what do you know? A whore *and* a king slayer. Your family must be very proud."

I couldn't take it anymore. Someone needed to teach this little shit a lesson, and I'd gladly do the honors.

I raised my fist to punch Kaspar square in the jaw, but a hand whipped out and grabbed my arm. Caught off guard, I looked over my shoulder. Hale's leather-gloved fingers were wrapped firmly around my wrist. Somehow, he'd stealthily made his way back through the crowd and joined us without my noticing. I struggled against his hold in a pathetic attempt to free myself, but the man proved unnervingly strong. Despite my best efforts, his grip didn't budge.

"Believe me," Kaspar continued, "if there were a better option, I'd happily take it. But if Astoria falls, that leaves our borders vulnerable. So with you here and out of Soren's way, you're no longer a distraction. He's free to focus on his warmongering, which means he's more likely to bring home a victory, which means my people will remain safe. I don't like it, but that's the way it has to be."

Kaspar spun on his heel and strode off, dragging his horse with him. Syrena gave me an apologetic wince before scurrying after him. Only when they had gone did Hale loosen his hold on me.

I ripped my arm from his grasp and rubbed it ruefully. "Your prince is a fucking asshole."

"Yes he is," Hale replied. He then jerked his nose to the twins, urging me to follow. I begrudgingly obeyed, muttering curses under my breath the rest of the way.

I STILL WANTED to throttle Kaspar, but I discovered it's difficult to remain in a bad mood when you're in awe of your surroundings.

I thought Astoria's castle was beautiful, but this was the most awe-inspiring place I'd ever seen.

We'd passed through the seaside village's outdoor markets and bustling harbors, coming to land at a magnificent work of art perched on the cliffs at the water's edge. The walled palace was filled with extravagantly carved pillars, luscious gardens, jeweled archways, and intricately painted tiles on every surface. Each room was draped in an array of breezy silks in warm colors, and everywhere I looked I found something gold-coated or ruby-encrusted.

"Home sweet home," Syrena sang as we passed through the emerald-studded entry hall. "This way, Lina."

I'd gotten distracted staring at an ornate mural on the high, domed ceiling of the foyer and hurried after the rest of the group.

"You'll be staying in our wing," Syrena continued as she led the way up a winding staircase at the center of the main hall. "It's the wing closest to the water, top floor. I hope you like an ocean view."

I nodded dumbly, tracing my fingers over the swirling gold and orange paint decorating the bannister. Never in my life had I seen anything so painstakingly detailed.

"You'll be the first room at the top of the stairs. If you need anything, both me and my brother's bedrooms are at the end of the hall, and Hale's is halfway between yours and ours."

Like a good little guard dog, I thought with a smirk.

When we arrived at the top of the stairs, Hale held up a fist to stop us. He then ducked around the corner. After a few seconds, he returned.

"All rooms are clear," he stated.

I raised an eyebrow. "How did you check them that fast?"

Hale's eyes darted to me, his lips pressing together firmly. Though he said nothing, his point was clearly communicated: *Don't ask questions.*

"Hale is very good at his job," Syrena cut in, threading her arm through mine. "Come on, I'll show you where you'll be staying."

The princess and I turned the corner, and she proudly opened the first door we came to. The decor was similar to the main portion of the palace, with breezy drapery, gold accents, an intricate mural, and large pillar candles placed on every surface to illuminate the room in a golden glow.

"Washroom is through that connecting door, and the wardrobe is stocked with all the latest fashions," Syrena said, not-so-subtly scrutinizing my outfit a final time. "So now you can change out of... that."

"Would you like to burn it after?"

"Could I please?"

I chuckled a little.

"By the way..." Syrena hesitated for a moment before giving my arm a tender squeeze. "I wanted to say I'm sorry for what Kas said earlier. He's..." She sighed and raised her eyes to the ceiling, searching for inspiration somewhere among the rafters. "Well, I'm not saying his behavior is acceptable, because it's not. And believe me, I *will* pummel him later for how he's been treating you. But... please understand, it's been hard for him since our parents disappeared. It's been hard for both of us, but him especially."

Her normally bright eyes dimmed, the sight making my defensive walls lower slightly.

"What happened to them?" I asked. I didn't expect her to be willing to share, but to my surprise, the princess shrugged sadly.

"We don't know. One day they were here, the next they were gone. No one's seen or heard from them since."

She averted her eyes and became absorbed with one of her bracelets. "Part of me still thinks they'll show up one day. It's why Kas and I haven't accepted the title of king and queen yet. My brother and I... we weren't ready to rule, but we had no choice. The pressure we're under feels overwhelming at times. It's even worse with the threat of war looming. Kas isn't as good at handling everything as I am."

Syrena finally looked up and painted on another one of her

dazzling smiles before airily waving away the somber moment. "Anyway, what I'm trying to say is please be patient. He'll warm up to you, I just know it."

Her brother may be horrible, but the princess seemed genuine, and it was clear what she'd just told me hadn't been easy for her. My heart went out to her, so I nodded and smiled.

"I'll try."

Syrena beamed and gave my arm another squeeze before starting for the door.

"I'm sorry I didn't say thank you."

The princess stopped in the doorway and glanced back over her shoulder. "For?"

"Taking me in. I know you didn't want to, and for whatever reason it wasn't easy playing nice with Soren, but I appreciate you putting your feelings aside and doing it anyway. Even... even after everything I've done."

Syrena studied me, her pretty eyes narrowing slightly. "You and Soren... you two really care for each other?"

I love you, Lina Calder. With every fiber of my being.

I pushed down a stab of heartache and nodded earnestly.

The princess stared at me a little while longer, her mind somewhere else. Eventually, she shook her head and turned to go. "Well, you must see a side of him others don't."

"Syrena?"

"Yes?"

"Do you have a library here?"

"Of course. Why?"

I looked down at my hands, distracting myself from the emotion that started bubbling up by picking at a hangnail. "It's my little brother. Wynn."

"The one taken by the Nethers?"

"Yes." I swallowed hard. "I know he's out there somewhere, but I have no idea where to find him or how to get him back. No one's seen him since Samhain, so I've been looking for information that could give me some idea of where to start. But I haven't found anything yet."

Syrena nodded thoughtfully. "Well, you're welcome to take a look in our library. If you can't find anything there, you might have better luck at the one in the palace of Merimaya. They have the largest collection of texts in the five territories. Kas and I will be visiting there next month to celebrate Imbolc. You're welcome to join us if you want."

"I'd like that."

Syrena dipped her head, gave me one last blinding smile, and left the room.

I crawled onto the bed and pulled Soren's dagger from my waistband, placing it on the pillow next to me as I lay down. Slowly, I ran my fingertips along the silver vine filigree around the hilt, desperately wishing it were Soren's face beside me that I was tracing my fingers over instead. His words echoed in my ears until I fell asleep.

I love you, Lina Calder.

I HADN'T CONSIDERED how lonely my time in Lerian would be.

Back in Astoria, I'd had my morning training sessions with Xavier, as well Meer and the Sprites to talk to in order to keep my thoughts from wandering. Even though finding Wynn was still at the forefront of my mind, and my deceased brothers still weighed heavy on my heart, my friends had kept my days filled with activity and laughter, which in turn had kept me from losing myself to my sadness. But in Lerian, I had no one. Nobody, not even the staff, would speak to me or even look me in the eye. Something in my gut told me they'd been instructed not to. Kaspar's handiwork, I assumed.

The days blurred together, and eventually the dark thoughts began to creep in again, especially at night when the world went quiet.

I should have done more to protect my family.

I didn't tell Dominic I loved him enough.

I should've had more patience with Jaras.

What if I never find Wynn?

More people are going to die because of you.

I could do nothing about the past, but Wynn wasn't a lost cause yet. I could still save him. I *had* to save him, or I feared it might actually kill me.

To occupy my mind, I spent the majority of my time curled in a quiet corner of the palace library, searching for any information that might help my brother. It kept me busy, but it couldn't distract from the constant aching in my heart. I missed my brothers, I missed Soren, I missed my friends, and I missed the life I'd started to create for myself in Astoria.

I was a stranger in a strange land once again.

On top of everything else, there was an odd feeling in Lerian I couldn't shake. Every time I walked down an empty corridor or sat alone in the library for too long, the hair on the back of my neck would prickle and a chill would run down my spine. It felt like someone's eyes bored into the back of my head, but whenever I turned to look over my shoulder, there was no one there. The sensation was nagging and constant, and it followed me everywhere. After a while it made me paranoid, and I obsessively examined the paintings and intricate tile mosaics on the walls, searching for spy holes, secret passages, *anything* that would explain my general sense of unease. Maybe Soren was to blame. After all, he had told me not to trust anyone in this court. Maybe my subconscious took those words to heart a little too much, and the feeling was entirely made up. But as the days wore on and the feeling never let up, I chose to trust my instincts.

Someone was watching me, and I was going to catch them.

One morning, I asked Syrena for a small handheld mirror. She'd taken it upon herself to stop by my room every morning before breakfast to help me choose my outfit for the day. She insisted it was because she wanted me to experience all the newest and most popular fashions Lerian had to offer, but I got the sneaking suspicion it was because I was under her care, and therefore a reflection on her, and she didn't want me to embarrass her by wearing something unacceptable. Something such as mens' trousers and a shirt two sizes too big, for instance. As much as I wanted to protest, I kept my mouth shut and continued to let her dress me up like a human doll. I needed friends, and she was the only one willing to speak to me, so my mild annoyance was a small price to pay for companionship.

I carried that mirror she'd gifted me everywhere. Whenever I felt eyes on the back of my neck, I would whip it out of my pocket to peer behind me, or I'd turn down hallways and wait, holding the mirror at the ready to see if anyone rounded the corner after me.

No one ever did.

The mirror tactic proved useless, so eventually I gave up on it. Instead, I analyzed everyone I came in contact with in a desperate attempt to discover the culprit. Syrena was immediately thrown out of my list of suspects; the woman wore so much jewelry that I'd no doubt hear it jingling and tinkling if she were ever trying to sneak up on me. My first guess was Kaspar; he was fairly quiet, spending most of his time drinking and brooding in his bedroom, and he'd made it known he hated my guts. But something told me the prince rarely got his pretty little hands dirty. If he wanted something done, someone else did the dirty work. And who would immediately jump to his master's side to obey? A guard dog.

Hale.

It made the most sense. The man was as silent as the grave, those calculating eyes meticulously evaluated every detail in every situation, and his sole job was to protect the prince and princess. I was a rival king's lover. Just as Soren had told me not to trust anyone in Lerian, they'd probably been told the same thing about me. I was a threat, and Hale had the sworn duty to stay aware of any threat to the royal family at all times.

One day, I finally snapped.

I'd been busy reading in the library, so I missed breakfast and lunch. It was only when I returned to my room to wash up that I noticed my stomach growling, so I headed down to the kitchen to scrounge up something to nibble on before dinner. When I exited my room and made my way down the hall, that familiar feeling appeared. My skin tingled, the hair on my neck rose, and my back tensed. I turned, but as usual, there was no one behind me. Maybe it was due to week after week of that constant unnerving sensation, or maybe it was just because I was hungry, but the feeling instantly set my blood boiling. Before I realized what I was doing, I was stomping back down the hallway and pounding furiously on Hale's door.

He didn't answer.

I glanced down at the crack beneath the door. No candle-light flickered beneath it, which had me wondering if he was even inside. But deep down, something told me he was.

I knocked on the door again, this time for longer. When I lowered my hand, I waited.

And waited.

And waited.

Finally, the door creaked open a crack, and Hale peered

out. He scanned me quizzically, his lips turned down in their usual frown.

"Yes?"

I opened my mouth to speak.

Stop following me, I wanted to screech. *Don't deny it! I don't know how you're doing it, but I know it's you! I'm not a threat, so knock it off because you're driving me insane!*

"Hello," is what I said instead.

Hale squinted at me suspiciously. "Hello."

"Are..." I licked my lips and swallowed, the intensity of his gaze making me feel considerably less brazen. "Are you... following me?"

Hale blinked in surprise. "What?"

"Are you following me?" I repeated more confidently.

"Following you?"

Growing impatient, I fought the urge to roll my eyes. "*Yes.*"

Hale's frown deepened as he analyzed my expression. "Why would I be following you?"

I crossed my arms. "Because you don't trust me."

"No one here trusts you."

Now it was my turn to blink at his abrupt words. I'd already suspected as much, but I hadn't expected anyone to simply come out and say it to my face.

"That's... that's..." I shook my head, annoyed with how flustered his words made me. Or maybe I was just flustered that the man's searing stare hadn't yet moved from my face.

"Well, that's just not true," I finally managed to sputter. "Syrena likes me."

Hale grunted.

"What the hell does *that* mean?"

Hale shrugged.

I sighed and tapped my foot against the tile floor. Hale

continued to stare blankly back at me, unaffected by my obvious annoyance.

"Why do you think someone's following you?" he asked, his head angling slightly. He sounded genuinely intrigued.

"I don't know. It's just a feeling. Like someone's always watching me." A small shiver ran down my spine, and I rubbed my arms. "It's uncomfortable is all."

"I'm sorry to hear that."

He sounded genuine about that too.

"Thanks," I mumbled.

Hale dipped his head and started to shut the door, but stopped when I made no move to leave. He hesitated, then cleared his throat.

"Is there something else you need?"

A friend, whispered a sad, lonely little voice inside me.

But I shoved the thought back down.

I shuffled my feet uneasily. "Can I... can I ask you something else?"

He opened the door a little wider. I assumed that meant yes.

"It's just..." I took a deep breath. "I feel like an outsider here. Which I understand. I'm the cause of a lot of terrible things, and Lerian and Astoria aren't on good terms, and I'm not supposed to trust any of you either—"

I flinched as the words spilled out. That last bit of information probably wasn't something Soren had intended for me to go around repeating. A small flutter of panic rose in my chest, and I warily peeked up at Hale to catch his reaction. To my relief, he seemed unimpressed by the statement. Like it was something he'd expected or already knew.

"And?" he pressed.

"Well... I know technically I'm welcome here, but I don't... *feel* welcome. And... I guess I just want to know when it gets better. When did *you* start to feel like you belonged?"

Hale studied my expression so long that I began to wonder if those dark eyes of his actually could see into my soul. It sure felt like it.

After what felt like an eternity, he tore his stare away as his face softened, revealing the first glimpse of emotion I'd seen from him.

"Never," he murmured.

A pang of sadness jolted through my heart as the memory of the villagers tormenting Hale as he walked by flashed through my mind. An interaction like that would make me want to hide away in a safe space, but if the palace wasn't that for him... Was there anywhere he could find peace and comfort? Did he have anyone to make him feel safe, the way I had Soren?

"I'm sure it'll be different for you, though."

Hale's words brought me back from my thoughts.

"Just give it time," he added gently. He thought for a few seconds before tacking on, "And for what it's worth... Syrena does like you. And... others do too."

I nodded and mustered a grateful smile. "Thank you."

He bowed his head politely, and before I could get another word in, he whipped the door shut.

After we spoke, the constant, eerie feeling of being watched went away. It was a strange coincidence.

So strange, in fact, that I suspected it wasn't coincidence at all.

Every day that passed, I anxiously waited for word from Soren, but it never came.

I hadn't received any letters or messengers, and of course none of the staff would tell me if they'd heard rumors of war in the other territories. Whenever I asked Syrena about it, she waved the comment away and said her brother knew more about such things than she did. So after weeks of maddening silence, I decided to swallow my pride and speak to the prince.

When I made my way to the end of the hall and stopped in front of a pair of opulent double doors, I grit my teeth, promised myself that no matter what happened I wouldn't punch the man in the throat, and knocked. A few moments later the door opened, revealing Kaspar wearing nothing but a haphazardly draped gold robe. Behind him, a young orange-haired servant I recognized from the kitchen yanked down her skirts.

"King Slayer." The prince smirked. "What can I do for you?"

I attempted to hide my disgust and willed my eyes not to drift lower on the prince's body. The man was horrible, but some twisted, feminine part of my brain was curious to see just how far those rippling muscles went down.

"If you're busy, I can come back," I said curtly.

"Or you could join." Kaspar adopted a devilish smile.

My eyes narrowed, and I sniffed the air between us. The sharp scent of liquor wafted up from his skin and stung my nostrils. "Are you drunk?"

The smile disappeared from Kaspar's face. When he spoke again, his voice had hardened. "I said what can I do for you, King Slayer?"

Don't punch him in the throat, don't punch him in the throat, don't punch him in the throat...

"Have you heard anything about Soren?"

Kaspar sniffed and crossed his arms, then leaned a hip against the doorway. "No."

I stared at him, expecting him to expand on the comment, but he just glared back at me.

"That's it?" I asked flatly. "That's all I get? Just no?"

The prince shrugged carelessly.

Do not punch him.

"Kaspar, *please*," I said, fighting to keep my words calm, "these are my friends. I'm worried about them. Imagine if Hale was away at war and no one would tell you anything. I just want to know if they're alive, that's all."

Kaspar remained silent for a few moments longer before letting out an irritated grunt. "Fine. Last I heard, there have been minor skirmishes here and there, but your precious king and his low-born pet have come out from each battle victorious."

I breathed a heavy sigh of relief. "Oh, thank the gods. So, what now?"

"What do you mean, what now?"

"We can't just keep sitting around and waiting to see who wins, can we?"

"We can, and we will."

"Why not send any of your own troops to help them?"

Kaspar shrugged again. "Why would I? Soren isn't my ally, so why should I risk the lives of my people for his sake?"

My blood was starting to heat again.

Do. Not. Punch. Him.

"If you're so worried that Astoria is going to fall and leave Lerian vulnerable to Erith and the Nethers, then you should aid Soren in whatever way you can so he's more likely to pull off a victory."

The prince rolled his eyes. "So now you're an expert on military strategy?"

"It's not military strategy," I barked, "it's just common sense and basic human decency!"

"Well, I'm not a human, am I?" Kaspar bit back. His gaze changed. His eyes shuttered and licked me up and down as he took a step towards me. "But that doesn't bother you, does it? In fact, I think you like that about me."

"What?" I snapped.

The prince stepped again, bringing his lips uncomfortably close to mine, but I refused to give him the satisfaction of seeing me flinch. I kept my feet firmly planted in place.

"You've developed a very specific taste, haven't you, King Slayer?"

Kaspar's breath was hot on my face, the smell of alcohol overpowering.

"Without Soren to give it to you, you're just *starving* for it, aren't you?"

One side of Kaspar's mouth quirked upwards in a wolfish grin.

"Come on, King Slayer," he whispered. "Go ahead. Take a bite."

I really, *really* wanted to punch him.

Instead, I lifted my chin and turned my attention to the servant in his bedroom.

"You deserve more than this," I called to her.

Then I spun and stomped back down the hallway, where Hale had poked his head out of his room to see what the commotion was. I hurled a finger at him as I passed.

"Same goes for you."

CHAPTER 15

I'D NEVER PAID MUCH ATTENTION TO THE FESTIVAL OF IMBOLC back home.

Supposedly it marked the beginning of spring, but in my world the weather always remained cold, snowy, and wet for at least another month, so it seemed pointless to celebrate. Here, however, aside from the occasional rainy day, the nights were still cool, but I required fewer layers to stay warm. By the time Syrena, Kaspar, Hale and I set off to Merimaya for the festival, I could comfortably wear simple, flowing dresses outside during the day and a shawl or light jacket during the evening. Here in the Fae realm, it did in fact feel like spring was upon us.

The palace of Merimaya, it turned out, wasn't far from Lerian's. It only took us four hours to pass through the rocky High Lands along the border and descend into a territory made up of lush valleys, thriving farmland, and mirrored lakes fed by the alpine streams that trickled down from the mountains in the north. It was because of the territories' close proximity, Syrena informed me, that the two had such a tight-knit rela-tionship. That, and the fact the prince and princess of

Merimaya, Ilmarien and his sister Ilora, were also a set of twins near in age to Kaspar and Syrena. The four had grown up together and spent every possible festival, holiday, and ball they could in each other's company. When we arrived at the palace, which was nestled beside a massive crystal-clear lake surrounded by dramatic green foothills, it became evident how close they all were.

Syrena stopped her horse in the courtyard of the palace and leapt off, sprinting eagerly towards a female who was scurrying down the white stone steps. The woman wore a lilac dress that popped against her dark skin and fluttered in the wind behind her as she ran, and her tight black curls were pulled away from her face with a gold cord, displaying her exquisite features. A swipe of gold shimmer across her high, defined cheekbones caught the sunlight as she threw her arms around Syrena, and her full lips parted to reveal a bright white smile as the two squealed and jumped up and down.

Behind them, a man nearly identical to the woman in purple sauntered down the steps.

"So it begins," he grumbled, covering his pointed ears with his palms and wincing.

"Good to see you too, Ilmarien," Syrena giggled, leaning in and pressing a familiar kiss to his cheek.

Kaspar pulled Ilmarien from his sister and hugged him, clapping him on the back before embracing the woman in purple.

"Ilora, you look good."

"Wish I could say the same about you, Kas."

Kaspar playfully flipped her his middle finger.

"You all know Hale," Syrena said, motioning to her captain of the guard, who stood slightly removed from the group, gently stroking his horse's muzzle.

Ilmarien and Ilora glanced at Hale and nodded brusquely, unease flashing over their expressions.

"But *this...*" Syrena continued, grabbing my arm as I dismounted my horse and eagerly dragging me over to display. "This is Lina Calder."

"*The* Lina Calder," Ilora said, shaking her head in disbelief. "In the flesh."

I managed an awkward wave. "Nice to meet you."

"I thought she'd be prettier," Ilmarien mused, thoughtfully rubbing his chin as he circled me. I defensively inched closer to Syrena.

"That's what I thought when I first saw her too," Kaspar snickered.

Ilora smacked her brother upside the head at the same time Syrena punched hers in the shoulder.

"*What?*" Ilmarien protested. "We're just saying, you'd think a woman who a king would go to war over would be stunning—"

Ilora smacked him again.

"Don't listen to him, Lina." Syrena drove daggers into the prince of Merimaya with her eyes. "You're beautiful, they're just trying to break down your self-esteem so you'll be easier to lure into bed."

Ilora nodded. "Fairy princes are little pieces of shit."

"All of them," Syrena added.

"So this is the human?"

We turned towards the new voice. A man and woman strolled our way. They were by far the oldest Fae I'd seen during my time beyond the veil; to human eyes, they looked to be in their late forties, which meant their true ages were probably somewhere closer to the thousands, if not more. Still, they were stunningly beautiful and dressed in breezy robes of teal and purple, with simple gold circlets resting on their heads.

"Welcome, Lina," the male Fae said. "I am Ilris, and this is my wife, Ivari. I see you have already met our children."

Queen Ivari gently took my hand. Her palm was warm and soft, as was the look in her golden brown eyes. "We want you to know you are safe here, Lina. Merimaya has long been a territory of peace and neutrality, and we are happy to offer you sanctuary."

"Thank you, Your Majesty," I said, respectfully bending my head.

"Thank *you* for joining us for the festivities." King Ilris slid a loving arm around his wife's shapely waist. "Do your people celebrate Imbolc?"

"Yes, Your Majesty."

"Not like this, I bet," Ilora stated proudly. "Merimaya's celebrations are legendary. You'll see."

I smiled. "I can't wait. Thank you for having me."

Queen Ivari patted my hand. "It is our pleasure. We still have much to prepare, so please make yourself at home, and we will see you tomorrow night for the celebration."

"It was lovely to meet you, Lina," King Ilris called over his shoulder as he led his wife away.

The two sets of twins followed them, enthusiastically talking among themselves about the upcoming festivities. They disappeared inside without a second glance back. I went to join them, but hesitated when I considered what would happen next. Just like when I came to Lerian, I'd be peppered with countless questions about my life in the human realm and my experience in Astoria. I'd force smiles, fake laughs, and brush off snide comments from Kaspar. I'd be the center of attention and a source of entertainment, which some days I had the energy for, but now, after weeks of grief and loneliness weighing on my soul, the peace beside the lake was considerably more appealing.

A presence came up alongside me, and I looked over to see Hale. He too seemed relieved by our newfound silence. His shoulders were slightly more relaxed than usual, and his frown considerably less downturned.

"You're not going with the others?" I asked.

"No," Hale said tightly. "The royal family of Merimaya prefers me to keep my distance as much as possible."

He didn't say it, but I knew what he really meant. They were afraid of him.

Hale wandered closer to the lake, his eyes fixed on the setting sun in the distance. I followed him, admiring how the rays of the sunset caught the surface of the water, the light sparkling and dancing in its turquoise waves. Together we stood in easy, comfortable silence, letting the soothing birdsong and rhythmic lap of the water wash over us and rinse away our worries.

When Hale finally spoke, his voice was so quiet that at first I wasn't sure I'd heard him. "What do you have planned for the evening?"

"Oh!" Finally realizing what he'd said, I faced him and chewed the inside of my cheek while I thought. "Just the usual, I guess. Wander around the palace, maybe try to find the library and read a book. I, uh..." I let out a laugh. "I don't really have many hobbies."

"What did you do back in the human realm?"

"Worked."

Hale's face remained stoic, but a puff of air rushed from his nose. His version of dry laughter, I assumed.

"Let me rephrase. What did you do for *fun* back in the human realm?"

I considered, then shrugged. "I didn't really have time for much else. When I wasn't working, I was making meals for my family or teaching my little brother to read."

At the mention of Wynn, my fingers absentmindedly traced the black scar running down my wrist. Memories of Samhain flooded my mind, the image of my brother screaming as Jaras bled out in front of him lingering longer than the rest. I swallowed hard and tugged my sleeve over the mark.

"Your little brother Wynnric?"

I looked up at Hale in alarm. I hadn't known he cared enough to learn my brother's name. He still faced the lake, but he was peeking at me out of the corner of his eye, a hint of compassion coloring his typically stern expression.

"That's his name, isn't it?"

"Yes. We call him Wynn."

"I was sorry to hear about his abduction."

I mustered a grateful smile. "Thank you."

Hale gave me a once-over, that unwavering gaze of his analyzing and assessing.

"You worry about him," he observed.

My throat tightened. "Yes. I do."

Hale hesitated, a muscle in his jaw ticking as he weighed his next words. It seemed like he was going to swallow them and allow the silence to settle around us, but eventually he muttered, "They won't harm him, you know. He's valuable to them. They wouldn't have taken him otherwise. They'll treat him well."

Soren had told me the same thing, and hearing someone else confirm it had hope cutting through the worry in my heart.

I breathed a sigh of relief. "Good."

Content with my response, Hale nodded and turned back to the water. The sunset caught his eyes once more, changing them to a warm, deep chocolate instead of their usual dark espresso.

"Maybe you can find a hobby besides worrying during your stay in Lerian," he said to the horizon.

A laugh bubbled out of me, taking me by surprise.

Did stone-faced Hale just crack a joke?

A peek in his direction found him fighting it, but a hint of a smile tugged at one corner of Hale's mouth.

"Yes," I said with a grin of my own, "maybe I can."

"What are some of your interests?"

"Before I left Astoria, Xavier was teaching me how to fight with a dagger."

"You should ask Syrena to continue your lessons, then. She's incredibly skilled with a blade."

There was pride in Hale's voice, which had me wondering if he was the one who taught her.

"Good idea. Maybe I will."

"Anything else?"

I rubbed at my collarbone while I thought. "I'm not sure. To be honest... I was never really allowed to have interests."

Hale glanced my way again, and when I met his gaze he raised his eyebrows. A silent request for more information.

I looked away and shuffled my feet, suddenly nervous to share.

"Growing up," I began, mustering my courage, "I was told that one day I would become someone's wife and bear their children and that was it. I didn't need to know anything else besides how to care for my future family. But... even as a child, that wasn't something I wanted. I remember my mother making me cook and clean and sew, but I'd stare out the window all day and wish I could be outside climbing trees and scraping my knees along with the boys. I wanted to do something, *anything* else. I didn't know what, but I at least wanted the chance to find out. People thought I was strange for that, for not wanting what they told me I should."

Hale nodded as he watched the last few rays of the sun dip

beyond the horizon, those last shards of light decorating his irises in flecks of gold.

"It's difficult to find a place to fit when the world sees you as different," he murmured.

Slight movement at the ground made me glance at our feet. A strange black mist had bloomed at Hale's heels and begun snaking around his legs like vines on a pillar. It flowed gracefully, the breeze catching its wisps and making them ripple and curl like silk in water. Fascinated, I watched it until Hale noticed my gaze and followed it down. When he saw the mist, it evaporated, and a hint of color rose in his cheeks as he hastily cleared his throat.

"My apologies, Miss Calder. I think I'll retire for the evening. Have a good night."

"Lina."

"Lina. Right. Sorry." He politely bent his head, turned, and darted towards the stairs into the palace.

"Hale?" I called after him.

He froze on the palace steps, then warily looked back over his shoulder.

"You don't have to hide it around me. The..." Unsure of the term, I swirled a finger towards my feet. "That. If you want to let it out, you can. It doesn't scare me."

Hale blinked, then averted his gaze to stare intently at the ground. Several weighted seconds passed before he spoke again.

"It makes everyone uncomfortable."

Something deep in my heart tugged at his words and the obvious pain behind them.

"Well, not everyone." I gave him an earnest smile. "I think it's pretty."

Hale stared at the ground a few more seconds before bowing his head one last time and continuing up the stairs.

Maybe it was my imagination, but I could have sworn I saw that hint of a smile again, only this time it tugged at both corners of his mouth instead of one.

THE PALACE of Merimaya was simple in its elegance and made entirely of marble, which I thought was beautiful at first, but ended up cursing. All the pillared corridors had minimal decor and looked nearly identical. Before I knew it, I'd gotten pathetically lost.

My internal compass scrambled even more when I stumbled across a servant who, to my eyes, had a faint blue sheen to his skin. Apart from the Nethers, it was my first instance meeting someone in this realm who couldn't pass as human. I was taken aback at first, but the poor creature seemed more frightened of me than I was of him, so I shook off my alarm, adopted my friendliest tone, and asked him which way to the library. He mumbled something about turning right before bolting back towards the lake-view terrace he'd been mopping. With those vague instructions in mind, I took the right at the end of the hall, but eventually came to a dead end. Confused, I backtracked and went left down the hallway instead, but *that* led me down a spiral staircase with another maze of corridors at its base. Soon I was starting to panic because I'd wandered into a long darkly lit room lined with columns three times my size, and I'd managed to convince myself I was never going to find my way out and this was, in fact, going to be my tomb.

I let out an exasperated grunt and sank into a corner, burying my face in my hands and desperately trying to think of where I could have taken a wrong turn. It was then that a door creaked open, followed by low voices and the pad of footsteps at the other end of the hall. I clambered upright, mentally thanking the gods for sending someone to save me, and stepped out from the shadows to ask whoever was in the room for help finding my way back.

But something grabbed me and ripped me back into the darkness.

I started to scream, but a hand clapped over my mouth, and when I struggled, something pressed up against me, pinning me against the nearest pillar. I would have melted down into full-blown panic if my sight hadn't adjusted to the dark, and I found myself staring into a pair of eyes so brown they were nearly black.

Hale jerked a finger to his lips, urging me to be quiet. I nodded obediently. He scanned my features, and when he seemed assured I meant it, he eased his hand away.

Movement near the floor caught my attention. The mist from before had reappeared. It wafted up behind Hale, growing thicker and thicker until it shielded us with a dense wall of black, rendering us virtually invisible in the darkened corner. All of a sudden, Kaspar's words replayed in my ears.

Your secrets aren't safe, even if they're whispered in the dark.

Because the dark is always listening, I realized.

Hale's eyes darted towards the hall as the voices neared. They were of a male and female, and after listening for a few seconds, I recognized them.

"The human seems nice enough," Queen Ivari said.

"She does," King Ilris replied with a sigh, "but I am afraid that does not change anything."

"I am not especially fond of either option. Do we have to choose?" Worry strained the queen's voice.

I glanced at Hale, hoping he would give me some idea of what they were talking about, but his focus stayed on the king and queen.

"She is insisting."

"Merimaya has never had to pick a side before. Why must we start now?"

"Who will defend us if we refuse her?"

"Lerian would."

Hale shifted, better angling his ear towards the voices as they faded down the hall. It made his hips push further into mine, abruptly reminding me the two of us were still pressed together. I peeked down, my cheeks heating at the sight of our flush chests. But Hale didn't seem to notice our proximity. His attention remained locked on the receding voices.

"They are practically children, Ivari. They are inexperienced and entirely unprepared for war. You think Kaspar could command a legion?"

"True. Nevertheless, we should think on it."

"I worry we will not have much time *to* think on it."

"I pray you are wrong, my love."

The second the footsteps shuffled out of earshot, Hale's shield of black dissipated. He whirled and started after the king and queen, barking over his shoulder to me as he did.

"Follow this hallway all the way down and you'll find the others. They'll show you where to go. And Lina?"

Hale stopped walking and looked back at me, his eyes narrowing. In the shadows, they were nothing but shards of obsidian glinting in the dark.

"You never saw me," Hale declared.

Before I could nod yes, he turned and crept around the corner after the king and queen like a cat stalking its prey.

THE NEXT MORNING, I somehow managed to find my way to the dining room by myself, although I was late to breakfast because I ended up lost three different times. By the time I arrived, Ilmarien, Ilora, Syrena, and Kaspar were already seated and helping themselves to an assortment of eggs, meats, cheeses, pastries and fruit.

"Good morning," I greeted them, slipping into the empty chair beside Syrena.

"Morning," she replied, pouring a cup of fragrant tea and sliding it in front of me. "Sleep well?"

I'd had a nightmare the creature that killed Meer was standing over me while holding Soren's severed head.

"Yes, very well."

I accepted a plate from Syrena and started loading up on eggs and fresh fruit. Hale wandered into the room and wordlessly took a seat at the far end of the table away from the rest of us. Ilmarien and Ilora immediately tensed at his presence and stole critical glances in his direction. Their behavior had fiery rage flaring inside me, prompting me to set my jaw, face Hale, and give him the biggest smile I could muster.

"Good morning, Hale," I chirped.

Hale nodded to me, a flicker of surprise and gratitude in his eyes. "Good morning."

I looked back at the prince and princess of Merimaya and adopted my most innocent, doe-eyed expression. The twins exchanged glances before Ilmarien shrugged and turned his attention to me.

"So, Lina. Tell me..." He lifted a slice of coffee cake from his plate and took a bite. "How many men have you slept with in the human realm?"

Syrena dropped her fork, the clatter echoing throughout the room. Kaspar choked on his drink from laughter. Ilora just rolled her eyes.

"Seriously?" she sighed.

Ilmarien shrugged a shoulder. "What? I was just curious

how they compare to the Fae. I've heard legends that the human male has a tiny shriveled—"

"Ew!" Ilora gagged. "I'm *eating*, Ilmarien!"

"Don't answer him, Lina," Syrena demanded.

Ilmarien glared at her across the table. "It's a valid question! For *research*."

"That's not something you discuss at the breakfast table!"

"It's not that different."

Everyone fell silent and looked at me.

I daintily lifted my teacup to my lips. "It's not that different. Fae men aren't special."

I slurped the steaming liquid, masking my delight at the insult on Ilmarien's face. At the other end of the table, Hale saw right through my act and hid the smile trying to sneak onto his own lips by taking a large bite of toast.

It was a blatant lie, of course. Soren was significantly, mind-bogglingly, leg-shakingly superior to any of the men I'd been with in my world. My insides still twinged at the memory of the night in his tent. In fact, I'd touched myself to the image last night. Repeatedly.

But the prince of Merimaya didn't need to know that.

"Well," Ilmarien huffed, brushing crumbs from his hands, "I think that says more about Soren's skills in the bedroom than anything else."

He and Kaspar snickered.

"Well, we all know *that's* not true." Ilora tutted, scraping thick cream onto a scone. "As I recall, in your youth you both lost out on *many* a lover thanks to the former prince of Astoria. And from what they told me, he was *very* skilled in the bedroom."

She smirked at her brother and bit into her breakfast.

Insecurity swept through me. Had the night with Soren not been as good for him as it was for me? Was I painfully inferior to the countless Fae women he'd been with before, just as all the human men I'd been with now were? Was *that* the reason I hadn't heard from him?

Syrena plunked a sugar cube into her cup before aggressively swirling it with a teaspoon. "Could we *please* change the subject? After all, we're talking about Lina's... um..." Her brow crinkled, and her head tilted to the side. "What exactly is he to you, Lina? Are you two betrothed?"

"No..." I fiddled with the napkin on my lap. "No, we're..."

What *were* Soren and I? Everything had happened so fast, we hadn't gotten the chance to discuss it.

"We're... um..."

"She's Soren's human whore."

Everyone turned to look at Kaspar. He grabbed a berry from a nearby platter and popped it into his mouth, shooting me a smug grin.

Ilmarien stifled a laugh.

I could have sworn a puff of dark fog snaked around Hale's knuckles as his fingers tightened around a fork.

And if looks could kill, I was absolutely slaughtering the prince of Lerian.

"Kas!" Syrena scolded. "Ignore him, Lina. The lover comment struck a nerve."

"What's wrong, Kas? Sore topic?" Ilora chimed in. "You know something else that's sore? All the women you *didn't* bed, because they were busy warming Soren's."

"With all due respect," Hale interjected, softly but loud enough for everyone to hear, "this probably isn't Miss Calder's favorite topic of discussion."

He was right. And while I was grateful for him coming to my aid, I refused to let Kaspar see me bothered. So instead, I faked a cool smile.

"It's fine, Hale. My brothers tease me all the time."

My accidental slip dawned on me, and I flinched. The heavy weight of grief settled in my chest, and I gulped and lowered my gaze to my plate.

"I mean... they *did*. They're gone now."

Another tense silence fell over the group. Eventually, Ilmarien cleared his throat and clasped his hands in front of him. "Well, you certainly know how to liven up a room, don't you?"

Ilora chucked her half-eaten scone at her brother's head as Syrena stood, grabbed my hand, and yanked me to my feet.

"That's it! We'll be taking our breakfast somewhere else."

"Somewhere more civilized," Ilora spat.

"Hale, teach these boys some manners while we're gone," Syrena ordered, dragging me out of the room with Ilora not far behind.

THE MORE CIVILIZED location we took our breakfast was the deck of a large sailboat anchored in the shallows of the lake, complete with a panoramic view of the castle and its surrounding hills. We feasted on pastries and fruit with cream, along with a bottle of something fizzy and sweet that Ilora insisted was a necessity when having breakfast with other women. It tasted like peaches and honey and made me giggle more than I had in a long time.

"This is *much* better," Ilora declared, leaning her head back and shutting her eyes to savor the warmth of the day. She stretched out a long, lean leg, the sun highlighting her dark skin in a way that made her look like she was glowing from the inside out.

"Life is so much better without any men around, isn't it?"

I laughed, but a pang of longing for Soren shot through my heart.

"Well," Syrena said, "I could do with *some* men, just as long as they're not our brothers."

"I'll drink to that!" Ilora cheered, pouring herself another glass.

"Again, I'm sorry about Kas." Syrena put a hand on my knee and sighed wearily. "He's been horrible to you, and it's unacceptable. I'll speak to him about it. *Again*."

"He really hates Soren, doesn't he?" I asked, sipping at the fizzy drink.

"I'm afraid so."

"How come?"

Syrena frowned and waved the comment away with a flick of her wrist, her gold bangles jingling. "I told you, fairy princes are little shits. *Everything* has to be a competition. And our whole lives, more often than not, Soren won. If there's something my brother hates more than anything, it's losing."

I considered her words. "That's it? Just jealousy and boys being boys?"

Ilora glanced at Syrena, her face growing serious. "You need to tell her."

Syrena's eyes widened, and she grunted at Ilora, motioning for her to be quiet.

"Tell me what?" I asked, my gaze bouncing from one woman to the other.

Syrena looked up at the sky and exhaled. The breeze loosened an ebony curl from her twisted updo, and she hooked it around a finger to tuck it behind her ear.

"Alright, fine," she conceded. "The issue Kas has with Soren is... he thinks Soren might have had something to do with our parents' disappearance."

Ilora sighed and hung her head.

"*What?*" I practically shrieked. "That's insane!"

Syrena stubbornly pinched her lips. "Is it? Astoria holds sway over the majority of trade in the five territories. If Soren had access to our harbors, *everything* would be his."

My brows knit together. "Sorry… maybe I just don't understand trade and commerce, but I don't see how this points to him abducting your parents. Soren *doesn't* have access to your harbors, does he? They're not part of his territory."

"What happens to a territory if one day the rulers just vanish?" Before I could attempt an answer, Syrena threw her arms over her head and blurted, "The whole thing goes up in flames! It's chaos! The territory would be vulnerable, and could easily fall victim to an invasion. We all know Astoria's army is strong enough to do it."

"*Did* Soren invade?"

"Well, no." Syrena sat taller. "My brother and I stepped up. We got things under control before anything bad could happen."

"This theory is a bit of a stretch," Ilora said, narrowing her eyes at her friend.

The princess of Lerian quickly averted her gaze, but haughtily lifted her nose to the sky. "You can't deny that crowns keep falling, and Soren is the thread connecting them."

I laughed. They *had* to be joking.

But my laughter died off as Syrena leaned in, her face grave.

"Lina, did he ever tell you about his father?"

I thought back to that moment in Soren's study weeks ago, when Soren sat barefoot in front of the fire, small cracks in his normally tough facade allowing glimpses of fear and sadness to shine through.

"A little. He said his father died a few years ago on a diplomatic trip to Lerian."

Even though we were the only ones around, Syrena lowered her voice. "He died under mysterious circumstances."

"What do you mean?"

"He drowned."

I stared blankly at the girls, then blinked. "And that's mysterious because...?"

"Stelios was a *king*," Syrena clarified. "He had powerful magic, he could heal himself. He was *not* the type of Fae to be taken out by something as minuscule as drowning. It doesn't make sense."

"Supposedly, he was drowned by a Merrow," Ilora explained. "They're crafty but relatively harmless Nethers found in large bodies of water."

"And although they've been occasionally known to lure men to their deaths, some fish bitch would be no match for a Fae king."

Ilora snorted. "Fish bitch. Good one."

"The story doesn't add up. Someone else *has* to be responsible."

I absentmindedly skated my fingers over my collarbone while I thought. "Well, who in Lerian would have wanted Stelios dead?"

"No one in particular. But someone in Astoria might."

"Someone who would benefit from all that power," Ilora added.

I balked. "You think *Soren* had his own father killed?"

Syrena took a loud, pointed slurp from her glass.

"No! No, he wouldn't do that."

Ilora squinted at me. "Are you sure?"

"Yes!"

"How well do you really know him?"

"Very well!"

"Oh?" Syrena leaned in, her gold earrings tinkling. "*How*

long have you known him? We've known him over a hundred years."

"I just know! He wouldn't. What would he have to gain?"

"The crown, obviously." Syrena examined her nails. "And with that, control of trade routes—"

"Power and prestige," Ilora cut in.

"Not to mention any woman he wants."

"Alright!" I snapped. "I get it."

I skipped my glass and took a pull straight from the bottle instead.

"Also Soren hated his father."

I lowered the drink and looked to Ilora, confused. "What? He loved his father."

Ilora shook her head. "He might have loved what his father was, which was a well-respected ruler, but he wasn't a good father. Soren was the best at everything because he *had* to be. There was no other option. As a child, Stelios used to beat him within an inch of his life if he did anything wrong. Him and his little brother, Silvain. That's why he was so protective of him."

Soren had never mentioned that. Gods, my heart ached for him. I desperately wished he were here with me. We could fuck through the night, and afterwards we would lie in bed, naked and tangled up in each other, while I ran my fingers through his hair, whispering to him over and over that he was safe as he dozed off. He'd become my safe place, maybe I could be his too.

I furiously shook my head. "Even with that being the case, I *know* Soren didn't hurt his father. We talked about him. I saw the pain in his eyes when he said his father made ruling look easy."

Syrena snorted. "Men will say and do all sorts of things to get a woman into bed. Fae men especially. They know exactly how to twist things."

"Yes they do," Ilora agreed, finishing off her drink.

I sniffed and pulled my knees to my chest. "Well, there's one thing they have in common with human men."

At the mention of human men, Ilora eagerly shot upright, her eyes brightening. "Alright, be honest... are they *really* just as competent in the bedroom as the Fae?"

I nibbled my bottom lip, looking back and forth between the two of them. "Promise not to say anything to the boys?"

Ilora solemnly raised her hand. "Never. I swear."

"Me too," Syrena said, raising her glass in salute.

I let them wait with bated breath for a few seconds before giggling. "Good gods, humans don't even come close."

The girls squealed in delight, and we all decided it was time to dive in to another bottle.

Chapter 16

When I came down from my room that evening for the Imbolc celebration, I expected something similar to the balls Soren held in Astoria, or at the very least a festive bonfire like my village used to hold.

I was severely mistaken.

Syrena had set aside a white dress for me, complete with a plunging neckline, a deep slit up the thigh, and a silver vine embellishment gathering the waist. When I put it on, I felt powerful, confident, and attractive, and I decided maybe, just maybe, the princess knew a thing or two about fashion. When I arrived in the great hall of Merimaya's palace, however, all my confidence leapt out the window.

Everyone was dressed in white, same as I was, some more revealing and some less, but all were emphatically participating in excessive drinking, gluttonous feasting, and boisterous song and dance. Fire-spinners stood on the tables, acrobats twirled in silks dangling from the ceiling, and seers huddled in the corners reading fortunes by way of cards and rune stones.

I had never felt so out of my element.

Syrena saw me across the room and squealed in delight, running over to throw her arms around my neck.

"Lina! You made it!"

She was dressed in a tight, one-shouldered gown and reeked of wine, but I didn't mind. The silly grin on her face was contagious and instantly made me forget how out of place I felt.

"I'm *so* happy you're here," Syrena slurred, pushing her face close to mine. "And I'm not just happy you're here here, but I'm happy you're *here* here, you know what I mean? Because my brother didn't want you to come stay with us, did you know that? We got in the biggest fight about it, but I insisted! I did! I told him, 'I don't care if she started a war, it's not her fucking fault! It was a stupid man's decision to do it, and she shouldn't be fucking punished for that,' you know what I mean?"

I nodded, biting the inside of my cheek to keep from giggling at her drunken babbling.

Syrena clapped her hands on either side of my face, smushing my features together as she drew me nearer. "You're amazing, you know that? I see why Soren likes you. I'm not going to lie, at first I didn't. At first I thought, really? *Her? Why?!* But now I see it. I really, really do."

Now I didn't know whether to laugh or be insulted.

"Thank you, Syrena, I... appreciate that."

Syrena beamed. "You're so welcome. Do you want anything to drink? There's wine!"

"I think I'm alright for now."

"Are you sure?"

"Lina!"

Ilora, wearing a sleek white two-piece set that bared her toned midriff, stumbled over just as inebriated as the princess of Lerian. She flung an arm around me.

"You're finally here! You look beautiful!"

"I picked out her dress!" Syrena stated proudly.

"You did? It's perfect! You're amazing."

"No, *you're* amazing."

Ilora and Syrena giggled and began to kiss passionately.

"Oh!" I desperately looked around the room for an escape. "Sorry, I... I should... go."

The women paid me no mind as I squeezed past them and wandered aimlessly through the room, dodging fire, dancers, and raucous displays of affection and intoxication. I'd decided to hide in a corner near a cheese platter and distract myself by nervously stuffing my face, when a hand landed on my arm. I jumped and whirled around.

"You look terrified," Kaspar laughed. "Are you alright?"

The prince of Lerian's wrists, neck, and fingers were bedecked in his usual jewelry, but he'd chosen to attend the party shirtless, instead decorating his defined abdomen and chiseled chest with swirls of gold paint.

"I'm fine," I lied.

Kaspar raised a skeptical eyebrow.

I sighed. "Your sister and Ilora just surprised me is all. I think they wanted a moment alone."

"Oh, that." Kaspar rolled his eyes. "Sorry, I should have told you to expect that."

"I didn't know they were—"

"A couple?" He chuckled. "They're not. They're too much alike, they'd kill each other. They just do that sometimes when they're drunk."

"Oh." I nodded. "Right."

I was *so* out of my element.

"I'm actually glad I ran into you." Kaspar grabbed my elbow and pulled me to a quieter corner of the room, lowering his voice. "Look... I think we got off on the wrong foot. Syrena made me realize I haven't been fair to you, and I'm sorry for that. I want to make amends."

"Amends?"

"Yes." His head angled to the side as he squinted at me. "Would you want you to get out of here? Ilmarien and I are hosting a smaller, much more private celebration of our own. Less noise, more conversation. It's just personally more our style. I wanted to extend the invitation to you in case all this isn't really your thing either." He gestured to the frenzy around us.

"Um..."

I anxiously massaged my neck and surveyed the room. The sea of white morphed into one stifling, writhing mass, and the roar of laughter, song, and shrill conversation became a deafening roar in my ears. The last time I was in a crowd this size, all hell had broken loose. And with how cramped this room was, there would be nowhere to run and no space to fight if the worst were to happen. My body went rigid at the realization, the adrenaline in my veins surging wildly with the frantic need to get out. To run. To be *safe*.

I faced the prince again and sheepishly ducked my head. "It *is* a little overwhelming..."

Kaspar flashed a charming smile. "Then follow me."

He started through the crowd, and I rushed after him. Together we pushed past a dance floor of blissfully unaware couples sensually swaying and gyrating to a fast-paced melody the musicians played on stringed instruments.

When we'd migrated out of the great hall and it was slightly easier to breathe, Kaspar led me down a maze of corridors, each one more dizzying and confusing than the last. Finally, we arrived at a door. The prince turned the handle and politely held the door open for me, beckoning me inside.

"Ladies first."

Finally behaving like a prince should. Maybe there's a chance for the two of us to be friends after all.

I entered a large suite, with a living area situated on one side while a bedroom sat on the other. Ilmarien was the only one inside. He stood next to a table full of liquor bottles near the chaise lounges in the corner, and was similarly dressed to Kaspar.

"Where is everyone?" I asked.

Kaspar walked over to Ilmarien and accepted the drink he offered. "Looks like you're the first one here."

"Wine?" Ilmarien asked, holding up a bottle and giving it a shake.

I shook my head. "I'm alright, thank you."

Ilmarien poured a glass and handed it to me anyway.

I frowned and hesitantly reached for it. "I... guess one won't hurt."

"That's what I always say." Kaspar winked at me and took a swig. "So how have you been enjoying your time in Lerian?"

"And be honest," Ilmarien added.

"Well..." I thoughtfully tapped my finger against the side of my glass. I considered making up something vague about the beautiful coastline and perfect weather, but settled on honesty instead. "Enjoying isn't really the word I'd choose."

Ilmarien threw his head back and cackled as he playfully shoved Kaspar. "Hear that, Kas? Your territory is shit!"

"She didn't say that!"

"It was implied." The prince returned his gaze to mine. "Merimaya is far superior, isn't it?"

"It's... different."

Kas shoved Ilmarien back. "That means it's just as bad."

"So you prefer Astoria, then?" There was a sudden edge to Ilmarien's words. Sharp and resentful.

I turned my attention to the ground, trying to think of the best way to answer without upsetting either man. "All the territories I've seen so far are beautiful in their own ways. But... at least in Astoria I had friends."

"You have friends here, too!" Ilmarien draped an arm around my shoulders and gave me a firm, almost painful squeeze. "You've got Syrena and Kas, and now you've got me and Ilora."

I smiled politely and went to pull away, but Ilmarien held on tight.

Someone knocked at the door.

"And here's a chance to make some new friends," Kaspar said, his eyes lighting up with excitement. "Come in!"

At his command, two Fae women entered the room. Like the princes, they wore gold body paint, which was prominently on display thanks to gold chain tops that barely covered their chests, and sheer, embellished scarves strung loosely around their hips.

"Ladies, thank you for joining us." Ilmarien beckoned them over, a dazzling smile spreading over his handsome features.

The women each sidled up to a prince, forcing me to look at the ceiling to keep from witnessing their most intimate parts.

"Lina, this is Parvani and Celestine," Kaspar said, his gaze lingering on Parvani's ample bosom. "They're going to be helping us out tonight."

My gaze flicked from the men to the nearly naked women and back again. "Helping us with what?"

Ilmarien's fingers began to rub small circles on the bare skin of my shoulder. For some reason, the movement made the hair on the back of my neck prickle with unease, and when I caught Kaspar staring at the high slit in my dress while he licked his lips, it finally dawned on me.

I cleared my throat and attempted to maneuver out from under Ilmarien's arm again. "You know what? I'm going to go. I think there's been a misunderstanding."

"Has there?" Ilmarien's arm slipped down to my waist, drawing me back to him.

I immediately shoved him away and jerked my hand forward, splashing my wine in his face.

"*Yes*," I snapped. "There has."

I set the empty glass down, turned, and headed for the door, but Kaspar caught me roughly by the wrist and yanked me back to him.

It was the same thing Lord Olin had done.

It was the same thing the marauder on Samhain had done.

But I wasn't the same girl I'd been then.

I whirled and grabbed the wine bottle off the table, smashing it against the corner before pinning Kaspar against the wall and raising the jagged shard to his neck. Behind us, the women screamed and took cover behind Ilmarien.

"Let's get one thing *very* clear," I hissed through gritted teeth, driving the bottle into Kaspar's throat enough that it pricked his skin. "I am *not* a whore. I am a king slayer, but I'll happily make an exception for a prince. Got it?"

A drop of scarlet bloomed at the shard's edge and dribbled down the side. Kaspar's eyes were cold, but his throat bobbed as he swallowed nervously. "Got it."

"Good."

I dropped the piece of glass, letting it shatter on the floor at our feet, then stormed out of the room. It was only when I had slammed the door behind me and was sure the men weren't following that my hands began to shake. I took a shuddering breath and slid to the ground, hugging my knees to my chest. At that moment, I wanted nothing more than to be wrapped in the safe haven of Soren's embrace.

"I wish you were here," I whispered, praying that somehow, somewhere, he could hear me. "I miss you. And I think about you all the time. I hope you're safe, and you come back to me. And... I... I love y—"

A pair of worn, dusty shoes shuffled in front of me, pulling me from my thoughts. When I looked up, one of the seers who had been reading rune stones in the great hall stood before me. She appeared even older than King Ilris and Queen Ivari, and had the same dark skin and regal stature. This woman, however, had fiery red hair gathered into a long braid reaching all the way to the floor, with bones, feathers, and charms woven throughout.

The woman knelt in front of me and lifted her hands to either side of my face, taking my cheeks in her palms.

"No, that's alright," I said, attempting to push her away as politely as possible. "Now isn't really the time. I don't want my fortune told, thank you though—"

"Lina Calder," the seer whispered.

I shut my mouth at the same moment I caught sight of the woman's eyes. A cloudy glaze blanketed them.

She was blind.

"A girl torn between two worlds." The woman ran her fingertips over my face, tracing my lips, my nose, and my cheekbones. "She searches for the Netherworld prince, but her path is one of darkness and pain. A great evil is growing, unable to be contained by one world alone. The Slayer of Kings will return before the end."

A chill rippled through my body. I wriggled out of the woman's hold and scrambled to my feet. She followed suit, opening her mouth to say more, but I bolted, watching her over my shoulder as I rushed down the hall. She faded into the distance, but I couldn't outrun the ominous sensation her words left in their wake. I was jolted back to reality when I turned a corner and two hands caught me by the shoulders. I yelped and whipped my head around, prepared to put up another fight, but once again I found myself staring up into Hale's piercing gaze.

"What's wrong?" he asked urgently. "Are you alright?"

"I just want to get out of here," I panted. *Please.*"

Hale clocked the intensity on my face and nodded. "I can show you back to the party—"

"No!" I shook my head frantically. "No, please! It's just... it's too much for me right now. I can't be around all those people. Is there..." I looked around helplessly. "Is there somewhere quiet I can go?"

Hale's eyes softened, and somehow I got the feeling he knew exactly how I felt.

"Follow me," he said.

We passed through another set of disorienting hallways and climbed a winding staircase before Hale led the way to a pair of giant carved wooden doors and pushed them open. When we walked in, my mouth dropped open. With its sky-high vaulted ceilings and towering wall-to-wall bookshelves, the room was a cathedral of books, complete with sporadic cozy corners furnished with plush sofas, pillows, and chairs to read in.

I spun in a circle, admiring the vast space. "You found the library!"

"I did."

"Was I anywhere close to it yesterday?"

Hale sniffed, that hint of a smile reappearing at the corners of his mouth. "Not even close. Good effort, though."

I chuckled.

Hale peeked at me, then unfastened the buckles on his leather jacket.

I took a wary step back. "What are you doing?"

He jerked his chin to my hand. "You're bleeding."

I glanced down at my palm. A bloody gash was sliced across

its center. I must have cut myself on the wine bottle when I broke it earlier.

Worth it.

Hale pulled off his jacket, revealing a black linen undershirt. He ripped the bottom hem and tore off a long strip of the fabric, then cradled my hand in his and began wrapping the cloth around the wound. For someone so strong, his grip was surprisingly gentle. I barely felt a thing as his fingers worked.

"Thank you," I muttered.

Hale nodded. "What happened?"

"Oh. Uh..." I tried to think of a good lie, but once again, Kaspar's words replayed in my ears.

Your secrets aren't safe, even if they're whispered in the dark.

Hale was bound to find out. Either the prince would tell him, or he'd somehow find out on his own. So I resigned myself to the fact there was no point in keeping secrets, and sighed.

"I broke a wine bottle and threatened to stab Kaspar with it."

Hale kept his eyes fixed on the makeshift bandage, revealing nothing about his opinion of the information. "May I ask why?"

"I guess the holiday has him feeling more... amorous and aggressive than usual."

Hale's jaw clenched.

"Good girl," he murmured, tying the linen in a firm knot and releasing my hand. When he met my gaze, his face darkened. "If he ever lays a finger on you again, cut it off."

My brows arched. "That doesn't sound like something a captain of the guard should say about the prince he's sworn to protect."

"Well, the prince deserves it if he tries that shit again." Hale shrugged his jacket back on and readjusted the buckles. "I'll leave you to your own devices. Good night."

He turned towards the door, but I caught his elbow.

"Wait!"

Hale froze, his eyes darting to my hand on his sleeve. The way every muscle in his body seemed to tense hinted that he wasn't used to being touched. I loosened my grip, but kept a hold on him.

"Will you stay with me?" I asked feebly. "We don't have to talk or anything if you don't want to, I just... I don't want to be alone right now."

Hale thought for a few moments before peeling his gaze away from my hand to look me in the eyes. A brusque nod followed.

"Thank you," I breathed, relaxing slightly.

I shuffled over to the nearest reading nook and curled into a plush armchair. Hale followed, briefly hesitating before easing into the chair across from me. He shifted uneasily in his seat, refusing to make eye contact.

How long had it been since someone asked him to spend time with them like this?

Had anyone ever asked him?

Eventually, Hale cleared his throat. "Well, you found your library. What do you want to read?"

I scanned the room, overwhelmed by the amount of space to cover. "I've been trying to find a way to help my brother ever since Samhain, but so far I haven't come across anything useful."

"What have you been searching for?"

"Any information on Changelings."

Hale considered for a few moments, then stood. "Changeling is a broad term. A human child taken by any crea-ture of this realm, Fae or Nether, will be labeled a Changeling."

He wandered over to a bookcase and browsed the spines. "You should try searching for information on the ones who took him. Those women. From what I've heard of your story, their appearance and pack mentality vaguely resembles that of the Sluagh."

Hale ran his leather-gloved fingers over the binding of a dusty tome and pulled it from the shelf. He walked back to the chairs and held it out to me. "Try looking for information on them. S-l-u-a-g-h."

I accepted the book and smiled up at him. "Thank you."

Hale dipped his head and returned to his armchair.

"So you know a lot about the Nethers, then?" I asked.

"I am a Nether."

The bitter statement hung heavy in the air between us.

A small ache formed in my heart at Hale's pained expression. I fiddled with the text on my lap, running my fingertips over its tattered cover as I searched for the right words.

"I've met a lot of them," I finally said, "over these past few months. Nethers, I mean." I peeked up at Hale, and caught him already looking at me. "You're nothing like them."

"Most people would disagree."

"Then most people are wrong."

Hale went quiet and turned his attention to the rug at our feet. He shook his head.

"You're too soft, Lina," he mumbled. "Our world is going to chew you up if you're not careful."

I settled back in my chair and folded my arms. "Well, it's certainly been trying, but it hasn't succeeded yet. So maybe I'm not as soft as everyone thinks."

Hale sniffed, and that tiny smile of his made another appearance. "I think maybe you're right."

When he looked back at me, another silence fell over us. But the quiet wasn't awkward or unnerving as we stared at each other. With him it was comfortable. Peaceful.

Safe.

Hale's face abruptly fell, his head tilting as he listened to something I couldn't pick up with my own ears.

"What it it?" I asked, sitting upright. "What's wrong?"

Hale's eyebrows drew together. "I don't know."

He threw out his arm, and the same thick dark mist he'd shielded us with the day prior extended from his palm. It slithered across the marble floor like a snake, staying close to the shadows to remain camouflaged before it slipped through the crack under the door and drifted into the hall. A distant look came over Hale's eyes, like he was lost in a memory from years past. He stared off into nothing for a few tense breaths before speaking.

"It's Syrena."

The ribbon of mist evaporated, and Hale leapt to his feet, bolting for the exit. I rushed after him. When he flung open the library door, we came face-to-face with the breathless princess.

"There you are," she panted, sobered up slightly since the last time I saw her. "I've been looking everywhere for you!"

"What's the matter?" Hale demanded, his eyes roving over her. "Are you hurt?"

Syrena shook her head. Her worried eyes darted to me, then back to Hale. "We... we just received some news."

A pit formed in my stomach before she even said the words.

I took a step forward. "Is it about Soren?"

Hesitantly, Syrena nodded. She looked to Hale again, trying to communicate something with her eyes.

"Syrena, what is it?" I snapped.

Syrena flinched at my tone. "Erith and Soren's forces clashed in the mountains bordering Kylanthia and Radomir. It..." She wrung her hands. "It was a bloodbath."

The pit in my stomach was growing by the second. Somehow, I knew. Something deep in my soul already knew.

"Is he alright?" I choked out.

Syrena glanced at Hale again, silently pleading.

"*Is he alright?*" I shrieked.

Syrena took a shaky breath. "So far... they haven't found any survivors."

It felt like the floor had been knocked out from under me. My stomach dropped, my knees buckled, and an agonized sob ripped out of my throat as I crumpled, Hale catching me in his arms just before I hit the ground.

Chapter 17

The night we heard the news, I sobbed uncontrollably until I'd cried myself to sleep. When I woke up, though, I was numb. I couldn't feel hunger, I couldn't feel thirst. I just stared into empty space, unintentional tears occasionally leaking out my eyes, but otherwise there was nothing except for a constant weight in my chest.

Kaspar and Syrena chose to cut our visit to Merimaya short, and something that *did* finally give me a flicker of feeling was seeing Kaspar with a black eye and split lip. Judging by the way Syrena rode ahead and refused to look at him, I guessed she was the one who had inflicted them. It seemed she'd found out about Kaspar and Ilmarien's attempted Imbolc activities with me, and she was just as displeased with their intentions as Hale had been. Although the Fae blood in Kaspar's veins meant his face had healed by the time we arrived in Lerian, it did my heart good to see him suffer some form of consequence.

Hale was the only reason I made it back to Lerian in one piece. He rode behind me the entire way, his eyes glued to the back of my head. I could feel them on me, his gaze intense and unwavering. Whenever I stared off into the distance for too long, growing so numb from my sadness that I couldn't feel the wind on my face or the reins in my hands or the horse beneath me, I would unknowingly start to slide off the saddle. Hale would ride forward, catch me, and drag me upright before retreating and preparing to repeat the cycle again and again.

When we arrived in Lerian, I didn't say a word to anyone before disappearing into my bedroom, locking the door, and refusing to come out. I stayed there for days. I slept some of the time, cried most of the time, but the rest of my time I spent staring blankly at the ceiling, my mind replaying images of those I'd failed. Soren told me that the horrible things happening weren't my fault, but with how many bodies were piling up, it was hard to think otherwise. My nightmares had transformed from ghoulish monsters to my loved ones glaring at me with hurt and betrayal in their cold, dead eyes.

Brothers asking why I'd failed them.

Kings begging me not to kill them.

Friends telling me I should have done more to save them.

When I was awake, I could think of little else besides the last time I saw Soren.

I love you, Lina Calder.

Those words repeated in my mind. Everything had happened so fast in the moment, I was still processing what he'd said and what I was feeling when he'd turned and vanished into the camp. The days following, I had racked my brain, trying to figure out if I loved him too. I'd never been in love before, and had no idea what it felt like.

Love to me had always meant getting married.

Getting married meant becoming a wife.

Becoming a wife meant becoming a mother.

And becoming a mother wasn't something I wanted, so love wasn't something I'd ever welcomed. It was something I feared.

But as I pictured Soren's expression as he said those words and felt the unrelenting sting of regret for not saying them back, I decided that if it hurt this bad, then it had to be love.

So I *did* love him.

I loved him, and I'd lost him.

The days blurred together so I stopped counting them, but I assumed I'd been lying in my bedroom for nearly a week when someone knocked at the door. I miserably crawled out of bed, so shaky from not eating that I almost fainted. On wobbly legs I fumbled towards the door, unlocked it, and cracked it open, blinking at the light pouring in. When my eyes adjusted, I saw Hale standing in the hallway.

"Wasn't sure if you were dead or not," he said tightly. "Had to check."

I squinted. "Are you trying to make a joke? Because it's hard to tell with you."

Hale's mouth twitched. "It wasn't a joke, but if you found it amusing, I'll consider it a small victory."

His eyes scanned me, head-to-toe. I still wore the same clothes from the ride back from Merimaya, and I hadn't bathed or brushed my hair, but Hale wasn't repulsed. Instead, he nodded knowingly, as if he understood or had been here himself once or twice before. The stern expression on his face softened and he brought a leather-clad hand from behind his back, extending an apple.

"Please eat."

Judging by his tone, it wasn't a suggestion. It was a nicely worded command.

I sighed, too exhausted to put up a fight, and took the piece of fruit. When I went to shut the door, Hale's voice stopped me.

"He could still be alive, you know."

I shifted my gaze to the floor, fighting another round of

tears that pricked behind my lashes. "If he were alive, wouldn't he have sent word by now? To tell me he's alright?"

Hale frowned. "I'm sure he has reasons if not."

"Or he's dead." I forced myself to meet Hale's eyes and shrugged helplessly. "There's no denying it now. I'm Lina Calder, the King Slayer. At least it's got a nice ring to it."

I went to close the door again, but Hale slid the toe of his boot in the way before it shut.

"Don't give up hope, Lina," he said, his voice uncharacteristically gentle. "Without hope, we have nothing."

Hale brought his other arm from behind his back and poked something through the crack in the doorway. In his hand was the book from the library in Merimaya. I'd been too distraught in the moment and completely forgot about it. Which meant Hale must have gone back for it before we left.

I accepted his offering. Hale pulled his foot from the door and continued down the hall towards his own room. I watched him disappear behind his door, then clicked my own shut and examined the manuscript in my hands. A ribbon of black linen had been placed at its center. I opened the book to the marked page and read the title of the chapter.

The Sluagh.

I set the book on my bed, took a bite of the apple, then went to take a bath before settling in to read.

IT TOOK me an entire day of rereading the chapter on the Sluagh for any of the information to stick. The language was dense and confusing, half of it sounding more like a riddle than anything else, but the knowledge I could glean was this: if the Sluagh had taken something to the Netherworld and someone made the journey there to bring it back, then the Sluagh no longer held dominion over it. That information alone gave me enough hope to pull me out of the pit of despair I had been wallowing in. If my brother was in the Netherworld, and I somehow managed to find a way there, then the enchantment the Sluagh had over him would be broken, and come Samhain we could finally return home.

Filled with renewed purpose, I went to breakfast the next day, ate the first full meal I'd had in a week, and asked Syrena to continue my fight training where Xavier had left off. She practically leapt out of her chair with excitement.

The princess was a fascinating woman. On the outside, she looked like an angel. She was stunningly beautiful, poised, and polite. Behind closed doors, however, she was tough, fiery, and cursed worse than a sailor. And Hale had been right; Syrena was an incredible fighter.

She insisted on sparring with dull blades first so she could determine my skill level, and I foolishly thought I might have a shot at landing a few blows. But unlike Xavier, Syrena never took it easy on me. She got the better of me every single time, even when I gave it my all, and by the time we finished, she hadn't even broken a sweat.

"Great!" Syrena smiled as she popped one hand onto her hip and twirled one of her daggers in the other. "You've got a decent foundation. Now we're going to build on it."

Bent over with my hands on my knees, I attempted to catch my ragged breath. "We're not done for the day?"

"No, silly." Syrena strode over to a table at one end of the courtyard and picked up two more blades. "Sparring is just the warmup."

"That was a *warmup*?"

"Yep!" She handed me a second dagger. "Here. Killing with one blade is fine, but two? That's much more fun."

There'd been times when we were training that I thought

Xavier's lust for violence was frightening, but Syrena might have him beat.

"Ready?"

I glared up at her, still breathless. She sighed and impatiently tapped her foot.

"Fine. Two minutes. Get some water."

"Thank you."

I jogged over to the table and guzzled two glasses before dumping the third down my neck.

Spring had most definitely arrived in Lerian. The weather was warm and sunny, and combined with the physical activity, it was making me sweat profusely. I didn't mind, though. It was nice to feel *something* besides heartache again, even if it was discomfort.

When I'd sufficiently cooled down, I returned to Syrena, who was absentmindedly flipping the two long daggers in her hands as she waited for me.

"Can I ask you something before we start up again?"

"Of course."

"How might someone get to the Netherworld?"

Syrena stopped playing with her knives and raised a defined eyebrow. "Why?"

"I think my brother might be there."

The princess blew out a puff of air and shook her head. "Gods, I hope not. There'd be no finding him if he was."

My heart sank. "What?"

Syrena nodded. "The Netherworld is just a myth. The story was made up so they could give a name to all the evil creatures here."

"Where did all the Nethers come from, then?"

She shrugged, readjusting one of her bracelets. "Where did any of us come from?"

I frowned. "But... it's not an impossible concept, is it? I

mean, a veil separates the human realm and this one, and I thought it was just myth. Who says there isn't another veil separating this world and the Netherworld?"

"It would have been found by now. The Fae have been searching for the Netherworld since the dawn of time."

"They have?"

"Of course. If you find it, then you might be able to destroy it. No more Netherworld, no more Nethers, and we'd finally have peace." Syrena swept an arm around her, gesturing to our surroundings. "But clearly, no one has been successful yet. So peace is still a long way off."

I nibbled the inside of my cheek as I considered her words, trying not to let the hope I'd scrounged up get smashed to pieces. "Where did they look for it?"

"Everywhere. There was a theory for a long time that the Nethers escaped out of a crack in the ground deep in the heart of Kylanthia, but no one ever found anything."

"Kylanthia is Erith's territory, isn't it?"

"That's right."

"So don't you think that's a strange coincidence? That she's allied with the Nethers *and* her territory is where they thought the entrance to the Netherworld is?"

Syrena sighed. "No, I don't think it's strange. Erith has always been power hungry. Since I can remember, she's been trying to align herself with whoever she thought held the most sway. She even tried to seduce Soren once."

A brief twinge of possessiveness shot through me. "Really?"

"Yep. She told him that if they married, their two armies combined could take control of the entire realm. And not just the five territories. The lands beyond the sea too." Syrena's eyebrows arched. "Crazy, right? Thankfully, Soren thought with his head instead of his dick for once and told her no." She winced. "Sorry, I shouldn't be talking about him."

I redirected my gaze to the ground. "It's fine."

But the ache in my heart disagreed.

Syrena walked over and slid a comforting arm around my shoulders. "They haven't found his body, you know. Much of his army is still unaccounted for too, so it's likely he's still alive."

I nodded, the pain in my chest lifting slightly at her encouraging words. "That's a relief."

Syrena peered at me curiously. "I thought that would make you happy."

"It does! Really, it does. It's just... why hasn't he made contact? If only just to tell me he's alright. It's not hard to send a letter. He has to know I'm worried about him."

Syrena frowned. "I... I don't know."

I hung my head. "I can't help but think something's wrong. Or what if..." Gods, it hurt to say. "What if we had our time together, and he's just... done with me now? Just like that?"

Syrena stared at me, her eyebrows knitting sadly. She opened her mouth to say something but decided against it, choosing instead to wrap her arms around me and give me a firm hug.

"No matter what," she said in my ear, "I want you to know you have a friend in me. I'll be here for you whatever the outcome, and you will *always* be welcome in my court."

I tightened my arms around her. "Thank you, Syrena."

The princess pulled away and patted my cheek. "You're welcome." Her eyes glistened eagerly. "Now quit stalling and get in position."

OVER THE NEXT month and a half, I threw myself into training. It felt good to get my mind off Soren, who I continued to hear nothing from. Syrena even said she'd heard rumors he and his forces were seen, alive and well, in the mountains just beyond Kylanthia's border, but I received no contact from him. The longer the silence stretched, the more intensely I trained. Still haunted by nightmares of my brothers and bloodthirsty monsters, my nights continued to be difficult, but during the days I channeled my grief and the growing hurt and anger at Soren's deliberate absence into my lessons with Syrena. Soon I could keep up with the princess relatively well in our sparring sessions, even though she remained impossible to beat. How someone could be so beautiful *and* talented was beyond me.

Lerian buzzed with excitement and anticipation as it prepared for the upcoming spring equinox. Syrena explained the festival was held in celebration of the first crops of the season being sown, and it was one of the only events the royal family put on that was open to the general public. Men, women, and children of all ages and castes were encouraged to partake in the festivities. Because of this, it was the biggest event of the year, and Syrena put me to work nearly a week in advance, helping her finalize decorations, menu options, games, and music selections.

The festival was held in a field just outside the city limits, and when I arrived the evening of, I saw all our hard work had paid off. Roaring bonfires and colorful paper lanterns dotted the space, illuminating the rows of long tables laden with impressive assortments of breads, cheeses, fruits, roasted vegetables, with a grand display of wild boar at the center. Flowers in shades of yellow and violet adorned every surface, while the scent of lilies hung heavy in the humid night air. Fiddlers walked the grounds playing merry jigs, and groups of children carried baskets of crocuses and daffodils to hand out to whoever they deemed worthy. The celebration was full of such cheer that it could warm even the coldest heart, and from the moment I walked in, I couldn't stop smiling. For the first time in months, the weight in my chest was almost nonexistent.

My presence in Lerian still had to remain a secret, so unlike the harvest celebration in Astoria, tonight I chose to wear something simple to avoid too much attention. I hadn't done anything to my hair except run a brush through it, making sure it stayed down over the rounded ears that would give away my identity. I'd chosen to wear a pale yellow dress whose neckline, thin straps, and hem were decorated in small appliqué flowers and butterflies. The skirt was comfortable and flowed easily, so no one could tell I had my dagger stashed there. I couldn't go anywhere without it now. Too much had happened, I had been defenseless too many times, and even though there was no foreseeable threat, having the blade on my thigh lessened my anxiety considerably.

As soon as I arrived at the festival, a small Fae child around Wynn's age took my hand, pulled me down to her level, and placed a coronet of yellow crocuses and daisies on my head.

"Thank you," I said softly.

The little girl beamed up at me and nodded, then merrily skipped away.

My heart swelling with joy, I stood and watched as the child joined her friends. I didn't even see Syrena glide up beside me.

"What do you think?" she whispered in my ear.

I turned to face her. The princess was breathtaking in a lavender gown with intricate beading on the bodice and a cascading skirt that reminded me of the petals of a flower. Her long dark hair had been piled on top of her head and studded with violets, with several dark ringlets falling down to frame her face. The look would have overpowered anyone else, but Syrena was elegant, alluring, and commanded attention.

"It's amazing." I smiled at a group of children who ran by

playing chase. "I've never seen so many happy people in one place."

Syrena's eyes lit up even more. "Right? It's my favorite holiday. Seeing everyone like this..." She looked around the party and let out a sigh of contentment. "It makes everything worth it. All the stress, all the pressure. Tonight my people are happy, so I am too."

A young Sprite boy, maybe twelve years of age, ran up to Syrena and extended a daffodil to her, bowing extravagantly as he did.

"Oh, why thank you, kind sir!" she cooed, taking it before responding with a deep curtsy. "Will you save me a dance later?"

The boy blushed and nodded before scurrying away.

I grinned as the princess sniffed the flower appreciatively. "They're lucky to have you."

"Well, they need at least *one* ruler who cares about them."

"Speaking of, where is your brother?"

Syrena rolled her eyes. "Probably off fucking in a field and claiming it's a fertility ritual for this year's crops."

I snickered and shook my head. "Fairy princes. Little pieces of shit."

"All of them," Syrena finished.

We fell into a fit of giggles.

"I'm sorry," she finally sighed. "Don't get me wrong, I love my brother. I just want to strangle him sometimes."

"Believe me, I understand."

I thought about Jaras, and said a bittersweet prayer that he knew more peace in the afterlife than he had in this one.

"Well, I'm going to make the rounds." Syrena placed a hand on my shoulder. "Will you be alright on your own?"

"I'll be fine. Go." I nodded to a group of more Sprite boys

approaching with armfuls of flowers. "Your adoring subjects await."

Syrena chuckled and squeezed my arm before heading in the children's direction.

Again, I turned to survey the crowd. It was a sea of flowers, pastel colors, and contagious laughter, marred only by a single fleck of darkness at the edge of the party. I made my way towards it, coming up beside the figure dressed in his usual black leather jacket.

"You look very festive," I teased.

Hale gave a wry sniff, but his sharp eyes continued to scan the crowd. "I'm on security detail. There's no need for finery when you're assigned to the shadows."

I considered his words for a few moments. Then I snapped one of the yellow crocuses off my flower crown, stepped forward, and wedged it into one of the buckles on Hale's coat before he could shrink away from my touch.

"There." I beamed up at him. "Even the shadows need a little light."

Hale blinked down at the flower. Maybe it was the swaying paper lanterns playing tricks on me, but I could have sworn a bit of color rose in his normally pale cheeks. He quickly composed himself, though, and returned his attention to the party. His arms stayed crossed, but he traded his typical stillness for repeatedly shifting his weight from one foot to the other.

"Everything alright?" I asked. "You seem on edge."

Hale's frown deepened. "We're in the open out here."

"So? Isn't this where the festival is held every year?"

"Yes, it's just..." He shook his head. "Never mind."

"What?"

Hale shrugged in an attempt to hide his clear discomfort.

"Nothing. It's just... something feels off. It has for awhile. And it's getting worse."

I followed his gaze over the sea of partygoers. "Did you talk to Kaspar and Syrena about it?"

"They said I was just being paranoid." Hale grunted and raked a stray piece of hair from his eyes. "So far, nothing seems out of the ordinary, so maybe they're right."

"Maybe you just need to get your mind off it," I offered. "You should go dance."

He arched an eyebrow at me.

"Do I look like I dance?" he asked flatly.

"Hmm..." I playfully squinted at him. "I think you dance alone in your room when no one's watching."

Hale chuckled, the noise startling me. I'd never truly heard him laugh before. It was a nice sound. Deep and gravelly.

"I do know how to dance," Hale said. "I grew up here. I learned all the customs. But..." His frown returned. "People have always preferred I keep my distance. No one wants to be dancing beside a demon. So I stay here, out of sight and out of mind."

Hale stared out at the crowd, his dark eyes glinting with repressed pain. Fiery rage rose inside me as I was struck with the overwhelming desire to destroy anyone and anything that had ever hurt this man. In that moment, I wanted nothing more than to soothe his battered soul and shine light into all the darkness swirling inside. I didn't understand the feeling or where it had come from, but it took control of my mind and body and had words bubbling up before I could rethink them.

"Dance here, then. With me."

Hale turned to look at me, his hardened expression overtaken by one of surprise.

"What?" he croaked.

I held out my hand. "Dance with me. In the shadows."

Hale's gaze flicked to the partygoers, then back to me. "I can't. If they saw me touching you, they would think I was..." He trailed off, unable to bring himself to say it out loud.

I stepped closer. "I know you're not what your father was, Hale. I know you won't hurt me."

Hale exhaled sharply, and for a moment I thought his eyes went glossy. He stared at my outstretched palm, then slowly reached a gloved hand towards mine. He tried to disguise it, but the man was trembling.

Just when his fingers were about to brush mine, Hale jerked back like I might burn him and clenched his hand into a fist.

"I can't," he blurted. "If they saw, they'd call you a witch."

"I don't care."

Hale shook his head adamantly. "No. I'm sorry."

My heart sank, although I wasn't sure if it was from the haunted look in his eyes or because, in the short amount of time it had been an option, I'd grown strangely attached to the idea of dancing with him. Regardless, I masked my disappointment and smiled reassuringly.

"Maybe next time, then."

I turned back to the festival, pushing away the ache in my chest and my fury at the world for failing this man so badly. Beside me, Hale remained frozen, staring blankly at the ground. In my peripheral vision, I glimpsed him swallow and lift his head. He cleared his throat, and when I glanced back at him, he stepped further into the shadows so he was veiled in darkness. There, he raised his hand. A puff of black fog accumulated in his cupped palm, growing larger and thicker until it overflowed and drifted to the ground. Then it rose into a swirling mass his same height, moving in a way that looked like it was bowing to me.

I let out a small laugh and followed him into the shadows. The mist sidled closer, but still warily kept its distance. I raised my hands the way I would if someone were about to sweep me into a waltz, one hand on top of an imaginary shoulder and one in their imaginary palm, before repeating the steps Xavier had taught me.

Step back. To the side. Forward. To the right. Turn.

The black fog followed along, flowing so it never touched me, but still led the dance. With the mist concealed by the shadows, from an outsider's point of view, it would have looked like I was dancing alone in the dark. But I didn't care. I laughed and swayed and twirled with Hale's darkness while he watched, and when I peeked over at him, a smile brightened his face.

Not a hint of a smile at the corner of his lips.

Not a smirk.

A *real* smile.

And it was one of the most beautiful things I'd ever seen.

An otherworldly screech echoed around us, followed by the piercing scream of a child.

Dread swept over me.

Suddenly, I was back at the Yule Ball, hearing that same screech, seeing my friend's severed head dripping blood, and feeling more terror than I had in my entire life.

Not again. Oh, gods, please not again.

CHAPTER 18

II*T WAS* HAPPENING AGAIN.

Only this time it was worse, because the crowd was full of children.

Their chilling screams cut through the air, saturating the night with the nauseating cries of innocence lost. Hale's mist instantly dissipated as he snatched two knives from the sheaths on his legs. We turned to see a swarm of Nethers viciously descending on the celebration, savagely clawing, cleaving, and hacking anyone, young or old, who crossed their path.

"Syrena!" Hale exclaimed.

He bolted towards the figure in purple at the other end of the party, but stopped in his tracks. He looked back at me, then back at the princess, torn between which one of us to defend.

I decided for him.

I hiked my dress up to the thigh and ripped my dagger from its home.

"Go!" I demanded. "I can take care of myself."

Hale blinked in surprise but nodded. His gaze then shifted to something behind me, and before I could bat an eye, he hurled one of his knives in my direction. It hurtled through the air, whizzed by my ear, and lodged in the face of a Nether who had materialized behind me. The monster collapsed to the ground, lifeless.

"Use that one too," Hale ordered, pointing to his knife. He then unsheathed another blade and dove into the frenzy.

Hale tore through the crowd, expertly and effortlessly taking down Nethers like he did it every day. He was the most lethal weapon I'd ever seen, moving swiftly and fluidly, as if he were created solely for the purpose of destruction. Most of his victims never even saw him coming. When he neared Syrena, who was cornered with a group of Fae children she'd been valiantly protecting, Hale cast out his mist, engulfing every-thing around them in dense black fog. He threw himself into the darkness, and although I couldn't see what was happening inside, the Nethers' shrieks of fear and suffering informed me Hale was making quick work of our enemies.

I stooped and ripped Hale's dagger from the skull of the Nether at my feet before looking around to see where I could be most useful. Movement flashed to my left. In a shameful moment of hesitation, I paused.

Kaspar battled two of the corpse-like creatures I had encountered in the woods of Astoria, while the fallen body of a pretty Fae noblewoman lay near his feet. Part of me grimly wondered if Kaspar had pushed her into the Nethers' path to save his own skin, but I shoved the thought from my mind and ran to the prince's aid.

By the time the Nethers heard my footsteps, it was too late. I flung myself at them, stabbing the blade of Soren's dagger high into the back of one, while I used Hale's knife to slice low at the other's legs, slashing it behind the knees so it crumpled to the grass. Then I finished it off by driving both blades solidly into the center of its chest, a sickening squelch confirmation that they'd found their mark.

I met Kaspar's wide-eyed gaze.

"You're welcome," I panted.

A scream of terror jerked my head up to scan the area. When my eyes locked onto the source of the sound, my stomach dropped.

The little girl who'd given me the crown of flowers was cowering beneath a table, her friends' bodies scattered around her. She sobbed feebly, cornered by a giant Nether.

... A Nether who was shrouded in black, with an elongated, skeletal face and antlers.

My breath caught, fear gripped my chest, and dread gnawed at my stomach.

But it was fury that raged through my body like wildfire, catapulting me into action.

Without a second thought, I tightened my grip on both daggers and sprinted towards the monster. I passed other Nethers along the way, but I barely glanced in their direction before cutting them down. I had eyes for one thing only, and it was looking at an innocent little girl like a wolf looks at a lamb. Slowly, it drew a long scythe-sharp claw from its billowing black sleeve and prepared to strike.

I screamed and threw myself through the air, tackling the Nether just before the blow landed, sending us both tumbling across the ground. My knives flew from my hands and scattered in two different directions.

Once I'd pushed myself onto all fours, I tried to regain my sense of direction. The Nether rose too, and as it brought itself up to its full height, I gaped in horror.

It was triple my size.

The creature roared and lunged towards me, aiming the points of its needle-sharp antlers at my head, but I rolled to the side, narrowly dodging them. The Nether landed beside me, its antlers embedding in the ground.

A sliver of silver glinted in a nearby tuft of grass, catching my eye.

Soren's dagger.

I crawled out from under the Nether and scrambled towards the blade. Just before I reached it, the creature tore itself free from the dirt and hurtled towards me, forcing me to throw myself to the side to keep from being skewered. This time, when its antlers stuck in the ground, I hauled myself upright and kicked it in the face. Then I kicked again, harder. The monster bellowed and ripped its head free, one of its antlers tearing off in the process, fixed in the ground.

The Nether employed a different tactic. It swiped an arm at me, wind whooshing by me as its blade-like claws narrowly missed my abdomen. I backed away, dodging and ducking as it swung. When it lunged, grappling at me with both arms this time, I dove between its legs and rolled out the other side. The Nether screeched furiously and whirled to face me. Again, I fumbled through the dirt towards Soren's dagger, the pounding of my heart blending with the pounding of the creature's footsteps as it charged after me.

The world seemed to slow.

I wouldn't make it to Soren's dagger in time.

In a panic, I looked around for the closest weapon. My gaze landed on the antler. Just as the creature was almost on me, I latched my fingers around the ivory and frantically dug it loose. The monster pounced, its bellowing victory cry ringing out through the night like a deafening clap of thunder. I flipped onto my back, held the antler out in front of me, and slammed my eyes shut as we collided.

I waited for the bite of pain, but it never came.

Carefully, I opened my eyes and found myself staring into

two empty sockets as the Nether twitched and spasmed on top of me, impaled on its own antler.

"Lina!"

Footsteps rumbled towards me, and Hale came into view. He shoved the Nether off me like it weighed nothing and knelt by my side.

"Are you alright?" he asked breathlessly. "Are you hurt?"

The screaming and screeching had stopped, which meant the onslaught of the Nethers had ceased.

Slowly, I pushed myself to sitting and blinked at the body on the ground next to me. Without saying a word, I clambered upright and staggered over to Soren's knife, shakily lifting it from the ground before returning to the body in the grass.

"What are you doing?" Hale's voice was a distant echo in my ears.

I fell to my knees and straddled the creature, raising the dagger high. Then I drove the blade firmly down into its neck.

Then I did it again.

Then again.

Again.

I moved faster each time, stabbing savagely and relentlessly. Thick blood sprayed from the monster's neck, soaking my face, hair, and dress, but I didn't care.

"Lina, stop," Hale muttered, resting a hand on my shoulder.

I shrugged him off and continued to hack at the corpse beneath me.

"Lina," Hale repeated, sliding both hands to my shoulders this time. "Stop."

I picked up speed and intensity, grunting and slicing furiously.

Hale dropped his arms to my waist and wrapped them around me, lifting me up from my knees. I struggled against him, flailing and kicking like a madwoman.

"No!" I screamed. "I need its head! I need its fucking head!"

"Stop," Hale whispered in my ear, dragging me away from the body. "It's done. It's gone."

"I need its head!" I said again, my voice breaking. Tears streamed down my face, but I had no idea when they'd started. "I need its head…"

Hale ignored my cries.

I went limp, and the Nether's body disappeared into the distance as Hale towed me back to the palace. Somewhere along the way I drifted into the familiar daze that happens after experiencing violence, where time and memory doesn't exist. Before I knew it, Hale was hauling me back into the great hall of the palace. The prince and princess rushed towards us.

"What the hell was that?" Syrena asked. Blood stained the front of her dress, but none of it was hers.

"Erith must have sent them," Hale replied. He finally released his hold around my waist and placed me on two feet. I had to catch the wall to steady myself, leaving a bloody hand-print against its gilded surface.

"But why?" Kaspar's voice was panicked and his bottom lip quivered. "We haven't sided with Soren! We should still be on good terms with her!"

"Erith doesn't give a shit about who's siding with who anymore!" Syrena barked. "Don't you see that? She wants everything! The whole realm! And the Nethers are helping her get it. We either side with her, or we get slaughtered. Tonight was her way of telling us that."

Kaspar wiped blood from his lip before his eyes fell on me and hardened. "This is all your fault! We've spent thousands of years avoiding this, then suddenly you show up and everything goes to shit!"

Hale moved between us, blocking me from the prince's view.

"That's enough," he stated calmly.

Kaspar sidestepped him and flung an accusatory finger in my direction. "You know how many people would still be alive if it wasn't for you? You're a disease, King Slayer! You're a fucking disease!"

Kaspar went to take another step forward, but Hale flattened a hand to the prince's chest, holding him back.

"Enough," he repeated firmly.

Kaspar gave Hale a rough shove backwards. "Don't fucking touch me, Night Sylph!"

Across the room, Syrena gasped. Hale went rigid, staring at Kaspar for a few tense beats before he took a deep breath and slowly released it through his nose.

"Everyone cool off," he said, his voice dangerously steady. "Bathe, cry, scream, drink, fuck something." He glared pointedly at Kaspar. "Whatever you need to do, go do it. *Now*."

He practically snarled the last word, which was enough to make the prince recoil in fear before begrudgingly shuffling out of the room towards the stairs.

Syrena watched her brother go, then cleared her throat. "Hale, will you walk me to my room, please?"

She started for the the door, but when she heard no footsteps following her, she glanced over her shoulder. Hale had stayed where he was. He wasn't even looking at her.

Instead, he was staring at me.

Syrena's expression changed. I couldn't tell if it was hurt or anger coloring her features, but when she spoke again, her words were armed with a sharp edge.

"*Hale.* Walk me to my room. That's an *order*."

I met Hale's gaze. He quickly blinked and looked away, hesitating a few seconds longer before dutifully shuffling after his princess.

I took Hale's advice and bathed, and when I'd finally managed to scrub away the Nether's blood, I crawled into bed. There I tossed and turned for hours before deciding I desperately needed something to help me relax and silence the phrase *you're a disease, King Slayer* that was playing over and over in my mind.

Shrugging on a silk dressing gown, I tiptoed down to the empty kitchen. An unattended bottle of wine rested on the counter, and after grabbing an empty cup from the cupboard, I poured myself a generous amount and gulped it down. Then I refilled my glass and slid into an empty seat at the table in the center of the room. I sipped the wine this time, savoring its rich, oaky taste that carried a slight burn as it slid down my throat.

"Oh."

Startled by the voice, I yelped and jerked my head up. When Hale materialized in the doorway, my body instantly relaxed.

"I'm sorry, I didn't know anyone was in here," he muttered to the floor.

His gloves had been removed, and his unbuckled leather jacket hung open, revealing the black undershirt beneath. Half the buttons were undone, exposing the toned muscles on his chest. His hair was still tied back, but the strands that escaped and hung in front of his eyes were slick with bathwater.

"That's alright," I said, setting my cup down and gesturing to the empty seat beside me. "Would you like to sit? I have wine." I shook the bottle.

Hale glanced over his shoulder. "I, uh... usually prefer something stronger..." He trailed off.

I had learned enough about him to know in Hale language that meant yes.

I stood and grabbed another cup from the cabinet while Hale slid into the chair next to mine.

"Thank you," he said as I poured him a glass. He was so quiet, no one would have heard the response if they weren't looking for it.

"Of course." I gave him a smile as I settled back into my seat beside him.

Hale hesitantly sipped the wine before nodding his approval. Silence settled over the room as my new drinking partner became transfixed by anything and everything that wasn't me.

Eventually, I cleared my throat and asked, "Is the princess alright?"

"She's shaken up, but she'll be fine."

"Good."

"You?"

"Fine now. Thank you. What about you? How are you feeling?"

"Fine."

Hale returned to drinking in silence.

Gods, does he ever get chatty? I frowned. *Maybe if he drinks enough.*

I topped off his drink and shot him a sideways glance. He immediately sensed my attention on him and looked up. I quickly averted my gaze to the ceiling and took another sip.

"Something you want to say?" he asked.

I sighed and set my wine down. "Yes, actually."

"Go ahead."

I propped my chin on my fist. "Promise to answer truthfully."

"No."

I chuckled. Hale's face didn't move, but his dark eyes sparkled at my acknowledgement of his joke.

"Well then, here goes nothing." I looked down at the table-top, absentmindedly picking at a crumb stuck to its surface with my fingernail. "I'm just curious... what's going on between you and Syrena?"

I peeked up at Hale again. His face betrayed nothing as he cooly swirled the wine in his cup.

"I'm her captain of the guard. I oversee the royal family's safety and remain aware of any threats in the palace—"

"Yes, I know the professional answer. I want *your* answer." I searched his face for any clues he would give me. I found none. "Tell me the truth. Do you have feelings for each other?"

One of Hale's eyebrows arched. "After a near-death experience, this is what goes through your mind?"

I gulped down more wine and licked my lips. "After a near-death experience, one might realize there are *many* things that deserve our fear, but talking about feelings shouldn't be one of them."

Hale sniffed and sat back in his chair, nodding as he ruminated on my words. We fell into silence once more, and just when I'd convinced myself to give up trying to have a real conversation with him, he spoke hesitantly but honestly.

"She was the first person here to show me kindness."

He didn't meet my gaze, choosing instead to keep his attention glued to the inside of his cup.

"When I came to live here," he went on, "the response wasn't the best. The queen knew my mother. She knew how difficult her life had been because of me. But the queen never extended a hand to help. Then my mother was killed, and the queen felt guilty. So she took me in to ease her conscience. Repay the debt, so to speak. She didn't actually want me here. No one did. I make people uncomfortable. Always have."

He shrugged and took two gulps of wine.

I inched closer to him. "But you didn't make Syrena uncomfortable?"

A puff of miserable laughter slipped from Hale's lips. "No, I did. But she decided to push past that and get to know me. No one had ever done that before."

The wine was beginning to take effect. At least, that was what I blamed for the boldness of my next question.

"And she liked what she found?"

Hale paused, his eyes glazing over as he lost himself in a memory.

"I thought she did once," he murmured. His lips pressed into a tight line. "But apparently it was just a passing fancy. A mistake."

He shook his head, and his eyes returned to their normal luster. "Now she views me as a trusted friend and protector, which I'm honored to be."

I shrugged and refilled both of our cups. "Well, Syrena's a fool."

Hale finally looked at me, his eyes flashing.

"Careful," he warned.

"It's true."

Hale grunted and used his free hand to rake the loose strands of hair from his face. "Anyone ever tell you that you speak your mind too much?"

"Anyone ever tell you that you don't speak yours enough?"

Hale narrowed his eyes at me, analyzing my expression for a few moments before sitting back and folding his arms. "No holding back tonight, I see."

"Nope." I crossed my arms too.

Hale jerked his chin at me. "Go on, then."

"Fine." I leaned forward again. "You sensed something was wrong tonight. You felt like something bad was going to happen, but you let the prince and princess do what they wanted anyway. Why?"

Hale shrugged. "When they make up their mind about something, no one can convince them otherwise."

"But you—"

"Especially someone like me," he snapped.

I flinched at his abrupt words. Hale winced at his outburst, and his eyes softened.

"They appreciate my opinion, but it's just that. An opinion. Ultimately, they're going to do what they want, and I have to follow along whether I like it or not. That's just who I am. That's who I have to be."

The ache in my heart started up again as Hale lifted his drink to his lips and downed the rest.

"I'm a bastard born of a monster," he said bitterly, wiping his mouth. "When anyone looks at me, they still see my father. But monsters don't sit back and be quiet. They don't bow their heads and submit to their masters. So that's what I do, Lina. I prove I'm not him, even if it kills me."

Hale's head drooped even further as he stared at the tabletop. Black fog materialized from beneath his jacket and began swirling at his hunched shoulders in waves, gently caressing the back of his neck, almost as if it was comforting him. It made me think about the way I rubbed my collarbone when I was uneasy. Maybe this was his own form of self-soothing. To offer him some relief, I changed the subject.

"Can you feel it?" I asked.

Hale looked up and blinked, snapping back from some distant place in his mind. "Hmm?"

I pointed to the wisps of darkness at his back.

"Oh." He shrugged at the mist, and it disappeared. "I'm sorry, I didn't mean to—"

"Don't be sorry. It's pretty, remember?"

Hale swallowed hard, a slight flush appearing along the sharp edges of his cheekbones.

"So?" I pressed. "Can you?"

"Yes. A little."

"What does it feel like?"

He sat back in his chair, his head tilting as he considered. "I never really thought about it before. It's always just been there."

He was quiet for a few moments, and the darkness reappeared, coiling in and out of his knuckles like a delicate ribbon.

"It's cold," he mused. "Well, not cold exactly. But it's cool. And there's a slight weight to it. Like when you step outside on a foggy night and the air is crisp and dense around you."

He lifted his hand off the table and took turns curling his fingers, sending the mist swirling and dancing between them.

"It's beautiful," I said softy.

The blush in Hale's cheeks returned.

"Can I touch it?" I reached a finger towards the swirl of black, but it immediately dissolved.

"Sorry," Hale muttered, clenching his hand into a fist and lowering it to his lap, "it prefers to watch."

I raised an eyebrow. "Is it something besides you?"

He ran his fingers through his hair again, but a few of the shorter pieces still fell forward to graze his chin. "It's complicated."

"I've got time." I took a sip of my wine, staring over the edge of the cup at Hale and batting my eyelashes playfully. "Please?" I sang.

Hale let out a barely audible chuckle.

"Fine," he conceded, shifting in his seat. "It's not a separate entity, if that's what you're asking. It can see and hear, but it's more like... an extension of me. My mind, my consciousness. My soul, I guess."

I nodded, slowly grasping the concept. "So... part of you is cold and dark."

Hale's eyes flicked up to meet my gaze. "Most of me is."

"And part of you is afraid to be touched?"

He flinched slightly and looked away. He didn't have to say anything else. I already knew the answer.

And it broke my heart.

"I, uh..." Hale cleared his throat. "I think I should go check on the princess."

He went to stand, and before I realized what I was doing, I'd grabbed his branded hand. "Wait!"

Hale stiffened, his forearm tensing as my fingers closed around his.

I wasn't exactly sure what I wanted to say. I'd acted on impulse, and suddenly all I could think about was how much warmer Hale's skin was than I'd expected it to be, and how the edges of the brand weren't rough like they looked, but soft as silk.

Somehow, the words found me.

"You shouldn't be," I said gently. "Afraid, I mean."

Hale looked like he was considering standing again, so I tightened my grip to hold him in place. "I mean it. I'm sorry the others make you feel like you're less than them. Because you're not. You're incredible."

He was quiet for a long time, refusing to meet my gaze. Finally he shook his head, and for a moment I thought moisture glistened in one corner of his eye.

I leaned in. "It doesn't matter where you came from, Hale, or who your parents were. All that matters is what's in here."

I raised my other hand to the center of his chest. His heart hammered furiously beneath my palm.

"You're *good*, Hale," I said earnestly. "You've gone through so much. You've lived through things that would've broken anyone else. You put your life on the line for others every day. You give and give without getting anything in return."

Hale finally lifted his gaze off the table and let it meet mine.

My stomach dropped as I got that feeling again, that he was seeing every dusty corner of my mind and soul, and my mouth went so dry I had to lick my lips before speaking again.

"I stand by what I said before. I adore her, but Syrena's a fool if she doesn't appreciate what's right in front of her. Someone like you shouldn't be pushed aside like you're nothing. You should be..." I exhaled a puff of air, searching for the words. "Hell, you should be worshipped."

We stared at each other in silence for a few weighted seconds. Then Hale's eyes shifted back to the table. I followed them down.

I was still holding his hand.

Immediately, I dropped it and sat back in my seat, Hale doing the same.

Clearing my throat, I quickly finished off what was left of my wine and stood. "I should probably get some sleep."

Hale jumped to his feet, politely dipping his head. "Yes. Me too. Good night."

"Good night," I said, offering an awkward curtsy before scurrying out of the room.

When I was out of sight, I groaned and smacked a palm to my forehead.

"Seriously?! A *curtsy*?" I hissed. I'd never curtsied to anyone in my entire life, not even when I was in Astoria. And in my *pajamas* no less? Gods, Hale was probably in there laughing his ass off.

Once again, I swore I'd never touch a drink again. I cursed that damn wine. I cursed it for giving me loose lips, for making me perform that pathetic, fumbling curtsy, and I especially cursed it for sparking the heat now spreading through my entire body. But as the heat spread lower, headed towards the spot between my thighs, I knew it wasn't just the wine.

I shut my eyes at the thought of loose strands of jet-black

hair and that half-unbuttoned shirt. I took a deep breath and exhaled slowly, trying to force myself to think of someone else instead.

Soren.

I frowned as I arrived at my bedroom and pushed the door open. Was I a fool for still holding on to the idea that he and I would be together? It had been nearly three months and I still hadn't heard anything from him. Should I be grieving him? Or was he just avoiding me? He was a king, after all. And what was I? Just a lowly human girl, a *disease*, who brought nothing but death and destruction everywhere she went. Now that I was out of the way, maybe he realized how much better life was without me in it. Maybe that was the reason I hadn't received so much as a letter. Maybe he was trying to tell me he no longer wanted me without actually having the conversation.

My frown deepened as I entered my room and removed my dressing gown, revealing the short silk nightgown underneath.

I'd experienced similar situations with men before. They'd have their fun with me, insisting they truly cared for me, but then I'd hear nothing from them for weeks until I received word they were betrothed to another or had only used me as another conquest to brag about in their local tavern.

Maybe Fae men really weren't so different from human men after all.

I sighed, threw back the covers on the bed, and crawled inside, staring up at the ceiling where I prayed sleep could find me at last. But deep down, I knew slumber would be impossible tonight. Partially because of the adrenaline still pumping through my veins thanks to the Nether attack, but also because the warmth remained fixed between my legs, creating a distracting ache at its center.

CHAPTER 19

HALE PACED THE ROOM LIKE A WILD ANIMAL WHILE HIS DARKNESS swirled furiously around him. The mist whispered to him incessantly, bringing to light the forbidden thoughts he usually shoved deep inside himself. He frantically shook his head, arguing with the words in his ears.

"It didn't mean anything... She belongs to another... She was just being kind... No... *No*... It was just your imagination..." He threw his head back and let out a furious growl. "Dammit, Hale! Shut up, shut up, *shut up*!"

His outburst caused the fog to explode into thin air.

Hale dragged a hand through his hair, trying to clear his mind of the image of Lina looking up at him with those bright eyes. But there was no forgetting that, or how her hand had felt as it gripped his. She hadn't shied away from his touch or the symbol that tarnished his skin. She'd even held on tighter when he tried to run. He had no idea how, but she could see right through him, clear as day, despite the wall he put up to keep everyone out.

Hale sighed and hung his head.

"She belongs to another," he repeated. "And Syrena..." He trailed off.

Lina's voice echoed in his ears.

Syrena is a fool if she doesn't appreciate what's right in front of her.

Syrena hadn't looked at Hale that way in years. Not since that day in the library when they were young, when they shared that one and only kiss. She'd barely even looked him in the eyes since that day. Probably too ashamed of even touching a creature like him.

You should be worshipped.

Lina's words repeated over and over in Hale's mind. He shook his head and beelined for the hallway, grabbing the bottle of wine as he went. He took a large swig as he stormed down the hall, eager to dull his racing thoughts. This was his new plan of action: drown himself in liquor until he passed out and pray that tomorrow things felt different. Because right now... right now he didn't trust his feelings.

Hale neared Lina's bedroom and had no plans to stop. But as he passed, his steps slowed. He tried to move away from the door and continue down the hall, but it was as if his feet were glued to the spot. He stared at the door, hyperaware of every-thing happening around him.

An owl hooted in the distance.

Footsteps scuffled two floors below.

His frenzied heartbeat thrummed in his chest.

And the black mist appeared at his fingertips, aching to slip forward and listen at the door.

Hale took a deep breath and let out a shaky exhale.

"No," he whispered.

His darkness vibrated in protest.

"No," he repeated.

It took all of his willpower to walk away, but he did.

He forced himself to pad down the hall and retreat to his own bedroom. When the door was shut, Hale threw his mist over the candles in the room, their wicks hissing as its moisture doused flames, thrusting the room into complete darkness. He ripped off his jacket and shirt and tossed them to the floor before lying back on the bed and gazing up at the ceiling. His fingers twitched as the dark fog swirled restlessly around them.

He should go to sleep.

He should forget about tonight.

He should forget the human a few doors down who belonged to another.

Hale lifted the wine to his lips and chugged. When the bottle was empty, he tossed it to the floor with his clothes and continued to stare blankly at the dusty, splintered rafters. The mist around his hands intensified, gliding up his arm to his neck and twirling around his ear as it whispered his own argument to him. This time, Hale considered the idea proposed. Taking this as an invitation, the tendril of fog spread from his body and expanded to the door.

"Wait!" Hale blurted.

The mist stopped.

Hale frowned, guilt tugging at him but not dissuading him. "Just a look, alright? Just for a second."

If the fog could nod, it did before slipping beneath the crack under Hale's door and floating into the hall.

I TOSSED and turned in my bed, not the slightest bit tired. The distracting ache between my legs hadn't let up and was now starting to pulse. I sighed. There was no way I would be getting any sleep without taking care of it. I shut my eyes and tried to relax, then started tracing my hands up my thighs as I pictured Soren and the last night we spent together in his tent.

His mouth, kissing and nipping at my neck.

His broad, muscular chest pressed on top of me, fusing his bare skin with mine.

His fist in my hair while his branded hand cupped my breast...

My eyes snapped open at two things: the image of Hale that had popped into my head, and the feeling of someone else in the room.

I scrambled upright and frantically looked around. I hadn't heard the door open, and we were too far up for anyone to climb in through the window, but the hair on my arms and the nape of my neck stood at attention, just like it would if someone was watching me. My heart pounded in my chest, but I was unsure if it was from fear of an unseen foe or arousal at the image of Hale my mind had unintentionally conjured.

Assuring myself that I'd imagined the sensation, I took a deep breath and settled back into the pillows. I rolled to my side and was about to return to my fantasy when I saw it.

Near the door, beside the armoire, it was darker than usual.

I blinked, thinking maybe it was just sleep deprivation making me imagine things, but no. It was light enough in the room that I should have been able to see through the shadow, but instead it was thick and dense and black as night.

Hale's voice echoed in my ears.

It prefers to watch.

"You little pervert," I muttered to myself, chuckling at the memory.

I should tell him off. I should tell him this was disgusting and inappropriate and he should be ashamed of himself. But when I opened my mouth to speak, what came out instead was, "If you wanted to watch, you should have just asked."

The shadow jumped.

Relishing my victory, I smirked.

Caught him.

Could anyone else say the same? Had he ever been found out before? Had he ever watched me like this before? Oh gods, what if he'd seen me doing what I was just about to!

But to my surprise... I didn't hate the idea.

Instead, the thought of Hale watching while I pleasured myself caused the ache in my center to leap. I squirmed a little and forced the image from my head.

The darkness remained frozen in the shadows.

I laughed and crossed my arms. "You're not fooling anybody. I know you're in here." I nestled further into the pillows and raised a taunting brow. "Well? Are you staying or going?"

After about ten seconds of tense silence, a puff of darkness shamefully seeped from the shadows as it was dragged back towards the crack under the door. It sounded like another person said the words, "Too bad."

But there was no one else in the room. It was only me and the mist, which froze as soon as those words left my mouth, just as stunned by them as I was.

My heart raced as I imagined Hale here doing the same, fixed in place and staring at me intently, searching my eyes to determine what I was hinting at.

What *was* I hinting at?

The twinge between my legs screamed the answer.

HALE HAD NEVER BEEN CAUGHT before.

He was good at his job. Damn good. Thousands of guests listened in on in the palace, and no one had suspected a thing.

But tonight a human sat in her bed, staring him down through the darkness with a smug grin of victory.

Hale gulped and considered his options. He *should* reel his power back in, run down the hall to her room, and beg for her forgiveness outside her door.

You ran off so fast, I wanted to make sure you were alright, he would insist. Which was the truth.

Partially.

He also wanted to know what was going on in her head, secretly hoping it matched what was in his.

Shame washed over him. He'd watched her when she first came to Lerian, but keeping tabs on her when she was in the library or wandering through the castle was one thing. This? This was a violation of her privacy. He would apologize profusely, then never speak to her again. Hell, he'd even request Kaspar and Syrena transfer him somewhere else until she left Lerian. Whatever he had to do to make her feel comfortable, he'd do it.

Hale groaned and buried his face in his hands. He couldn't believe he'd been so weak. After she'd just told him that he was a good man, here he was proving her wrong...

"Too bad."

Hale's head snapped up. Did she just say what he thought she did?

He peered through his darkness and studied her closely, watching the way she readjusted in her bed, the way her flushed chest rose and fell as her breathing quickened, and the way she stared into the shadows with bright eyes. Those eyes held no anger or revulsion. They were playful, taunting, and... dare he say it, lustful?

Hale shook his head at that last one. It couldn't be.

"She belongs to another," he repeated.

That phrase was starting to become his mantra. And yet...

I LICKED my lips and crossed one leg over the other, the friction between my thighs making my body scream with need. I attempted to focus my attention on the shadows.

"Was there something you were hoping to see?" I asked coyly.

I can tease him a tiny bit, can't I? This kind of behavior deserves a little punishing, right?

I feigned being flustered and fanned myself. "Gods, it's hot in here, isn't it?"

I pushed back the blankets on the bed, revealing my nightgown. It was a cool evening, and a salty breeze from the ocean wafted in through the window. When the air hit my skin, my nipples peaked beneath the silk pulled across them. The eagle-eyed captain of the guard missed nothing, so he definitely noticed. I grinned at the thought.

HALE'S JAW DROPPED.

He'd known she was beautiful, but...

"Fuck," he breathed, his gaze sliding over Lina's bare legs and paper-thin nightgown before alighting on her firm breasts. They were the perfect size, each one just enough for a handful, and just imagining yanking that nightgown down and gripping them in each hand, taking them into his mouth...

Hale groaned and began pacing frantically.

"Leave," he mumbled to himself. "Then go to her door and apologize. Tell her you made a mistake."

Hale returned to his separated consciousness and watched as Lina let out a low chuckle and slipped one of the straps of her nightgown off her shoulder.

Hale exhaled sharply.

He could *not* go to that door.

He knew for a damn fact that if he left this room, he wouldn't be able to resist temptation.

I PULLED one of the straps of my nightgown off my shoulder, smiling to myself at the thought of Hale watching me intently, those dark eyes of his drinking this all in.

Getting a good look, Captain?

My fingers found their way to the hem of the nightgown and slid it slightly higher. I peeked at the fog on the ground. It was as still as a statue, but I knew he was watching.

I *felt* him watching.

I squirmed against the mattress and uncrossed my legs, the heat between them almost unbearable. It was pulsing, aching, begging for relief.

Tell him to go, I thought to myself. *Tell him to leave so you can take care of this.*

I peeked at the mist. It seemed to shudder, confirming Hale really was there and I was having some kind of effect on him.

My aching center leapt again.

Then realization hit me like a tidal wave.

I'd begun this as a joke to taunt him, but... I liked it.

A lot.

I liked his eyes on me.

I wanted him to see me in this way.

I wanted...

Him.

... Oh gods, I actually wanted him.

Bad.

SOMETHING IN LINA'S gaze changed.

Hale searched her eyes, trying hard not to focus on the way his cock was swelling in his pants. Gone was her playful expression. Now she stared into the shadows with her mouth set in a determined line. She'd made up her mind about something, but what?

When her hand dipped between her legs, he got his answer.

THE BLACK MIST skittered for the crack under the door.

"Wait, don't go!" I blurted.

The darkness hesitated, halfway into the hall.

I swallowed nervously. "Not... not unless you want to, of course. But... I want you to stay."

The fog fidgeted at the base of the door, as if contemplating whether to stay or go. I leaned back into the pillows again, trailing my hand lower.

"You said it prefers to watch, didn't you?"

I angled my hips towards the mist.

"So watch."

When my fingers slipped between my thighs and found their mark, I tilted my head back and moaned.

HALE HAD STOPPED PACING.

Transfixed by the woman writhing on her bed with a hand between her legs, he practically shook with desire. His eyes shifted to Lina's lips and watched them part as she moaned. He imagined those soft pink lips around his hardened cock, moving up and down every inch of him.

Hale undid a button on his pants, providing some space to relieve the swollen object pressing painfully into his waistband, begging to be let out.

Lina brought her fingers to her mouth and sucked, wetting them before sliding them back between her legs.

Hale's fingers undid another button.

Then another.

Then he couldn't resist any longer.

He reached in and stroked himself, groaning at the pleasure and desperately wishing he could rip that tiny teasing nightgown off Lina's body and bury himself inside her. He imagined he was the one making her moan and squirm instead of her own hand, that it was his length she threw back her head and gasped at instead of her own fingers.

"Fuck," Hale muttered, watching Lina turn and bite the pillow to keep from making too much noise. "*Fuck.*"

My BACK ARCHED as I neared my climax.

I gripped the sheets with my left hand and bit the pillow, my hips bucking as my fingers brought me closer to release. When I was nearly at my peak, I released the pillow and threw my head back.

"I wish you were here!" I panted. "I wish it were you inside me! *Oh, fuck, Hale!*"

That mental image finally sent me over the edge, bliss rippling through my body and leaving me limp and breathless in its wake. When the waves of pleasure subsided, I chuckled breathlessly and looked over to the mist at the door.

But it was gone.

I sat up and looked around. There was no sign of the darkness watching me.

My cheeks immediately flushed with humiliation.

It had been too much.

I'd gone too far and scared him off.

I groaned and buried my head in my hands. I could never face that man again. My heart sank at the idea of having made him more uncomfortable than he already seemed to be at every hour of the day. I sure as hell wouldn't be sleeping now. Not with the anxiety of seeing him after all this eating away at me.

"I'll just apologize," I mumbled. "I'll apologize tomorrow at breakfast."

But I wasn't sure I was capable of having that conversation with him. Not unless I had *a lot* to drink before that.

I slipped out of bed and hurried to the desk on the other side of the room.

"It's fine," I tried to assure myself. "I'll just write a note and slip it under his door for him to find first thing in the morning."

Was it a cowardly move? Maybe. But I hoped if anyone would appreciate that I took the least confrontational path, it would be Hale.

I found a piece of stationary in the desk and scribbled out a quick apology:

I'm sorry. I shouldn't have done those things. Please forgive me.

Short and to the point. A man of few words would appreciate that.

I nervously chewed at my bottom lip, praying to the gods I hadn't traumatized the poor man even more than life already had. Pushing my guilt aside, I rushed to the door, eager to drop off my message and, hopefully, start repairs for the damage I'd inflicted.

I gripped the handle and tore the door open, coming face-to-face with Hale.

CHAPTER 20

The air was tight between us as we stared at each other.

Hale was shirtless, his bare chest rising and falling rapidly and his defined abs slick with a thin layer of sweat. The only thing covering him was a pair of dangerously low-slung pants unbuttoned at the top. There were vicious scars of varying shapes, sizes, and colors scattered over his body, and another brand was seared into the skin near his lower right hip, but it did nothing to distract from his unique beauty.

My brain turned to mush as I blinked up into his unflinching gaze. I opened my mouth in an attempt to speak, but Hale beat me to it.

"What I did was a violation of your privacy and your trust," he said, his stony face betraying nothing. "I apologize."

"It's alright," I replied. "I... ended up enjoying it."

Hale just stared.

My pulse quickened, and I licked my lips. "I'm sorry if I made you uncomfortable—"

"You didn't," he blurted. "I swear, you didn't."

"Good."

Hale finally broke my gaze, his eyes drifting achingly slow down my lips, my neck, my chest, my legs. He looked at me like piece of art, drinking in every last detail.

"You belong to another," he murmured.

I wasn't sure if he was saying it to try and convince himself or me, but his choice of words made me bristle.

"First of all, I belong to no one but myself." I lifted my chin. "Second, the *other* you're referring to hasn't spoken to me in months. If I *am* his, he has a funny way of showing it."

"Good point."

He stepped towards me, entering the room, but I didn't move. Our faces were close now, our bodies even closer. Heat radiated off his sweat-misted torso, and as his gaze continued to rove over my body, I wondered if he could hear the way my heart was racing.

"You used a phrase earlier," Hale said, his voice low and raspy. My stomach dipped at the sound. "You said I shouldn't be pushed aside, that I—"

"Should be worshipped," I finished for him.

Hale nodded, finally peeling his eyes from my skin to meet my gaze. "Did you mean that?"

"Yes," I whispered.

The door slammed shut behind him.

"Then get on your knees."

A shiver raced down my spine at his commanding tone, my body instantly thrumming to life with desire. Slowly, I sank to the floor, looking up at him the whole way.

"I want to hear you say it." His deep, rumbling voice sent another chill rippling through me. "What do you want?"

My lips curved into a smile. "All of you."

And with that, he undid the final button on his pants, letting his cock spring free. My insides leapt at the impressive length, already aching for it.

Hale stroked himself, paying special attention to the tip, but still kept his eyes glued to mine.

"Go on, then," he said with a jerk of his chin. "Worship me."

I grinned and eagerly obeyed.

Without breaking eye contact, I grabbed him in both hands and ran my tongue along the underside, base to tip.

Hale shuddered.

I then trailed my tongue in circles around the head, causing him to groan in pleasure.

When I took the whole of him deep into my throat, he gasped and grabbed the wall for support.

"Shit!" he hissed.

I moaned at his taste, earning another groan of pleasure from Hale. Then I repeated everything I'd just done, faster this time. Hale threw his head back, his free hand finding its way to my hair and balling into a fist.

"Fuck, Lina!"

Gods, I liked my name on his lips.

I greedily repeated he movements, moving faster and faster each time and loving every second of it. Soon, Hale's melody of moans and groans and muttered curses had me dripping with want. He must have sensed it because he suddenly pulled himself from my mouth and hauled me to my feet, crushing me in a kiss as he guided me towards the bed.

When the back of my thighs hit the mattress, Hale shoved me onto my back and crawled on top of me. We kissed passionately, his tongue eagerly exploring my mouth before migrating down to my neck, my chest, my stomach. He already had me quivering by the time he lifted my nightgown and began to devour me. My back arched when his tongue expertly found the perfect spot that jolted pleasure through my core, prompting Hale to grip my neck with his branded hand, pinning me in place.

He held me there, fervently lapping up and down and around, leading me closer to a climax with each stroke. My hips lifted off the mattress, angling up so Hale's tongue could hit me better. His speed increased to match my grinding hips, and my breathing became increasingly ragged as he brought me to my peak. At the last second, Hale pushed two fingers inside me and curled them upwards, sending me spilling over the edge. I cried out in ecstasy, tangling my fingers in his hair to steady myself as I shook uncontrollably.

Hale didn't miss a beat and pushed my hips back to the mattress before dragging his tongue up my body from navel to neck. Too impatient to hold off any longer, I hauled him into a desperate kiss, breaking away only to gasp, "I need you. *Now*."

Hale responded with a hungry growl and spread my legs wide, positioning himself over me. He angled his tip at my opening and was about to push in—

Knock. Knock. Knock.

I jumped at the rapping on the door. In the blink of an eye, Hale was off of me and wedged in a shadowy corner of the room, camouflaged by a shroud of black fog that rendered him invisible. It took me a few dumbfounded seconds to even process what had happened.

The knock sounded again. I yanked my nightgown over my hips and smoothed my hair.

"Uh..." I cleared my throat. "Who is it?"

"Kaspar."

There was a mumbled curse from the shadow in the corner.

"What do you want?" I asked, trying not to sound too breathless.

"You're needed downstairs," Kaspar said. Even through the door I could hear tension in his voice.

"Can't it wait until morning?" I asked, glancing at the corner. "I'm... sleeping."

"It's urgent."

A brief moment of panic. "Is it more Nethers?"

"No."

I huffed a relieved sigh. Irritation returned, and I rolled my eyes. "Alright, then what could possibly be so urgent that you need to see me at this exact moment—"

"*Lina.*" His voice was firm now. "It's Soren."

I sat upright, my stomach lurching. A lump formed in my throat, and I swallowed hard, bracing myself for the worst.

"You've heard news?"

"No," Kaspar replied. "He's *here.*"

By the time I'd composed myself, thrown on a dressing gown and slippers, and arrived in the great hall, Kaspar, Syrena, and Hale were already there. The latter had somehow found enough time to return to his bedroom and wash up. His damp hair had been re-wet, and he was dressed in fresh, pressed clothes. No one would have guessed what we'd been up to not ten minutes before.

My face flushed as I banished the heated memory from my mind and focused my attention on the far end of the room. A blue-cloaked figure stood with their back to me. My heart was pounding so hard I could feel it in my throat, and when they turned and removed their hood, my knees went weak.

Soren smiled at me, his weary expression and the dark bags under his eyes doing nothing to diminish his handsome features.

"Hello, Lina," he said softly.

Tears welled in my eyes. I walked towards him, my steps growing faster and faster. He started for me too, eyes shining with emotion as he opened his arms to wrap me in a warm embrace.

I slapped him.

Hard.

The sharp clap echoed off every surface in the room.

Tears spilled down my cheeks, and my bottom lip quivered as I glared up at Soren, waiting for him to say something. When he remained silent, eyes glued to the floor, I smacked him again.

"Where were you?" I demanded, my voice wavering.

Soren rubbed his jaw ruefully, but still didn't say anything.

"*Where* were you?" I repeated, my voice stronger.

When he didn't reply, I pushed him.

When he didn't move, I balled my hands into fists and furiously beat at his chest.

"Where the fuck were you?!" I shouted.

Soren's calm exterior finally cracked. He roughly grabbed my wrists and yanked them down to my sides, holding them tight while I fought against him.

Hale subtly moved his hand to the hilt of one of his daggers.

"Gentlemen... lady..." Soren grunted as he struggled to contain me. "Do you mind if we have some privacy?"

"I think it's best if we stay," Kaspar said, casually examining his nail beds. "If one of you ends up killing the other, I'd like to know right away. Wouldn't want the blood to set into the tile."

Once I realized my struggle was in vain, I let myself go limp in surrender. When Soren seemed sure I wouldn't hit him again, he released his hold.

"One letter," I whimpered, tears continuing to flood from my eyes. "Where were you that made it impossible to send *one* letter?"

Guilt riddled Soren's face, but he stood his ground and

proudly lifted his nose high. "I told you I wouldn't be able to have much contact."

"It's been *three months*," I spat. "Not a word to anyone. For all we knew you were dead!"

I wanted him to wrap me in his arms, bury his face in my neck, and whisper an apology over and over. But instead his eyes went cold, and he faced Kaspar.

"You told her I was dead?"

The prince raised his brows innocently, but the ice in his eyes matched Soren's. "I did nothing of the sort. I just left out the fact that you were alive."

Soren growled, snatched up my hand, and dragged me towards the hallway.

"Come on," he ordered. "We'll talk about this while you pack."

"*Pack?*" I ripped my hand from Soren's grasp and backed away. "You show up out of nowhere in the middle of the night and expect me to just pack up and leave?"

Outwardly, Soren remained calm. But as he carefully articulated each syllable in his words, I could tell he was struggling to keep his composure.

"I told you all of this before. I said you'd have to move, in secret, from territory to territory, and I had no idea how often I'd have contact."

"We haven't had *any* contact!"

Soren sighed and grit his teeth. "I'm losing my patience, Lina."

I recoiled at the subtle threat behind his words. "What the hell happened to you?"

"What happened to me? What happened to *you*?" Soren snapped. "You were fine with this before!"

"Yes, before she learned to think for herself, " Kaspar mumbled.

Soren spun and flung an accusatory finger at him. "Stay the fuck out of this! You've poisoned her against me enough!"

"You've done that all on your own," the prince bit back.

"This was the only reason you agreed to take her in, wasn't it? You just wanted to use her so you could get back at me."

Kaspar took a menacing step towards him. "Where was this conversation three months ago when you were practically throwing her my way, begging me to get her away from you?"

"That's not how it happened!"

"Gentlemen," Hale cut in, his voice quiet but potent enough to command the attention of the room, "with all due respect, there are ladies present. Perhaps we save this conversation for another time?"

Both Soren and Kaspar bristled, but the former backed down.

"Fine. Another time." Soren turned to me and motioned to the doorway. "Let's go."

I stood firm, barring my arms over my chest. "Maybe I don't want to."

A muscle in Soren's jaw twitched. "What?"

"You keep telling me what we're doing, but you haven't asked what *I* want to do." I shrugged. "Maybe I like it here. Maybe I want to stay."

"That's not your decision."

"She's welcome here," Syrena said tightly, coming up beside me and standing tall. "She can stay as long as she wants."

Soren stared at Syrena for a few weighted seconds, then returned his gaze to me. "This is *not* what we agreed to."

"I didn't have a choice the first time," I countered. "Again, you just told me what we were doing instead of asking."

"You wanted to stay with me, which was impossible!"

"It still would've been nice to have been asked!" I shrieked.

Silence swept over the room.

Soren looked at Kaspar, then Syrena, then Hale, then finally back to me. He took a deep breath, balled his hands into fists, and shut his eyes.

"What would you like to do, Lina?" It sounded like it physically pained him to speak so calmly. "Please keep in mind that the longer you stay here, the more dangerous it is."

"Lina's safe with us," Syrena cut in defensively.

Soren barked out a laugh. "That's not what it looked like when I passed what was left of your spring equinox."

"I took care of it," Hale said. He was still calm, but his voice had begun to sound eerily similar to an animal's warning growl.

Unaffected, Soren shook his head. "It's only a matter of time before Erith and the Nethers target Lerian seriously. If they find out you've been harboring Lina too—"

"Then she flees to somewhere safe, and we ready our army and fleet," Syrena said with a shrug. "Simple."

When Soren faced me, I forced myself to be strong and meet his gaze. It was clear he was angry, but the more I looked at him, the more I caught glimpses of confusion and hurt.

"Is this what you want, Lina?" he asked.

"I..." My voice cracked. I swallowed, my gaze shifting from Soren to Syrena and Hale. I could think of nothing to say but the truth.

"I don't know what I want," I whispered.

Syrena slid a comforting arm around my shoulders. "Listen. It's been a long, difficult evening. Everyone is exhausted, and tensions are high. Why don't we talk about this tomorrow after a good night's rest and a hot meal?" She looked to Soren. "I'll have our finest quarters made up for you. Do you have any belongings with you? I'll send one of the servants to retrieve them."

Soren didn't answer. He just stared at me for what felt like an eternity before storming out of the hall.

"Soren!" I called after him, my voice breaking. The flood-gate released, and tears spilled down my face in torrents, which Syrena took as her cue to rub my back as she led me in the direction of my bedroom.

When we were out of sight of the men, she lowered her voice.

"You smell like sex."

My stomach lurched. "Do you think Soren noticed?"

"Yes."

KASPAR STORMED over to Hale and sniffed him. Hale didn't want to meet his prince's gaze, but forced himself to anyway.

"Shit!" Kaspar hissed, turning away. He began to pace and roughly raked his fingers through his curls in frustration. "What the *hell* do you think you're doing?"

Hale kept his expression blank. "To what are you referring, Your Highness?"

"You know exactly what the fuck I'm referring to!" Kaspar whirled to face him, his eyes hard as steel. Even the air around him seemed to vibrate with rage.

Hale squared his shoulders and lifted his chin. He refused to show the shame he felt... not so much at what he'd done, but mainly at the fact he'd gotten caught.

"Things with Soren are bad enough, and now you have to go and fuck his—"

"It didn't come to that."

"*Would* it have?"

Hale's mouth clamped shut.

Kaspar groaned and ruefully rubbed the back of his neck.

"Gods, this girl is going to be the death of me. What is it about her, anyway? Why is everyone losing their minds over a *human*?"

Hale frowned. Where should he start? He could go on and on about Lina's kindness, her humor, her strength despite all she'd been through, those eyes made up of every shade of blue and green and amber imaginable, the look of ecstasy on her face right before she—

"It was a single moment of weakness," Hale stated, clearing his throat. "It won't happen again."

"It better not." Kaspar's eyes bored into him. "If you need a release, Hale, just tell me. I could have one of the Sprites from the kitchen in your bed at the snap of a finger—"

"I don't need your help getting my cock sucked, thank you very much." Hale's tone came out rougher than he'd intended. "I'm perfectly capable of achieving that myself. Not everyone finds me as repulsive as you and your sister."

"We don't..." Kaspar trailed off, and his head tilted as he studied Hale. "Is that what this was? You wanted to punish Syrena for never sleeping with you, so you dirtied her new toy?"

"*No!*" A flash of rage bubbled up from the deep, dark place Hale usually kept it in. "It had nothing to do with Syrena! I'm not some lovesick puppy obsessing over your sister every second of the day!"

"Really? Because from the moment you set foot in this palace, that's all I've seen you do."

Hale ground his teeth. "Well then, I guess I've finally come to my senses."

"Or you've grown even more delusional." Kaspar brought his face close to Hale's again. "You're playing with fire, and it's going to get us all burned. We need to do what's best for the territory, and that means not pissing off a king we're already on thin ice with. You're smarter than this, Hale."

Kaspar finally softened and clapped a hand on Hale's shoulder, making him flinch.

"Whatever this is with the human," the prince added, "I swear to you, she's not worth it. Let it go."

"I told you," Hale ground out. "It won't happen again."

"Good." Kaspar nodded and removed his hand, brushing it off on the leg of his trousers before stuffing it in his pocket and backing away. "Now if you'll excuse me, I need a fucking drink." He headed for the stairs, calling back over his shoulder, "Follow Soren. Make sure he's not setting fire to the drapes or anything."

CHAPTER 21

I BARELY SLEPT.

By the time the first light of dawn crept over the horizon, I was already dressed and pacing my room. I rubbed my neck raw, gnawed at my fingernails, and constantly smoothed the buttons down the front of my dress as I once again found myself anxiously waiting for contact from Soren. I told myself I shouldn't be ashamed of what had happened with Hale; I wasn't promised to Soren, and his silence over the past three months had led me to believe he wanted nothing to do with me. But still the guilt ate away at me, and I couldn't unsee the pained look in his eyes when he asked me what I wanted. I also couldn't unsee Hale, shirtless and looking down at me from above, calmly commanding me to worship him. The two images warred in my mind, and it caused me more stress than I knew what to do with.

When someone rapped at my bedroom door, I jumped, my heart nearly exploding out of my chest.

"Come in," I squeaked.

I expected Soren or maybe even Hale, but Syrena carefully slipped into the room.

I let out the breath I'd been holding, groaned, and collapsed in a miserable heap on the bed. Syrena climbed onto the mattress and nestled in beside me.

"How are you doing?" she asked softly.

"How do you think?" I moaned, my face buried in a pillow.

Syrena tenderly rubbed my back. We were quiet for a long time before she finally lay down beside me.

"Lina?"

I lifted my head slightly to peek up at her.

"I have to ask..." The princess picked at a piece of lint on the bedspread. "The one you were with last night... it was Hale, wasn't it?"

I pushed myself into a sitting position. My lips parted as I desperately tried to find words, but nothing came out. The silence spoke for itself, and Syrena sniffed and nodded.

"It makes sense," she said with a casual shrug, "that you and him have connected over the past few months. You both feel like outsiders. That's a strong bond. I understand. Really, I do."

"He said there was nothing between you two—"

"Oh, *gods*, no," she laughed, waving the comment away with a hurried flick of her wrist. The movement sent her stack of bracelets clanging. "No, I'm not... *no*. That's not why I'm here. I'm just worried about *you* is all."

"Why?"

"It's just..." She nibbled her lip. "I want you to be careful. I mean, Hale *is* half Night Sylph, after all."

A sudden wave of anger washed over me. "Hale's not like that."

Syrena's forehead wrinkled in concern. "It's in his blood, Lina. He might not think he's like that, but—"

"*I* know he's not like that," I barked. "And *you* know he's not like that! He's served your family for years, how can you even say that about him?"

Syrena's lips pinched as her eyes grew cold. "Have you ever asked if we've had any issues with him? Hmm?"

I wilted.

"No. You haven't." Something in Syrena changed. Her words became a weapon, each one landing with a venomous strike. "You don't know him better than I do, Lina. No one knows him better than I do. And I'm telling you, for your own good, stay away from him."

I tensed at her tone. Regret flickered over the princess's face, and the hard shell she'd adopted quickly melted away. The edge in her voice dissolved and she sighed.

"I'm sorry. I just... I want you to realize what you have in front of you." She slid my hand into hers. "You have a man who loves you, Lina. A king of all people. One who has everything to lose. And without a moment of hesitation, no matter what it might cost him, he chose *you*. Do you know how special that is? How *rare* that is?"

A lump formed in my throat, and my eyes pinched from unshed tears.

"You have something most of us could only ever dream of, Lina," Syrena continued. "So from one friend to another? I think you should choose him in return."

Syrena gave my hand a tender squeeze, slid off the bed, and with one last smile thrown over her shoulder, she exited the room. Her heels clicked down the hall, but stopped suddenly.

"Oh! You."

"Me. Good morning, Your Majesty."

"Not Majesty. Just Highness."

"My apologies."

"That's alright. It happens a lot. But I haven't taken the title of queen yet, because... well, just because."

"I see." There was a beat before the voice coughed. "Um... is Lina—"

"In her room?"

"Yes."

"She is."

"Wonderful. Thank you."

"You're welcome."

"Good day, Your Highness."

"Good day to you... whatever your name is."

"It's—"

Syrena's footsteps retreated.

"Never mind, then."

I glanced at the door to see who the voice belonged to, anticipation sitting heavy in my chest. When a pair of forest green eyes and a head of dark brown curls peeked around the door, I bounced off the bed.

"Xavier!"

I hurtled across the room and threw myself into his arms. He squeezed me tight, but when I pulled away and looked him up and down, I gasped at how his clothes hung loose on his body. He was alarmingly thinner than the last time I saw him.

"Gods, what have they been feeding you?"

"Winters in the mountains of Kylanthia aren't kind," Xavier said grimly, but he still managed to give me one of his signature winks. "Don't lie, though. You know I still look good."

I laughed and pulled him into another fierce hug. "Gods, I missed you. Really, though... how are you?"

Xavier let out a long, slow exhale and nodded solemnly. "I'm alright. War is terrifying. And miserable. And lonely. But all things considered, I'm good. At least I'm alive, and so is Soren. Speaking of Soren..." He raised an eyebrow in my direction.

I gulped. "Is it bad?"

Xavier grimaced and rubbed the back of his neck. "It's been a difficult few months. He was already on edge, so needless to say, this hasn't gone over great."

My heart sank. "I didn't hear from him! I thought he'd lost interest, or worse—"

"You don't have to explain yourself to me. I understand." Xavier's normally bright eyes grew dark. "He lost himself out there. The war consumed him. He didn't let himself focus on anything else. I barely recognized him half the time." He sighed. "Soren does that. He disappears in battle, becomes someone else. In his mind, the only thing that exists is violence and vengeance. I knew that about him, had seen it a few times too. But this... this was so much worse than ever before."

Xavier looked at me and tried to smile, but it fell flat. "So you're absolutely right. Soren should have sent word. He should have written a letter every week to keep you informed about the situation. But after seeing him out there... I understand why he didn't. You wouldn't have known that man, Lina. *He* didn't even know who he was."

Somehow, my heart broke even more.

"I have to see him."

Xavier winced. "I don't think that's a good idea. He's working through some things. He'll come to you when he's ready."

"Well, *I'm* working through some things too," I snapped, standing and planting my hands on my hips, "and I'm sick of waiting around for him. Where is he?"

"Lina..."

"*Where is he?*"

Xavier rolled his eyes and flung his hands to the ceiling in exasperation. "Fine! He's in the suite they prepared for him."

I lowered my arms, curled my fingers into determined fists, and stormed out of the room.

"If you tell him I told you, I'll deny everything!" Xavier called after me.

I stomped furiously down the hall with my head held high, and when I arrived at the guest quarters, I threw open the door without knocking. I found Soren in the middle of getting dressed, his fingers still in the process of fastening the buttons on a blue silk shirt. He looked up in surprise as I entered.

"We are going to talk, damn it!" I said through gritted teeth.

Soren's jaw clenched and his eyes iced over. "You want to talk, Lina? Fine. Let's talk." He stalked over to me and jabbed a threatening finger in my face. "Don't you *ever* lay your hands on me again, do you understand?"

I smacked his hand away. "Then don't abandon me and treat me like I'm nothing to you if I'm not."

Soren scoffed. "You know you're not nothing to me."

"No, I don't!"

"I told you I loved you!"

"Words don't mean anything if you don't prove them!"

"*You don't think I'm proving them?*" he roared, shoving his face in mine.

But for once I didn't recoil. I stayed right where I was, my feet fixed to the floor, my chin raised defiantly, refusing to back down as he raged.

"For the past three months I've been on the front lines spilling blood to protect *you,* Lina! I've been keeping quiet, lying low in the mountains, starving and miserable all winter so I can win a war *for you!* I didn't *touch* other women, I didn't even *think* about other women! It was *you* I thought about at night when I stroked myself, *your* face, the feeling of *your* lips, the taste of *you!*"

Soren's chest heaved, his breath puffing against my lips. "I *have* been proving it, Lina."

"And I didn't know!" I barked. "There was no way for me *to* know. Can't you see that?"

Soren took a shaky breath, calming slightly. His eyes softened, the anger replaced by sadness.

"Well, now you do," he muttered weakly.

I stared up at him, at the pain etched on his face and the emotion glinting in his eyes, and tried desperately to think of how to respond. Words failed me like they too often did, so instead I chose to do something I'd thought about for the past three months.

I grabbed his face and kissed him.

When his lips met mine, Soren froze in surprise, but soon his arms wrapped around my waist and yanked me closer. Suddenly it was as if no time had passed, and I was back in the warm, safe space I'd craved every night since we'd been apart. Soren's hands moved up my back and buried in my hair, pulling me deeper into his kiss. My hands roved over his chest, eagerly exploring every inch of him, relearning every muscle and curve. Soren's lips and tongue grew more demanding, and soon we clawed frantically at each other, making up for lost time.

Feverishly entwined, we stumbled backwards and collided with a nearby desk. Soren pulled away and caught the front of my dress with both hands, ripping firmly, and I gasped as the buttons burst to expose my bare skin. A low, lustful groan rumbled out of Soren's throat as he took both of my breasts in his hands and brought them to his mouth, taking turns tracing his tongue in circles around each of the peaked tips before sucking one into his mouth and sinking his teeth in. I threw my head back and moaned at the perfect amount of pain and pleasure, to which Soren responded by shoving me flat on the desk. He then fell to his knees, gruffly shoved my skirts up to my hips, and buried his face between my thighs.

I let out a quivering breath as his tongue worked me. I'd forgotten how good he was at this. *Gods*, was he good at this.

Soren licked two of his fingers and slipped them inside me, gently curling them in and out while he lapped at me, his tongue moving in ways that had my eyes rolling back in my head. I squirmed, my breath growing more ragged as the pleasure swelled. I fumbled for something to hold on to, knocking quills and ink off the desk.

"Oh *fuck...*" I moaned. "Don't stop, Soren. Please, don't stop."

Soren's fingers and tongue moved faster, pulling another moan from my mouth.

"Yes," I panted. "Oh, *gods*, yes!"

I wove my fingers into Soren's hair and pulled as the intensity built. At the last second, he sucked firmly, sending me hurtling over the edge. My back arched, and I cried out as pleasure rippled through every inch of me.

I was still trembling when Soren stood and lifted me into a seated position. He grabbed my face in one hand, forcing me to look at him, while the other loosened the lace on his pants. He held me there as he pulled out his length, positioned it between my thighs, and firmly thrust inside me. We both gasped at the sensation.

"You want to know how much I thought about you?" he breathed.

I moaned as he thrust again, this time harder.

"Every fucking second I thought about how perfect this feels."

Again, he pounded into me. I groaned, digging my nails deep into his back.

"Then fuck me like you missed me," I demanded.

Soren let out an animalistic growl and shoved me back down on the desk, slamming into me again and again, harder and faster each pass. I cried out in pleasure, gripping the sides of the desk to hold myself in place so he filled me to the brim. My legs shook as the pleasure built, and Soren lifted me to a seated position once more, holding me close as he nipped and sucked my neck the way I liked. I tore my nails down his back, forcing him to mutter a curse and hammer into me until I was screaming his name at the top of my lungs. Only when I climaxed and frenzied waves of bliss exploded through me did Soren allow himself to let go too, shoving himself as deep as he could and roaring as he shuddered and released.

We clung to each other, panting heavily, for only a few seconds before Soren slid himself out of me and pulled up his pants.

"There's something I need to take care of," he said brusquely.

He then stomped out of the room, slamming the door behind him. I stayed splayed on the desk with my mouth agape and my dignity gone, my mind even more scrambled than before.

AFTER FOLLOWING Soren all night as he stormed around the castle grounds to blow off steam, Hale needed to find a release of his own.

There was one brothel in town that would serve him, but under one condition: he could only use one of the low-caste girls, and she'd cost the price of their highest earner. Usually, it wasn't worth the trouble or humiliation. Over the years, Hale had found plenty of success on his own; rebellious Wood Sprites were notorious for seeking him out in the summer to antagonize their parents. But Hale desperately needed an outlet. So he paid the price, bent the prostitute over her dresser, and fucked her as quickly as possible. When he finished, he tipped and thanked the girl before proceeding to the closest tavern and drinking himself into a stupor. He woke up in the alley behind the establishment the next morning with a black eye and scattered memories of being jumped by a group of spiteful middle-caste Fae men still on edge from the Nether attack. Hale, however, had fared better than they had. His black eye would be healed within the hour; the damage he'd inflicted on them would last days.

Hale had just shuffled back into the palace and was busy formulating a strategy on how best to get back to his bedroom to wash up without running into Lina, when a hand grabbed him by the collar and dragged him into a darkened corridor. He was roughly thrown against a wall, and Hale instinctively reached for one of his knives, but froze when he saw who pinned him.

"It's you, isn't it?" Soren snarled in Hale's face. "You're the one she's fucking."

Hale kept his mouth shut, breathing sharply through his nose. The king smelled like Lina. Fucker probably just left her. Probably planned this because he wanted to get a rise out of him. Hale dare not lay a hand on a Fae king, but it was going to be *really* hard not to.

Soren shook him so hard Hale's teeth rattled. "Say something, you Nether bastard!"

"It didn't get that far," Hale grunted.

Soren wrapped a hand around Hale's throat and tightened his grip, cutting off the air to his lungs. He held him there until stars scattered across Hale's vision, before eventually letting out a furious growl and releasing him.

The king pushed away from the wall and stepped back, glaring at the ground and shaking with contained rage, but there was pain in his voice when he spoke next.

"Do you love her?"

Hale just stared at him as he attempted to catch his breath.

"Because *I* do." Soren looked up, meeting Hale's gaze. "She's gone through hell these past few months. She deserves to have something good." He swallowed hard, anger melting away to reveal an expression of pain and sincerity. "Could you give that to her?"

Hale's heart skipped a beat.

"What?" he croaked.

"You heard me."

Hale paused for a moment, searching Soren's face for a sign this was some sort of trap, but he found none.

"Could you?" Soren pressed, emotion glistening in his eyes.

Hale took a deep breath and answered honestly. "I... I don't know."

Soren nodded and looked away, toying with his signet ring pensively. "I knew I could love her the moment I watched her offer her own life in exchange for her brother's. I made my choice then, and it was the easiest decision I've ever made. I'd make it over and over again. Because she's worth it."

"What are you asking me, Your Majesty?"

"I'm asking you if you're capable of giving Lina your heart. Because if you can, if you are *certain* that you can, that it's possible for you to give her your love, wholly and completely..." He swallowed, his voice breaking. "Then I'll step away, and you two will be free to explore whatever it is you have. But..."

All the vulnerability Soren had shown abruptly dissolved as the edge returned to his words, and he took a threatening step towards him. Once again, Hale fought the urge to reach for a knife.

"If there is any sliver of doubt in your mind that you are capable of giving Lina your heart, if you are not as certain as I've been since the night I met her, then I'm asking you to do what's best for her."

Could he love Lina? Fuck, did he even deserve someone like Lina?

Hale frowned.

No. No one deserved Lina, least of all someone like him. He wasn't even sure a creature like him was capable of love. He'd have to be delusional to think there could be anything between the two of them.

So Hale ignored the ache in his chest, wiped his expression blank like he had infinite times before, and squared his shoulders.

"You have my word, Your Majesty. I won't come between you two."

Soren's eyelids flickered, and he let out what sounded like a sigh of relief. Then, he extended his hand. "Do we have a bargain?"

A dark pit formed in Hale's stomach.

"You won't lay a hand on her?" Soren pressed.

Hale took a deep breath. What he wanted, how he felt, didn't matter. This was for Lina's own good.

"I won't lay a hand on her unless her life is in danger," he amended.

Soren considered and nodded.

There was no turning back now.

Hale accepted the king's hand. "Yes. We have a bargain."

AFTER I RAN BACK to my room, clutching my ruined dress to my body to protect my decency, I washed up and redressed for the day, then headed down to breakfast.

When I arrived in the dining room, Syrena, Kaspar, and Xavier were already nibbling at their food in uncomfortable silence. I wasn't sure if I was relieved or disappointed Hale wasn't there.

I pretended not to feel everyone's eyes on me as I entered.

"Good morning," I said, feigning a happy smile and slipping into an empty chair.

"Good morning," Syrena and Xavier chirped at the same time. They turned to look at each other and blinked in surprise.

Even though it was morning, a large goblet of wine sat in front of Kaspar's plate. For a moment, I considered asking him to pour me one as well. Gods knew I could use it.

When Soren entered the room, Xavier rose respectfully, and Syrena forced a cheerful smile onto her face.

"Good morning," she said, gesturing to the seat beside me. "Will you be joining us for breakfast?"

"No." Soren clasped his hands behind his back. "I'm leaving."

"What?" Xavier and Syrena exclaimed simultaneously.

I pushed back from the table. "What do you mean you're leaving?"

"I need to get back to my troops. Erith's forces could be regrouping. I need to be there to command them if she strikes."

"But we've only just arrived," Xavier said.

Soren shot him a sideways glance. "You're not coming with me. You're staying here."

"*What?*" Xavier and Syrena shrieked together.

"I want someone here to protect Lina."

Syrena crossed her arms. "Hale is perfectly cable of protecting us."

"I want someone else here too."

Judging by the stubborn glint in Soren's eye and the way he held himself, with his back rigid and his chin high, I knew there would be no point in trying to reason with him. He'd made up his mind, and any argument, no matter how strong, would fall on deaf ears.

"But…" Xavier tried to remain stoic, but his expression looked more like that of a wounded puppy. "I go where you go."

Soren shook his head. "Not this time."

Xavier seemed ready to argue, but after a stern frown from Soren, he wilted and attempted to appear cool and unaffected as he bowed his head. "Yes, sir."

Soren's gaze then drifted to me.

"I'd prefer it if you moved to a different location like we originally discussed, but something tells me you want to stay here."

I hesitated for a moment, thinking about leaving Hale and Syrena and starting over again in a new place. Everything I'd grown accustomed to suddenly uprooted, in-depth interrogations about being human, the agonizing loneliness…

Soren was right. I *didn't* want to do that again.

Soren nodded solemnly, understanding my pensive silence. "As long as you're happy, Lina. That's all I want. For you to be happy."

I stared at him, trying to make sense of the chaos in my heart. I wanted to be angry with him. Hell, I *was* angry with him. He'd kept me in the dark and expected me to follow along blindly with whatever he said like a loyal dog following dutifully behind its master. That alone should have hardened my heart, but as I stared at Soren now, his shoulders slumped in defeat and his gaze more sincere and honest than I'd ever seen, it screamed at me to let him back in.

The pull to him was undeniable. And looking back, it always had been.

Even when I'd decided to hate him for giving Wynn to the Sluagh, I'd had to physically fight against the desire to be close to him when we drank by the fire in his study.

When Xavier was in trouble, I had run to Soren.

When I'd recovered from the attack in the woods, I went to Soren.

Good or bad, happy or sad, it was Soren I ran to because something about him felt right.

More than that, he felt like home.

And I'd really been missing home.

I walked over and tenderly slipped my hands into his.

"Lina..." Soren lowered his voice so he was speaking solely to me. "I'm sorry. For everything. You were right, I should have asked you if you wanted to come here. I should have written to you while I was away. I should have done a lot of things differently. I just..." His brow furrowed as he struggled to formulate the words. "I don't know how to do this. I don't how to be a king and a warrior and a decent lover all at the same time. I've never done it before. But I want to learn, and I'd like to learn with you, if you'll let me. You don't have to love me back, but—"

"I do," I blurted.

Soren's eyes widened.

I gave him a small smile. "I *do* love you, Soren."

Soren sniffed and tucked a rogue strand of hair behind my ear before dragging me into a kiss. When he broke away, he wrapped his arms around me, and I nestled into my favorite spot at the center of his chest.

"I'll come back to you," he murmured, pressing his lips to my neck one last time.

I shut my eyes, relishing the feeling. "You better."

He chuckled, the noise vibrating through his body and into mine. When he pulled away, he embraced Xavier, clapping him firmly on the back.

"Take care of her," he commanded, his voice stern.

"Yes, sir."

The men broke away and nodded curtly, their feelings for

each other unspoken but understood. Then Soren turned and bowed to the prince and princess.

"Your Highnesses, thank you for your hospitality. This time, I *will* be in touch."

Without another word, the king of Astoria left me for the second time.

Chapter 22

(100 years prior)

Soren slipped out of the coatroom, smoothed his hair, and tucked in his shirt. He glanced cautiously in both directions to make sure no one from the ball was casually meandering down the hallway before opening the door wider to allow a voluptuous Fae woman, also in a state of disarray, to sidle out behind him. He didn't even know her name. All he knew was he'd seen her across the dance floor, given her a charming smile and a wink, and within the hour they'd ended up here. Like most of his conquests, she was an easy, meaningless target, but a fun one nonetheless.

"Thanks again," the woman tittered. She pressed her body against Soren's and walked her index and middle fingers up the front of his chest. "You won't forget me, will you?"

Soren kissed her hand before slipping one of her fingers

into his mouth and sucking firmly. The woman blushed and giggled.

"How could you say that?" Soren asked with a lopsided grin. "I would *never*."

He would.

"You really meant what you said before?" the woman asked, looking up at him with a heavy-lidded, starry-eyed gaze.

Most women gave him that look. To be honest, it was becoming a little dull. Sure, it was fun in the moment, but after all was said and done and he looked back on everything, Soren couldn't help but feel a little disappointed. It had all been so easy. Too easy.

"Of course I did," Soren purred. In his peripheral vision, he was still warily keeping watch for any prying eyes. "I meant every word."

He hadn't.

"Go on now," Soren commanded, giving the woman a brief peck on the lips before spinning her around and sending her off with a smack to the backside. "And remember, this is our little secret."

The woman giggled once more and pranced into the depths of the palace. Soren let out a weary exhale and headed in the other direction, back towards the merry music and laughter coming from the ballroom. Lerian always threw the best parties. It was one of the few things they did better than Astoria, and Soren was eager to get back and see what other sumptuous pleasures he could indulge in while he was here.

Soren checked his trousers were buttoned one last time before starting for the ballroom. When he passed a darkened doorway, a scoff sounded from the shadows. He spun, instinctively grabbing for his sword before remembering he wasn't wearing it tonight.

"You're fucking unbelievable."

A figure with white-blonde hair and angry blue eyes slipped out of the darkness. Erith, sipping liquor straight from the bottle, wore a long sleeve dress that clung to every crevice and curve on her body. Soren might have actually found her attractive tonight had it not been for that typical scowl polluting her stunning features. Such a waste of beauty.

"Is it even possible for you to think with something other than your cock?" Erith asked, her upper lip curling in disgust.

Soren gave her a dazzling smile, a response sure to get her blood boiling. "You know, Erith, I've noticed every time I talk to you, you seem to bring up my cock."

She took a swig from the bottle and wiped her mouth. "Well, it's certainly busy."

"Busy with everyone except you."

Erith's eyes narrowed as she crossed her arms. "You couldn't handle me."

Soren chuckled. "I could, I just *really* don't want to. And that drives you crazy, doesn't it?"

Erith pursed her lips and stood a little taller, looking down her nose at him. "Does it ever get tiring being such an arrogant prick?"

"No. Does it get tiring being a frigid bitch?"

Erith glowered at him. The hand that wasn't holding the bottle tensed, sending her long nails digging into her arm. Soren twisted the dagger even further by taking a step towards her and gently brushing a knuckle against her cheek in a loving caress. It was a move he'd used on countless women, and it always, without fail, brought them to their knees.

"Of course not," he murmured, looking Erith up and down appreciatively. "That's just how they make you lot up there in Kylanthia, isn't it? Cold and harsh, just like that territory of yours."

Erith smacked his hand away. "One day you'll get what's coming to you, Soren. And I personally can't wait to watch."

She stormed off in a huff, but Soren had heard her pulse quicken, and seen the way his touch had caused her breasts to peak beneath that skintight satin.

Too. Fucking. Easy.

He snickered to himself and continued on his way.

When Soren arrived in the ballroom, he scanned the crowd, his gaze wandering over the couples dancing, the fire-spinners, the contortionists, and luxurious decorations, until it landed on a mop of ash-brown curls in the corner. Soren was surprised to see his brother right where he'd left him: locked deep in conversation with Princess Ilora of Merimaya. Silvain said something, and Ilora touched his arm as she threw her head back and laughed heartily. Soren tilted his head curiously and focused on his brother. Silvain's blue eyes sparkled and a ruddy flush appeared in the apples of his cheeks. Sure, it could have been from the drink, but as Soren glanced between his brother and the princess, he sensed it was something else. His suspicions were confirmed when Ilora brushed a curl from his brother's face and tucked it behind his ear, causing the pink in Silvain's cheeks to deepen. Soren chuckled under his breath and shook his head.

Good for you, little brother. She's one of the good ones.

"Silvain!"

Soren's gaze darted across the ballroom to see where the shout had just come from. Kaspar stormed across the dance floor towards Ilora and Silvain, his eyes glinting with rage. Silvain looked up and gave the prince of Lerian a friendly wave.

"Hey, Kas! What's—"

Kaspar shoved Silvain roughly, sending him stumbling backwards. "Where the fuck is your brother?"

Soren instantly bolted across the room towards the two of

them. He got to his younger brother just as Kaspar shoved him again.

"I said where is he?!"

"Hey!" Soren barked. Kaspar started to turn, but Soren caught him by the back of his jacket before he could twist all the way around and dragged him into one of the hallways branching off the ballroom. Silvain faced the crowd of curious onlookers who'd gathered and casually waved them away.

"Nothing to see here," he said brightly. "Carry on."

Once they were far enough from prying eyes, Soren tossed Kaspar forward, releasing his hold on the prince's collar.

"What the hell was that, Kas?" he hissed.

"You son of a bitch!"

Kaspar tackled Soren to the ground. The prince was stronger than he looked, and he got a few decent blows in before Silvain and Ilora caught up.

"Kas!" Silvain stooped and grabbed Kaspar from behind, hoisting him off his older brother. "Stop! What are you doing?!"

Kaspar managed to wriggle free, whirled, and punched Silvain in the nose, the resounding crack echoing down the empty hallway.

Not wanting to hurt Kaspar, Soren had been holding back up until now. But that sound of his brother's bones breaking... he'd heard it too many times when they were young, and it ignited something deep inside him.

Now all bets were off.

Soren threw out his hands and flicked his wrists, releasing one pump of his magic, which blasted into Kaspar and sent him hurtling through the air. The prince collided with the opposite wall and slid to the floor, groaning in pain, but Soren wasn't finished. He charged over, grabbed Kaspar by the throat, and hoisted him to his feet.

Silvain rushed up behind his brother and put a hand on his shoulder. "Soren, it's alright. I'm fine, really!"

No. No one hurt Silvain. *No one.* Not anymore.

So Soren shrugged his brother off and tightened his grip around Kaspar's throat.

"Don't you ever," he began, his voice quivering with rage, "*ever* lay a hand on my family again, do you understand me?"

"That's rich coming from you," Kaspar croaked.

Soren searched Kaspar's eyes. A maddened, instinctual fury flared in them. The realization finally clicked, and a hint of panic fluttered in Soren's chest.

He'd been caught.

Soren dropped Kaspar to the floor. The prince crumpled, coughing and rubbing his neck, but still managed to look up at Soren with an icy glare.

"I never want to see your face in this territory again," he rasped.

Something formed deep in Soren's stomach. It was something he should feel all the time, but rarely did.

Guilt. Gnawing, stomach-churning guilt.

"Is *anyone* going to explain what's going on?" Silvain sighed, pressing the hem of his velvet tunic to his nose as blood dripped from both nostrils.

"Go pack," Soren said firmly. "I'll tell Father you and I are going back to Astoria tonight."

"What?" Silvain exclaimed, glancing over at Ilora. "But we just got here."

"*Now*, Silvain."

Silvain opened his mouth to protest, but decided better of it. Instead, he gave Ilora a half smile and shrugged helplessly. She looped her arm through his.

"Come on. I'll take care of that nose before you go."

They disappeared down the hall. When they'd gone, Soren

turned back to Kaspar and forced himself to meet the prince's gaze before clearing his throat.

"For what it's worth, I'm sorry."

Kaspar scoffed. "No, you're not. You're just sorry you got caught."

Soren sighed. There would be no reasoning with Kaspar, but he understood why. If their roles were reversed, Soren would feel the same. He wouldn't waste his breath on an argument. Instead, he headed back towards the party.

"You're not even going to try to explain yourself?" Kaspar's voice chased after him. "You're a fucking coward, Soren!"

At that, Soren froze.

Hot, stinging fury filled his veins and clouded his mind, and before he could stop himself, he spun to face Kaspar.

"I'm not going to waste my time defending myself to someone like *you*. Your family can hide behind all the riches you want, but everyone knows there's not a shred of magic among the lot of you. You're a pathetic excuse for royalty. Hell, you might as well be low-borns."

The second the words spilled from Soren's mouth, he regretted them. He didn't mean it. Kaspar was his friend, and Lerian had been Astoria's ally for thousands of years. He'd been angry and embarrassed and had lashed out, he didn't—

"Get out," Kaspar demanded. "*Now.* Whatever friendship we had is over. From now on, you're dead to me."

His godsdamned pride made Soren hold his head high and reply, "Good."

∼

(100 years prior, and ten minutes before that)

HALE CREPT INTO THE LIBRARY, keeping to the shadows as he silently padded down the stacks. Finally, he laid eyes on what he'd gone in search of.

A figure sat in the window seat in the corner, clutching her knees to her chest while her salty tears splattered the bodice of her elegant party dress. Hale took a deep breath to muster his courage and slid out from the darkness.

"Syrena?"

The princess's head jerked up, and she quickly wiped her face. "Shit, you scared me!"

"Sorry," Hale muttered.

"It's alright." Syrena sniffed and untucked her legs, smoothing her gown. "I just didn't hear you come in is all."

Hale frowned, looking her up and down. "What's wrong?"

Syrena's bottom lip quivered, but she forced it into an unconvincing smile and shook her head. "Nothing."

Hale slid onto the seat beside her. "You can tell me."

Tears filled Syrena's eyes, and she fidgeted with one of her bracelets. "Alright... promise not to tell anyone?"

"Who would I tell?"

"Kas." Syrena spat the name.

Hale put an earnest hand to his heart. "It'll be our secret. I swear."

Syrena nodded and gathered her strength. "It's... it's Soren of Astoria."

A pit formed in Hale's stomach at that name, but he kept his face blank.

"What about him?" he asked innocently.

"Well," Syrena began, a tear finally sneaking out and trickling down her cheek, "we've been spending more time together lately—"

"I know."

Hale winced. He couldn't let her learn how many times his

darkness had followed behind them. She'd be furious. She'd be so angry she'd probably never speak to him again, and Hale couldn't bear that.

"I meant..." He cleared his throat. "Go on."

"Well, over the past few months we've been spending more time together, and we've talked a lot about Astoria. I told him how beautiful I think the land is there, and how I'd like to visit more. Then he was saying how well I would fit in there. How good I would look among the ladies of his court."

More tears streamed down Syrena's cheeks, and Hale's heart ached. He wanted nothing more than to kiss them all away.

"He said the most beautiful things I've ever heard, and I was actually starting to think... well, that we might have a future. One with him as king of Astoria and me at his side as queen. I told him that, and he said he could picture it too."

The pit in Hale's stomach gouged deeper. "What happened?"

"I... I figured if he wants to marry me someday, then we should... you know... *be together.*"

Hale's blood heated with rage, but he shoved his emotions down.

"Did he hurt you?" he asked, deadly calm.

"No! Gods, no. It was wonderful."

Bile rose in Hale's throat.

"But... but then...." Syrena cried harder, her breaths coming in shallow gulps. "Tonight at the ball, I went to look for him and... I found him on the veranda... and this woman was on his lap... and he was telling her the exact same things he said to me."

Unable to hold herself together any longer, the princess broke down in hysterical sobs, throwing her arms around Hale and burying her face in his chest. He hesitated for a moment, then, holding his breath, gently slid an arm around the princess's shoulders. In the six years since he'd known her, she didn't shy away from his touch. Instead, she allowed him to hold her close until the tears had subsided.

"Maybe I just wasn't any good," Syrena finally said, smearing her nose on the sleeve of her gown.

"No," Hale snapped, "that's not it."

"You don't know that, you weren't there."

No. He'd been in his room beating the shit out of a pillow while his darkness watched from the crack beneath the door.

"Trust me. The problem isn't you. It's him."

Syrena miserably shook her head. "He has his pick of women. It was stupid to think he'd pick me."

"It's not stupid." Hale's heart pounded frantically as he took another deep breath and prepared himself to speak the words he'd wanted to say since he was fourteen. "I... I'd pick you."

"You're just saying that."

"I'm not. I mean it. I'd choose you."

One of his fingers found its way to Syrena's hair and twirled a curl without her noticing. "I'll always choose you, Syrena."

Syrena looked up, the intensity of her bright green gaze nearly making Hale melt. His stomach flopped and fluttered, but Hale did his best to remain cool and collected.

Syrena studied him. Then, achingly slow, she leaned in and carefully, cautiously, brushed her lips against his. Hale blushed and pulled away, ducking his head to avert his gaze, but Syrena sat up straight, grabbed Hale's face in her hands, and hauled him forward to kiss him again.

The princess kissed him furiously, gripping the collar of his leather jacket to drag him closer. Hale eased, losing himself in her smell, her soft lips, and her frenzied movements as he slipped his arms around her waist. He became so caught up that he lost control, and without realizing it was happening, the black mist slipped out of him and materialized around them. Syrena briefly opened her eyes, and when she saw the cloud of darkness, she immediately screamed and pushed Hale away. He opened his eyes too and gasped, the fog instantly evaporating.

"I'm sorry!" he blurted. "I'm sorry, I didn't mean to!"

"Get away from me!" Syrena scrambled to the other side of the window seat and cowered in fear. "Don't fucking touch me!"

"I'm so sorry," Hale choked, his throat tightening as tears stung his eyes. "I swear, it wasn't trying to hurt you—"

"Hey!" Kaspar strode into the library. "Did I just hear someone yell?"

Syrena glanced at Hale, her eyes wild with panic. He stared at her, silently pleading with her not to say anything. To his relief, Syrena smoothed her hair and sat upright, painting an alarmingly convincing smile on her perfect face.

"Hale was just telling me a scary story, that's all."

"Oh." Kaspar's forehead crinkled. "That's... weird. Anyway, Ilmarien and I are bored, so we're going to spike the punch bowl. I want to see what Mother and Father look like when they're..." He trailed off and squinted at Syrena. "Have you been crying?"

Syrena tossed her hair. "No."

"Yes you have."

"Have not."

"What happened?"

"Nothing!"

Kaspar turned to Hale. "Why is she crying?"

Hale's eyes widened as his gaze bounced between the twins. "It... it's not my place to say."

"Tell me."

"Don't tell him, Hale!" Syrena begged. "Please!"

Kaspar raised himself higher. "As your future king, I command you to tell me what's wrong with my sister."

Syrena rolled her eyes. "As your future queen, I command you *not* to tell him!"

"Tell me!"

Hale shut his eyes, shaking his head. "I... I can't..."

Kaspar stepped forward and shoved him. "Come on, demon, just spit it out!"

"Syrena slept with Soren of Astoria!"

Syrena gasped.

A tidal wave of shame washed over Hale, and he frantically racked his brain for a way to backtrack. But before he could, Syrena leapt to her feet and ran out of the room.

"Syrena, wait!" Hale called after her. "I'm sorry!"

But she was gone.

When Hale turned back to Kaspar, the prince's eyes had grown dark.

"I'm going to kill him," he declared.

CHAPTER 23

———————

A HUNDRED YEARS LATER, HALE SAT IN THAT SAME LIBRARY, IN that same seat by the window, staring out at the moon as it appeared on the horizon and began its rise over the palace.

He heard Lina before he saw her.

He could hear the pounding of her heart, could hear her footsteps on the tile floor even though she was tiptoeing towards him, and he could hear her shallow, anxious breaths puffing in and out as she tried not to make a sound. Hale could easily disappear into the depths of the palace to dodge another interaction with her. He'd been doing it all day. But he decided against it. He couldn't run from her forever.

"There you are. I've been looking everywhere for you."

Hale didn't respond. He kept his gaze on the moon, too afraid to look at her. He was worried that if he did, if he lost himself in those beautiful eyes, then he'd lose all control and tell her everything. He'd tell her about the bargain he'd made with Soren, reveal the feelings he'd shoved down to do it, and admit he was a monster incapable of love, but because of her, because she had never treated him that way, he'd foolishly started to think that maybe, just maybe, he might be capable of it after all.

But he'd made his choice. If it meant Lina would be happy and loved and taken care of, then he could suffer. He'd suffered his whole life, what was a little more?

Hale continued to stare out at the night sky as Lina sat on the other side of the window seat. She was wearing a sleeveless emerald dress, cut low in the front and the back. Gods, she looked beautiful. Painfully so.

"Are you coming to dinner?" she asked quietly.

"Not tonight."

Lina nodded and glanced down at her hands in her lap, absentmindedly picking at a fingernail. It was a nervous tick she'd developed, Hale had noticed. That and rubbing her collarbone. Hale sneaked a glance at those collarbones, on display for the world in that maddeningly revealing dress. Gods, if only he could have touched her one last time.

"You weren't at breakfast this morning either."

Hale refocused on the moon. "No."

"Are you avoiding me?"

"Yes."

Lina sighed. Hale didn't have to look over at her to know she had tears in her eyes. She was always crying about something or other, but he didn't mind. She felt things so deeply, so fully, and wasn't afraid to show it.

Hale respected her for that. It took courage. More than he had.

"Hale," Lina began, her voice cracking slightly, "I have to tell you—"

Hale cut her off. "You don't have to say anything. I already know."

Lina chuckled. "Of course you do."

Despite what she hinted at, for once he hadn't gleaned the

knowledge by watching and listening from shadowy corners. Syrena was how he'd found out that Lina and Soren had worked things out. She'd found him after Soren left and informed him about the exchange at breakfast.

"I'm happy for you," Hale said. "When you find Wynn, you two will live a very comfortable life in Astoria. If you choose not to return to the human realm, that is."

He felt her eyes boring into him.

Don't look at her. Don't you dare look at her.

"How is it so easy for you?"

"What?"

"Not feeling anything?"

Hale couldn't fight it any longer. He turned his gaze to hers, softening under the emotion in her eyes. "I feel, Lina. I feel everything so much it scares me. I have to bury it in a cold, dark place just to get through the day."

Lina's eyebrows pinched. "Why bury it at all?"

"Because if I start to let it out, I won't be able to stop."

"Is that such a bad thing, though?"

"It could get me in trouble."

"But..." Lina's throat bobbed. "Maybe something wonderful could happen too."

"Wonderful things don't happen to me," Hale replied bitterly.

"They should." Lina's bottom lip trembled, the watery shine in her eyes only amplified by the silver light of the moon. "You deserve something good, Hale."

Hale's heart ached as a tear slipped out and trickled down Lina's cheek. He instinctively reached out to brush it away, but remembered his bargain with Soren in the nick of time. Hale curled his fingers into a fist and returned it to his side.

Lina sniffled as another tear fell. A lump formed in Hale's

throat. He wanted to touch her. He *needed* to touch her. He needed to take away that pain shining in her eyes.

Without thinking, Hale allowed his darkness to materialize. His heart pounded as he sent the fog forward, rolling and curling like waves on the ocean. Lina looked up as it swirled towards her.

She wasn't afraid.

She didn't pull back or scream.

Instead, when the darkness sidled up to her, she smiled. Hale coaxed it to waft over Lina's cheek in a delicate caress. Lina shut her eyes at the cool breath of mist against her skin, her smile stretching wider.

Hale's gaze drifted lower, and the darkness followed, brushing along Lina's jaw, then down the side of her neck. Judging by the way Lina's skin pebbled with goosebumps as she leaned her head to the side and let out a barely audible moan, she liked it.

She liked it a lot.

A twinge of arousal stirred in Hale at that moan, and he ordered the tendril to repeat what it had just done. It licked at Lina's skin, making her breathing pick up speed. Then it moved between her shoulder blades and skimmed down her spine, making her shiver. The tongue of darkness returned to her neck, then circled those flawless collarbones before lapping at the dip between them. Eyes still shut, Lina leaned her head back and let out a small whimper. The fog stroked up the center of her neck, then her chin, then up to her mouth. A hazy finger of black traced the delicate skin of Lina's lips, making them quiver with desire.

When the mist pulled away, Lina exhaled sharply, opened her eyes, and met Hale's gaze. Her chest quickly rose and fell, and her body quaked like she'd been caught in the cold. Hale was breathing heavy too, and as he stared back at her, he knew.

He never should have let her go.

Hale swallowed hard. He had to tell her. He had to tell her everything.

"Lina, I—"

"There you two are!"

The mist dissipated, and both Hale and Lina whipped their heads to the doorway. Syrena strode towards them.

"Dinner's been on the table for ten minutes. What are you doing in here?"

Lina cleared her throat and stood, smoothing the front of her dress. "Sorry, we just..." She glanced at Hale, then ducked her head and brushed past the princess. "Sorry."

Syrena watched Lina exit the library, then turned back to Hale and raised an eyebrow. "That was odd."

Hale didn't respond. He just stared out the window again, sinking back into his previous state of melancholy.

Syrena wandered over and lowered herself onto the cushioned seat beside him. "Will you be joining us?"

"No."

Syrena sighed. "This is for the best, Hale."

"I know."

They sat in silence until Syrena slowly reached out and slid her hand into Hale's. He jumped at her touch, looking down at their joined hands in surprise.

"Maybe..." Syrena nervously licked her lips. "Maybe this just opens up other opportunities for you. With other people."

She looked up at him, her bright eyes hopeful.

Hale's brow furrowed. "What do you—"

Before he could finish, Syrena leaned in and pressed her lips to his. Hale let her kiss him for a few seconds, but eventually pulled away.

"What are you doing?" he muttered.

"What does it look like I'm doing?" She leaned in again, but Hale dodged her.

"Why?"

"What do you mean, *why*?" Syrena laughed. "You know I've always had feelings for you."

She shut her eyes and leaned in again, but when her lips were about to graze Hale's once more, he spoke.

"And now that someone else wants me, it's safe to show them?"

Syrena's eyes snapped open. "No, that's not... I..." Her words fell flat on her tongue.

Carefully, Hale maneuvered out of her grasp and rose to his feet.

"I love you, Syrena. I always have, and I always will. But not like that. Not anymore."

Syrena scoffed bitterly and crossed her arms. "Really? Because of *her*?"

Hale frowned. "No. Because of me."

He started for the exit, leaving Syrena behind on the window seat. A sniffle made him freeze and glance back over his shoulder. Same as she had a hundred years prior, Syrena tucked her knees to her chest and began to cry when she thought no one was watching.

SYRENA WAS in a foul mood the next morning for our training session. More foul than the rest of us, which was saying a lot. Xavier was still pouting about his "demotion," as he referred to it, and I had tossed and turned all night worrying about Soren, fantasizing about Hale's darkness grazing the skin on more intimate parts of my body, and feeling guilty for thinking about both things at the same time.

But the princess of Lerian had us both beat as she stormed into the courtyard without saying a word, rolled up her sleeves, snatched up two long daggers, tossed her braid over her shoulder, and took a fighting stance. She jerked her head towards the weapons table, silently ordering me to arm myself.

"Good morning to you too," I mumbled, grabbing two blades of my own.

Xavier leaned against a nearby pillar, still chomping on a sticky bun from breakfast as he watched the two of us take our places.

"Shouldn't we stretch beforehand?" I asked.

"No."

Syrena lunged at me without warning. I barely had enough time to block before she expertly knocked one of my daggers out of my hand and kicked my legs out from under me. I landed on my back with a grunt.

"Move your feet," Xavier called across the courtyard, his words garbled as he spoke around a mouthful of pastry.

I groaned and rolled over onto my side, pushing myself upright. "If I want your input, I'll ask."

Xavier shrugged and took another bite, licking the sugar from his fingers afterwards. "Suit yourself."

I stood and composed myself.

"Are you alright?" I asked Syrena, slightly taken aback by the steely glint in her eyes.

"Perfect. Never better." Her voice was alarmingly chipper.

The princess lunged again. This time I was better prepared, but Syrena attacked with such ferocity that she quickly got the better of me, disarming me of both daggers before finishing me off with a solid kick to the chest. I was knocked backwards, the wind whooshing from my lungs as I slammed into the ground.

Xavier jerked upright and stomped over, his face stern.

"Hey!" he snapped. "That was a cheap shot."

Syrena glared at him. "It was not. It was a real-life scenario. She has to learn what to do in situations like this."

Xavier scoffed. "Oh, please. Your bullshit might work on other people, but I see right through you, Princess."

Syrena's eyes narrowed. "I don't know what you're talking about."

"Yes you do." Xavier lowered his face to hers, forcing her to take a step back. "If there's one thing I hate more than anything, it's a bully. So back off, or deal with me."

Syrena cackled in disbelief. "Are you *threatening* me?"

"No, I'm challenging you. Learn the difference." Xavier snatched one of the daggers out of the princess's hand. "Pick on someone who actually knows what they're doing."

The patronizing way Syrena looked Xavier up and down would have crippled anyone else's pride, but not Xavier.

"*You?*" Syrena sneered.

"What's the matter, Princess? Scared?"

Syrena bristled and backed away from him. "Fine."

"Fine."

The two took defensive stances, but not before Xavier ripped off his shirt. He'd lost weight in Kylanthia with Soren, but his muscles were still impressively defined. She tried not to show it, but Syrena's gaze flicked over his body, lingering just a little too long on the v-shaped outline low on his hips.

Xavier clocked the princess's stare and jerked his chin to her, a cocky half smile alighting on his lips. "You're welcome to take yours off too."

Syrena's expression hardened.

Without breaking eye contact, she squared her shoulders, brought her fingers to the buttons of her blouse, and unfastened them. She viciously tore off the top, revealing a lacy corset underneath, and tossed it at Xavier's feet. For once, the man was speechless.

I peeled myself off the ground and cautiously backed away from the oncoming storm.

Xavier managed to pry his eyes from Syrena's chest and cleared his throat. "Ready, Your Highness?"

"Are you?" Syrena cooed.

Xavier let out a low chuckle. "Oh, I was born for this, Princess."

"That makes two of us."

Syrena attacked with a vengeance, Xavier meeting her half-way. The two collided, transforming into a flurry of slicing, grunting, stabbing, and blocking. They expertly matched each other, both often attempting a thrust or guard, but the other reading their mind and meeting them there. Finally, Xavier was able to switch up one of his moves at the last second and disarm one of Syrena's knives. She responded with a furious growl and savagely flung herself at Xavier, knocking one of the knives from his hand as well before kneeing him in the stomach. Xavier coughed as the air whooshed out of him, but he didn't miss a beat, expertly dodging Syrena's next attack before kicking her second weapon out of her hand. When Xavier went in with the finishing blow, Syrena ducked out of the way, grabbed his wrist and twisted, flipping him firmly onto his back. She fell to her knees, straddling him, and angled his own knife to his throat.

The two stared at each other, breathing heavily, for a few long, tense beats. Eventually, Xavier grinned and gave Syrena a lustful once-over.

"Not bad, Princess. Next time take everything off. You'll have better range of motion without that corset."

Syrena's eyes narrowed and she opened her mouth, but hurried footsteps in the distance cut her off.

Soren barreled into the courtyard, his chest heaving and his eyes wide.

"Soren!" I gasped, running to him. I traced my hands over his shoulders and abdomen in an anxious hunt for any wounds. "What's wrong? Are you hurt?"

"No," he panted, shaking his head, "I'm not hurt."

"Then what are you doing here?"

"I came back as soon as I saw it."

Xavier and Syrena both scrambled up off the ground, the latter grabbing her shirt and hurriedly clutching it to her body to protect her modesty.

"What happened?" Xavier asked.

Soren's face darkened. "It's Erith. She's attacked Merimaya."

SOREN HAD ME, Kaspar, Syrena, Hale, and Xavier gathered in the great hall.

He leaned forward on the table, hands braced on either side of him, his expression grim.

"I'd just passed over Kylanthia's borders when I happened to look back. I saw smoke on the horizon, and decided I had enough time to go scout out what it was. When I arrived, Merimaya's capitol was in flames. They were caught completely by surprise. I picked off whoever I could on the outskirts, but they need reinforcements. That's when I turned back to give you the news."

Kaspar started pacing while Syrena fretfully wrung her hands.

"What of the royal family?" she asked, her voice tight with panic. "Are they alright?"

Soren shook his head. "I'm not sure."

Syrena groaned and ran a hand through her hair, then faced her brother. "Kas, what do we do?"

"You send troops," Soren stated. "They're your friends, your allies. You go to help them."

"Don't tell me how to run my own territory!" Kaspar spat, whirling on Soren. "You've run your own into the ground, I don't need you doing it to mine too!"

Soren took a menacing step towards the prince, the contempt and fury radiating off of him practically palpable. "At least I don't run and hide in the corner at the first sign of trouble like a fucking child!"

"No, of course not!" Kaspar snarled, not backing down. "You just charge in and take, don't you? No thought for others or how it will impact them. Whatever Soren wants, Soren gets!"

"Both of you, knock it off!" Syrena shouted.

The men turned to look at her.

Syrena stood tall and proud. The princess had disappeared, and a queen now stood in her place. "You two can be fickle and petty and bicker like little girls on your own time, but right now our friends need us."

Kaspar grumbled something under his breath, but Soren quickly bowed his head in bitter acknowledgement of his poor behavior.

"We'll send reinforcements," Syrena continued. "How many soldiers did Erith send to attack the city, did you see?"

"Not many. They had the upper hand due to the element of surprise, not because of their size."

"Then we'll send three squadrons." Syrena peeked at Soren, uncertainty briefly flickering over her face. "That should be enough, right?"

"It should, but who do you plan on having command that squadron? Him?" Soren jerked his chin towards Kaspar and scoffed.

Syrena glanced at Kaspar. He looked back at his sister, the two of them having a silent conversation only a brother and sister could understand. Finally, Syrena sighed and returned her attention to Soren, banishing the glimmer of fear from her eyes as she did.

"I'll lead them."

"*What*?" Xavier nearly shrieked. The two silver hoops at the top of his ear clinked together as he shook his head in disbelief. "I'm sorry, tell me I didn't just hear what I thought I did."

Syrena ignored him and continued to speak directly to Soren. "Hale will join me. He's been trained by Lerian's best, so he'll act as my second in command."

The stone-faced captain nodded dutifully and silently slipped out of the room to prepare. Anxiety gripped my chest at the idea of Hale putting himself in harm's way, and I desperately tried to catch his gaze before he left, but he refused to look at me.

Xavier huffed and stomped his foot, staring at Soren pointedly and waiting for him to interject. When the king remained silent, Xavier glared at Kaspar.

"So what are *you* planning on doing during all of this?"

Kaspar leaned a hip against the table and shrugged. "Someone needs to stay here to look after the city."

Xavier let out an incredulous laugh. "You can't be serious! You're telling me you're going to send your own sister into battle while you just sit around with your thumb up your ass?"

Kaspar's eyes flashed. "Watch your tongue, low-born, or I'll have it cut—"

Xavier lunged forward and punched Kaspar square in the nose.

A loud crack rang through the room, and Kaspar yelped and crumpled to the floor, cupping his face. Without a shred of remorse in his eyes, Xavier stepped back and stuffed his hands into his pockets.

"Your sister has bigger balls than you ever will."

And with that, he stormed out to the courtyard. I peeked over at Soren and caught him struggling to rein in a smug grin.

Kaspar groaned and stood upright, wiping a smear of blood on the sleeve of his kaftan. "You better pray that low-born scum dies in battle, Soren, because if he shows his face in my territory again, I'll—"

"Oh, shut up, Kas," Syrena sighed wearily, walking across the room and snatching a bottle of wine off a nearby cart. She yanked the cork from the top with her teeth and spat it out before taking a long swig and offering it to me. I gladly accepted. After I'd taken several pulls to calm my nerves, I lowered the bottle and looked over at Soren. "I'm going with them."

"Like hell you are!"

"Ilora is a friend, and the king and queen welcomed me with open arms." I lifted my chin stubbornly. "I sparked this war, the least I can do is fight for the ones who showed me kindness."

"You're not a soldier, Lina," Soren hissed, grabbing my arm and drawing me forward so his face was close to mine. "You have no idea how a true battle works. You'll only get in the way, or worse, you'll get yourself killed. You are *not* going with them."

I ripped my arm away. "You can't keep ordering me to do things. I'm not one of your loyal subjects. I get a say, and I say I'm going."

Soren grunted in exasperation and looked to Syrena in a silent ask for her to intervene. The princess simply shrugged.

"Lina's become more than proficient with a blade. When the Nethers attacked, she fought valiantly and saved a score of my people. I would be honored to ride alongside her into battle."

I glanced at Syrena, and she gave me a hesitant smile. I nodded, whatever feud we had earlier forgiven and forgotten.

Soren rubbed his temples. "This is ridiculous."

"Maybe," Syrena said, her tone clipped, "but it's what we're doing."

"And the longer we stay here arguing, the longer Merimaya is under attack," I added.

"Right." Syrena started for the door. "Everyone get dressed and be ready to ride within the hour."

Syrena exited, followed by a sullen and bloodied Kaspar. I turned to Soren.

"I'm sorry," I muttered. "I know you want me to stay out of harm's way, but I can't just sit around and do nothing. Ever since Samhain I've had to rely on other people to take care of me. This is the first time in my life I can actually *do* something."

Soren was quiet as he stared at the ground, his fists clenched at his sides. My heart pounded as I braced myself for his wrath.

But instead, Soren let out an exasperated exhale and cupped my face in his hands.

"You, Lina Calder, are maddeningly reckless." He shook his head. "But gods, I love you for it."

A slow smile spread across his lips, and I relaxed, breathing a sigh of relief as he leaned in to kiss me gently. When he broke away, Soren added, "So that's why I'm coming with you."

"What about your army?"

"I'll return to them after. I need to know you're safe, and the best way I can do that is if I'm there beside you."

I shook my head and slipped my arms around his waist, pressing my chest into his. "You, Soren of Astoria, are maddeningly stubborn and overprotective." I grinned. "But I love *you* for it."

Soren chuckled and dragged me into another kiss, this one

deeper. I wanted to stay in that moment, locked in the safety of his embrace for all eternity, but he eventually pulled back.

"Go on," he said, nipping my bottom lip. "Get dressed before I take you right here on this table."

"That's terrible motivation to leave," I murmured against his mouth.

Soren chuckled and steered me towards the doorway. "Go."

I giggled and exited the great hall, then jogged up the staircase towards my bedroom. When I pushed open my door, however, I froze.

Resting on the center of my embroidered silk bedspread was a box.

I glanced over my shoulder, trying to catch a glimpse of who'd delivered it, but saw no one in the hallway with me. Warily, I padded into the room and carefully lifted the lid of the package. Inside was a note. I held it up to the light so I could read the hurriedly scribbled handwriting.

Not the head, but the next best thing.

I peeked back into the box. When I reached my hand in, I pulled out a small hand-carved knife. It was made of something smooth and white, carved from bone or...

Antler.

My heart skipped a beat as I realized what I held in my hands.

The knife was made from the Nether I'd killed on the spring equinox. The same one who'd murdered Meer. The one whose head I'd lost myself trying to tear off as payment.

I curled my fingers around the blade, then clutched it close to my chest.

"Thank you, Hale," I whispered.

A shadow in the room swirled to say, "You're welcome."

CHAPTER 24

Merimaya's capitol was still on fire when we arrived.

Neither Erith's forces nor the Nethers were anywhere to be seen, but the decimation they'd left was everywhere. Syrena ordered her soldiers to spread through the city, finishing off any stragglers they found or helping where they could, while she, Hale, Soren, Xavier and I headed straight for the palace.

We found Ilora on the palace steps, covered in blood, dirt and ash, and tending to the wounded as best she could. When I was here before, I hadn't realized she was a healer like Meer had been. She was in the middle of shining a cool, blue-toned light over a Merimayan guard's shattered leg when we found her.

"Ilora!" Syrena yelled, leaping off her horse and running to her friend.

Ilora's head jerked up, her light disappearing from her palms as she cried out in relief. She threw herself into Syrena's arms.

"We came as soon as we heard," Syrena said, squeezing her tight.

"How did you hear? They were picking off all the messengers we sent out!"

Syrena pulled away and gestured to Soren on the horse beside me. Ilora blinked in confusion.

"He was passing through on his way to Kylanthia," Syrena explained. "He and his troops have been hiding in the mountains there, taking Erith's forces by surprise when they could."

"Well, it seems Erith learned a thing or two from you." Ilora's eyes dimmed. "They came out of nowhere. We were completely blindsided."

Syrena searched Ilora's face. "Something's wrong. What aren't you telling me?"

Tears slipped from Ilora's eyes and streamed down her cheeks, and though she tried not to, she let out a strangled sob.

"Ilora, what is it? We can help!" Syrena wiped her friend's tears and rubbed her back.

It was then that Hale turned his attention to our surroundings, his eyes scanning the smoldering buildings.

"Where's the rest of your family?" he asked.

Ilora choked on another sob and sank further into Syrena's arms.

Syrena gasped. "Oh, gods... Ilmarien, is he—"

"Gone." Ilora pointed a shaky finger towards the lake. There, a limp body rested on the shore, respectfully shrouded in a sheet now soaked through with blood.

My heart dropped to my stomach as I thought about the last time I'd seen the prince of Merimaya. He deserved a goblet of wine to the face on Imbolc, but not this...

"What of the king and queen?" Soren asked urgently.

"That's the strange part." Ilora sniffled and wiped her eyes. "The soldiers just took them."

"They took them as hostages?"

Ilora shrugged helplessly. "They just came in, grabbed

Mother and Father, and dragged them out. No explanation, nothing. They took them and went northeast."

"Towards Kylanthia?"

Ilora nodded.

"What would Erith want with King Ilris and Queen Ivari?" I asked Soren.

"It could be a way to get to Lerian," he replied. "She'll demand their allegiance in exchange for sparing the king and queen's lives."

"Or it could be another way to get at you," Xavier suggested. "She'll expect you to retaliate. Maybe she thinks you'll move your troops before they're ready, and she'll have the upper hand."

Soren frowned. "Either way, we need to find them before they reach Erith." He returned his attention to Ilora. "When did they leave?"

"Four, maybe five hours ago."

"Then there's still time."

Soren hauled on his horse's reins, spinning it in a circle. "I'll track them into Kylanthia. When darkness falls, I'll ambush them and take the king and queen back."

Hale nudged his horse forward, coming up alongside the king of Astoria. "I'll go with you. I can scout ahead."

He released a tendril of mist, sending it snaking into the shadows.

Soren tensed at the darkness, but nodded nonetheless.

"I'm coming too," I declared, riding up between the both of them.

Soren opened his mouth to protest.

"I'm coming too," I repeated firmly.

He promptly pressed his lips shut and glared at me, his frustrated sigh confirmation I'd gotten my way.

"Well..." Xavier shrugged and clicked his tongue, urging his horse to take the spot to Soren's right. "I suppose if I'm Lina's nanny now, I have to go wherever she does. I'm in too."

I made a mental note to smack him for that comment later.

... *If* we survived.

Syrena's eyes bounced between all of us. Finally, she hauled herself back onto her horse.

"You're going to need every blade possible. Ilora, my soldiers will stay here and help tend to your wounded. Command them as you would your own."

Ilora dipped her head. "Thank you. Thank you all."

Syrena nudged her horse into a trot, looking back over her shoulder as she passed us. "What are you all waiting for? Let's go!"

WE RODE as hard and as fast as we could for hours, only stopping to briefly water our horses. Otherwise, we pressed on relentlessly, headed straight for the jagged silhouette of Kylanthia's mountains on the horizon.

As we crossed the border between Merimaya and Kylanthia, the terrain instantly changed. Instead of Merimaya's lush, green landscape, the world became dry, barren, and cold, lacking color and life. I couldn't imagine anyone living here and being happy about it, and for a moment I thought I might understand why Erith was so angry. She was the queen of a wasteland, pushed to the far corners of the world, out of sight and out of mind, while the other territories lived in excess. I would be angry too. Not enough to align with the Nethers, though. Nothing could get me to form an alliance with those creatures.

As far as alliances went, one proving more stressful than I'd anticipated was the one between Soren and Hale. I rode behind them the entire way, watching their tense shoulders as they stared straight ahead and refused to look at each other, even when one had to grumble orders or mutter an important piece of information to the other. Again, I had to remind myself I'd done nothing wrong and had no reason to be ashamed, but it didn't help when my memory kept replaying heated moments with each of them over and over in my mind. I tried to force myself to think of something else, but when I did, I dwelled on the fate of King Ilris and Queen Ivari, and the fear of the unknown we were riding towards.

As we neared the mountains, Soren called back to let us know many of the tracks had fallen away, but the ones that remained led up a canyon into the peaks. That was our heading, and as we began our ascent and I gazed up at the towering rock looming ahead, there was no easing the dread that swept over me.

What waited for us in those precarious peaks?

What horrors slept in this corner of the world where no one ever dared to go?

And what would happen if we woke them?

As we ascended, signs of life started to appear in the form of evergreen forests and scraggly underbrush, but the land continued to feel empty. We rode deep into the mountains until the sun dipped beyond the crags in the distance. When the light had faded and our horses were too exhausted to continue, we made camp for the night. Here it still felt like winter, and even huddled around a fire with Soren's arms draped around me, I shivered uncontrollably. It brought to mind that night in the woods with my brothers all those months ago, hunched around a fire just like this, blissfully ignorant of the horrors I'd been about to endure.

That night seemed like a lifetime ago.

Since then I'd lived in palaces, dined and danced with royalty, learned to fight like a warrior, fallen in love with a king, been hunted and tortured, watched my family and friends die, and taken a few lives of my own along the way. I'd experienced more joy than I had in my entire life, and more pain and sadness than I ever thought possible. If that frightened girl from Samhain could meet me now, I'm not sure she would even recognize me.

I fell asleep curled against Soren's chest, his arms and furs wrapped around me to block out the bite of the cold. Xavier had proposed he and Syrena should sleep the same way, prompting the princess to chuck a pinecone at him. It forced him to retreat to the other side of Soren, but not before offering her his cloak. She'd begrudgingly accepted, but it was only because, she'd repeatedly assured him, she could use the extra warmth. He'd responded with blowing her a kiss, and *she* had responded by scavenging another pinecone to hurl at his head.

Hale offered to take first watch, and while we rested, he perched on a nearby boulder that overlooked the valley we were poised to enter come morning. When I woke sometime during the night he was still there, staring out at the vast blanket of stars twinkling high above. I wriggled out from under Soren, taking care not to wake him, and clutched a wolf pelt around my shoulders as I padded over to the dark figure hunched on the rock in the distance.

"Hey," I whispered. "You're still up?"

"You all need your rest," Hale replied.

"So do you." I settled on the boulder beside his. Our breaths came out in dense white puffs. "Go get some sleep. I'll take next watch."

Hale glanced over his shoulder at the figures lying around the fire. "Fae have nightmares about waking to a Night Sylph. I won't subject them to those dreams becoming a reality."

A heavy pang of sadness shot through my heart.

"You know that's not what you are, Hale."

He shrugged and returned his gaze to the stars. I shifted on the rock, rubbing my arms to ward off the chill already nipping at my skin.

"We'll make Xavier keep watch, and you can sleep next to me."

Hale let out a miserable chuckle. "I can't do that, Lina."

"Because of Soren? It's freezing out, he'll understand it's just for warm—"

"I *can't*, Lina," Hale repeated, his voice firm.

Even in the darkness, I caught the glimmer of pain in his eyes, and just like on the spring equinox, I felt the overwhelming desire to take it away. I didn't know how, I wasn't even sure if I could or if he'd let me, but I wanted to.

I shimmied the fur off my shoulders and gently draped it over Hale's back. He flinched for a moment, but eventually settled.

"Thank you," he mumbled.

"Of course."

It was then I noticed the long, winding trail of black fog bubbling out from Hale's feet and snaking down the mountain where it disappeared into the depths of the night. I gestured to it.

"See anything?"

Hale nodded. "The ones we've been tracking."

"Are the king and queen with them?"

He nodded again.

"Unharmed?"

"Seems so."

I breathed a sigh of relief. "Thank the gods."

"They're camped at the far end of the valley. We should catch up to them by tomorrow."

I squinted into the darkness. "The far end of the valley? Your power can reach that far?"

"Apparently."

I raised an eyebrow. "You don't know how far you can reach?"

Hale shook his head.

"You've never tried to see?"

"No."

"How come?"

Hale glanced down at his hands, allowing a puff of darkness to pool in his palms. "There's never been anyone I wanted to see from that far away."

He peeked over at me, and like they always seemed to, our eyes locked. I lost track of how long we stared at each other, but my heart picked up speed as it anticipated the words I wanted to say. Before I could talk myself out of it, I forced out, "Do you think you could reach all the way to Astoria from Lerian?"

There was a pause.

"Maybe," Hale finally replied, that unflinching stare of his making the chill of the night seem a little less bitter. "Is there anyone in Astoria who will want me to see them?"

I hesitated, then nodded.

A small sad smile appeared on Hale's lips. "Maybe I will, then."

He looked like a painting, crouched on that rock, silhouetted against the sky, blending into the night save for the stars reflected in his eyes and his pale skin illuminated by moonlight. I could have stayed up all night admiring the dark beauty of that image, but Hale's voice brought me back to reality.

"Get some sleep, Lina. Tomorrow's a big day."

Reluctantly, I rose. "Good night, Hale."

I reached out to give his shoulder a squeeze goodbye, but when he jerked away from me, I wilted, dropped my hand, and returned to the fire to settle in beside Soren. Despite the cold, with Soren's arms draped over me and the knowledge that Hale was keeping watch over us, I fell into the deepest, most peaceful slumber I'd had since I passed beyond the veil.

WE WOKE to Hale urgently whispering, "They're moving."

The first rays of morning were barely brightening the sky as we scrambled to our feet and hastily packed up camp. With Soren's dagger strapped to one thigh and the antler knife Hale had gifted me on the other, I hauled myself onto my horse and mentally prepared for another battle. Even though I had fought Nethers before and come out victorious, the cold claw of anxiety was still embedded in my chest, my hands still shook, and my stomach still roiled at the thought of clashing with them. Did this ever get easier? Both Soren and Hale flew into skirmishes without hesitation. Surely they didn't get nervous after all this time. But as I watched Hale's shoulders grow increasingly tense while Soren repeatedly adjusted his grip on his horse's reins, I had the sneaking suspicion killing never did get easier.

The trail down to the valley was considerably more steep and narrow than the one we were following, so we were forced to slow our pace to avoid slipping and tumbling to our death. In some areas we even had to dismount and guide our horses down on foot.

Hale continued to scout ahead with his darkness, keeping it close to the shadows of the sparse evergreens to avoid detection. He insisted we were gaining on Erith's soldiers, though, and once the land leveled out, we would finally catch up and overtake them.

When we touched down in the valley, the land opened up to reveal a large alpine lake. Syrena, Xavier, and I filled our canteens and let the horses drink their fill while Soren and

Hale scoped out the tracks that led to the other end of the lake. When they returned, their faces were grim.

"We have to leave the horses behind," Soren declared.

"Why?" Xavier asked.

Soren beckoned for us to follow him. At the far end of the lake, the water funneled into a series of raging rapids before careening down a sheer cliff face.

"There's a path off to the side," Soren shouted over the crash of the water. He pointed to a precarious trail to the left of the waterfall. Carved into the cliff, it consisted of countless dizzying switchbacks that led to the ground far below.

"They went that way. The horses won't make it, so we'll have to go the rest of the way on foot."

Syrena eyed the trail and groaned.

"What's wrong?" Xavier asked.

"I just hate heights, is all," the princess mumbled. She nervously adjusted Xavier's cloak still pinned around her shoulders. She hadn't given it back to him yet, even though there had been plenty of opportunities to do so.

"I could carry you," Xavier offered.

I think he genuinely meant it, but Syrena rolled her eyes and gripped Hale's arm to steady herself as we began our descent. I did the same with Soren, and Xavier, pouting slightly, brought up the rear.

By the time we reached the base of the waterfall, its roar was deafening and we practically had to scream to hear each other.

"Where's the trail?" Xavier hollered, squinting against the spray of water as it pounded into the rocks in front of us.

Soren looked at the gravel beneath our feet, his brow furrowing as he searched for prints. "I'm not sure. Hale?"

Hale carefully scanned our surroundings. "Give me a minute."

He extended both hands and let his darkness flow from his palms, growing larger and thicker until it was nearly as tall as the evergreens around us. He then flung his arms forward, flooding the black mist over the boulders and trees and cliffs. It slid into every crack and crevice, swirled around every branch and bush, and coated every inch of the ground beneath us.

A few seconds passed before Hale's eyes lit up, and he contained the darkness before jogging towards the waterfall.

"What is it?" I asked, slipping and sliding along the algae-slick rocks as I ran after him.

"There's something back here," he called over his shoulder.

The rest of the group followed us, and when we caught up with Hale, who had his back pressed against the cliff face, we followed his outstretched finger to see what he was pointing at.

In the wall of rock behind the waterfall was a vertical fissure that led into a pitch-black cave.

I glanced at Syrena. "A crack in the heart of Kylanthia..."

"It can't be," she breathed, taking a step closer. "Do you think it's really—"

"The Netherworld?" Hale frowned. "Only one way to find out."

And with that, he stepped forward into the darkness, the rest of us following warily behind.

I clung to Soren as we shuffled behind Hale, who used his mist to see ahead while we waited for our eyes to adjust. When they did, my jaw dropped.

The path led us into a massive cavern with dripping stalactites hanging from the high ceiling and a pool of dark water surrounding us. A single beam of sunlight shot through a gap in the rocks high overhead, shining down like a beacon on the stone path, which abruptly stopped at the center of the pool.

"Everyone stay alert," Soren ordered.

"I don't like this," Syrena mumbled, peering around the

cave. She palmed the hilt of one of the daggers at her side and subtly inched closer to Xavier.

"Wait!" Xavier commanded.

We all turned to him, and he tapped his ear with his index finger. "Listen."

We fell silent, focusing intently. That was when it hit me...

There was nothing to hear.

There was no echo of our voices, no splash from the water dripping off the stalactites. Even the roar of the waterfall behind us was muted. It was as if something thick and dense was absorbing all the noise throughout the cave.

"Nethers?" I asked worriedly.

Soren nodded, eyes cautiously roving over the slick gray stone of the cave walls.

"Something else too," Hale added. "Not sure what, though."

"Keep your weapons at the ready," Soren ordered, drawing his sword.

Xavier followed his lead, and after a nervous gulp, Syrena unsheathed her two long daggers. I kept the knife Hale had given me in its sheath at my thigh, but drew Soren's dagger, trying not to focus on how badly my hands were shaking. Ahead of us, Hale pushed on, his mist spreading over the ground in front of him while his fingers hovered and twitched over the knives at his thighs, ready to jump into action at the first sign of trouble.

We neared the end of the path, and Hale held up his fist, stopping us in our tracks. He stared straight ahead, his eyes narrowing as his head tilted curiously to the side.

I crept up beside him and tried to follow his gaze, but I couldn't see anything worth noting.

"What's wrong?" I whispered.

"I don't know," Hale murmured, his eyes still fixed on nothing.

When we edged closer, something changed.

My head started to pound, my heart raced faster, and I began sweating profusely at the same time every hair on my body stood at attention. Something wasn't right. This didn't feel like normal anxiety or fear. Those I knew far too well. This was something else. Something was so wrong in this place, so *off*, that my body was having a visceral reaction.

"Are you feeling this too?" I croaked, wiping my brow with my sleeve.

Hale nodded grimly.

I looked back at Soren. Judging from the sweat beading on his forehead and the way his hand trembled on the hilt of his blade, he felt the same. Behind him, Syrena had swallowed her pride and clung to Xavier like her life depended on it.

I turned back to Hale. Slowly, he sent his darkness creeping past the end of the path. The fog went only a short distance before billowing up as if it had hit a solid wall.

Hale frowned, then tried again. Still, his mist refused to go on. Hale changed tactics and spread his darkness out horizontally, but still it pressed up against an invisible barrier.

Hale shook his head in disbelief. "I've never seen it do this before."

Cautiously, he eased forward and reached out past the path's end. As Hale raised his palm to where his darkness had stopped, the air seemed to wobble and vibrate as if it were made of water and he'd just sent ripples flowing across the surface. He paused, his frown deepening, then reached further. The air trembled again, more aggressively this time, and Hale's hand disappeared.

I gasped, and Hale yanked his hand back, his eyes wide.

"Lovely." Xavier grimaced. "Who wants to go through the creepy invisible wall first?"

I glanced at Soren.

Then Hale.

Then I set my jaw.

"Lina!" Hale shouted as I took a step.

Soren whipped out a hand to pull me back.

But he was too late.

I'd already passed through.

IT FELT LIKE WATER.

Thick water so cold it chilled me all the way down to my bones, my teeth, my organs. It was so cold it scrambled my mind, and for a moment I forgot everything I'd ever known: my name, how old I was, where I was, and what I was doing. My feet were heavy and slow, like I was trudging through waist-deep mud, but when I peeked at the ground, I saw none. All the nightmares I'd had where I was trying to run but couldn't go fast enough, or trying to scream and no sound came out, had suddenly become a reality. For a split second, I felt like I'd died and this was the Underworld, but it was over as quickly as it began, and I stumbled forward, collapsing into a shallow stream.

I lifted myself onto my hands and knees and retched, my body quaking from the strange purgatory I'd escaped from. When I'd successfully emptied the contents of my stomach, I wiped my mouth and looked up. My jaw dropped, and I shakily hauled myself to my feet.

I was in a low-ceilinged tunnel with a stream running through its center, stalactites and stalagmites covering every surface, much like in the cave before. Here, however, a glowing blue-green algae dappled the surface of the rock, its bright turquoise light illuminating the entire chamber. The cool light bounced off every surface, making the stalactites appear more like icicles, while the water adopted the refreshing cyan hue of a cloudless summer sky.

Behind me, water sloshed. I spun and seized my dagger to hold at the ready. Soren and Hale materialized out of thin air, stumbling forward the way I had. Not far behind them, Xavier trampled through with Syrena holding his hand.

When everyone had recovered, they took in our surroundings. Their mouths immediately went slack.

"Gods," Syrena gasped, her eyes aglow from the turquoise light reflecting in them. "What is this place?"

"I've never seen anything like this," Xavier murmured, squinting curiously at a luminescent stalactite. "Soren, have you?"

Soren shook his head, his fingers wrapping around the hilt of his sword so tight his knuckles turned white. "Don't let your guard down. We don't know what else is here with us."

His warning snapped all of us out of our daze, and immediately we were on high alert once more. Hale padded forward down the tunnel, Soren beside him, and together the two of them stealthily waded through the water without a sound. I followed, trying to mirror their movements as best I could.

As we trekked deeper into the passage, the stream we trudged through shallowed. Soon it was just a trickle of water in the gravel beneath our feet. The algae dotting the rock, however, thickened as we went, and before long, the entire tunnel was splattered with bright blue light. Cracks marred the stone ceiling and walls, and when I peered closer, I saw moonflowers sprouting upside down from the majority of them. Strangely, though, instead of their traditional lemony aroma, the faint scent of night-blooming jasmine filled my nose.

I would have been in awe of the unusual beauty around me if it weren't for the way anxiety gnawed at my stomach and the hair on the back of my neck still prickled with unease. As we pressed on, the scent of jasmine grew stronger, while the tunnel widened around us. The rock gradually changed from dark stone to something lighter, practically white, and more smooth, and the luminous blue-green flecks of algae grew more abundant with each passing step.

Finally, the tunnel opened into a colossal cavern, its towering arched ceiling almost too high up to see, with flower-entwined pillars carved from pale moonstone lining its edges. Other passages studded the walls behind the pillars, but with their doorways darkened, there was no way of knowing where they went or what was inside. The aroma of jasmine had become overpowering, almost sickening, and the anxiety I'd had since setting foot in this place multiplied. My breathing picked up speed at the same time beads of sweat began to glide down my lower back and both my temples.

Something is wrong, my mind, body, and soul were screaming. *Something is seriously wrong.*

I couldn't ignore the unease any longer. Everything in me was saying we should turn back. We would find another way to reach the king and queen, or we'd return with reinforcements. Somehow, we'd figure it out. But right now, we couldn't be here. We needed to get out. *Now.*

I frantically tugged Soren's sleeve, opening my mouth to tell him what I was thinking, when motion ahead caught my eye. I turned, only for my breath to catch in my throat.

A woman had stepped out from behind one of the pillars.

A disturbingly thin woman draped in an old gray shawl.

A woman who simultaneously looked like youth and death.

"You," I breathed.

"You," she replied in a voice that was half old woman, half child. Her smile exposed a row of grimy teeth. "He's been waiting for you." The woman's sunken eyes roamed over Soren, Hale, Xavier and Syrena. "He's been waiting for all of you."

A tiny sliver of hope fluttered in my chest at her words. I immediately scanned the room for a sweet freckled face and a mess of curly blond hair.

"Who's been waiting for us?" Soren asked. His voice still commanded respect, but the woman didn't flinch at his tone the way she had on Samhain. Instead, her smile spread wider.

Then another woman appeared from behind a different pillar.

Then another.

And another.

The hope in my heart was ripped away as Nethers of all shapes and sizes materialized from the passageways in the walls, each more grisly and garish than the last, their weapons drawn and their fangs bared.

I spun. Nethers stood there too, including a row of creatures who seemed to be half man and half goat lined up with their crude bows drawn, angling the points of their arrows directly at our heads.

We were completely surrounded.

When I turned back to the woman, she slowly extended a long, crooked finger and pointed towards the other end of the cavern.

"*He's* been waiting," she said.

The legion of Nethers parted, revealing a figure at the far end of the room.

It was larger than the horned beast I'd battled on the spring equinox.

It was larger than the old-growth trees in Astoria's forests.

It was larger than any living, breathing thing I'd ever seen.

It wore a billowing gray hooded cloak, and where its face should have been, there was nothing but a swirling mass of black. Two red eyes peered out from the darkness, their haunting glow searing into us from across the room. It had no feet, and instead floated above the ground like a phantom.

This creature wasn't a Nether. This was something else entirely.

Something much, much worse.

When the figure spoke, though, the voice that rang out was sickeningly sweet, just like the smell of jasmine around us, and somehow that made it even more terrifying.

"Hello, Hale," it purred. "Welcome home, son."

CHAPTER 25

For a moment, Hale thought his heart stopped beating.

A deep laugh rumbled out of the creature at the end of the room, so loud it vibrated the ground they stood on.

"Oh, yes," it chuckled. "I know you, Hale. I know you very well."

Hale was hyperaware of everyone's eyes on him. Not just Lina's, or Soren's, or Xavier's and Syrena's, but the eyes of the Nethers too.

Whatever he did, he couldn't show weakness.

Hale squared his shoulders and steadied his voice. "How do you know me?"

The laugh rang out again, louder, causing Hale's knees to buckle slightly as it shook the floor.

"I sired you, as I've sired all the creatures of the Netherworld."

"My father was a Night Sylph." Hale spoke calmly, but his fingers inched towards the blades at his thighs. "I don't know what you are, but you sure as hell aren't one of those."

The being's red eyes flashed, and the swirling black of its face grew darker.

"I can be whatever I like." Its fiery gaze shifted to Lina and flared. "I can be whatever *she* likes."

Suddenly, the creature spun into a dense cloud of black smoke. When it dissipated, a figure identical to Soren stood in its place, dressed in fine black robes embroidered in gold, complete with a jagged crown of obsidian shards on his head.

"How about this?" the replica asked, a smile spreading over his handsome face. "Does this better suit you, my dear?"

Hale glanced at Lina. The color had drained from her cheeks, her eyes were wide, and the dagger in her hand shook. Hale's own terror became overshadowed by the frantic urge to take away hers.

"Or what about this?" The creature raised a mischievous eyebrow and became swirling smoke once again, and when the cloud disappeared, an image of Hale stood there instead. He was dressed in the same luxurious black robes as before, the dark crystal crown perched atop jet-black hair that grazed his chin.

"Maybe," the imitation said, pensively tapping his finger against his lips, "*maybe* you would prefer a mixture of both?"

Once more the smoke erupted, and when it cleared, a stranger stood in front of them. He was a disturbing combination of both Soren and Hale, with Hale's angular face, black hair, and the brand on his neck, as well as Soren's square jawline, hooded navy eyes, and broad shoulders adorned in regal pelts. There were knives strapped to the man's thighs like Hale, and a broadsword at his side like the king.

"Is this the ideal scenario?" the stranger asked, giving Lina a seductive smile. "Is this what you *really* want?"

Hale sneaked another peek at Lina. She was doing well, all things considered. She was gritting her teeth and holding her head high to hide how frightened she was, but Hale had no doubt everyone in the room could hear the way her heart was hammering.

The hybrid in front of them chuckled and shook his head. "No, you're right. This is wrong. I have something else I *know* you'll love, though. One of my children saw this form recently, and I must say it has become one of my personal favorites to embody."

He vanished in a dark cloud one final time. When the smoke cleared, a Fae with pale skin, long white hair, and bright gray eyes stood in front of them. Hale didn't recognize him, but from the way Soren and Xavier tensed and Lina let out a horrified gasp, they clearly did.

MEER.

That *thing* had the audacity to turn into Meer.

I shook harder, but not from fear. Not anymore. Now I shook with repressed rage, and as I stared at the creature, I swore a silent oath that I would kill it.

I didn't know how.

I didn't know when.

Hell, I didn't even know what it was.

But I *would* kill it, or I'd die trying.

In front of us, Meer smiled sweetly. "What do you think, Lina Calder? Is it good to see your friend again?"

At the sound of my name, I recoiled.

His grin widened. "Oh yes, I know who you are too." His gaze drifted over the rest of the group. "I know all of you."

Meer's gray eyes landed on Soren, and he extended a hand to perform a grand, mocking bow. "Behold His Majesty, the charming warlord of Astoria, who has taken anything and everything he's ever wanted, but it never seemed to fill the void inside."

Soren's cheeks flushed, but I was unsure if it was from anger, humiliation, or a combination of both.

The creature's eyes flicked to Hale next. "And of course, my son. The Night Sylph bastard."

The muscles on Hale's back tightened like a wolf readying to pounce.

When Meer's form faced Syrena, he grinned hungrily. "And this pretty little thing here is the spoiled princess of Lerian, who hides behind a carefully crafted smile to hide the fear of her own inferiority."

Syrena gripped Xavier's arm tighter.

Meer's attention shifted to him next, his head tilting as he looked Xavier up and down curiously. "I was wrong. I actually don't know *you*, which tells me you're nobody. A dog in fancy clothes. Nothing but an insignificant waste of space."

Xavier's eyelids fluttered, but he clenched his jaw and stood proud.

When the creature turned to me, my stomach dropped. Those gray eyes held none of Meer's warmth, kindness, or compassion. His pupils were empty and lacking any form of empathy. This looked like my friend, but it was the farthest thing from him.

"And finally, here is the unexceptional human who searches for a Changeling boy. A woman who has accidentally fallen in love with a king... as well as a demon."

I had no control over the gasp that leapt from my mouth.

I knew I loved Soren, but... Hale? I barely knew Hale. Was I attracted to him? Of course. The night of the spring equinox had confirmed that. Did I care about him? Absolutely. He was so broken, had been so mistreated by this world and its people. I wanted to do whatever I could to take away his pain. I wanted to show him people could be kind and gentle. I wanted to make him realize he *was* deserving of love, but that didn't mean *I* loved him.

... Did it?

I felt both Soren's and Hale's land on me, but I couldn't bring myself to look at either of them.

"Oh," the creature said, his chin angling to the side as he batted his eyelashes innocently. "You didn't know? I thought everyone suspected." He motioned to Soren with a graceful, sweeping hand. "The king certainly did."

I looked to Soren. Now *he* was the one ignoring *my* gaze.

Hale seemed to be the only one of us capable of forming words.

He took another step forward and demanded, "Who are you?"

The creature laughed heartily. "Did I not introduce myself? How rude of me! Please forgive my poor manners. I don't receive many guests, I'm afraid." He stretched his arms wide and adopted a cheerful smile. "You may call me Aedan. Welcome, friends, to the Netherworld."

Aedan approached us then, his gilded black robes billowing behind him. "Come. Join me for a meal. You must be hungry after your long journey."

He snapped his fingers, which immediately sent the Nethers into a frenzy. Somehow they produced a long table and dragged it into the space between us and Aedan, covering it in an impressive assortment of otherworldly foods. Five seats were placed around the table, but at the head they set a massive chair adorned with large spikes of quartz and obsidian.

Aedan strode over to the gemstone throne and lazily draped himself across it, gesturing to the table.

"Sit," he urged.

Soren, Hale, Xavier, Syrena, and I exchanged glances.

Finally, I swallowed my fear and uneasily came forward, the others following my lead. Beside me, Soren leaned into Xavier's ear and whispered, "Don't. Eat. *Anything.*"

Slowly, I lowered into the seat closest to Aedan. He looked me up and down, impressed I'd willingly chosen to be so close to him.

Good, I thought bitterly, *underestimate me. It'll make killing you that much sweeter.*

The others took their seats; Soren beside me, Hale across from me, Syrena beside him, and Xavier at the other end. Aedan beamed out at us.

"Well, this is nice, isn't it?" He popped a strange, purple-spiked berry into his mouth, then beckoned to the Nethers still prowling around us with their weapons at the ready. "Please excuse my children. They're quite protective of their home. They're not welcome anywhere else, you see. In your world, they're treated like pestilence, hunted down and slaughtered like animals. You'd know all about that, though." His gaze lingered on Soren. "I heard something a few months ago. What was it again?" He tapped his index finger against his chin, his lips curling into a smile. "Oh yes, that's right. 'You tell them Soren of Astoria is coming for them, and he will not rest until he slaughters every last one of you.'"

Aedan let out a condescending laugh and shook his head, popping another piece of fruit into his mouth and gnashing it between his teeth until its juice dribbled onto his chin.

I glanced at Soren. His clenched hands shook, and a vein had appeared along the side of his neck. He looked ready to snap. Either someone needed to change the subject, or Soren was going to tear Aedan's head off and we'd be at the mercy of the bloodthirsty Nethers circling us. I took the responsibility on myself and cleared my throat.

"So, Aedan," I said as pleasantly as I could manage, "are you the king here?"

Aedan chuckled. "My dear, if that is the only word your simple human mind can come up with to make sense of it, then yes, you may call me the king of the Netherworld."

I bristled at the venomous words, but forced myself to keep a straight face.

"But kings are bound by the laws of their land," Aedan continued, his eyes gleaming with excitement. "I *am* the law. I *am* the land. I am *everything*, older and more powerful than you could even fathom."

I sniffed and poked at a berry on the plate in front of me. "Humble too, I see."

To my surprise, Aedan threw back his head and laughed, clapping his hands in delight. "How wonderful! You still have that sense of humor! Amazing. Even when my children feasted on your flesh in the forest it remained, same as it does now. That's good, Lina. I admire that. I can see why they like you." He angled his head to Soren and Hale. "Well it's that, as well as that delicious scent of yours."

He leaned forward, pushing his face unnervingly close to my neck. It took every ounce of courage in my body not to pull back in fear. The scent of jasmine became so strong the back of my throat constricted, and I desperately willed myself not to retch.

Aedan inhaled deeply, shutting his eyes as he savored whatever he scented on my skin, then let out a low, appreciative moan.

"Human," he drawled. "Absolutely delicious. So alluring to the Fae, like predators drawn to the kill. It's the only reason you're desired by so many, you know."

He sat back, popping another piece of fruit into his mouth, clearly amused by the confusion in my expression.

"What?" he asked with a smirk. "You didn't actually think they wanted you because of your beauty or charm?"

I shifted uncomfortably in my seat, and Aedan threw back his head and cackled, then gestured to Syrena. "When creatures that look like *her* fill their world? You're nothing, Lina! Absolutely nothing!"

I didn't care if he currently looked like Meer, I wanted to take my blade and slit this creature's throat like I had Valdir's. Only this time, I'd relish every second.

"No, my dear," Aedan said, wiping tears of merriment from his eyes, "I'm afraid it all comes down to the fact that you, a human, are so much slower and weaker, and therefore make ideal prey. On some deep, primal level everyone just wants to take a bite."

"That's not true," Soren barked.

Aedan's eyes lit up, and he eagerly leaned forward. "Finally, the brute speaks! You disagree, Your Majesty?"

"Yes," Soren snarled through his teeth.

"Oh?" Aedan raised an eyebrow. "The moment you saw her you, wanted her, didn't you? You saw the wounded deer in the forest and wanted to devour her. You needed to have her as your own even though you didn't understand why, and once her flesh touched your tongue, you were addicted. You developed a maddening, insatiable appetite for no one but her. You, the mighty Soren of Astoria, who could have and *has* had anyone he wants, obsessed with *that*."

He spat the last word as he gestured to me.

At last, Soren's gaze met mine.

"Think about it," Aedan pressed. "*Really* think about it, Your Majesty. It's the only thing that makes sense."

Soren's brow furrowed as he searched my eyes. In that moment, I swore my heart cracked as I realized what he was doing.

He was trying to determine if Aedan's words held any truth, if he really *did* love me or if his attachment to me was just a deep-rooted, animalistic part of him that only saw me as a victim.

I could do nothing but mentally send all of my love to him and pray he could feel it in the very depths of his soul the way I did.

But Soren looked away and stared down at the plate in front of him in a daze.

The crack in my heart deepened.

"Come on, Your Majesty, say something!" Aedan urged. "Give us some of those flowery words you were so well known for in your youth! Pretty words that could lure anyone into your bed, including the beautiful princess of Lerian."

Soren's head snapped up, and across the table Syrena gasped. My stomach lurched, and I whipped my head towards her. That wasn't true. She would have told me. *Soren* would have told me.

Syrena quickly averted her gaze to the tabletop. When I turned to Soren, he refused to make eye contact too.

"Oh, dear." Aedan tutted. "You didn't know that, either?" He sighed, grabbed a crystal-encrusted goblet off the table, and raised it to his lips. "Average beauty and below average intellect. How disappointing."

His words sent the strangest combination of humiliation, pain, and anger rippling through me, and I didn't know if I wanted to cry, scream, throw up, or stab something.

"Anyway..." Aedan sniffed and nodded to Hale. "At least my son could resist the urge to go back for seconds once *he* had a taste. Must be the Night Sylph in him once again proving that my children are more evolved than the Fae."

"Why do you keep saying that?" Hale mumbled.

Aedan turned to him and smiled brightly. "Saying what?"

"Your children."

He gestured to the Nethers lurking around us. "Because you are my children."

Hale opened his mouth to speak, but Aedan cut him off.

"No, I didn't truly sire you. You are a Night Sylph's son, make no mistake." The Netherworld king eagerly leaned forward on his elbows. "But long ago, at the dawn of time, I created these magnificent beasts; the Night Sylph, the Sluagh, the Merrow, all of them. And over the years, I've watched them survive in a world that sought to destroy them." He glanced up, his eyes roving over the Nethers and gleaming with the pride of a father. "My creation. My proudest accomplishment. And that includes you. In fact, you might be my favorite so far."

"He's not one of you!" I blurted without thinking.

Aedan's eyes locked on me and went cold, but his lips curled upwards into a grin. "Oh no?"

I sat taller in my chair. "No."

"Both you and the princess think you know him," Aedan said, propping his chin on his fist, "but you don't. Not really. Only I do."

My blood boiled hotter. "That's a lie."

Aedan raised an eyebrow at me. "Then you'll know the Night Sylph bastard delivered you here to me."

Xavier, Syrena, and Soren tensed, and across from me Hale's eyes went wide.

"I don't know what you're talking about," he ground out. His nails dug into the table, and I could tell it was taking everything in him not to grab a knife and hurl it into Aedan's face.

Aedan looked over at Hale, his eyes softening as he clicked his tongue. "I know you don't, son. I wish I could have revealed everything to you. Believe me, I wanted to. I wish I could have let you know that you felt broken and alone your entire life... but you were never truly alone. Because whenever you used the power your father gave you, the power *I* gave you, I was right there with you."

Aedan leaned forward, his eyes blazing with delight. "When *you* looked through the darkness, *I* could see through too."

Hale's face paled.

"I was there when you hid in the cellar at fourteen and watched from the shadows as the villagers dragged your mother from your home and slaughtered her, calling her a witch and saying she purposefully fucked the demon of the night to create *you*, an abomination. I was there six years later when you watched beneath the door as the princess of Lerian gave herself to the silver-tongued Soren of Astoria, and you desperately wished it were you taking her maidenhead instead of him. And I was there once again when a human girl knew you were watching and touched herself anyway, coming with your name on her lips instead of the king who started a war for her."

A flush rushed to my cheeks as Soren's eyes landed on me. I ducked my head and prayed the floor would open up and swallow me whole.

"So you see, Hale?" Aedan continued. "You've helped me more than you know. For thousands of years I tried to find a way to overthrow the Fae, but then you came along! A son of a Night Sylph, turned captain of the guard, unknowingly an invaluable part of my crusade. It was because you looked in on King Stelios of Astoria during his diplomatic mission to Lerian that I learned of his plans to go sailing in the bay before he returned home. So I sent a horde of Merrow there to bid him farewell. You frequently listened in on your guardians as well, and it was because of that I learned the route the king and queen of Lerian planned on taking to Merimaya one evening. It made them an easy target for my flesh-hungry children to intercept along the way."

Aedan's eyes flicked to Syrena as he sipped innocently from his goblet. "They told me the Fae meat was so decadent that they ate *everything*, including the bones."

Without warning, Syrena snarled, grabbed her daggers from her sides and launched across the table towards Aedan. Xavier leapt out of his seat and caught her by the waist, dragging her back, kicking and screaming, to his seat, where he held her firmly on his lap and whispered things in her ear that calmed her slightly. Aedan watched the exchange with an amused smirk, then lifted his glass to Xavier in salute.

"You know, you might be smarter than you look, boy."

I'd never seen Xavier look more terrifying than when he glared back at the king of the Netherworld.

Aedan refocused on Hale. "So you see, son? What you view as a curse is in fact a glorious gift. Because of you, the Fae realm is ripe for the taking. It's led by inexperienced and arrogant rulers, constantly bickering and picking sides like petty children. Now is your chance to get what you deserve. Finally, we can emerge from the depths and seize the land you've been chased out of for millennia. All of these creatures will live normal lives, all thanks to you."

A heartfelt smile spread over Aedan's face. "You're the lowly demon spawn no longer, Hale. You're a *savior*."

Suddenly, all the Nethers surrounding us bent their knees, fell to the ground, and bowed their heads. Hale surveyed the crowd kneeling before him, his eyes growing wider than I'd ever seen them. For the first time since I'd known him, he seemed shaken. I tried to catch his eye, but couldn't.

"Hale, look at me," I demanded.

Hale's gaze fluttered over to meet mine. His eyes glistened with tears, his features twisted with confusion, guilt, and shame.

I leaned in. "You're not one of them, you hear me? You're good, Hale. You are *good*."

Aedan slammed a fist onto the table, the resounding *bang* causing all of us to jump.

"Who said my children aren't good?" he asked, his voice eerily calm. "I'll tell you who. The Fae decided that. Just because my children didn't look like them or act like them."

My nails dug into the arms of my chair, and I spoke through gritted teeth. "They decided that because your children are violent and cruel."

Aedan scoffed. "More lies spun by the Fae."

"I've seen it!" I snapped. "You said yourself, your children feasted on my flesh in the woods! Your children slaughtered my friends in their own home on Yule, and your children found an innocent, scared little boy in the woods and stole him away from his own sister!"

Aedan's eyes flashed. "Did you ever ask my daughters why they took your brother?"

My brow furrowed. "I... well, no—"

"They witnessed the attack in the human realm." Aedan leaned back in his seat and crossed his arms. "They saw your brothers fall, then saw you pinned by a man who planned to have his way with you. When your little brother ran, they took him in as an act of mercy and spellbound him so he'd forget the horrors he witnessed. They took him under their wing so he'd remain unharmed throughout the night."

I blinked and shook my head. "No, they wouldn't give him back—"

"Because they saw who you aligned yourself with." Aedan abruptly sat forward, his eyes shooting to Soren. "A violent, prejudiced Fae king. They felt they could provide the Changeling a better upbringing than he could."

"That wasn't their decision," I barked, leaping from my seat.

The Nethers around us hissed and chittered as they prepared to strike.

"He doesn't belong to them!" I pressed on. "He's not a piece of property, he's my family and I want him back!"

Aedan stared at me for several long, tense beats. Finally, he leaned back and chuckled.

"You're right. Forgive me. You made the perilous trek to the Netherworld, Lina Calder, which means my daughters no longer have dominion over him."

The Sluagh women surrounding us grumbled their disapproval.

"I know, I know," Aedan told them, shrugging helplessly. "I don't like it either. Alas, rules are rules. Where is the Changeling?"

A murmur spread throughout the room as the Nethers talked among themselves.

Finally, the crowd parted.

Time seemed to stop when a head of blond hair appeared in the distance and bobbed towards me.

"Wynn!" I screamed, pushing away from the table and sprinting towards him.

I threw myself to my knees and flung my arms around my brother. Gasping sobs of relief tore out of my body as I squeezed him tight, while the tears springing from my eyes soaked the black silk robe shrouding him.

"I found you," I wept pitifully against his shoulder. "I finally found you."

Hands casually stuffed in his pockets, Aedan stood from his crystal throne and wandered over to where my brother and I embraced.

"It's a shame," he sighed. "I had high hopes for this one."

I pulled away from Wynn just enough to look up at Aedan as he smiled and gently stretched out a single alabaster finger to caress my brother's cheek. Melancholy washed over his face.

"Goodbye, little princeling. I'll miss you dearly." The king of the Netherworld's eyes shifted to me. "He is yours, Lina Calder. Go, and be at peace."

"Thank you," I whimpered. "*Thank you.*"

Aedan dipped his head and turned, starting back towards his seat. When he reached it, however, he stopped in his tracks, thought for a few seconds, and glanced over his shoulder.

"Actually... I think I might have phrased that wrong."

Dread washed over me. "What... what do you mean?"

"What I *meant* to say was, he is yours... *if* you can make it out." Aedan's lips curled into a delighted smile. "And I'm afraid my children have no intention of letting you leave."

At his words, the Nethers stood and snarled in our direction, prompting Soren, Hale, Syrena, and Xavier to jump up and draw their weapons.

"We aren't leaving without the king and queen of Merimaya, anyway," Xavier declared.

Aedan's eyebrows arched in amusement. "Oh, is that so? Well, why didn't you just say that! My love?"

We followed Aedan's gaze. The crowd parted a second time, revealing Erith striding towards us, leading a bound and gagged King Ilris and Queen Ivari behind her on a tether. The queen of Kylanthia stopped beside Aedan, glaring out over all of us with disdain. She wore gray satin like she had at the harvest celebration, but this time her only accessories were the raw diamond circlet on her head and a long curved sword strapped to her back.

"Erith," Soren said, walking forward and stretching out his hand like he was taming a wild animal, "please, don't do anything rash. We can talk about this. Just think about what you're—"

"Go ahead," Aedan interrupted with a flippant wave.

Without hesitation, Erith yanked her sword from its sheath and brought the edge of the blade to Ilris's throat, slicing quick and deep.

The movement was so fast I didn't process what had happened. But then the king crumpled to the ground, twitching and gurgling as blood bubbled out of his body like a spring. His eyes held the same terror Jaras's had on Samhain, the same terror Valdir's had on Yule, and those memories partnered with Ivari's screams finally made the realization hit.

The queen of Merimaya wailed as scarlet pooled beneath her husband's body. In response, without a flicker of regret or compassion in her eyes, Erith turned and assigned her the same death sentence, cutting her throat while the rest of us were still processing our shock and horror.

Syrena cried out and buried her face in Xavier's shoulder, and I instinctively clutched Wynn's face to my chest so he couldn't witness the slaughter.

"Oops," Aedan giggled, shrugging. "It looks like you won't be leaving after all."

Then, he raised his right hand and snapped.

Wynn instantly shoved me away and walked towards Aedan. I scrambled after him on my hands and knees.

"Wynn? Where are you going? *Wynn!*"

I latched onto my brother's robe, but he pried my fingers off and pushed me back with unnatural strength, then continued forward to take a place at Aedan's side.

Aedan lovingly stroked Wynn's curls and shifted his eyes to Hale. He extended his other hand. "Come, son. Take your rightful place among your brothers and sisters."

The Nethers edged closer.

Hale glanced at me, eyes full of turmoil.

"Let your old life die," Aedan pressed, "and let your new life begin."

I tried to read the look on Hale's face, but it revealed nothing.

Don't listen to him, I thought desperately.

There was no way he could hear me, but I still had to try. Maybe, just maybe, he'd understand.

I stared at Hale pointedly.

Listen to me, Hale, I willed to him. *This wasn't your fault. This is not who you are. You are good, Hale. You are **good.***

Tears appeared in Hale's eyes.

Suddenly, Soren charged, tore his sword from its scabbard, and swung it wildly over his head before bringing it down with a solid crunch into the chest of the Netherworld king.

Aedan gaped and went still.

My heart skipped a beat.

He did it. Soren actually did it!

But the victory was short-lived.

Across the room, Erith began to laugh.

Aedan groaned, fastened a hand around the hilt of the sword, and slowly drew it from his chest. He glared up at Soren with fire in his eyes.

"Fool!" He bellowed, the word shaking the cavern. "You think your weapons can kill me? I am a god, boy! Nothing can kill me!"

Soren's eyes went wide. Thinking fast, he extended his hands and flicked his wrists, unleashing the full extent of his power on Aedan and the Nethers.

But nothing happened.

Erith laughed even harder.

Soren's expression changed from one of surprise to one of terror. He whipped his head down to stare at his hands and flicked his wrists again.

Then again.

Then *again*.

Still, nothing happened.

Aedan joined in with Erith's cackling. "Oh dear, that's not going to work either. Different worlds, different magic, I'm afraid. Your powers are useless here, Your Majesty."

Soren backed away, his eyes darting frantically between the Nethers and Aedan, his expression disturbingly similar to that of an animal caught in a trap.

Somehow amid my rising panic, I felt someone's eyes on me.

I looked to my right. Hale stared at me over his shoulder, his gaze round and intense, like he was trying to communicate something. When his eyes flicked to my thigh, his intention finally clicked.

The knife he'd given me wasn't Fae, it was made from a Nether.

Then Hale tucked his arm behind his back so only I could see it, and opened his palm.

An airy black cloud accumulated in the center.

Hale was half Night Sylph. Part of him belonged to this world.

So he still had his power.

CHAPTER 26

I nodded to Hale, and he nodded back.

Then, at lightning speed, his darkness hurtled through the room, engulfing the entire space in pitch-black fog.

The Nethers erupted in angry screeches and sent arrows whizzing from their bows, their razor sharp points glancing off the moonstone near our feet. It was so dark I could barely see my hand in front of my face, and I had no idea where my friends were in relation to me, but I didn't care. I was dead-set on one thing and one thing only, and I had memorized where he'd been standing just before Hale released his power.

I ducked low to the ground to avoid the second barrage of arrows hurtling through the air and bolted towards the last place I saw Aedan. I accidentally stumbled head-first into his throne, colliding with a crystal spike. Stars scattered across my vision while throbbing pain shot through my skull and scrambled my thoughts. I pushed past the discomfort and wildly flung my arms around me in search of the Netherworld king and the human boy in his clutches.

But the throne was empty.

I turned and continued fumbling through the dark, my hands furiously searching for any sign of Aedan.

"Lina, to your left!" Hale shouted. He must have been peering through the darkness and caught a glimpse of the Netherworld king. I lunged to my left, my arms outstretched, clawing feverishly for the shapeshifter. My hands landed on something, but when I stepped closer, I came face-to-face with the glowing yellow eyes of one of the Nethers who had tortured me in the woods. It opened its mouth and let out a chilling screech before piercing its claw into my shoulder, unleashing agonizing, paralyzing pain.

My body went rigid as a spasm shot through me, and suddenly my mind began to replay memories of the past few months.

I saw myself laughing with Dominic and Wynn on Samhain.

I saw every moment spent with Soren dancing and fighting and fucking.

I saw myself giggling on the boat with Syrena and Ilora.

And I saw myself in the library with Hale while his darkness licked at my neck and back and lips.

Just before my vision went black, something deep inside me stirred. It woke from the place it had been slumbering and exploded up, jolting through my veins and propelling me into action.

Fight, Lina, the voice screamed, *fight like hell.*

I mustered what strength I had left and forced my tensed, trembling fingers up to the creature's face, then with a final push of willpower, I jabbed my thumbs deep into the sockets of its eyes. The Nether screeched and released its hold on me, bringing an abrupt stop to the pain. When the Nether crumpled, clutching its face in its hands, I saw my opportunity and pounced.

I kicked the creature solidly in the chest, just as Syrena had done to me when we were sparring, which sent it flying backwards onto the ground. I then leapt onto the monster, straddled its chest, and took its face in my hands. It roared again and gnashed its teeth up at me, hunting for a piece of flesh to sink into. I let out a furious battlecry and jerked the monster's head to the side with a nauseating crack. It immediately went limp beneath me.

In the distance, Syrena cried out in pain. My stomach lurched, but I fought the urge to run to her rescue and forced myself to focus on the task at hand.

I stumbled forward through the dark once more, flailing my arms in front of me in search of the Netherworld king. My hands met something solid, and my breath caught. I prepared for another brush with a Nether, but when my fingers tangled in a mess of curly blond hair, relief flooded through me.

"Wynn!" I whispered urgently, wrapping my fingers around his arm. "Come on! Hurry!"

I turned, dragging Wynn in the direction I could hear my friends clashing with the Nethers, but I collided with something else. It fastened a hand around my throat and lifted me off the ground. I released Wynn as I gasped and choked and sputtered, kicking and clawing at whoever was holding me. They leaned forward, and I froze when a pair of cold gray eyes came into view.

"Enough," Aedan snarled, giving me a rough shake. "I found you amusing for a time, but all toys eventually lose their luster. It's time for you to go."

My fists beat at Aedan's chest in an attempt to free myself, but I weakened as he continued to cut off the air to my lungs. My chest burned, and my vision clouded with bright, bursting stars.

"Goodbye, Lina Calder," Aedan said with a smile. "Do say hello to your brothers for me."

My mouth opened and shut, gaping like a fish out of water, and my vision faded to black.

Then, echoing far in the distance as if I were in a dream, Hale's voice called to me.

"The knife, Lina! The *knife!*"

Those words hurtled through the darkness, jolting me awake. In the midst of it all, I'd forgotten what was strapped to my left thigh. I forced myself to hold on to consciousness a few seconds longer and stretched my hand down to my side, groping feebly for the antler blade. Just as my vision had nearly gone dark, my fingers found the cool, smooth handle and latched onto it, and with the last bit of strength I had left, I wrenched it from its sheath, plunged it deep into the Netherworld king's stomach, and twisted.

Aedan let out an ear-shattering shriek that rattled the world surrounding us. Something warm and wet spilled over my hand, the smell of jasmine in the air suddenly mixing with the sharp, metallic tang of blood. I released my hold on the hilt of the knife, leaving it buried deep in Aedan's abdomen as he dropped me to the ground and stumbled backwards, screeching in agony. I crumpled onto the cold moonstone floor, coughing and hungrily gasping in air, but somehow managed to scramble upright, grab Wynn's wrist, and yank him deeper into the fog.

My brother and I staggered blindly through the darkness until something grabbed me from behind. I yelped in alarm and spun, preparing for another fight to the death, but to my relief I found Hale firmly gripping my shoulders.

"Come on!" he urged.

I nodded, and together the three of us pressed on through the dark. When we located Xavier, Soren, and Syrena, who had a nasty gash across her forehead that was oozing blood, they were defending themselves against a furious onslaught of monsters descending left and right. Hale leapt to our friends' aid, making quick work of their attackers, then rounded us up and guided us through the dark.

"The passage is this way! Hurry!" he ordered. He shoved me, Syrena, and Xavier forward, while Soren hauled my brother over his shoulder and darted after us. Hale brought up the rear.

We dashed into the tunnel we'd entered through, pushing our legs as fast as they would carry us. I tried not to think about the adrenaline firing through my veins, my shallow breaths, or the roars of the Nethers as they realized we'd escaped. Instead, I focused my attention on the glowing passageway ahead. All we had to do was pass through the veil that separated the Netherworld and the Fae realm, come out on the other side in the cavern behind the waterfall, and we would be safe.

A round of the Nethers' arrows shot through the air, forcing us to duck and weave. I was sure we'd successfully navigated them all when a single rogue arrow sped through the air and embedded itself deep in Xavier's shoulder. He grunted and crumpled to his knees in pain. Then a second arrow hissed past me and pierced his side, wrenching an agonized scream from his throat as he fell to the ground, face-first.

His voice brought Syrena to a skidding halt, and she sprinted back towards him. A bug-eyed Nether leapt out of the dark, savagely descending on Xavier, but Syrena rushed in with a brutality I'd never seen from her and butchered the creature in a matter of seconds. She then slung Xavier's good arm over her shoulder and hauled him upright before helping him stumble onward.

When the stream trickling through the tunnel deepened, I looked up and recognized the cracks in the ceiling with moonflowers sprouting from their depths. We were coming up on the end of the cave.

Soren splashed through the water ahead, and in the blink of an eye, he and Wynn disappeared into thin air. My heart leapt.

They'd passed through the veil.

My little brother was finally out of the Netherworld, and the Sluagh no longer had dominion over him.

After all these months, Wynn was finally safe.

Syrena and Xavier sloshed through the stream after them, and they too disappeared through the invisible veil.

Hope swelled inside me.

This is it! We made it! We made it out!

Out of nowhere, an arrow shot through the air.

... And found its mark deep in the center of Hale's back.

He gasped out and collapsed to the ground. I immediately stopped in my tracks and scrambled back towards him, slipping my arm around his waist, gritting my teeth, and hauling him upright.

"Come on!"

Hale groaned in pain, but staggered on.

Behind us, I could hear the Nethers gaining as Hale and I limped down the tunnel. With each step, the agony etched into his face cut deeper.

Pushing aside my fear, I readjusted my hold on his waist. "Almost there. Just a little further."

Suddenly, another arrow whizzed through the air, successfully embedding beside the first.

Hale grunted and stumbled forward out of my arms, collapsing onto his hands and knees in the stream. I knelt beside him, frantically trying to drag him back to his feet.

"Get up!" I demanded. "Hale, get up! Come on!"

I tightened my grip around Hale's arm and lifted him from

the water, but he let out a guttural groan of pain and went limp, forcing me to drop him.

"*Get up!*" I repeated, tears stinging my eyes. "You have to get up!"

Hale peered up at me through the sweat-drenched strands of hair clinging to his face, pain and emotion clouding his eyes. His breathing became ragged as liquid rattled in his chest.

"Go," he wheezed, nodding to the end of the tunnel a few strides away. "Go back through the veil, Lina."

Again I attempted to haul him to standing, but Hale remained on the ground.

"Get up, damn it!" I shouted, my voice breaking.

I wrapped my arms around his waist and tried to lift him, but he was too heavy.

"Lina," he gasped, the arrows in his back quivering with the word. "*Go.*"

Tears spilled from my eyes as I furiously shook my head. "I'm not leaving you."

The rattling in Hale's chest grew louder. He coughed, splattering flecks of blood onto his lips.

"Please," I whimpered, my breath shuddering as I wiped the blood from his mouth with my sleeve. "Please, Hale. Get up."

Hale's eyes softened. Slowly, he reached out a trembling hand and wiped the tears streaming down my cheeks. Then he clasped my jaw and smiled that radiant smile I'd only seen once before.

"Thank you," Hale whispered, his voice cracking. A single tear slipped out one corner of his eye. "Thank you for everything."

Then he pulled me forward and pressed his lips to mine.

The world stood still as Hale kissed me deeply, with one hand cupping my face while the other wrapped around my waist. When he finally broke away I was left breathless, and I barely had time to realize what had happened before Hale mustered his remaining strength and firmly shoved me towards the end of the tunnel. I stumbled backwards, my arms flailing as I struggled to stay upright. Hale then rose to his knees, threw both of his hands above his head, and sent his darkness tearing into one of the cracks that snaked through the ceiling of the cave. He grunted as mist poured out of him, anguish contorting his features as he strained. The column of black barreled into the crevice above until the stone began to grumble and groan as it cracked further. Soon the entire tunnel rumbled, shaking loose stones that started raining down around us.

I ducked as a piece of the ceiling crashed down beside me. When I stood upright, my hands curled into determined fists at my side. I wasn't leaving this place without Hale. Everyone had failed him his entire life, but that ended today.

I would not run from him.

I would not abandon him.

I would not fail him the way this world had.

So despite his demand for me to go, I gathered my strength, stepped forward, and reached out to drag Hale to his feet a final time.

But before my hand could grasp the back of his jacket and pull him to his feet, Soren materialized back through the veil, wrapped his arms around my waist, and dragged me through.

We passed through that thick, stomach-wrenching cold, emerging on the other side in the cavern behind the waterfall shivering, retching, and screaming.

"Hale!" I shrieked, thrashing wildly in Soren's arms as he hauled me towards the exit. "We have to go back! We have to go back for Hale!"

The massive cavern around us shook, causing stalactites to crack and crumble from its roof and walls. I managed to wriggle out of Soren's grasp and dashed back towards the veil, but a giant boulder smashed down in front of me, Soren dragging me out of its path in the nick of time.

"It's not safe!" Soren yelled.

I tugged furiously against his hold. "We have to go back for him! Please!"

A spike of rock careened down from the ceiling, and Soren barely managed to yank me out of the way before it speared me.

"Soren, *please!*" I sobbed.

Soren glanced over his shoulder at Syrena, Xavier, and Wynn making their way out of the cave towards safety, then turned back to me and growled in frustration.

"We go together. Hurry!"

I nodded, and the two of us sprinted back towards the veil. Just as we were about to pass through, a wall of rock broke free and tore towards us like a tidal wave.

"Shit!" Soren shouted, throwing his hands up and using his magic to push the avalanche backwards, buying us enough time to run back the direction we'd come to avoid being crushed. Once we were out of harm's way, Soren again took my hand and pulled me towards the exit.

"We can't go back, Lina," he stated. "This place is coming down any second!"

"We have to try!" I wailed.

I continued to struggle as Soren dragged me away, but as boulders quickly piled up where we'd just stood, I knew he was right.

Nothing and no one would be coming through the veil ever again.

The tears flooding my eyes clouded my vision, forcing me to cling blindly to Soren as he led us out from behind the waterfall to join the others. The ground shuddered beneath us, causing our knees to buckle. We looked back in the direction of the cave. Stones at the top of the waterfall began to tumble down with the current.

Syrena gasped. "That whole thing is going to come down!"

Soren immediately scooped Wynn onto his shoulder. "*Run!*"

I ducked under one of Xavier's arms while Syrena did the same, and together we bolted into the forest, dragging him with us as we leapt over rock, bramble, and stream while the deafening roar of water and collapsing rock chased after us. I dared to glance back for a half second, only to see the mountain behind us crumble in the distance, the water from the alpine lake above gushing down and flooding the surrounding area.

I faced forward and urgently called to Soren, "We're not going to make it! We have to get higher!"

Soren skidded to a halt and frantically searched the forest.

"Everyone find a tree," he panted. "A sturdy one. Climb as high as you can."

Syrena and Xavier obediently hobbled over to a nearby evergreen and began scaling it while Soren and I did the same, both of us taking turns hauling Wynn up through the branches. The roar grew louder, trees in the distance bending and breaking as a wall of water ate through the forest.

"Hold on!" Soren commanded, wrapping his arms around me and Wynn and pinning us to the tree trunk.

I shut my eyes, gripped my brother with all my might, and braced for the impact.

The flood barreled through the forest and knocked into the base of our tree, causing the wood to creak and shake violently. I cried out in fear, certain the trunk was going to snap so we'd be hurled into the rapids below and swept away with the current.

"Don't let me go," I begged Soren.

His arms tightened around me. "Never."

We clung to each other, waiting for what felt like hours to

hear that final crack that would plunge us to our deaths, but miraculously the tree stood strong. Over time it shook and creaked less, and the roar of water gradually quieted. Before I knew it, Soren was patting my hand.

"Lina," he whispered, "it's over."

I eased one eye open, followed by the other, and peeked down at the ground. All that remained of the flood was a sheet of slow-moving, ankle-deep water trickling across the forest floor. The land had been transformed into a battered marsh, our tall, gnarled old tree one of the few still standing. Not far away, Syrena and Xavier's perch had made it through too, but just barely. The base of the trunk was cracked, and the tree leaned perilously to the side, but my friends still clung to its branches.

"Everyone alright?" Soren called across to them.

Xavier nodded listlessly. Beads of sweat dappled his forehead.

"We're alive," Syrena shouted back, "but we need a healer. I don't think he's going to make it back to Merimaya."

Soren nodded calmly, but panic flashed in his eyes. I'd seen that same look in him back in Astoria when Xavier had been wounded by the Nethers.

"I left my army camped southeast of here," Soren said. "The healers there can help him. Wynn too."

I frantically looked down at my brother, running my hands over his body in search of injury. "Wynn? What's wrong with..."

My stomach dropped.

His eyes.

My brother's lids drooped and a white glaze coated his irises. In the darkness of the Netherworld I couldn't see it, and afterwards I'd been too focused on not dying to notice.

Wynn was still spellbound.

"We'll find a way to fix it," Soren said, giving my arm a reassuring squeeze before starting his descent down the tree. I took a deep breath, slipped my brother's hand into my own, and carefully made my way down after Soren, praying to the gods he was right.

We started our trek through the mountains, but with Xavier draped over Soren's shoulders, drifting in and out of consciousness, we didn't get far. By the time dusk fell, Xavier was disturbingly pale, Soren was drained from carrying him, and I was sick with worry.

"We'll stop here," Soren finally said, grunting as he lowered Xavier to the ground and propped him against a boulder. "Lina, make a fire. I'm going to run ahead. Hopefully I'll be able to find some of my scouts. We'll send horses for you."

"Soren, you're exhausted." I placed a hand on his shoulder. "You need to rest—"

Soren shrugged me off and continued into the forest without a second glance back. "I said make a fire, Lina."

He broke into a jog and disappeared from sight. Begrudgingly, I focused my energy on gathering twigs for kindling. After a while, I felt a presence shuffle up beside me.

"Lina?" Syrena asked hesitantly.

I ignored her and continued foraging.

"Lina, is Hale—"

"Gone."

A tiny, stifled whimper was her only response. After a few moments of silence, Syrena bent and started gathering wood too. She sniffled, but when I peeked at her out of the corner of my eye, the princess was cool and collected, refusing to let the emotion show on her face.

"Did he..." Syrena cleared her throat. "Did he suffer?"

The image of Hale on his knees, two arrows in his back, looking up at me with tears in his eyes and blood rattling in his lungs flashed into my mind.

Yes, he suffered. He suffered his whole life and never got to experience even a shred of the kindness and love and joy that he deserved. That I wanted to show him.

"No," I lied. "It was quick."

Syrena nodded. "Good."

We gathered in silence again. Finally, Syrena took a deep breath.

"Lina, I... I should have told you about me and Soren—"

"Yes, you should have." I grabbed a fallen pine bough and snapped it over my knee.

"I didn't..." Syrena trailed off and sighed. "I didn't mean to keep it from you. At first I thought Soren must have told you, and when I realized he didn't, I... I just didn't know how to bring it up, or what to say. It was so long ago, and it was just the one time—"

"I don't want to hear about it, Syrena," I muttered. "I don't want to hear about anything. I just want..."

I wanted Hale back.

I wanted Soren to apologize for not telling me about his past.

I wanted my brother to look at me with clear eyes and hug me tight and tell me he'd missed me.

I wanted this agonizing pain in my heart to go away.

I wanted to go home... even though I wasn't exactly sure where home was anymore.

"I want to be quiet," is what I said instead.

Syrena wilted, but respectfully dipped her head and backed away. "I understand. I'll leave you alone, then."

She offered me a sad smile and retreated back to where Xavier and Wynn sat. Syrena tucked Xavier's cloak around him, then tenderly pushed one of his sweat-drenched curls out of his face before settling in beside my brother.

No one spoke the rest of the evening.

Not as I built the fire.

Not as the night wore on and we stared into the woods for hours on end.

And not when torchlight appeared in the distance as Soren's scouts rode to our aid.

~

SOREN HAD LIED.

We couldn't seem to find a way to fix my brother.

No matter what any of the healers did, they couldn't make the light return to Wynn's eyes, couldn't make him speak, couldn't bring back any part of my brother that I knew. Their suggestion was that I locate a witch who could break the spell, but no one had any idea where to find one, at least not here in Kylanthia.

Thankfully, we received much better news in regards to Xavier. The healers said we were lucky to get to them when we did, but after an hour in their hands, color was already returning to Xavier's cheeks. Soren sat dutifully beside his cot the entire time they worked.

I left them there and took Wynn to Soren's tent. Together, we curled up on the pile of pillows in the corner, where I draped a fur around my brother's shoulders and held him close as I sang him lullabies. I hoped it might awaken that part of him that lay dormant, the sweet little boy I once knew who was still locked inside him somewhere, but it was just wishful thinking. Wynn stayed catatonic and limp in my arms for the rest of the night.

He was still nestled there when dawn came and the tent flap pulled back to allow Soren entry.

"Have you slept?" he asked softly.

I shook my head. "You?"

"No."

"Xavier?"

Soren lowered himself onto a large tufted pillow beside me. "He's going to be fine."

I let out a grim chuckle. "He's going to think he's invincible and can't die."

"I know," Soren sighed. "It's going to make him even more reckless. I have no idea what I'm going to do with him."

He smiled at me, but it was pained. He quickly looked away, and an uncomfortable silence settled over us. I focused my energy on smoothing Wynn's hair. It had gotten longer since I'd seen him last, but he still had that one curl at the back of his head that refused to be tamed.

At least there was one thing about my brother I still recognized.

Soren and I were quiet for what felt like an eternity. Eventually he cleared his throat, but still couldn't meet my gaze.

"Aedan... revealed some things."

I swallowed hard. "Yes, he did."

Soren nodded and began spinning his ring in circles around his finger. "I... I think... maybe we both need time to process them."

I'd thought the pain in my heart couldn't get any worse, but it did.

Because I knew what Soren was going to say. I knew because I was thinking it too.

But that didn't make it hurt any less.

"You think I should return to Lerian with Syrena while you and Xavier go back to Astoria."

Soren finally lifted his eyes to mine.

"It's alright," I said. "I've been thinking the same."

"It's just... I need to rebuild and help Merimaya get their affairs in order, and with Valdir and Erith gone, who knows what's going to happen with Radomir and Kylanthia, and I..." Soren's throat bobbed as he swallowed, a glimmer of emotion shining in his eyes. "I just... need to think about some things."

My throat tightened, but I channeled the princess of Lerian and plastered a calm, cool expression on my face to hide my pain. "Me too."

Soren hesitated for a moment but nodded and cleared his throat once more before pushing himself off the ground. He then bent and placed a tender kiss on my forehead before starting for the door. He pulled back the flap to exit, but stopped and glanced over his shoulder before he did.

"I'm sorry for your loss," he said earnestly. "Hale, he... he was a good man."

At that, my cool facade broke, and my bottom lip quivered. "Yes. He was."

Soren nodded again, his brow furrowing as the pain returned to his eyes. "Goodbye, Lina Calder."

"Goodbye," I whispered.

Epilogue

It was a year to the day since I watched my brothers die. A year since my world had been flipped upside down.

Samhain.

The holiday that once brought me joy as a child now sent a chill down my spine, one the shrieks from the Nethers in the distance only worsened. We'd collapsed the entrance to the Netherworld, but the Nethers who'd remained in the Fae realm at the time were still here, spending their days getting picked off by the Fae and growing angrier and more violent than ever as a result. I was told the holiday this year would be a particularly bloody one for any humans the Nethers came across, so my dagger stayed at the ready in my right hand while my spellbound brother's stayed fixed in my left.

I'd lost Wynnric a year ago, and although I had him back physically, mentally he was still missing. None of the healers in Lerian could help, no amount of begging or crying or shaking him had helped. I had no other option left.

We were returning to our world.

I gripped Wynn's hand tighter as I stood on the bank of the

river and looked across to the forest beyond. Over there somewhere was an ancient burial ground that marked the boundary of the veil, as well as a clearing with my brothers' remains. That glade was my first stop once I passed over. Wynn and I would say a quick prayer for Dominic and Jaras, sing one of my mother's old songs to honor them, and we'd continue onward to our village. I had no fear of it anymore, no fear of the predatory old lord who would be there on my return. I had killed monsters with my bare hands. That lord could try to hurt me, but I could confidently say he would fail, and it would be the last thing he ever did.

"Are you sure that's all you want to take?"

I glanced over my shoulder at the newly appointed queen of Lerian, who was staring at the humble pack on my back with a deep frown of disapproval.

"I just don't see why you couldn't take what I bagged up for you," Syrena grumbled.

"Right," I laughed. "A peasant woman returns from a year in the woods with a sack full of gold and rubies. That's not strange at all."

I shot her a playful grin.

"I already told you," Syrena huffed. "You make up a story about marrying some exotic wealthy lord, then say he died and left you his fortune. Problem solved."

I giggled and shook my head. "The answer is still no."

It had taken a long time for me and Syrena to be on good terms again. We hadn't spoken when we returned to Lerian, and we'd avoided each other in the halls of the palace, which was difficult to do because we'd both frequently paid visits to the same bedroom door. Multiple times a day, I'd find her doing exactly what I did: staring down at the crack under Hale's door, expecting to see a swirl of black mist creeping through. I had been on my way to do just that when I found Syrena already there, sobbing pitifully on the floor. When she heard my footsteps, she'd looked up, but she hadn't wiped her face or masked her pain like she usually did. She'd let me see the tears, let me see her weakness, let me see *her*, for the very first time. We'd stared at each other for a few moments before she finally stood, ducked her head, and returned to her own room. The next day I'd found her at breakfast and asked her to spar with me. And that day, she'd let me win.

After that, it was like nothing had ever happened between us. She'd slowly gained my trust back, and was now a dear friend. It was going to kill me being apart from her, but I had to do this. For Wynn.

"You weren't planning on leaving without saying goodbye, were you?"

A giant smile spread over my face at that voice. I whirled to face it. I'd recognize that lopsided grin and floppy mop of dark curls anywhere. I handed Wynn off to Syrena and ran forward, tackling Xavier with a ferocious hug.

"You made it!" I squealed, squeezing him tight as he spun me in a circle, just like he had at the harvest celebration almost a year prior.

"Of course I made it!" Xavier chuckled. "I wouldn't miss it."

He set me down and dipped his head curtly to Syrena.

"Your Highness," he said stiffly.

"It's Majesty now," she snapped back.

Xavier rolled his eyes. Syrena rolled her eyes too. I just sighed.

I had seen this song and dance of theirs at Ilora's coronation in Merimaya this past summer. Eyes sparkling fondly, Xavier had pushed through the crowd and approached Syrena, and she had, for reasons unbeknownst to me, acted aloof and coldly indifferent to him. Put off by her reaction, Xavier had responded by giving her the exact same treatment she'd given him, so I spent the whole evening watching them both go out of their way to show each other how much they definitely *didn't* care that the other *didn't* care.

They fooled no one but themselves.

But just as I had on that day in Merimaya, I looked over Xavier's shoulder as he stood before me, hoping to catch a glimpse of someone else. And same as that day, I didn't see him.

"I'm sorry, Lina," Xavier said, reading my expression. "He's not with me."

The ache in my chest that had been a constant these past six months grew heavier, the way it always did when I thought about Soren.

I hadn't seen or spoken to him since that day in his tent after we returned from the Netherworld. He hadn't come to visit or sent me any letters while I was in Lerian. In his defense, I hadn't sent him any letters either. I could have. It wasn't like before when I hadn't known where he was. I knew very well he was in Astoria, attempting to settle unrest among his people, as well as the people of Radomir, which was still without a ruler thanks to my actions during Yule.

I must have written a thousand letters to Soren but had torn them all up. How do you pour your heart out on paper? How do you make sense of all the confusing, conflicting emotions inside and put them into words so someone can feel exactly what you do?

I love you, Soren, one letter had said, *I love you so much it hurts. And maybe I might have loved Hale too. But it was different for each of you. The love you and I have is special; it is ours, and ours alone. It is its own, unique thing, and I would never want to change it, nor would I want to change you. And the love I had for him was its own unique thing too, and it was wholly different from the love you and I have, because that one is ours, and he had another, and I don't know why but they're both love, but they feel different because you're different, and that's good, and both loves are good—*

And that was when I tore that letter up, because I realized I wasn't making a shred of sense. I'd then written *I love you, but I'm mad at you* on a scrap of paper and handed it to Syrena to send off, but she'd ushered me back to my room and told me to sleep on it. Wise advice, because in the morning I'd torn that paper up too.

I *was* mad at Soren. I was mad at him for not speaking to me, I was mad at him for keeping his past with Syrena a secret, I was mad at him for doubting his feelings for me in the Netherworld, and I was mad at him for pulling me through the veil away from Hale, even though I knew he had only done it to protect me.

I was also ashamed.

I was ashamed because Soren had given me so much. He had protected me and fought for me, yet I could barely find the energy to write to him because I was mourning someone else.

In those first few months, there'd been weeks I couldn't get out of bed. I couldn't eat. I could barely talk. After those passed, I'd spent many a day and night drinking myself into a stupor in a pathetic attempt to take away some of the pain. I couldn't shake the feeling that I'd failed Hale, and not just in those final moments. I felt like I should have done more for him. More to make him smile. More to bring light into his dark world.

I should have picked more flowers and stuck them in every damn buckle in his jacket.

I should have danced with his darkness every night.

I should have brushed those loose strands of hair out of his face every time they fell forward into his eyes. I'd have been pushing them back all day long if that were the case, but I wouldn't have minded.

It was because these thoughts consumed me that I couldn't

find it in myself to write to Soren. But as I searched the woods behind Xavier, hoping he was playing a cruel trick on me and Soren actually *had* come to say goodbye, I knew what my letter would say if I were to write it now.

I love you, Soren of Astoria, it would read, *and I'm sorry for the pain we've caused each other. I miss you desperately, and I'll never forget you. I wish we could have worked out. I wish our story could have had a happy ending.*

"Did you…" I swallowed the lump that had formed in my throat. "Did you tell him you were coming to see me?"

Xavier's eyes filled with compassion, and he nodded sadly. "I did."

"Did he at least tell you to give me a message or anything?"

"No, Lina," Xavier said softly, reaching out and giving my shoulder a tender squeeze. "He didn't."

I nodded, inconspicuously wiping a tear from the corner of my eye by pretending it was nothing but a loose eyelash. It was a little trick I'd learned from Syrena, and she immediately recognized the move and put a comforting arm around me.

"Last chance for that bag of jewels," she teased.

I laughed and sniffled, pulling her into a hug. "For the last time, *no*. Wynn and I are going to go back and live a normal life."

Xavier snorted. "Good luck with that. You, Lina Calder, are the farthest thing from normal. And I mean that as a compliment." He winked.

I flicked one of the curls dangling in front of his left eye. "Shameless."

Xavier chuckled and pressed a fond kiss to my cheek.

I took Wynn back from Syrena, then readjusted the straps of my pack. "Alright. I think… I think I'm ready."

Syrena pouted and fiddled with one of her emerald bracelets to distract herself from the tears welling in her eyes.

She probably would have let herself cry had Xavier not been here, but since he was, she put up her usual front.

"Now, don't forget..." The queen tossed her hair and popped her fists on her hips. "You promised to meet me here next year. We have one evening to catch up, and I am *not* traveling all the way here just to find out you missed it."

I gave my friend a warm smile. "I won't forget."

"And don't forget your training either," Xavier added. "You've got to practice regularly, or you're going to lose all the progress you've made. I'm not going to reteach you the footwork next year, so you have to stay on top of it. Alright?"

"I will, I promise. I'll even do it shirtless in your honor."

Xavier grinned and winked once more. "I've taught you well, human."

Syrena uncomfortably pulled her shawl over her chest as Xavier glanced her way, the twinkle in his eye most likely the memory of her holding a knife to his throat while wearing nothing but a lace corset.

"Well..." I sighed. "If I put it off any longer, I might convince myself to stay, so I'm just going to say it." I stood tall and lifted my chin. "*Goodbye.*"

"Goodbye," Syrena and Xavier replied simultaneously. They immediately glared at each other.

I laughed and shook my head, then started for the river, looking back at them over my shoulder one last time. "By this time next year, you two have better figured this out."

"Figured what out?" they asked in unison.

I giggled again and shuffled onto the bank, sheathing my dagger and hoisting Wynn high into my arms before wading into the shallows. A year ago I had been lying in this same spot, half-submerged, as a Nether's venom coursed through my veins. I still had that long raised black scar from its teeth on my wrist, but the sight didn't bother me as much anymore. It was a reminder that I'd survived. It was a reminder of my own strength.

"Um... Lina?" called Syrena's voice behind me.

I kept my attention on the water tugging at my hips, carefully navigating the precarious riverbed underfoot. "I'm not going to spell it out for you two. You have to figure it out on your own. I'm honestly amazed you haven't already."

Miraculously, I made it through the swift current without slipping or being swept away. I trudged out of the water and up the steep, muddy bank on the opposite side of the river.

Finally, after an entire year, Wynn and I were on our way back home.

"Lina!" Xavier yelled.

The urgency in his voice made me freeze.

Was it Nethers? Maybe some of the Sluagh had managed to remain in the Fae realm and wanted Wynn back? Or was it the slimy green monstrosities I'd first met a year ago, hungry for another taste of my blood?

Instinctively, I lowered Wynn to the ground and tucked him behind my back as I ripped my dagger from its home at my thigh. My muscles tensed as adrenaline pumped through my veins, preparing my body for one last fight.

But the forest wasn't deathly quiet, and I didn't hear an otherworldly screech or inhuman roar.

All I heard was a horse's hooves.

I turned. Syrena and Xavier stood with their backs to me, staring into the forest. I followed their eye-line, and my heart nearly stopped. A figure in a blue, fur-trimmed cloak rode towards us on a large steed. He yanked on his horse's reins, pulling it to a stop, and leapt off, barreling past Syrena and Xavier straight towards me. I hurriedly shrugged off my pack and lunged into the river, frantically splashing across as fast as possible before throwing myself, sopping wet, into Soren's arms. He lifted me off the ground, clutching me tighter than he ever had. There was no stopping the tears that burst from my eyes and streamed down my face.

"I didn't think you'd come," I choked out.

"I'm sorry." Soren's voice wavered. "I'm sorry, I didn't know how to say goodbye. I didn't want to."

He lowered me to my feet and took my face in his hands. "But I couldn't let you go without telling you. I should've said it then, but I didn't. I doubted myself. I'm ashamed to admit that, but I did, and I'm sorry. I've done nothing but continue to fail you, and I'm so, so sorry—"

"Soren, slow down. What are you talking about?"

Soren took a quivering breath, his hands trembling against my cheeks. "In the Netherworld. Aedan said you were prey and that's why I wanted you, but that was a lie. I know that because you're *not* prey, Lina. You're not a victim, you're a survivor. A fighter. You are resilient and brave and strong, and *that* is why I am completely, recklessly, hopelessly in love with you."

His words burst the dam holding back my emotions, turning my tears into hiccuping sobs. Through heaving breaths I managed to gasp out, "I love you too."

Undeterred by my pitiful blubbering and dripping nose, Soren dragged me in and kissed me the way he had that very first time: passionately, unashamed, and like he'd been starving for it his entire life. When he finally tore his lips from mine, he pulled me to his chest and wrapped his arms around me.

"I want you to stay," he mumbled into my hair.

"Soren—"

"No, listen. Please." Soren returned his hands to my face and forced me to look deep in his eyes. "I don't deserve you. I've failed you more times than I can count, and I hate that I've brought you so much pain and heartache. And I swear to you, I will spend the rest of my life trying to make up for that."

I studied his expression. "What are you saying?"

Soren took a shaky inhale, his hands trembling even more than they were already. I had seen this man cut down monsters out of my worst nightmares without batting an eye, and here he was cowering before *me*.

"I'd like to start making up for my past indiscretions by giving you and Wynn a place to call home. I want you to live here in Astoria. With me."

"What? *No!*" I pulled away from him. "No, I don't want to live with someone because they feel like they owe me."

"No! No, I didn't mean it like that, I..." Soren grunted in frustration and rubbed his face. "*Shit!* None of this is coming out right. Why isn't this coming out right?"

Not only was he trembling, but the silver-tongued Soren of Astoria was tongue-tied in front of me.

"Forgive me, I'm just..." Soren took another quivering breath. "I'm afraid to lose you."

I softened, and Soren slipped his arms around my waist to draw me closer.

"I don't want you to live with me because I owe it to you. I want you to live with me because I love you. I want to wake up next to you, and come home to you, and hear your laughter echoing down the hall. I want to watch you fight with Xavier, and I want to dance with you, and I want to find you playing in the garden with your little brother. If you stayed here, we could find Wynn the help he needs, and when he's well again we'd get him the finest tutors in the five territories. Eventually we'll teach him how to defend himself, and he could grow up to be a mighty warrior like his sister. The two of you will never have to want for anything ever again."

It sounded perfect, it really did. That was all I'd ever wanted for my brother. But something continued to gnaw at me.

"I don't know, Soren…" I swallowed. "I think… maybe too much has happened."

Hale. Hale had happened. Not to mention the months Soren and I had spent without speaking to each other, the constant doubt and distrust, the painful secrets kept shamefully hidden away…

"I agree things haven't been… ideal." Soren frowned, then tightened his hold. "But I know without a shadow of a doubt that what we have is worth fighting for. I'm more sure of this than I have been of anything in my entire life."

"Soren," I murmured, gently cupping his cheek in my hand and running my thumb over the raised white scar along his cheekbone, "my brother and I don't belong here. We don't belong in this world."

Soren took my hand and brought it to his heart, squeezing it tight. "You, Lina Calder, belong with *me*. In my arms. In this world, your world, or any other."

I shook my head. "You love me now, but what happens when I start to grow old? I'm not like you. I'll wither and die eventually, and you'll just have to sit there and watch."

"And I'll still view myself as the luckiest man in the world because I got to spend those few precious years with the most amazing woman I've ever known."

"But what if—"

Soren silenced me with a determined kiss. When he broke away, he pressed his forehead to mine. "The answer is you, Lina," he whispered. "I'm never going to stop choosing you."

That look came over his face, the one I'd learned meant nothing and no one was going to change his mind. He made his decision look so easy, but I was finding mine anything but.

Here, in this strange, perilous land, I was out of place. I had seen and done horrific things. I spent my days looking over my shoulder, unable to relax because something terrible always seemed to happen when I was least expecting it. My nights were spent tossing and turning, haunted by nightmares of what I had endured and could very well endure again if I stayed.

But in the human realm, I had nothing. I was a single orphaned peasant who was, as my brother Jaras once said, well past a marriageable age. My world was not kind to women like me. If I went back, I would still have to fight and claw to survive like I did here, just in a different way. Could I even stand being in the real world now? Was it even possible to go back to a normal life after all I had seen and done? Would I spend the rest of my life in misery, constantly wishing I were in this world instead, with the people I loved, wearing gorgeous gowns and wielding blades and dancing in grand ballrooms and darkened shadows?

I glanced over at Wynn. He sat slumped against a rock on the opposite shore, staring off into the distance at nothing.

My brother had been my priority from the start. His safety and well-being were the most important part of this decision. It needed to be for him, not for me. The human realm might hurt me, but the Fae realm had hurt him.

So I turned back to Soren and kissed him one last time, long and slow. Then I moved my lips to his cheeks, his nose, his forehead, his temples. My fingers followed behind, tracing the spots I'd just left. I memorized every line, every freckle and scar, every piece of this man that I loved and locked them away so I would never forget them. Soren searched my eyes, silently pleading with me to choose this life, this world. To choose *him*.

But this decision wasn't his to make, it was mine and mine alone.

So I turned and sloshed through the river to where Wynn was seated on the shore, shouldered my pack, scooped my brother into my arms, and made my choice.

Acknowledgments

The Veil wouldn't be possible without my dear friend Kari. While sipping wine under a full moon, I told her about an idea for a book. If she hadn't fallen in love with the story then and there and begged me to tell it, I don't think I would have. Her love for The Veil silenced my self doubt, and her belief in its potential encouraged me to take the leap into publishing. There is too much to thank you for, Kari. Your support means so much to me, I can't even begin to get into it here or it'll take up the whole page. So for now I will say this: you've changed my life. I'll say the rest to you over another bottle of wine under the next full moon.

This book also wouldn't be the same without my editor, Nia. I told her to hack it to pieces so it could be the best version of itself, and by god, did she. It is her incredibly hard, detailed work that took this book from clunky manuscript to full-fledged novel, and I am so thankful the universe brought us together. For the sequel, I'll try to make life easier for you and use less filter words, Nia.

Thank you to my dad, who has always wholeheartedly supported me in whatever endeavor I pursue. When I told him I'd started writing a book, he simply said, "Great. When are you publishing it?" Then he insisted on reading said book, despite my protests about the dirty bits. I feel so incredibly blessed to have you, Dad. My entire life, you have never, ever trampled out a single spark of my creativity, and instead do everything in your power to stoke it into a blazing inferno. You see the fire inside me and don't run from it, but celebrate it. That means the world to me. *You* mean the world to me. I love you.

A big shoutout to my beta readers Kylie, Alex, and Ricbre. You ladies read some rough, *rough* drafts, but your encouragement and thoughtful insight was invaluable in making it the product it is today. Thank you for being the first ones to pass beyond the veil.

And lastly, thank you reader. Thank you for going on this rollercoaster of a journey with Lina. Thank you for feeling her pain and crying her tears and fiercely loving the people she does. Thank you for creating magic of your own by bringing this story to life every time you picture it in your mind. I am truly honored that you chose to pick up this book, and I can't wait to give you more of Lina's story.

This is only the beginning.

Resources for Survivors

- NSVRC - National Sexual Violence Resource Center, nsvrc.org
- National Sexual Assault Hotline 1-800-656-4673
- RAINN - Rape, Abuse, & Incest National Network (they have a text chat option as well as a telephone hotline), rainn.org
- RALIANCE - Directory of rape crisis centers, raliance.org
- RCNE - Rape Crisis Network Europe, rcne.com
- NASASV - National Association of Services Against Sexual Violence (Australia), nasasv.org.au
- For those wanting to provide support to loved ones who have experienced sexual violence, remember to listen without judgment, offer supportive reassurance, acknowledge their pain, remind them it wasn't their fault, be present, and accept their decisions on healing. For more details, visit rainn.org/TALK